'This is a wonderful first book from K A Hitchins – touching, poignant, inspiring and beautifully written. I was captivated from the start and raced to the denouement, knowing I'd need to read it again to appreciate fully its many nuances and challenges. Like Vincent, the author's sympathetic yet shallow narrator, I don't think I'll ever see life in quite the same way again, thanks to the extraordinary Sarah Penny, one of the most memorable and unlikely heroines ever created.'
Michele Guinness, author of Archbishop

'K A Hitchins has crafted a touching and insightful love story that will warm any heart. I can't wait to see the movie!'
Sean Paul Murphy, award-winning screenwriter, The Encounter, Sarah's Choice

'A compelling read.'
Editor's Desk, Authonomy

For Nandi
with every blessing

The girl
at the end of
the road

K A Hitchins

K A Hitchins

instant
apostle

First published in Great Britain by Instant Apostle, 2015.

Instant Apostle

The Barn
1 Watford House Lane
Watford
Herts
WD17 1BJ

British Library Cataloguing-in-Publication Data

A catalogue record for this book is available from the British Library

This book and all other Instant Apostle books are available from Instant Apostle:

Website: www.instantapostle.com
Email: info@instantapostle.com

ISBN 978-1-909728-39-4

Printed in Great Britain

For Graham

Acknowledgements

I am indebted to a number of people and organisations who have encouraged me in my journey as an author.

Firstly I must thank my husband, Graham, who believed in me and nagged me to start writing even though I told him once I began I wouldn't be able to stop! Next, I must thank our children, Lizzie and Harry, who have had to put up with the inconvenience of a mother whose head is often elsewhere. Also, thanks must go to my sister and brother-in-law who were the first people to read this book and who gave me feedback with tact and kindness. My dear friend, Deidre Lansdown, has been a constant source of inspiration and encouragement, helping to clarify my ideas and sharing with me wisdom gained from a life well lived. I am in her debt.

I would also like to pay tribute to Carers in Hertfordshire, a wonderful organisation which supports carers with information, advice and stress-busting activities. They enabled me to attend four creative writing courses delivered by the Workers Educational Association. I am particularly grateful to my brilliant writing teachers, Lynne Garner, David Richardson, Pamela Mann and Clare Hobba, who teaches the BeauSandVer Writers on Monday nights. And of course my many, many writing friends who have shared their own work with me and given excellent feedback and generous encouragement. For friendship, editorial advice and proofreading completely free of charge, I would like to mention the Authonomy online community of writers, and the HarperCollins editor who gave me such invaluable feedback.

Special appreciation must go to the members of Park Street Baptist Church, Spectrum Girls and the Park Street dog walkers, who have travelled with me down some very dark footpaths and helped me to find my way back into the sunshine.

Last, but certainly not least, my utmost thanks to Manoj Raithatha and the Instant Apostle team for taking a risk and publishing the work of an unknown author.

I wrote this book to raise money for a small children's charity which, among other things, trains volunteers to work in a disability school in Togo, West Africa. All author's royalties will be donated to Mission Enfant pour Christ International.

You're blessed when you meet Lady Wisdom,
when you make friends with Madame Insight.
She's worth far more than money in the bank;
her friendship is better than a big salary.
Her value exceeds all the trappings of wealth;
nothing you could wish for holds a candle to her.
With one hand she gives long life,
with the other she confers recognition.
Her manner is beautiful,
her life wonderfully complete.
She's the very Tree of Life to those who embrace her.
Hold her tight – and be blessed!
Proverbs 3:13-18 (The Message)

Chapter 1

The drive home was endless. It was a journey I hadn't wanted to make and didn't want to end. Perhaps it was better to travel hopelessly than to arrive, I thought. Arriving would be the problem.

A mild hangover lingered, a subtle ache behind my eyes, a foul taste on the tongue, reminding me of the previous night when I had sat alone drinking vodka amidst the suitcases and boxes of my downsized life. I swallowed back a mouthful of bile at the memory of the lost deposit on my rented apartment, and turned up the music.

The great Friday afternoon exodus, heavy until the outskirts of the M25, gradually thinned. The red line of tail lights snaking ahead had fragmented down to three or four well spaced-out vehicles. The countryside on either side of the road flattened until there were no hills and no landmarks except for the occasional silhouette of a tree or a church tower. The sky stretched in all directions, darker ahead of me and paling to a cold brightness at the horizon where the sun had slipped away in my rear-view mirror. Eventually a solitary car in front turned off at a crossroads and I was alone, adrift in a great expanse of nothing.

The A505 was a boring stretch of road at the best of times, easy to coast along on autopilot while lost in thought. I knew I had left civilisation behind when the street lights disappeared and the darkness beyond my car headlights became a thing in itself, a presence, pressing close, forcing me to scrunch my eyes so as not to oversteer on the occasional bend and hit the mud verge.

That night it seemed I was travelling the same stretch of tarmac over and over, caught in an endless loop, moving forwards but never arriving, damned for an eternity of leather seats and Coldplay on the radio. Newly ploughed earth and rows of sugar beet flashed past in my headlights. How long had I been driving? How much further before I reached the junction?

Had I passed the pet crematorium yet with its memory of childhood desolation, or was that still to come?

I approached Bury St Edmunds. Another ominous chimney, this one belonging to the famous sugar factory, its floodlights casting the nearby industrial units into Dickensian gloom. A column of white vapour spewed 50 feet into the air, bright against the black sky and trailing westward, dissipating into the night. As a child I imagined cauldrons of sugar beets being stirred by grotesque demons. 'I wish we could burn calories like that,' my mother would joke every time she saw it.

From Bury it was a 12-mile drive eastwards to the village of Elmsford. The pig fields flashed by on either side of the road. Swollen shadows moved darkly amidst the corrugated iron sties. The smell was worse than the boiling beets.

I pulled into my old street just past seven o'clock and reversed onto the driveway. Mum had put the porch light on to welcome me home. The house was bathed in soft light, but my heart could not respond. This was unlike previous visits for birthdays and Christmas – nostalgic, expectant, carrying gifts and looking forward to being indulged for a couple of days before a welcome return to real life. No! This homecoming was as flat and dark as the Suffolk countryside I had just passed through. Intense self-pity, buried beneath the serious swearing and drinking sessions of the previous week, surfaced unexpectedly. I blinked angrily and flung open the car door.

The country air was shockingly cold. I breathed deeply, feeling its freshness scour my face and lungs of London's grime. I opened the boot to retrieve my small overnight bag. My parents must have been listening for my arrival, for as soon as I slammed it shut the front door burst open.

'Darling, it's so lovely to see you,' Mum exclaimed, kissing me on both cheeks.

To my surprise, Dad had grown a beard. It was almost white with darker streaks below the mouth, as though he was dribbling smoke.

'Dr Freud, I presume. Seriously, what happened to your chin, Dad?'

'I got tired of scraping it every day. I fancied a change... Welcome home, son.' Dad released me after a couple of firm slaps on the back and shook my hand. I slammed the front door behind me.

'It can't change back quickly enough for me,' Mum commented. 'It ages you by about ten years, Derek. And the scratching!'

'I feel ten years older. How was the journey down?' he asked.

'Slow at first, but the traffic improved by Duxford. I like the beard, Dad. You look distinguished. You've lost a few pounds too.' I punched him lightly in the stomach.

Elsie, my parents' arthritic pug, waddled into the hall. She sat at my feet looking up, her eyes bulging like black marbles. I gave her a scratch behind the ears. 'Hello there, girl.'

'I thought you were going to give us a ring when you reached the sugar factory.' Mum said, pulling the coat from my shoulders. I recalled the sweet, earthy smell that had insinuated itself into the interior of my BMW as I drove past Bury St Edmunds. For the second time that evening I swallowed back a sensation of nausea.

'Sorry.'

'Never mind.' Mum hung my coat in the hall cupboard. 'Your dinner's keeping warm in the oven. We ate earlier, I'm afraid. We can't eat after about 5.30 because of your dad's indigestion. It keeps him awake.'

It was hard to imagine anyone over the age of ten eating so early. It reminded me just how far out into the sticks I had come.

'Can I park the car in the garage now and leave the rest of my stuff there overnight? I'll unpack properly tomorrow, in the light.'

'Of course.' She turned to Dad. 'Open the garage door for Vincent, will you, darling, while I dish up his casserole?'

Dad grabbed a bunch of keys from the hook in the hall and I followed him out of the front door. He was in his slippers and shirt sleeves and shivered at the iciness of the night. 'Mum's really excited about having you home. Don't spoil it for her.'

'Who, me?'

'Yes, you. Let her enjoy herself. Try not to make it too obvious you'd rather be somewhere else.' He turned to open the double garage door. I remember my feet crunching on the gravel as I walked to my BMW; stones as loud as gunshot in the silence, the sound as sharp as glass. How I longed to jump in the driver's seat and race away into the night. But instead I reversed into the double garage and parked next to Dad's Ford Focus. He disappeared into the darkness at the far end and opened the door leading into the utility room. I slammed the metal overhead door shut.

Half-finished paint pots and mysterious garden implements crowded the shadowed walls. I remember thinking everything I owned was contained in that small space: my car, some designer clothes, a flat-screen bubble-wrapped TV balanced on top of a suitcase on the back seat, an iPod, laptop, CDs, DVDs, books, a few pots and pans and some bedding. How small my life had become, how few the places I now inhabited. My locker at the private gym had been given to somebody else. My desk drawers at work were empty; the files on my PC wiped clean. The loss of my office territory had been harder to bear than losing my flat and my space in Chloe's bed. What was I without my work? Jobless and insignificant! Pathetic and broke!

I stomped through the utility room and into the kitchen. The table was laid for one. Mum and Dad sat opposite me, eager to chat.

'The Berringers send their love, and Simon and Liz from number seven are looking forward to seeing you again.'

I ate quickly while Mum filled me in with news of friends and neighbours. I grunted and nodded at appropriate moments, half-listening, chewing over a growing sense of irritation, tired and longing to crash upstairs but knowing I would have to talk for an age before they would let me get to bed. And I didn't want to discuss the recent past – nor the future – just yet.

'Your nan will be pleased to see you –'

'That's if she remembers him,' Dad interrupted.

'What?' I asked surprised. 'Is Nan poorly?'

'Something like that,' Dad said.

'We didn't want to worry you,' Mum continued. 'She's been going downhill for a couple of months. She had a funny turn before Christmas and it left her a bit forgetful. She's not too good on her legs either…'

'If she lost a bit of weight, like the doctor said, her mobility would improve,' Dad grumbled.

'Well, it's not easy to lose weight at her age. Eating is one of the few pleasures left to her and she's too frail to exercise –'

'Too fat to exercise!'

'She's too frail, Derek! You know she is. She can barely walk across the room, let alone get up the stairs. She's got a stairlift now.' She turned pointedly away from Dad. 'A carer goes in twice a day to help her get up and to put her back to bed in the evening.'

'I hadn't realised…'

'If you had come home a bit more often –' Dad began, but Mum interrupted.

'He's home now. That's what counts. It's been a strain the last couple of months, I must admit. I've been popping in to see her most days after work to check everything is OK. It will be a nice change for her to see you instead.' My heart sank.

'I won't be sitting around doing nothing. Of course I'll visit Nan, but my time will be pretty much taken up with career planning for the next few weeks. Strategy without planning is hallucination! That's what Tony says.'

'What exactly are your plans?' Dad asked after an awkward pause. I swallowed my last mouthful of food and placed my knife and fork together on the plate.

'I need to brush up my CV and talk to some contacts. I imagine I'll be having quite a few meetings and interviews, travelling back and forth to London. "The only way is up", as they say.' I spoke in the confident tone I had developed for my clients. No one was fooled.

'Of course it is,' Mum said. 'But you'll still have time for Nana, I'm sure.'

I forced a smile. I didn't want my parents to guess how much it hurt that Tony had let me go. I was his best salesman. He had told me so many times.

'This credit crunch is affecting a lot of people, son. There's hardly a family in the village that hasn't been touched in one way or another. Simon's driving school is taking a big hit, for instance. Youngsters can't afford driving lessons or the cost of car insurance. Don't be surprised if it takes you a bit longer than expected to get the job you want. Lots of people are finding it a problem to –'

'There are no problems, Dad, just opportunities. Hopefully I won't be bothering you for too long.'

'You're no bother at all, darling,' Mum said. 'We love having you here. And it will give you a chance to have a bit of a break and catch up with your family and friends. You've been working much too hard. You're looking very thin and tired. I don't think living in London agrees with you. What you need is some good home cooking. I've got a copy of the *Bury Free Press* in the lounge, so you can look in the job pages after dinner.'

'I can't imagine there'll be anything in the local paper that would be of interest.' My tone was sharper than I intended.

'Beggars can't be choosers,' Dad said. I took a deep breath, steadying my anger.

'This is a temporary setback. London is where the financial services industry is, and I *will* be going back there as soon as I can. I like the buzz. I'm not cut out for country life.'

'I don't know why not. You used to like it.'

'When I was about ten years old, Dad! There's more to life than climbing trees, building camps and going fishing. I want a career, the chance to travel, make some money.'

'It's the dark space between the stars that makes them shine so brightly,' Mum said as she poured me another glass of orange squash.

'What have stars got to do with anything?' Dad asked.

'I'm just saying that it's at times like these we appreciate the good things in our lives.'

'What cra... I mean, what a dreadful cliché, Mum. You'll be telling me to count my blessings next.'

'It can't hurt, can it?'

'I'm not looking for cosy words to make me feel better. I've lost everything I've been working towards for the last 12 years. There are no bright stars for me. But rather than sitting about on my backside counting my non-existent blessings, I'm going to spend every moment of every day working to get my life back. I'll do whatever it takes!'

'I'm sure you will,' she said. Dad stood up abruptly and walked out of the room. Mum cleared my dirty plates. 'Your dad's a bit irritable at the moment. He needs a holiday. We both need a holiday. Now that you're home, perhaps we'll be able to get a late booking for half-term. You could look after the dog and keep an eye on Nana for us.'

'I don't know...'

'Of course, we can talk about it later. You've only just arrived home! It's wonderful to see you, love, to have you here with us.' She bent down and kissed my cheek. 'I know you'd rather not be here, but all the same I'm glad you've come. I've made a lovely steamed pudding for you, with jam, just the way you like it.'

I eventually extricated myself and carried my overnight bag upstairs. Thankfully my old room had been redecorated a couple of years earlier, all childhood traces eradicated. Sleeping in a single bed under my old Ipswich Town duvet cover would have been too much to bear. A pine double bed with a cream bedspread took up most of the space. Mum had arranged brown and gold scatter cushions by the headboard, and cream towels at the foot of the bed. Matching pine bedside cabinets, a wardrobe, dressing table and chest of drawers topped by an arrangement of silk flowers completed the room. Bland oblivion!

I hung up the shirt and trousers from my overnight bag. There was a box of my old books in the bottom of the wardrobe. I picked a paperback copy of *The Hound of the Baskervilles* from the top. A badly drawn picture of an enormous dog, blood dripping from its fangs, adorned the front cover. Curious, I rummaged further. *The Woman in White* by Wilkie Collins. *The Strange Case of Dr Jekyll and Mr Hyde* by Robert Louis Stevenson. *Frankenstein* by Mary Shelley. Bram Stoker's *Dracula*. They had been cheaply produced under the Adventure Classics imprint. All had startlingly vivid front covers coated with dust. The last book was *Lady Audley's Secret* by Mary Elizabeth Braddon. A white-faced woman with outrageously red lips stared from the cover, her grey eyes denouncing me for abandoning her to the bottom of a box. Some of the pages were coming loose from the spine, their corners curling and speckled by age. I remembered nothing of the story, but I had a vague recollection of nights spent reading with a torch under the duvet. Throwing the books dismissively back into the box, I slammed the wardrobe door. I kicked off my shoes, flung myself across the bed and texted Chloe.

Hi babe. How are u? I'm back home with old croaks, planning my escape. Sorry about what I said. Doesn't have 2 b the end. I'll b back in town before u know. Missing u. Vince.

Exhausted, I washed and changed quickly into an old T-shirt and joggers. My shoulders ached from emptying the flat of my personal possessions. My neck was still stiff from the drive. I stretched out under the duvet and waited for my body to relax. Something was niggling away at my subconscious. Silence hung thickly in the air, a kind of auditory darkness, suffocating, disorientating, startling in its intensity. After a few uneasy minutes, I realised the room was too quiet for sleep, so quiet I could hear the blood pounding through my ear as it pressed against the cold pillow. I was used to the comforting, near-constant drone of London traffic. Its absence made me anxious, as if I had forgotten something important like a wallet or passport. Something *was* missing. Then I realised what. My life!

Waves of emotion from the last few weeks pounded through my body, crashing and roaring against an implacable wall of injustice and bad luck. The eviction notice from my landlord. My last argument with Chloe.

Christmas spent drunk and alone because I was too proud to tell my parents I had lost my job. I had hoped to find another position quickly, so I told them I was working on Christmas Eve and the day after Boxing Day. Surely they could see it wasn't worth driving to Suffolk for two days. In any case, I explained, I wanted to spend Christmas with Chloe. In the event, she had driven to Hertfordshire to be with her family, fed up with the lavish pity party I was throwing myself. I spent the day on my own with a turkey ready meal and a bottle of whisky I unwrapped that morning.

It must have been the expensive gifts I sent which signalled my financial woes. My parents knew my instinct for disguise. I was compelled to tell the truth on New Year's Day, and they pressed me to come home. Unable to come up with a viable alternative, and with another month's rent looming, I crumbled. I should have stuck it out, stayed put and gambled on something turning up. But I was scared.

Through a crack in the curtains, I watched the dazzling dark of the Suffolk night. The stars were brighter than I had seen for a long time, brilliant points on black velvet, undimmed by the glare of city lights. I remembered what Mum had said: 'It's the dark space between the stars that makes them shine so brightly.' And it was true. They did shine more brightly in this dark place.

Chapter 2

That weekend we started to adjust to living together again. I unpacked my boxes and bags. Kitchen equipment and bedding were stored in the loft. I set up my television on the chest of drawers, relegating the silk flowers to the top of the wardrobe. Mum and Dad were tired after the working week. They had mundane jobs to do around the house – laundry and paperwork to sort out. It would have been rude to stay in the bedroom with my laptop but I felt awkward hovering downstairs. They tried to entertain me with a stream of small talk, as if I weren't quite one of the family but a guest in need of polite attention. Eventually, I decided to take a stroll round the village.

'If you're going past the library, perhaps you could return my books,' Mum called from the kitchen.

'Do I have to?'

'Yes, you do,' Dad shouted from living room.

I circumnavigated the village on my way to the library. There wasn't much to see. The village hall, the local Anglican church, a few shops. The front gardens I passed were neat. Hedges and shrubs had been trimmed and herbaceous plants cut back hard for the winter. The borders and paths were free of weeds. Early snowdrop shoots glimmered green against the damp earth. Cars gleamed on the driveways. A small cage for the delivery of milk bottles stood by one front door, with a little dial turned to indicate the number of pints required. A notice declaring 'NO HAWKERS OR TRADERS' adorned another door.

The smug respectability irritated me. Didn't the residents know that at any moment everything could be swept away by a sudden catastrophe – accident, death, or financial collapse? There were greater hazards to protect themselves against than unemployed boys selling dusters on doorsteps! Would they bother to sweep their porches or wash their windows if they knew of the dangerous precipice on which their lives teetered?

The front gardens perfectly personified the parochial mindset I longed to escape. Life in London was too hectic to worry about such tidiness. Gardens were for additional parking or for storing bins and recycling boxes – a bicycle chained to an iron railing, perhaps, or a broken skateboard on the garden path. Front doors and windows were covered with a dusty film deposited by the passing traffic. Time and money mattered. My neighbours had too much life to live to think about washing the front step. Who cared about the litter collecting in dark corners? It was survival of the fittest, not the smuggest.

I mooched towards the library, a 1960s flat-roofed box. I hadn't visited this library – any library – since leaving school. None of my friends in London read anything other than newspapers and magazines. We were the gaming and internet generation. If we needed information or entertainment we had smartphones, iPads and computers.

When I was a child, Mum insisted I borrow at least one book a week. I owned a brown cardboard library card back then which I showed to an old fogey at the desk. She would stamp the return date on the first page of the book with a satisfying clunk, startling the dusty silence which snoozed between the shelves. I had always been glad to escape.

I had been surprised to find the box of books in my wardrobe the previous night. There had been that one summer, a frenzy of heat and imagination, when I had glutted on jumble sale books and lost myself to another world. A passing phase, no doubt, fuelled by hormones and teenage idealism.

I pushed open the glass doors and stopped in surprise. The library appeared to be experiencing a mid-life crisis. Although housed in the same squat building, the wrinkles had been smoothed and the grey atmosphere eradicated by bright paint and strident noticeboards. The books were stored on the kind of funky shelving I imagined in Hollywood loft apartments. Rotating racks for paperbacks and DVDs lined up in front of a row of flickering computer screens. Newspapers and magazines were strewn invitingly on low white tables surrounded by squashy chairs. Nipped and tucked to accommodate contemporary tastes, the room had all the character of a fast food café. At least in the old days you could smell the books! I sank into one of the chairs and picked up a newspaper, suddenly self-conscious and feeling like the new boy at school.

I watched several ladies taking books to a couple of machines in the middle of the room. They swiped their cards, placed their books in a little alcove and appeared to be following instructions on a touch screen. After a moment they removed their books and placed them either on a bookshelf next to the machine or into their shopping bags. Receipts were automatically printed and ejected from a slit to the side of the alcove.

There didn't appear to be any staff at the help desk, though I did see a middle-aged lady speaking to a young woman with a buggy and toddler in the children's section. I wondered whether to linger and ask her to show me how to return Mum's books, or to watch a bit longer to see if I could work out how to do it myself – the preferred option, obviously.

A tall woman collected a pile of books from the returns shelf next to one of the machines and put them on a trolley. Walking back along the stacks, she took each book in turn, checked its spine and returned it reverently to its correct place. I watched her for some minutes. She refused to hurry what was clearly a tedious and routine job. She had her back to me. I couldn't see her face, but my eyes followed her progress. Something about the way she moved piqued my curiosity.

I found myself staring. Not the kind of stare men give women wearing skimpy clothes, nor the look you give when you are trying to catch a girl's eye to see if she's interested. It was the kind of involuntary second look you give when something seems familiar or puzzling. It had happened to me several times on the London Underground escalators. I would see a girl travelling on the opposite escalator going up when I was going down, or going down when I was going up. A turn of the head. The flash of a smile. It would seem for an instant as if I knew her a little bit more than all the other faceless commuters. There would be a jolt of something like recognition followed swiftly by a nagging regret that I would never see her again.

I continued to stare at the tall librarian, partly from boredom, partly from curiosity at her methodical deliberation. Her hair was a mousy blonde. Stray strands fell from a knot on the back of her head. A grey poncho was draped around her thin frame, long wool tassels swirling by her sides as she drifted along the aisle like a colourless jellyfish. A black skirt hung to her ankles, skimming a pair of lace-up boots – the type children wore in films about Victorian life. Everything about her was shapeless, frumpy, washed out. She was noticeable because of the very unnoteworthiness of her clothes.

From her back it was impossible to guess her age. She could be anything between 18 and 50 years old. She turned slightly and I saw her profile. A wave of disquiet washed through me. I looked away, unsettled. Suddenly I knew precisely how old she was... and who she was. Sarah Penny! We were in the same class at upper school. I automatically pulled the newspaper up to hide my face.

I forced myself to read an article about the euro crisis. She probably wouldn't recognise me, I reasoned. I silently congratulated myself on my transformation from overweight teenager to svelte businessman. My eyes tracked down the column inches of *The Times*... 'huge deficit'... 'rising unemployment'... 'bail out'... 'political will'... 'quantitative easing'. Words and phrases bounced off the page, detached from meaning and floating free. I was overcome by an inexplicable feeling of dread.

Sweat beaded my forehead, pushed through my skin by the anvil now hammering in my chest. I wiped my brow surreptitiously with the back of my hand, but couldn't stop my fingers shaking. I couldn't understand what was happening to my body; it was as though all the distress and tension of the last few weeks had suddenly hit my nervous system. I was engulfed by panic.

I don't remember how long I sat there. Customers came and went, their quiet footsteps lapping at the distant shores of my consciousness. I heard the roar of the sea in my ears, tasted salt on my lips. The blue carpet shimmered and heaved at my feet as I struggled to breathe. I clung to the newspaper like a drowning man until eventually my heartbeat steadied to the rhythm of a murmured conversation nearby. A couple of pensioners were discussing the best way to clean windows. Lemon juice... vinegar... screwed-up newspaper. The blurred words in front of me coalesced into meaningful sentences. Someone nearby coughed. A large lady sitting opposite pursed her lips and looked away. Unconsciously I had been tapping my foot to dissipate the adrenaline in my system. I folded the newspaper and tossed it onto the low table in front of me with a loud slap.

'If it doesn't kill you, it will make you stronger,' Tony had said as he ushered me out of his office. And I *was* getting stronger. I stood and picked up the reusable carrier bag with my mother's books inside. I might be unemployed and living with my parents, but at least I was no longer the awkward fatty who had escaped Elmsford all those years ago. Hadn't my career path proved I could handle myself in any social situation? It might be good to talk to someone from the past to remind me just how far I had come in the last few years, despite the current setback. Sarah Penny would probably be flattered I remembered her. What better time to pick myself up and be assertive? As Tony said, 'If it scares you – do it!'

I would be charming. She had been timid and unassuming at school, a little standoffish, in fact. She used to creep quietly round the edges of the class, avoiding eye contact with the other kids for fear of attracting their attention. But I had never joined in with the snide comments and teasing.

I walked to the end of a row. She was standing on a small step to return a book to the top shelf, her back to me. As she stretched, a flash of pale skin peeped between the top of her thick ankle sock and the hem of her shapeless skirt. 'Dowdy dressed means depressed,' my mother's voice echoed in my head. And who wouldn't be depressed working in Elmsford library?

She climbed down and disappeared along another aisle. I sauntered over, trying to look casual, glancing at the book titles on the shelves as I passed. Whether it was the after-effects of my adrenaline rush, or because I'd been sitting down for too long, I remember walking slowly as though wading through water, wanting to move fast but unable to muster the required energy.

I turned a corner to walk down the aisle she was stacking and jumped back in surprise as we nearly collided. She dropped the book she was carrying.

'Oh!' she exclaimed, glancing away when our eyes met. She bent to pick up the book and clutched it to her chest.

'I'm so sorry.' I stood my ground, not letting her pass, waiting for her to acknowledge my presence. She studied my brown leather moccasins for some moments before pulling her eyes to my chest.

'Can I help you?' A wave of nostalgia surged through my body. How could I have forgotten that voice – quiet, tightly controlled, with no trace of a Suffolk accent despite having lived here all her life.

'I need to return these and there's no one at the desk.' I pulled one of my mother's books out of the carrier bag.

She glanced at the cover. It was obviously a romance. A smile hovered, so quickly I couldn't be sure. Was she amused or merely being polite?

'You can return them yourself. Here, let me show you.'

'These are my mother's,' I gabbled. 'I might take out a book for myself if I see anything in my field. Perhaps you could direct me to the business section in a minute.'

'Follow me.'

'With pleasure!'

There was no answering look or smile, none of the usual stuff you might expect from a conversation between two people of the opposite sex. I had been facetious and we both knew it. We walked towards the machines. She touched a screen and selected the 'Return book' option and placed the book in the alcove.

'The computer recognises the bar code on the cover,' she said. The screen displayed the title and author of the book. She placed the second book on top of the first, and its title and author were added to the list. 'These are overdue. There's a fine of £2.50. You put your money here. It takes all denominations of coins, and notes up to £10. It gives change.' She spoke with deliberation, as though she were part of the machine.

'Right.' I fished around in my trouser pockets, dropping some coins in the process. I wanted to claw back the initiative and introduce myself, but fumbled as I put my money in the slot. She selected the 'Finish' option. The screen instructed us to place the books on the returns shelf to the right, which she did.

'Don't forget your receipt.' I took the slip of paper and stuffed it in my coat pocket. 'The business section is by the exit.' She pointed towards the shelves and stared at the floor, waiting for me to walk away.

'Umm... I haven't been to the library in ages, as you might have guessed. Could you tell me if my card's still active?' I reached for my wallet and pulled out a plastic card, the successor of the brown cardboard ticket of my childhood. It looked at least 15 years old, but had miraculously stuck with me all this time, along with a Bury St Edmunds' snooker club card and the phone number for a local taxi company.

'You'll need a new one with a bar code. We're fully automated now. Come with me.' I followed her to the librarian's desk. She typed my card number into her computer. While she was concentrating I examined her closely. Her face was pale, her eyes and lips lacking the definition of mascara and lipstick. There was no jewellery that I could see, certainly no rings on her long fingers.

'Do you still live at the same address, Mr Stevens?'

'Yes... Don't I know you? You look familiar.'

'No.' She didn't look up, but her expression tightened.

'I think we went to the same school.' She stared intently at the screen and made a few keystrokes. Her nails were short and unpainted, like small pink shells.

'Your mobile number?'

I reeled it off and she typed it in.

'King Edward's Upper School in Bury St Edmunds. Weren't we in the same class for a while?'

'I think I should let you know that the sort of person who asks, "Did we go to school together?" is exactly the sort of person I don't want to talk to.'

She spoke quietly, but I was taken aback by the rudeness of her remark. Had I been mistaken? Did she think I was spinning a line, some creep trying to chat her up? Perhaps that happened often in her job – sad weirdos looking for love. The earlier sensation of panic flickered at the edges. A woolly fog descended. My brain struggled to find the words that would pull me from the murk and the terror and place me back on solid ground where I was a genuine kind of guy, a good bloke with a life, not the type who had to visit a library to pick up women.

'Here's your new library card, Mr Stevens.' Eager to leave, I turned to walk away but she continued quickly, 'Yes, I went to King Edward's.'

'Then I *do* know you!' I spun round, smiling in nervous relief. 'I thought so. I never forget a face.'

'You don't know me. But we did go to the same school, yes.'

For the first time she looked at me directly. Pale grey eyes with a dark outer ring. Black lashes tipped with gold. A gaze of complete emptiness which sliced through me as though I wasn't there at all. It was the kind of direct, unknowing gaze you sometimes see on the faces of the very young or the very old, those who haven't seen anything to trouble them yet or who can no longer remember. I wondered if she was a little simple. I shivered. *You don't know me. But we did go to the same school, yes.* Was she stupid, or was she saying something more profound? *You might recognise my face but you never really knew me at all.*

'I'm sorry, have I done something to offend you? It's Sarah, isn't it? Sarah Penny? You probably don't remember me very well.'

'I recall you, Mr Stevens. I have an excellent memory.'

'Vincent, please.' In other circumstances I would have been flattered that a woman I hadn't talked to for more than 15 years remembered me, but my unease was turning to annoyance. She wasn't even attempting to

25

go through the motions of normal social interchange. Suddenly I felt a sickening thud in my stomach. Did she remember me better than I remembered her? *Had* I done something stupid in the past and blanked it out? Of course she wasn't simple! She had been exceptionally bright. How could I have forgotten? She was on some kind of gifted and talented programme, drifting in and out of normal lessons whenever she wished, her erratic attendance one of the reasons no one noticed she had left the school until some weeks after she had gone. She probably *did* have an excellent memory.

To hide my anxiety I tried a humorous approach. I wanted to clear the waters, bring the conversation back to some kind of normality so I could extricate myself and leave the library, never to return.

'Uh-oh! What did I get up to? I guess I was a bit of a lad. Was I a pain in the backside?'

'No.'

'That's a relief. What have you been up to since school? I've been working in London for the last few years, a firm in the city. Wheeling and dealing. You know the sort of thing.' I laughed, but she didn't join in. 'Anyway, I'm now taking some time away from the financial markets, letting things settle down in the global economy. No one wants to take risks any more, particularly with all the interference from politicians. I'm visiting my parents for a few days...' I paused, but she made no comment. 'So you're a librarian now. That must be interesting.'

'I'm a library assistant.'

'What's the difference?'

'I don't have the qualification.'

'Oh!' Perhaps she wasn't as bright as I thought after all. 'Are you studying for it?'

'No.'

This was hopeless! I tried again. 'Are you still in touch with any friends from the old days?' I flashed my most charming smile.

'I didn't have any friends...'

I'm not surprised, if this is how you talk to people, I thought. I needed to cut my losses – and fast. I didn't want to get sucked into some excruciating story about her miserable childhood.

'... much like yourself.' With that she picked up the book she had been returning, and walked calmly away.

Chapter 3

I spent the rest of the afternoon turning the incident over in my mind, thinking of clever things I should have said to put the stupid woman in her place. Why would she suggest *I* didn't have friends at school? She had been the outcast, the oddball, the alien in the classroom! I had been friends with Jimmy and his gang. I wasn't the one nobody would talk to. Didn't they give any customer service training at that library?

What was wrong with me that I was making such a big deal out of something so small? Why did her opinion even matter? Move on, forget her, I told myself a dozen times. After all, my whole life had just smashed into a wall and was lying in pieces at my feet. I had more important things to worry about than rude librarians. Perhaps that was it! Her words had hit me when I was down. It was no more than that. It wasn't personal. She wasn't to know that I was going through a bad patch. She probably didn't even realise she had offended me.

At dinner time, the incident still rankled. Mum cooked a mixed grill: pork chops, sausages, mushrooms, tomatoes, with baked potatoes done in the microwave (never as good as the ones cooked long and low in the oven so that the jackets become crisp and shiny). My parents chatted about mundane things: projects at work, jobs that needed to be done around the house, a charity fundraiser they were helping to organise in the village.

'Simon and Liz are coming round to play Scrabble tonight. You're welcome to join us,' Mum said. 'That'll cheer you up.'

'No thanks. I texted Jimmy Hodges earlier. We've arranged to meet up at the Railway Tavern this evening.' Jimmy was my old schoolfriend.

'What time?'

'8.30.'

'Good. You'll still have time for a quick chat with Simon and Liz before you leave,' Mum smiled. 'They're arriving at half-past seven.'

'Great!'

'There's no need to be sarcastic, son. It doesn't suit you. Simon and Liz are always asking after you. The least you can do is say hello. And don't drink too much tonight, or make a noise when you get home, either. Your mother and I will be getting up for church in the morning.'

'Give me some credit. I'm not a teenager any more.'

'Jimmy's got a reputation as a bit of a lad in the village. And you were always easily led.'

'What are you talking about?'

'You've got a knack of only seeing what you want to see. Why you idolised him I'll never know. You were twice the boy. Just because Jimmy didn't want to carry on with his schooling, there was no reason for you to decide not to go to university.'

'That's all water under the bridge now,' Mum said.

'Dad, Jimmy left school at 16, if you remember. I stayed on for sixth form. It was my choice not to go to university after A levels. I wanted to get out into the big wide world.'

'Because you saw Jimmy earning money, buying himself a clapped-out old car. You didn't appreciate then that a few more years of education would give you better prospects. After all, look at you now.'

'Derek! We *are* in the middle of a global economic crisis. Lots of people are losing their jobs, graduates as well. It's not Vincent's fault.'

'Thanks, Mum.'

But Dad was on a roll. 'All I know is that you could have been doing something a bit more meaningful the last few years than selling dodgy financial products. There's more to life than a quick buck – commission this and commission that. Why don't you think about retraining and getting a proper career?'

'Because I don't want to be a quantity surveyor, Dad, that's why. And I don't fancy years of studying.'

'Think of all the money you've wasted on that fancy apartment with nothing to show for it now. Rents will only go one way. Up! You need to get your foot on the property ladder.'

'That's virtually impossible for a first-time buyer in London.'

'Then live out of London. Find somewhere cheaper to start off with.'

'But my job's in London.'

'Not any more it isn't!'

'That's a bit harsh,' Mum said.

'I'm just saying it how it is. When we reach retirement age, your mother and I can sell this place, downsize and have a nice little nest egg to supplement our pensions. Renting's a mug's game.'

'Supposing you reach retirement age, that is.' I immediately realised the crassness of my statement. 'I didn't mean that in relation to you and Mum specifically. I'm sure you're both going to be fine and enjoy a long and happy retirement. What I mean is that you never know what's going to happen. You have to live your life for today, not just for tomorrow.'

'You remember Simon and Liz's youngest son, Jeremy? He had a gap year backpacking around the world. Then he went to university, had a great time, graduated with a poor degree and an enormous debt. He spent a couple of years working in bars, doing casual work, spending a lot of time lazing about on Simon and Liz's settee. Then finally, about 18 months ago, he applied to be a fireman. He got through the interview process and passed the training with flying colours. He worked on Green Watch for just under a year. He had plenty of time to follow his other interests with his shift patterns, even carried on doing a little bar work on the side. And do you know what happened?'

'He hasn't been injured, has he?' I asked, remembering a happy-go-lucky lad a few years my junior.

'No. He's in Australia on a career break. A career break, I ask you! He's hardly had a career! He's 26 years old and he's bumming around, picking up girls and topping up his suntan. No doubt he'll roll back into the village at some future point and start moaning he can't afford the deposit for a flat. At 26 I had a wife and child. I was working all hours back then to make ends meet. Because of that, we don't need to worry about the future now.'

'Life is like a swimming pool, Vincent. All the noise comes from the shallow end,' Mum said.

'What's *that* supposed to mean?'

'You've always gravitated towards those who want to make a big noise. In a swimming pool, all the noise comes from the children in the shallow end. You're a strong swimmer. You could make it to the deep end if you wanted.'

'I haven't got time for this,' I slammed my knife and fork together on the plate with a clatter.

'You've been underselling yourself, that's what I'm talking about,' Mum continued.

'You can't be serious. Underselling myself! Since I've been with Tony I've been pushing the envelope every day.'

'I don't mean that. You put on a façade for everyone to see – you're well dressed, you've been successful, had money in your pocket and a pretty girl on your arm – but underneath all that you're something else, something better.'

'What *am* I then, Mum?' I asked bitterly.

'I don't know. But perhaps that's what you've come home to find out.'

*****

Scrabble with Simon and Liz Addington was a fairly regular Saturday night fixture in my parents' social calendar. I had a sherry with them and made small talk for about 20 minutes. Liz was thin and very quiet. Simon's grey hair had receded since I last saw him. His eyebrows had grown bushier with age – two grey tufts reaching up as if to grasp any remaining hair before it slipped completely over the back of his head. His moustache was carefully clipped.

'Sorry to hear about the job, Vincent. Sometimes in life's journey you end up on a road you don't expect, but that doesn't have to be a bad thing. When I was made redundant 20 years or so ago, I decided on a complete change of direction. Look at me now! Of course, it's a bit of a bumpy ride for everyone in this economic climate. But I'm sure you'll be just fine. "Keep your eye on the road ahead," that's what I always say. Don't look back at what's in the past, that'll get you nowhere.'

'Thanks, Simon.'

'Take a little time to think about what you *really* want in life. I know your parents will support you all they can. You'll be back on the road to success in no time at all. And if things have stalled really badly, you can always consider becoming a driving instructor, like me. Be your own boss!' He gave a self-congratulatory laugh. Realising he was laughing alone, he cleared his throat and adopted a more serious tone.

'Of course, the driving lessons market is a bit swamped at the moment. Lots of people are having the same idea. They've crashed out of the fast lane and are looking for a new career. My business has certainly taken a double hit. Too many instructors and not enough pupils. Once the politicians sort out this mess and jump-start the economy again, all those young people who can't afford lessons now will suddenly join the queue. If my business can hang on in the short term, I see a rosy road ahead for

Addington's Autodrive. If you want to talk about a future as a driving instructor, Vincent, just pop in for a chat.'

*****

Jimmy was already standing at the bar sipping a lager and watching the football on a big TV when I arrived at the pub just after half past eight.

'Alright, boi?' he said, slapping me on the shoulder. 'Good to see yer. How's life?'

'Not so bad, not so bad. How about you?'

'Can't complain – though Oi do.' He laughed a little too loudly. I had forgotten how thick his Suffolk accent was, a soft burr that made him sound like a farmer's boy but delivered at full volume. I cringed inwardly at the parochial twang.

I looked around the pub. Not much had changed. Since the smoking ban, the atmosphere was fresher, but it didn't look as though the carpets and curtains had been cleaned or the walls repainted. Everything had a grimy nicotine tint. A mismatched collection of oak chairs and benches huddled in small groups around the room. The walls were covered with pictures of pigs in honour of the local pig farms: black and white photographs of pigs, cartoon pigs, pigs in oils, pig in pastels and watercolours, pigs in women's clothes…

'Still working at the sugar factory?' I asked.

'For me sins. What happened to yer, then? Big city chew yer up and spit yer out? Are yer back for good, laughen boi?'

I grimaced. 'Just passing through. I can't wait to get back to London. The financial crunch took a bite out of my organisation. They had to let people go. But my boss said I'd be the first to be asked back if things pick up. I'm not going to hang around waiting, though. I've got some other options to explore. It's all good.'

'Well, yer were probably due a kick in the pants. Yer can join the rest of us down here in the muck.' He changed the subject. 'Are yer still with yer woman?'

'It's a bit on and off at the moment. We're still in touch. I think we would both be open to a rematch, but at the moment I'm free to have a look around, see what's out there, if you know what I mean.'

'Good stuff.' Jimmy was looking at the TV. I managed to catch the barman's eye. He pulled me a pint and another for Jimmy and gave me the change. I took a long drink. We were both distracted for a moment by the match. A mixture of groans and sighs of relief were exhaled as the ball hit the crossbar and the moment of excitement passed.

'Fancy gorn out on the pull next Saturday night then, Chubbs?' Jimmy asked, reverting back to our previous conversation about women.

'It's Vince now. I'm not Chubbs any more.'

'Whatever yer say, boi, whatever yer say.'

'I'm four stone lighter than when we were at school. I work out at the gym. Chloe and I have been running together at weekends…'

'A bit of a goer, is she?' he leered. 'Anyway, how's about Saturday, then? Let's go and get ourselves some fee-males.'

'I thought you had a new woman. You said in your text you were seeing her last night.'

'Yeah, Oi did. She's a great girl, but it's not exclusive yet. Early days. She's gorn to stay with her sister in Birmingham next weekend. We can go out on the pull like the ol' days.'

I took another swig from my glass. The beer eased down my throat, ice cold and invigorating. 'Looking forward to it already…'

Unable to resist bringing up the subject that had been scratching away at my insides all afternoon, I said, 'Talking about the old days, you'll never guess who I met today.'

'Who?'

'Sarah Penny.'

'Sarah who?'

'Sarah Penny. She was in year 10 and 11 with us at King Edward's, then suddenly left. Tall blonde girl, kept herself to herself. A little odd.'

'Oi would have remembered anyone tall and blonde. What were her chest like?'

'Flat.'

'That's probably why Oi don't remember!'

'She was supposed to be very bright. She sometimes got up in the middle of lessons without asking and the teachers just let her go out of class. Don't you remember? We could never understand how she got away with it.'

'Yeah, it's beginnen to come back to me now… She were the one all the other girls hated.'

A loud cheer went up from a group of lads in the corner. Their team had scored. They punched the air in celebration. We watched the action replay.

'Why did they hate her?'

'What?'

'Why did all the other girls hate her?'

Jimmy paused and thought for a moment. 'Well, yer know women. Anything can set them off. Maybe she didn't wear the right shoes or fancy the right pop star. Oi were dating Catrina Pickard back then, and Oi know she couldn't stand her. She were always a bit creepy, don't yer remember? Where did you see her?'

'In the village library. She works there.'

'That's why Oi haven't bumped into her, then!' He laughed. 'What were you doing in the library, fatso?'

'Careers research, that kind of stuff.'

'If you want careers advice, yer should have come to me, mate.'

'Yeah, I'll remember that next time... Going back to Sarah, from something she said I got the feeling she had a hard time at school. Do you remember that?'

'Probably that thing in the girls' changing room.' Jimmy's eyes were returning to the big screen.

'What thing?'

'Don't ask, boi!' he smirked.

'Seriously, what thing?'

'Oi dunno what happened...' He saw my sceptical expression. 'Really, mate, I don't know. Catrina wouldn't say, but the girls were laughen about it for weeks. They were driving all the lads mad because they wouldn't let us in on the joke, don't yer remember? Our imaginations was running wild. Lots of girls getting changed after PE, group nakedness, showers... you get the picture.'

'I don't remember that at all. Are you sure it had something to do with Sarah Penny?'

'Oi think so. She dropped out of school a few weeks after that and Catrina was worried she were going to get the blame, get accused of bullying or somethen. But by that time I was sick of her winden me up so I didn't really listen. We split up soon afterwards.'

'Are you still in touch with Catrina?'

'On and off. She pulls pints in a club in Bury. She had a baby a few years back, so works evenens while her mum looks after the sprog. We run into each other now and then. We could go to the club she works at on Saturday night. Great idea! Oi'm glad I thought of it, Chubbs.'

We spent the rest of the evening talking about football and Jimmy's opinions about women's bodies and workers' rights. We made plans for a lads' night out the following Saturday. He had some mates in town; we could sleep on their floor so we wouldn't have to pay for a taxi back to Elmsford.

I walked home just after 11 o'clock. The night was bitterly cold. A bright moon shed a silver glow over the streets. Frost glinted on the pavements and I stumbled off the edge of the kerb and onto the empty road.

I checked my phone. There was a text from Chloe. She was out clubbing with friends. She slipped that in at the end of her message, as if an afterthought. I knew it was a carefully planted barb. I didn't like to think about where she was and what she was doing, in contrast to where I was and what I was doing – walking back to my parents' house before midnight on a Saturday night.

I was eager to get into the warm. Mum and Dad had already gone to bed by the time I quietly bolted the front door. I slipped off my shoes in the hall and crept into the kitchen, feeling like a trespasser. I snapped on the light, my feet shocked by the icy chill of the floor tiles, despite my socks. Elsie looked up from her bed.

'Some guard dog you are!'

I found a glass and quickly turned on the tap. A jet of freezing water shot into the stainless steel sink, spraying the front of my shirt. I cursed quietly, not wanting to wake my parents, and dabbed my chest with a tea towel. There was a bowl with a plate on the top in the middle of the kitchen table. A sticky note was stuck on the upturned plate. It read, 'Bread and butter pudding for your supper.'

I wandered clumsily into the lounge with the bowl and my glass of water, not bothering to turn on the light because the curtains were open and the moon was throwing a cold glance across the room. Sinking heavily into an armchair, I ate the pudding, swigging large mouthfuls of water in between each bite. Hopefully the bread would soak up some of the excess alcohol in my stomach.

My eyes adjusted to the gloom and the furniture began to extricate itself from the shadows. A handsome display cabinet filled with glinting silver and glass emerged from the corner. A tall vase of sticks, a tribute to some home improvement television programme my mother had watched, came into focus. A black and white wedding photograph stood at one end of the mantelpiece. A head shot of myself, taken when I was about 25 and skiing in Italy, was propped at the other end.

Even in the shadows, my parents' furniture looked solid and established, fixed and secure, as though the three-piece suite had sent down roots into the foundations of the house to hold it firm while the world around me shook and crumbled. The clock ticked. Apart from the vase of sticks, little had changed here since I was a child. Even the air smelt the same – polish and the faint, comforting whiff of dog. And just like the child I had been, I started to cry.

*****

I didn't sleep well that night. The sheets were cold and took a while to warm up. I thought about Jimmy, and how we had stayed in contact over the years, even though we didn't really have that much in common. I remembered our schooldays together. He had been a bit of a jack-the-lad and I had tagged along after him. Dad was right. I probably had been easily led.

I wracked my brains again to remember more about Sarah Penny's schooldays. Sometimes when Jimmy had a detention, Sarah and I would travel back to Elmsford on the train together. She never spoke much, preferring to gaze out of the window as the fields and farms flashed past. If Jimmy was on the train there was always some joke or prank which filled the carriage with laughter and annoyance; invariably, Sarah travelled in another carriage on those occasions. I remembered she had lived at the other end of the village with her mother in a bungalow. I wondered if she was still there.

What sort of a sad existence did she lead if things that occurred at school more than 15 years ago still haunted her? I barely remembered what had happened last year. Something really horrible must have taken place in the changing rooms. Girls could be cruel. No doubt it had been utterly humiliating. That was why she had been so rude when I asked if we had gone to school together. Then again, how sad was I to be giving the matter a moment's thought?

Exactly! I turned over and visualised myself landing a top job and moving into a new apartment. If I wanted it badly enough, it had to come true. But amidst the images of success, I saw again a knot of messy hair, a thin figure shrouded in drab layers of clothing. I remembered the shock of her pale eyes meeting mine and shuddered. I ran over the conversation in the library. I was just another customer, as far as she was concerned. I had seen a woman who didn't look like she received much male attention and had wanted to impress her with a façade of slick success. Instead she snubbed me. My ego had been bruised. *Get over yourself!* I scolded. Sure as hell she wasn't lying awake in bed thinking about me!

Chapter 4

The next morning was cold, even for January, even for East Anglia which was known for the cutting winds off the North Sea. Overnight a heavy frost had descended, whitening the earth, encrusting the garden beds and transforming the vegetation into serrated corals that glistened in the early morning light. The lawn was a crystal blanket, plump and pure as virgin snow.

The weather girl on the local radio explained that an area of high pressure over East Anglia was responsible for the bright sunshine and bitter temperatures. I was used to high pressure, I told myself, and decided to face the conditions head on. I would walk Elsie before breakfast. No doubt my parents would be looking for signs of my late night at the pub; I didn't want to give them the satisfaction of knowing I had a slight hangover.

I had noticed the previous day that Dad was not as active and alert as he had been. He was walking more deliberately around the house and hadn't washed his car – a weekly Saturday morning ritual for as long as I could remember. He didn't object when I suggested taking the early morning dog walks off his hands during my stay. It was important to inject a semblance of purpose into my routine, I told myself. I didn't want to regress into some kind of moronic teenage slob who lazed about in bed all morning. I wanted to look like an achiever, even if there weren't many people to notice.

The ornamental willow by our front gate was crying frozen tears. A silver birch in a neighbouring garden drooped mournfully under the weight of its icy branches. The air held a tremendous stillness, that quiet which only comes with extreme cold. The Sunday morning roads were empty. Turning down a narrow footpath between two houses, I walked past the fenced-off back gardens to a kissing gate which clanged loudly behind me. I was now behind the village.

A vast landscape stretched before me, fields spreading flat to a wide horizon. I could see for miles. I squinted into the distance, dazzled by the sun trailing low across the fresh blue of a winter's morning. The fields were tinted palest brown and green, all colour diluted by the covering of frost. Petrified grasses crunched softly underfoot as I walked into the first field. Tall weeds and teasels stood still and white as statues; the hedgerows were sharp and glittering as glass. To me it looked as though the whole world was in stasis, freeze-framed, left on pause.

A man walked towards me with a springer spaniel at his side. 'Morning,' he said as he passed. 'Bootiful day.'

'If you say so,' I replied, beginning to lose the feeling in my fingers.

The dry chill was hardening my cheeks and cracking the skin on my lips. Pulling my beanie hat down low and breathing into Dad's scarf, I marched at a military pace, filling my lungs with icy air and bracing myself to think positively about the future. I would make this enforced hiatus work for me. I would set myself some clear goals and think strategically, envisage where I wanted to be in five years' time, perhaps read up on the latest management techniques. I would send my CV to anyone and everyone, sign up with the best recruitment agencies and headhunters. It would only be a matter of time. And while searching for the perfect job, I would get to spend some quality time with my parents and childhood mates. Perhaps I might even get to see a couple of Ipswich Town matches at the Portman Road stadium. Without my hefty London rent, I would be able to get a handle on my credit card debts, which were not significant in the grand scheme of things, but were beginning to hurt.

An icy mist clung to the ground ahead. My pace began to slow. Up ahead, a small copse of trees interrupted the monotonous landscape. Even from a distance it looked unwelcoming. Stark branches stabbed at the sky. A large black bird – probably a crow – flapped out of the shadows, wheeled above the treetops and circled down again into the darkness of the coppice. The frost was thickest in the shadows cast by the trees across the field. I shivered as I walked out of the cold sunlight and into the shade, pulling Elsie behind me.

The trees on the outskirts of the copse were emaciated ghosts, their woody skins transformed by a shimmering pallor. Looking deeper into the coppice, the trunks were dark and clammy; patches of moss clung to the crevices. A cold mist lapped around the roots, trapped by the stillness within the small wood. I had no desire to explore. Even if I had, tangled around the edge of the trees was a bank of vicious brambles, their thorny stems stained deep purple, their few remaining leaves withered and livid as splashes of dried blood. As far as I could see, there was no accessible path through the undergrowth. I hurried past, shivering not only from the cold but also from the uncomfortable feeling, remembered from childhood, that there might be something monstrous lurking in the gloom.

I trudged onwards towards the next gate, slipped the blue nylon string off the post and let Elsie through into a ploughed field. The clods of mud in the recently tilled soil were hard as rock. Splinters of ice glinted in the tyre tracks left by a tractor. I had to be careful not to turn my ankle on the uneven ground. Designer trainers were not the best footwear, but I no longer owned any wellington boots. Elsie picked her way carefully along a narrow path made by walkers around the edge of the field, sniffing the hedgerow occasionally, her blunt nose powdered with crystals.

Chloe might not be in bed yet, I thought. She and her friends sometimes finished off a Saturday night with a cooked breakfast at a café near Euston station. I hoped this was the case, and she wasn't having toast and something hot in some other bloke's flat. I remembered what it was like going out with her on a Saturday night, having her by my side when we walked into a wine bar or restaurant. She always looked fit and sexy. She turned heads. She was the kind of girl I liked to be seen with, someone completely together and confident who wouldn't take nonsense from anyone. I did *not* like the idea that she might have been with someone else last night.

Suddenly I felt very insignificant and alone, a small person in the middle of a vast and empty landscape. I stood still and slowly turned around, looking in every direction. Behind me I could see the small village of Elmsford, neat houses and bungalows painted in the pastel shades favoured by Suffolk residents, a square-towered church, a large barn with a white, corrugated roof. I turned back into the sun. I thought I saw the silhouette of another dog walker at the far end of the field, wearing what looked like a cowboy hat and long coat. The shadow of an enormous dog loped ahead, stirring the mist into iridescent swirls. My eyes watered in the brightness; I couldn't be sure of the breed. Before I could get closer, the dark figure whistled and they turned and cut behind a hedge into another field.

After 20 minutes outside, Elsie was shivering. I had forgotten to put on her winter coat. I turned back to the village and made my way home for breakfast. Mum had pulled out all the stops: bacon, eggs and cereal. While I ate, she put a leg of lamb in the oven and prepared the vegetables for Sunday lunch, leaving them in saucepans of water.

'We're off to church at 10.15. Are you coming with us?'

'No thanks. I'm not in the mood to talk to more of your friends.'

'What's that supposed to mean? Have you got a problem with Simon and Liz?'

'No. I'm just not up to small talk at the moment.'

'It doesn't have to be small. We are capable of talking the big stuff you know,' Dad said.

'You're definitely coming to visit Nana with us this afternoon,' Mum insisted. 'It doesn't matter what you say to her – big, small, sense or nonsense. She'll just be glad to see you.'

*****

During lunch, Dad asked about my drink with Jimmy the previous night. I kept my replies deliberately vague. I knew he was looking for an excuse to criticise my choice of company.

'Did Jimmy have news of any of your other friends?' Mum asked during pudding.

'Not really.' I chewed for a moment. 'Well, we did talk a bit about Sarah Penny. She was in our class for a couple of years. I forgot to tell you I bumped into her in the library yesterday when I returned your books. I wondered if Jimmy was still in touch with her.'

'Yes, of course. Sarah Penny. I'd forgotten you were at school together. Is she friends with Jimmy, then? I wouldn't have thought she was his type at all.'

'No, they're not in touch. In fact, Jimmy had trouble remembering her. She wasn't in our school for very long. She left suddenly. No one knew why.'

'She always looks as though she's in her own world,' Mum said. 'I knew her mother, Eleanor, and was sorry when I heard she had passed away. She had a difficult life. Her husband died in his early 30s and she was left with Sarah. I always had the feeling there were some difficulties there. I don't know whether it was depression, or whether Sarah was a particularly problematic child, but Eleanor had an unusual parenting style. She kept herself to herself. Didn't mix in the village. She was a bit of an eccentric –

very clever, mind – but not really on the same planet as everybody else, if you know what I mean. It's no wonder Sarah turned out the way she has.'

'What do you mean?'

'She's quirky,' Mum lowered her voice as though someone might overhear, a habit acquired through years of discreet conversations with friends in public places. 'I've always thought there was something... I can't put my finger on it –'

'Gillian, you think half the village is peculiar,' Dad interrupted.

'Well, they are!' She scraped the last of the custard from the edge of her bowl and licked the spoon clean. 'But Sarah does very well in the library. Did she remember you?'

'At first I didn't think she did.'

'Was she a bit shy?'

'Something like that.'

'When I tried to talk to her about Eleanor's passing she was quite sharp, but it was probably because of the circumstances. Since then, however, she has been very helpful ordering books for me and such, though she's not very chatty. An introvert, I think.'

'What circumstances?'

'Pardon?'

'You were talking about the circumstances of her mother's death.'

Mum looked uncomfortable.

'Yes... well, that was all a bit mysterious. She'd been unwell for a couple of months, so in that sense it wasn't totally unexpected. I shouldn't really speculate. There were rumours she had been found locked in a room. Some people even said she was found in a cupboard, but that's absurd. People were very upset.'

'Found dead?'

'Yes.'

'Was there any explanation given?'

'Not that I know of. They called it natural causes in the local paper, and I'm sure it was. But she was a rather eccentric woman.'

'Who discovered the body?'

'I think it was the carer. Eleanor was ill, as I said, and needed help with personal stuff. Was Sarah a particular friend of yours?' Mum asked, changing the subject.

'No, not really. But you wouldn't wish that kind of thing to happen to anyone.'

'You know you can ask any of your friends to come back here while you are staying with us. We want you to feel right at home, don't we, Derek, though perhaps Jimmy would be the exception, particularly after last time...' She trailed off. I remembered how he had vomited in the fruit bowl after we had returned home jubilant from a football match a couple of seasons ago.

'I don't think I'll be seeing Sarah again while I'm here, but thanks for the offer.'

Dad looked at me closely. 'Elmsford is a small village. It's easy to bump into people.'

*****

Mum drove us to Nana's house. Dad had a stomach ache and sat in the passenger seat with a covered plate of cold roast lamb, potatoes, carrots and sprouts on his lap. I sat in the back, somewhere I'd not been since passing my driving test at the age of 17. I stared out of the window as we passed familiar streets, feeling like a child: dependent, lesser, carried somewhere I didn't want to go. Mum stopped briefly outside the local supermarket and I jumped out to buy Nana's Sunday newspaper.

There were very few customers. The girl on the checkout looked bored. She smiled as I approached. Behind her, rows of shining bottles lined the wall: beers, wines and spirits glowing blood red and gold. On the spur of the moment I pointed to a bottle of Scotch. She scanned the newspaper and whisky at the till and asked if I had a membership card. I shook my head and pulled out my wallet.

'Would you like to become a member?'

'No thanks. I don't usually shop in here.'

'You're not local, then?'

'Used to be, but not any more.'

'That's a pity.' She smiled. I looked at her more closely as she put my money in the till. Her hair was brown with a streak of artificial blonde at the front. Her hazel eyes were fringed with clotted lashes, a smudge of silver on the lids. She was curvy, even a little overweight under the unflattering polyester uniform. But still attractive. An overripe peach. She reminded me of a picture on the computer that had been dragged and stretched from the side; the proportions looked wrong but you could still see the original image. There was a slim, pretty girl in there trying to get out.

'Is there anything else I can get you?'

'No thanks.' I smiled back. 'Not now, anyway... maybe I'll be back tomorrow.'

'I'll look forward to it!' She flicked her hair behind her shoulder. 'Bye.'

I looked at her name badge. 'See you later, Lauren.'

I folded the newspaper under my arm and left the shop swinging my carrier bag. A nice-looking girl, probably ten years my junior, had flirted with me. I still had it! I took a deep breath of cold air. Life could still have its good moments, despite everything.

*****

Nana's chair had been pulled into the centre of the living room opposite the television. There were small tables on either side, one with a reading light, glasses and a magazine on top, the other with a box of tissues, her handbag and a jar of peppermints. The room was hot and stuffy. I stooped to kiss Nana. Her crêpey skin was as soft as chamois leather against my cheek.

Mum hurried into the kitchen to heat up the plate of lamb in the microwave. She had brought a box of cherry Bakewell tarts too, much to Dad's disgust. He stood by the living room window frowning at the overgrown garden. I sat at the small dining table, pushed against the wall to leave more space for Nan to manoeuvre around the room with her walking stick. She fumbled in her purse for some change.

'Here you are, Vincent. Here's the money for the newspaper, there's a good boy.'

'That's OK, Nana, you keep it.'

'Don't be silly. You deserve your pocket money, a good boy like you.'

I stood up to take it and sat back at the table.

'Thanks, Nan.'

Mum put a tray of food on Nana's lap. The bottom of the tray was padded to stop it slipping. Nana took a boiled mint she had been sucking out of her mouth and placed it on the table next to her before starting to eat. Mum tutted, picked it up in a tissue and retreated to the kitchen. She returned a few minutes later with a tray of coffees for us and a cup of tea and a Bakewell tart for Nana. After passing round the drinks she flopped heavily onto the sofa.

'What time did the carer come this morning, Mother?' she asked loudly.

'I'm not sure, dear.'

'Did you have a shower?'

'No, not today.'

'Why not?'

'The water's too wet, dear. I don't like it.'

'I know you don't, but you need to have a wash.'

'I'll have one tomorrow. Now I must pay the boy for my newspaper.' She reached across for her handbag on the side table, her hand shaking as she fumbled with the clasp. The tray on her lap wobbled dangerously and she accidentally knocked her glasses case from the table onto the floor.

'That's alright, Nan, I've got it,' I said, retrieving the case. 'You've paid me for the newspaper already.'

'Did I?'

'Yes.' We sat in silence as Nana finished eating.

'And did the cleaner come yesterday?' Mum asked, taking the tray and passing Nana her cherry Bakewell.

'Yes, but I told her to go away. I don't need her.'

'Of course you do. We've talked about this. You need some help to keep on top of the housework. I can't do it all for you. I have to work.'

'I might do a bit of hoovering later.' Nan deliberately brushed some crumbs from her lap onto the carpet.

'That's what the cleaner's for, Mother! You're not able to do it any more.'

'I don't like the cleaner. She can't be trusted.'

'Of course she can. She's a lovely lady.'

'No, she tried to trick me!' Nan replied, her voice trembling. 'Cleaners can't be trusted.'

'They can be trusted. Jodie comes to help you. She was just trying to show you how easy it is for other people to steal your money if you aren't careful.' Mum turned to me and explained. 'Nana left her handbag near the front door the other day. When Jodie let herself in she brought it into Nana and told her she should keep it out of sight. She was telling Nana about people who come to the door – you know, distraction burglars – who prey on elderly people. Nana didn't really understand, so to make her point Jodie did a little role play. She pretended that she was some kind of tradesman and took the handbag and walked out of the room.'

'Yes, she stole my handbag!'

'But she brought it straight back. She was just demonstrating how easy it is for someone to take your handbag if you don't keep it safe.' Tears welled up in Mum's eyes.

'I don't trust cleaners!'

'But Auntie Pat's a cleaner,' I said. There was a pause while Nan thought about that. She then looked sideways, avoiding our eyes like an obstinate child. 'I've always wondered about Pat...'

'Oh, for goodness' sake!' Dad exclaimed under his breath. Nan reached for her newspaper and her glasses. Mum carried our mugs into the kitchen. I followed her and together we washed and dried the crockery.

'She can't hoover!' Mum explained, sniffing. 'She can't work out how to plug it in, or remember how to switch it on, let alone push it around the room. But she forgets that she can't do these things any more. I can't be here all the time. That's why we've got the carers and the cleaner, but she's so stubbornly independent. I'm not even sure she can read the paper any more. I think she just looks at the pictures.'

Mum made a sandwich and put it on a tray with a glass of juice, a bowl of tinned peaches and another Bakewell tart.

'I've made you some supper for later,' she said loudly, returning to the living room and putting the tray on the dining table.

Dad had switched the television on and Nana didn't respond. She was staring at the screen, mesmerised by an advertisement for toothpaste.

'If you've got everything you need, we'll leave you in peace,' Mum shouted. 'Do you want Vincent to help you up to the toilet before we go?'

'No, I'm fine, dear. I just need to pay him for the newspaper.'

'You've paid me, Nan. Put your purse away.' I kissed her goodbye with relief.

Chapter 5

Mum and Dad had both left for work before I awoke the next day. Annoyingly, there was a note on the kitchen table to remind me to walk the dog and feed her afterwards. They already assumed I would forget my promise. Dad usually gave Elsie a quick run across the fields before his daily commute to Ipswich. He had worked at the same small quantity surveyors' office for more than 20 years, climbing his way up to a position where he could manage his work diary to fit around his home life. None of the other partners seemed overly career-driven or ambitious for the company. I imagined that his working life was pretty much the same as it had been when I was a child. What a rut to get stuck in! I hoped he wouldn't lose the habit of his morning walk now that I was here to do the honours for him for a couple of weeks. If you don't use it, you lose it, as they say.

Elsie was flopped on her bed. She watched with dark reproachful eyes as I made myself a black coffee. I couldn't face breakfast. I had managed to drink half the bottle of Scotch the previous night, swigging it in bed, then hiding the bottle in my underwear drawer so Mum wouldn't find out I'd been bingeing.

The day stretched endlessly ahead. I looked at myself in the mirror while I shaved. My skin was sallow. Pink capillaries zigzagged across the whites of my eyes. I had a vague headache, not bad enough for painkillers, but irritating nevertheless. I tried to see myself as others saw me: dark hair, brown eyes, tallish, not overweight but not slim either. Nothing out of the ordinary, but pleasant enough. It was a face you could trust. Who wouldn't want to give this bloke a job?

I bent to splash my face and stood up too quickly. Grasping the edge of the sink, I swallowed back a mouthful of bile. The chemical smell of the air freshener my parents used in their small bathroom caught at the back of my throat. Perhaps I should cut back on the drinking. I didn't seem to be bouncing back any more.

I studied myself again in the mirror. I was trapped. Stuck in a small world, entangled by the emptiness of my new life – nothing to do and nowhere to go. The only escape would be to refill my life with everything that had made it meaningful in the past – money, sex, the admiration of my peers. I straightened up. I would not allow myself to fall into despair.

I remembered Elsie's coat, but she still looked reluctant to leave the warmth of the house. Perhaps, like Dad, age was beginning to take its toll.

The sun was a low wattage light bulb behind dirty net curtains that morning. A hint of drizzle thickened the air. I walked quickly to keep warm. Once again, I saw the walker with the hat and the huge dog in the distance. This time it was racing across a field, running low and taking enormous bounds over tussocks of dead vegetation. From its outline, I deduced it was short-haired, lean and in great condition – possibly a Doberman, or even a Great Dane, though it seemed to be moving too fast to be the latter.

Its owner walked purposefully forward, head down and muffled in a large scarf, a dark figure against the pale sky. It was impossible to tell if it was a man or a woman. By the time I reached the end of the field they had gone through a gate and were walking behind the small copse of trees I had passed before – the opposite way from the path I was taking. Elsie showed not the slightest interest in the other dog. Perhaps it was too far away. Perhaps she just wanted to get back to her breakfast and a sleep on the sofa. I decided to walk to the end of the field then turn back to the village and make my way home for a late breakfast too.

I skirted the outside edge of the field until I reached the splattering of trees again with its vicious circlet of brambles. The branches reminded me of fingers clawing their way out of the earth. I quickened my pace as I passed. Suddenly something shot through an invisible gap in the briars and ran into the longer grass in the middle of the field. Before my mind had time to process what I had seen, an enormous russet-brown dog bounded from the shadow of the trees and raced across my path, legs at full stretch.

Lithe as a cheetah, its glossy coat stretched taut over muscle and bone, the dog thundered across the field, its paws reverberating on the cold earth like a galloping pony. Abruptly changing direction, it slowed, pounced forwards and skidded to a halt, spraying clods of mud in all directions. It nosed the ground. A piercing, unearthly cry shattered the silence. The dog raised its head with something dangling from its mouth, something brown and quivering, back legs kicking frantically. The dog trotted back towards the coppice, but stopped on seeing me. It threw the limp body of a rabbit a couple of times in the air, catching it adroitly and giving it a vigorous shake. Elsie took a couple of tentative paces forwards, paused, then watched from a safe distance.

The contrast between the two dogs was pronounced. One glorying in the power of its kill, adrenaline quivering through its thighs, beautiful, primitive, wild. The other, Elsie, standing obediently by my side in her blue hooded jacket, her face puckered in a quizzical frown, the definition of overweight domestication. At that moment a figure stepped from the copse through an invisible break in the thorns, a long black coat swinging to the ankles and a brown leather hat with a wide brim pulled down low. The dog walker stopped, startled. We looked each other full in the face. It was Sarah Penny!

'Damnation!' She looked from me to the dog and swore again. Not knowing how to respond, I followed her gaze. Her dog was proudly loping away along the line of the hedge which bounded the field, head high, ears pricked, tail wagging in triumph. Had her expletive been levelled at me or the dog? I experienced again the strange feeling that had come over me in the library, a mixture of fear and fascination, a sensation that I knew her but also that she was a stranger to me – a kind of déjà vu.

'Handsome animal,' I announced awkwardly. 'Is he yours?'

'Yes.'

'What breed is he?'

'A Rhodesian Ridgeback.' She looked away.

'Are they the dogs that were bred to hunt lions in Africa?' I persisted.

'Yes… Damn! I'll never get that rabbit off him now before he eats it.'

With relief, I realised she had been swearing at the dog.

'Is that a problem?'

'Apart from the fact that the rabbit could be riddled with some horrible disease, the last time he devoured one he vomited the whole lot back up on my kitchen floor a couple of hours later. Ears, feet, claws, fur. He swallowed it whole and that was how it came back up!'

'Charming!'

'It wasn't charming,' she replied seriously. 'It was very messy.'

'I meant "how horrible", obviously.'

48

There was an embarrassed silence. Should I just walk past and leave her to her dilemma? She pulled off her hat and dragged a hand through her hair in exasperation. I tried again.

'What's his name?'

'Bruce.'

'Does he bite?'

'Only rabbits... and sometimes ducks. Once a rat.'

'Well, why don't we try and catch him and take the rabbit off him?'

'I don't know... he will be very possessive. He won't let us near him. He will keep a safe distance until he has finished playing with it. Then he'll eat it. Last time I was stuck out here for over an hour before I could get him back on the lead.' She looked at her watch. 'I have to be at work soon.' The dog loped further away with the rabbit in his mouth.

'Let's try a pincer movement,' I suggested. 'You follow the dog –'

'Bruce,' she corrected.

'You follow Bruce, and Elsie and I will go round the field in the opposite direction. When we meet up, you grab his collar and I'll try and grab the rabbit.'

Sarah nodded, spun on her heel and strode towards Bruce who shook his kill vigorously and backed away. I turned and walked in the opposite direction, asking myself what the hell I was doing. It took about five minutes to circle the field so that Sarah's shrouded figure was walking towards me with Bruce trotting in front, head high and proud, the rabbit dangling from either side of his jaws. He spied me and stopped, unsure. Elsie and I walked a little way out into the field so he couldn't run onto open ground. We had to be careful not to walk too far from the hedge, otherwise he would shoot past. He feinted one way, wary. I followed his movement, cutting him off. He started in the other direction; I countered. He looked back at Sarah, who was approaching fast. In profile, his muzzle was deep and powerful, his body perfectly proportioned, the outline of his ribs just visible beneath his coat. He really was a beautiful specimen.

I began to move back towards the path by the hedge to cut off his escape route. Sarah continued to walk towards me. Thankfully, Elsie remained a little way out into the field so that Bruce was caught in a triangle between the three of us, his body quivering in anticipation, scenting the cold wind that blew across the field.

At that moment, Elsie's curiosity overcame caution. She toddled forwards, backing Bruce against the hedge. The two dogs eyed each other suspiciously, gradually circled and sniffed. Sarah and I moved quietly, unobserved. As soon as Elsie was close enough to smell Bruce's hindquarters, I lunged forward and grabbed his collar.

Immediately there was a tremendous struggle. I was taken off guard by his strength and found myself dragged to the ground as he sprang away. Pulling from his shoulders, he seemed unaffected by the collar digging into his neck. Determined to hold on, even though the collar was now cutting into my gloved hands and my knees had hit the rough ground, I shouted at Sarah for help.

'Steady, boy!' she ordered, grabbing the collar too and fumbling to connect the lead. Bruce thrashed from side to side. 'Steady!'

We were both on our knees, shoulders touching, struggling for control. Then she stood up, lead attached, winding it firmly round both hands and bracing herself as it pulled taut.

'Don't let go of the collar yet, or he'll pull me over!' she gasped. 'Gently, Bruce!' He shook the rabbit vigorously again, almost pulling my hand off as I clung on.

Catching the excitement, Elsie lumbered into his line of sight. He froze. The two dogs gazed into each other's eyes. I grabbed hold of the rabbit's legs, dangling from the jaws of the beast, and shouted, 'Drop!' I felt a momentary hesitation, a lessening of tension, and yanked with all my strength. I had it!

The body of the rabbit swung away. I stood up and let go of the collar. Immediately Bruce sprang forward. I threw my arm up to hold the rabbit out of reach. He lunged again. Sarah wrestled with the lead, trying to gain control. I was intensely aware of two rows of sharp, gleaming teeth, a massive, muscled body with hackles raised and enormous clawed feet. He was so large that if he wanted, he could have rested his front paws on my shoulders and looked me directly in the eye. A vision of a paperback book with a vicious hound on the cover flashed before my eyes.

'Off!' Sarah cried, struggling to hold on to the lead. 'Leave!'

Clutching the prize over my head, I frantically scanned my surroundings to see how I could safely dispose of the body. I could throw it over the hedge, but no doubt Bruce would try to drag Sarah through a thorny opening. There was a tallish hawthorn tree a few metres away on the boundary. I ran towards it, Bruce and Elsie following, Sarah pulled along behind as she tried to brace her feet on the slippery mud. Just as I felt his hot breath behind me, I threw the rabbit as high as I could up into the branches, praying it would catch in the tangled network. The rabbit flew to the top. It hit the highest bough and bounced down through the branches, stopping halfway, out of reach of man and beast.

I put my hand on my knees and bent forward, panting, winded by the struggle and by fear, my breath vaporising in cloudy gasps. From my bent position I looked sideways at Sarah and Bruce. He was jumping half-heartedly at the base of the tree, looking at the rabbit with longing, his bright intelligent eyes turning to me in an expression of vexation.

'Leave. Good boy, good boy,' Sarah said. She was panting too, her cheeks pink with exertion. 'I thought I was grabbing the collar! That's what you said.'

'I acted instinctively. The opportunity arose and I took my chance. We did it though, didn't we! Now the birds can eat it.' I couldn't control the huge grin spreading across my frozen cheeks.

'I like to stick to a plan,' she retorted.

I couldn't believe it. What was wrong with the woman! I had sorted her problem and saved her a lot of time and hassle, muddying my trousers in the process. I stared in disbelief. She must have picked up on my annoyance because she looked down at the ground for a moment before saying, 'I'm sorry. That must have sounded very rude. Thank you for helping me... Vincent.'

It was the first time she had acknowledged me by my Christian name. My pulse quickened. She looked at my muddy trousers for the briefest moment before glancing away. Her eyes were very pale and intense in her flushed face. She had a small drop of moisture – nasal condensation – hanging from the end of her nose. She wiped it away unselfconsciously on the back of her glove.

'I have to get back.' She looked up at the rabbit dangling in the tree, its eyes bulging open, a splash of red on its neck. She showed no sign of distress at the pitiful sight, and turned away dismissively. We both started to move in the same direction, taking the path back to the village. The dogs fell into step beside us, seemingly happy to trot along together. Bruce looked back at the rabbit hanging in the tree several times, but was calming down. I felt breathless, though physically my breathing was returning to normal. I tried to think of something to say. Drizzle, as fine as dust, began to fall on my hot cheeks.

'They like each other.' I remarked eventually.

'Yes.'

We continued to walk in silence, the dogs making better conversational progress than we were, if their body language was anything to go by.

'That's not your dog, is it?' she asked. 'I've seen it before with an older man.'

'That would be Dad. Elsie belongs to my parents. I'm staying with them for a few weeks.'

'Oh.'

'Do you still live in Moon Rise?' I said.

'Yes. But my mother died.'

'I heard. I'm sorry. That must have been very difficult.' I turned sideways to catch her expression, but her eyes were shaded by the large brim of her hat. 'You must miss her dreadfully.'

'Yes.'

'Do you have any other family?'

'I have Bruce.'

'Yes, but that's not the same –'

'It's another beating heart in the home. That's what counts.'

'Still…'

'Mum suffered a great deal at the end. I wouldn't want her back like that. I was glad when she was put out of her misery.'

I was shocked by the unfeeling way she delivered this statement, using a phrase more appropriate in a vet's practice than in a conversation explaining her mother's death. There was an awkward pause while I searched for a suitable response.

'Was she ill for a long time?'

'Not as long as I was told she might be. In the end she had a happy despatch.'

'Happy?' I exclaimed.

'It's all comparative. I didn't like to see her suffering so it was better in the end that she died more quickly than expected. The carer used the phrase "happy despatch". I was just happy it was over, though not happy she had gone.' She spoke without a tremor of emotion.

'It's good you can see it that way. I'm not sure I could in the circumstances.' I remembered what Mum told me about Eleanor Penny being found dead in a cupboard. It seemed too outrageous. I felt sure Mum must have got hold of the wrong end of the stick. Still, it wouldn't do any harm to pretend a degree of ignorance.

'Was she in hospital?'

52

'No. I was looking after her at home.'

'That must have been very hard.' I imagined her looking after her sick mother, seeing her in pain and feeling helpless and alone. I thought of how the strain of caring for Nana had taken its toll on Mum.

'I had a carer coming in to help. She kept Mum company when I was working.'

'And did that work out OK? My nan has carers at the moment but Mum has to spend a lot of time checking up on them and convincing Nan they're a good idea.'

'She kept Mum comfortable. She didn't like seeing her in pain any more than I did.'

'Perhaps you could give me the name of her agency. Mum keeps threatening to sack the ones we have. They turn up at any time they fancy. Sometimes they don't arrive to help Nana get out of bed until nearly midday, and at other times they want to put her to bed at half past five. It's ridiculous!'

'She doesn't work for an agency. She's just a girl in the village.'

'So... were you with your mum when... when...?'

Sarah looked at her hands, rubbing them together. She didn't respond for such a long time that I began to wonder if she had heard my question. When she did answer, her tone was abrupt.

'No. I wasn't. Why? Did you think I was?'

'I didn't... I... I was just marvelling how well you seem to have coped. That's all.' Her manner had been so controlled, so matter of fact up to that point, I had allowed myself to stray too far into private territory. Her face had a shuttered, almost secretive expression now, and she abruptly changed the subject.

'Why are you here?'

'I'm staying with my parents for a few weeks, taking a little holiday –'

'No. I meant why are *you* here in this field, instead of your father?"

'Oh... I'm giving him a break from the dog-walking. And I'm getting some fresh air before settling down to my computer.'

'You said you were on holiday.'

'I am, but I'm researching some new possibilities.' It began to rain properly. I gazed around at the flat countryside and oppressive sky. Despite the downpour I found my body relaxing after the recent drama with the rabbit. Bruce was walking with sinuous grace by Sarah's side, his shoulder blades rotating with every step. I realised his hackles had not

53

been raised during our struggle. He had a stripe of hair growing in a different direction along the mid-line of his back from neck to tail, topped with two crowns at the base of his neck. It was the ridge that gave Rhodesian Ridgebacks their name. A strange peace descended between us. Sarah didn't seem to feel the need to fill the silence.

I was struck again by her unusual appearance. Her clothes were odd, her expression masked. Today her hair was down, darkened with rain and hanging limply from beneath her hat. She kept rubbing her gloved hand as if it were cold.

We were nearing the village. The headache I had woken up with had miraculously vanished.

'You're probably wondering why I'm having a sabbatical,' I said.

'No.'

'Oh, well in case you were… I'm between jobs right now. I had come to the end of what I could achieve with my organisation, so we mutually agreed to part company. I had some ideas they liked but they couldn't implement them in the current economic climate. I'm looking to work in the kind of business that's open to some new, original input. It has come at a good stage in my game plan. I have no commitments. I have the freedom to take my time, have a good look around before I jump back into the rat race. Time to reassess.'

'So you're unemployed.' This was a little insensitive, but I nodded.

'In a nutshell.'

'Have you signed on for Jobseekers' Allowance? We have some leaflets in the library.'

I interrupted her before she could continue. 'I don't think things are that bad yet! There are a few opportunities coming up. I have good contacts, so I'm anticipating some useful conversations fairly shortly. Also, once it gets about that I'm available I'm expecting some of my old rivals in other firms to be in touch. It's all about who you know.'

'I thought it was about what you can do.'

'Well, yes, of course… it's about that too. That's taken as read.'

We reached the kissing gate which led out on to the lane. She stopped and examined her right hand. 'Are you all right?' I asked. She took off her glove.

'I had the lead wrapped around my fingers to help me hold on to Bruce, but he pulled it really tight when he was jumping up at the rabbit. My hand hurts.' I looked down and saw an angry welt forming across the middle knuckle of each finger. One knuckle in particular was badly swollen, almost purple and edged with red.

'That does look nasty. Perhaps you should come back to my place for some ice to bring down the swelling. My parents live just down the road. We could have a cup of tea, some breakfast, while we wait to see if it improves. It might be fractured. You might need to ring the library to say you can't come in today.'

'No, it's fine.'

'Don't worry. My parents will have left for work...'

'No.'

'... and I make a great cup of coffee.'

'I thought you said tea.'

'Tea, coffee. I'm great at both.'

'No. I don't go into strangers' houses, thank you.'

'Stranger! I'm hardly a stranger!' I exclaimed. She looked at her feet, her nose pink and moist, her hair bedraggled under her ridiculous hat, her coat hanging shapelessly from her shoulders. 'You are completely safe with me. I thought we established yesterday that we went to the same school and that you remembered me. Vincent Stevens, the one you apparently thought didn't have any friends – though why you should think that I don't know. I had friends!'

'I remember you, but I don't know who you are. I thought I used to know you, but you have changed.'

'Changed!' I spluttered. 'It's been 15 years since we've seen each other! Everyone changes. I've helped you catch your dog. You are hurt and I'm offering my help, just some basic first aid and a hot drink of some description. What *is* your problem?'

She stared at me intently for a few seconds, looking as though she were concentrating on a difficult puzzle. 'Are you offended?'

'Of course I'm offended! We used to come home from school together on the train. Don't you remember? You're treating me as if I'm some kind of pervert.'

'I'm sorry. My mother always told me not to go off with strangers. Old habits die hard.' She looked thoughtful for a moment. 'I'm not very good at talking to new people. You don't look like you used to look. You *have* changed. You're not fat any more, for one thing. And yesterday, what you were saying and what you were meaning seemed to be two different things. That makes me nervous.'

'What on earth are you talking about?'

'Yesterday in the library, you thought you were being friendly but really you were looking down on me. You didn't used to be like that. What you said and what you meant always used to be the same thing.'

'I wasn't looking down on you!'

'Yes, you were. And you were annoyed because I wouldn't play your game and be impressed by all your talk.' There was a long silence. Paralysed by embarrassment, I desperately tried to think of a way to extricate myself from this bizarre conversation. Sarah looked at her feet, scraping her wellington boot on the ground and leaving a scar in the mud.

'I'm sorry,' she said at last. 'Sometimes I feel there's a kind of conspiracy against me. Everyone else seems to know the right thing to say and the right time to speak... except me. I can't talk the way other people do. I either say things as they are, or I say nothing at all. My mother used to tell me, "Always tell the truth, but don't always be telling the truth."'

'Good advice,' I began. 'Honesty is an excellent quality, but –'

'Yes, it is. You have changed. You used to be sincere. What happened to you?'

'– but,' I continued, ignoring her question, 'honesty should not become an excuse for bad manners.' I took a deep breath. 'Look, I don't want to get into an argument. Obviously we have had some kind of a misunderstanding.'

'I don't think so. I understood what was happening yesterday. I think you misunderstand yourself.' She looked me directly in the face and smiled coldly as though she had made an interesting discovery on a microscope slide.

A wave of piercing longing struck me deep in the chest. I suddenly remembered a time when speaking with Sarah had been as effortless as breathing. She was right! What I said and what I meant were often different now. The black and white world of my youth, when life had been relatively straightforward and certain, had melted into a tangle of grey dishonesties. I *had* wanted to patronise her the previous day to make myself feel better. I *was* going through a charade of friendliness when I didn't want to be friendly at all. I had wanted to make myself feel good and build up my fragile self-esteem at the expense of her own.

'I'm sorry if I've upset you. It wasn't my intention.' She shrugged. 'You are very perceptive.'

'I have always been able to see things other people don't see. All the little details. Sometimes I can sense what people feel before they realise it themselves.'

'That's a gift?'

'Or a curse. I can get overwhelmed by everything that's going on, people's expressions and the way their bodies move. Sometimes when they look at me it hurts because I can see all their emotions at once.'

We were way outside the usual rules of casual conversation. I was beginning to wonder if she was crazy or on medication. Yet I also knew that for the first time in a long while someone was speaking honestly to me.

'I've been going through a difficult time recently,' I blurted out. 'I've been trying to put a brave face on it, pretending everything's OK. But you're right. I'm putting on a front. What I'm saying and what I'm feeling inside are different. I've lost my job and I've had to move back with my parents. My girlfriend's decided she doesn't like me so much now that I can't afford to take her out to fancy clubs and restaurants. I feel like last night's leftovers. Perhaps we can forget it and move on.'

She didn't reply, but continued to look down and rub her injured hand while I spoke. 'You may want to drive yourself to A and E if that bruising doesn't improve. If it's broken it shouldn't be left unattended or it could cause you all kinds of problems in the future.'

'I don't drive. I wish I could.'

'Let me to drive you down to the hospital in Bury. It's the least I can do. You could be there in 20 minutes. This time of the morning, Accident and Emergency should be fairly quiet.' There was a long silence before her eyes flicked to mine. 'Oh, right,' I said, suddenly understanding. 'I suppose your mother told you not to get into cars with strangers too.'

Unexpectedly, she laughed. 'You're right! But thank you for the offer. I think I'll survive. Thank you for getting rid of the rabbit, and thank you for telling the truth. Next time we meet, we won't be strangers. Goodbye.' She walked away without a backward glance, Bruce padding sinuously by her side.

Chapter 6

I regretted my honesty immediately. What was I thinking? Why had I opened up to some crazy woman who thought anyone in trousers was trying to entice her back to their place? Or was it just me in particular she suspected of having designs on her virtue? I had revealed private things to Sarah that I hadn't even told my parents. OK, I had been irritated by her suspicious nature and wanted to prove her wrong, but that was no excuse. What a catastrophic lack of judgement. *I* was the one who had been trained to gain the confidence of others through body language and tone of voice. *I* was the expert at reflecting back the things people said to make them believe I shared their point of view. Usually I was extremely cautious about sharing emotions, especially when it came to people who might demand more from me than I wanted to give. Yet without using any clever tricks, Sarah Penny had opened up a chink in my defences. I felt as though I had been scammed by an amateur crook.

The ankles of my jeans were soaked where they had brushed against the wet grass; my knees were stained with mud. I was cold and jittery by the time I arrived home. I stripped off and showered, towelling my damp hair and gelling it into dishevelled spikes. I pulled on a pair of wool trousers and changed my jumper for a chunky cardigan I'd bought in the Portobello Road. 'Image is everything,' Tony always said. 'Dress to be the best!' I cooked a plate of eggs, bacon and toast to calm myself down.

I spent the morning on my laptop, purposely not thinking about Sarah. It was time to fine-tune my CV and I was pleased with the finished result. I had placed a photograph of myself at the top of the first page. It had been taken the previous autumn at a conference. I was giving a presentation, standing in front of a screen upon which a graph with an upward financial trend was projected and looking away from the camera towards the audience, the top of whose heads could just be seen in the bottom corner of the picture. My stance was authoritative. I was wearing one of my favourite suits, dark blue, with a crisp white shirt. I still had the suggestion of a tan from my summer holiday in Portugal.

My parents didn't have broadband. I had to plug my laptop into their telephone jack to connect to the internet. It was frustratingly slow. I toyed with the idea of taking a memory stick and working down at the library but dismissed the thought almost immediately. I had seen enough of Sarah for one day. Gritting my teeth at the sluggish technology, I sent my CV to as many recruitment agencies as I could. I then searched through the job sites, sifting the rubbish for anything worthwhile. It didn't look very encouraging. Most of the big firms were downsizing rather than recruiting.

In a moment of weakness, and despite the wait between each search, I Googled 'Eleanor Penny' and read the small article in the local newspaper about her death. There was nothing there I didn't already know, except that she was 58 when she died and had worked at the Elmsford Library for more than 30 years. The penny suddenly dropped. *She* had been the old fogey who had stamped my library card all those years ago.

I then searched for Sarah. She was nowhere to be found. No Facebook account, no Twitter feed. It was as if she didn't exist.

*****

Mum arrived home just after 4.30. I made her a cup of tea and we sat down at the kitchen table.

'How was your day?' she asked.

'OK. I've been looking at job sites on the internet, getting my CV out there. As you don't have broadband, I unplugged your telephone jack to plug in my laptop. I hope you don't mind.'

'I wondered why the line was engaged when I tried to ring you at lunchtime.'

'Sorry about that. What did you want?'

'I was going to ask you to visit Nana this afternoon. But I popped in quickly on my way home from school.'

'I've been busy, you know. It's important stuff.'

'Nana's important.'

'I know that.'

'If our telephone bill's huge this quarter, your dad might ask you to chip in,' she added.

'That's fine by me. I'll be happy to pay my way.' I would have a new job by the time the next quarter's telephone bill arrived. Money would be no problem by then. 'I'll contribute towards the housekeeping too. Tomorrow I'm going to ring some old mates to see if they know of any openings.'

Mum stood up. 'You can tell me all about it later, darling. I'm a bit behind now because of Nana. I must get on with the dinner. Your dad will be home soon and he can't eat late. Then I'm off to kickboxing class.'

'Kickboxing! When did you start that?'

'About 18 months ago. It was either kick the punchbag or kick your father. I've started Zumba classes too.'

'What brought this on?'

'I don't know. Midlife crisis. Empty nest. Going through the change...'

'OK. I get it.' I didn't want any more specifics.

She took a packet of chicken thighs out of the fridge and began to brown them in the pan. 'Marriage isn't easy, you know. It's not all rainbows and dancing unicorns.' She sipped her tea in between chopping up an onion, a red pepper and a punnet of mushrooms.

'I never said it was. But I thought you and Dad were happy.'

'We are. In our way. I know I can be a bit much, sometimes. I don't mean to be. It's just been hard seeing Nana go downhill. And now Dad's started picking at his food. I keep making all these pies and cakes but he's not interested. Perhaps I'm losing my touch –'

'You're a great cook.'

'You didn't used to think so.'

'I was watching my weight. That's all.'

'Sometimes I wonder... you know... whether your dad's losing interest in me as well as my food.'

There was an awkward silence while I digested this. 'Don't be ridiculous. He adores you.'

'Maggie Jordan's husband lost a lot of weight. She was delighted until it turned out he was seeing a hairdresser in Stowmarket behind her back.'

'Dad would never do anything like that.'

'Of course not. I know that really. But he's not been himself. I'm so glad you're here, Vincent. I know you've got better things to be doing. There's not much for you in Elmsford. But we have missed you.'

'I know.'

She gave my shoulder a little squeeze. 'Underneath all that wheeling and dealing and wining and dining, there's a kind and sensitive boy. An extraordinary boy. I'm allowed to think that, aren't I? You can be anything you want. Remember that.' She put the chicken and vegetables in a casserole dish and poured over a can of tomatoes. 'Didn't you want to be a teacher once?'

I shrugged. 'I don't think that's really me, do you? Corduroy jacket, brown shoes, sideburns.'

'No... perhaps not.'

She put the casserole in the oven and began moving between the kitchen, the utility room and the freezer in the garage collecting the rest of the ingredients for the evening meal. She returned to the subject of Nana. 'When I arrived, she was trying to get herself some tea. She had a dinner plate with a slice of fruit cake, a cherry Bakewell, two fairy cakes and a jam doughnut.' Mum walked into the utility room, raising her voice so I could still hear. 'When I asked her whether she thought it was a suitable meal for a diabetic, she told me it was what she fancied.'

She returned with a bag of potatoes and put a couple of pans of water on the hob to boil. 'After I had helped her back to her chair, I hid all the cakes in the tin apart from the doughnut, which needed to be eaten today in any case. I made her a ham and tomato sandwich with a little bit of salad on the side. When I took it in, she said "That looks nice, dear." I don't think she even remembered all the other cakes. She's getting worse, I know she is.' She disappeared into the garage.

I drained my cup and put it in the sink. Suddenly there was a scream. Mum rushed back into the kitchen, flushed and frightened. 'Vincent! I think there's a rat!'

'A rat? Did you see it?'

'No! Thank goodness.' She shuddered. 'I was getting some cooking apples from the box. It's baked apples and custard for dessert. The newspaper your father wrapped them in has been shredded and one of the apples is gnawed, actually gnawed. I can't bear it, I really can't!'

'Calm down. Let me have a look.' I went into the garage. On top of the spare freezer was a box of Bramley apples, picked from the tree in my parents' garden the previous autumn, each one wrapped in newspaper to prolong its life. In one corner was a partially unwrapped apple with an inch-wide crater on the top. Looking closely, the surface of the hollow was made up of minute facets, the work of tiny teeth feasting on the fruit. Chewed-up scraps of newspaper lay on top of the other wrapped apples. I noticed a couple of small brown droppings. I picked up the bitten apple, threw it in the green recycling bin and returned to the kitchen. Mum was sitting at the table, one hand to her throat. 'You have a mouse.'

'Not a rat?'

'No.'

'Oh no! I hate them. I can't abide them. Are you sure it's not a rat? I'm not going out there until it's gone. You must throw away the rest of the apples. We can't eat them now.'

'Mum, you're overreacting. Only one apple's been nibbled. The rest are fine. You're going to wash and peel them anyway.'

'No! They have to go. I can't have them attracting vermin. You must run down to the shop before it closes and get some poison. We need to move quickly before we're completely infested.'

'It's just a little field mouse, crept in to get out of the cold. Can you blame him, the weather we've been having lately?'

'It's horrible!'

'He won't harm you. I'll sort it out, I promise. The shop will still be open.'

I walked down to the supermarket and bought a box of mouse poison. It promised 'humane and effective mouse control'. I doubted the humane part but it was preferable to a trap. I felt sorry for the little fella. Putting it to sleep was better than breaking its spine.

As I hurried along the dark street, tightening my scarf against the wind, I noticed two women on the other side of the road. One was riding a mobility scooter, the other wore a green bobble hat. We were travelling in the same direction, but I was drawing level fast. To my horror, I realised the one in the hideous woollen hat was Sarah. I slackened speed instantly, not wanting her to see me. Unfortunately they stopped beneath a street light, outside a small house with a ramp up to the front door.

A tumult of emotions surged through my body: fear of being seen, embarrassment at my disclosures that morning, dread of introductions and small talk, annoyance that I couldn't step out of the house without bumping into her. They were chatting, apparently about to part company, but taking their time about it. My steps slowed further. Perhaps they were discussing the rabbit incident that morning or talking about me. I didn't want to have to acknowledge her, but equally I didn't want Sarah to think I was ignoring her. I could stop and tie my shoelace but, damn, I was wearing slip-ons. I prayed she would be invited into her friend's house and would be inside by the time I drew level.

The low rumble of a diesel engine reverberated behind me. I glanced back to see a lorry approaching on my side of the road. Just at that moment, a bus turned into the street ahead and approached the lorry from the opposite direction. If I was lucky and timed it right I could pass the women at the moment the vehicles blocked me from their view. I speeded up, shielded by the lorry which had drawn level. Both vehicles slowed as they eased past each other. I broke into a jog. By the time the lorry accelerated away, Sarah was behind me and I was hurrying away, my beanie hat drawn down and my scarf pulled up. I looked straight ahead, fighting the temptation to turn round. She might have resumed her journey and be following me on the other side of the road. Hopefully she wouldn't recognise my back. In any case, I could now genuinely pretend I hadn't seen her.

My heart was still thudding when I arrived home. Now that the danger was past, I couldn't believe I had been so stupid and cowardly. What was it about Sarah that intimidated me? Why was I skulking about the streets? I had nothing to be ashamed of. How I hated this place! Elmsford was bringing out the worst in me, resurrecting all my past insecurities. If only I could hide away and forget my problems, find somewhere quiet and disappear.

My sympathy for the mouse increased with each tray of blue pellets I placed around the garage. He was trying to survive in a cold climate, like me. I didn't begrudge him one apple.

Chapter 7

I dreamed of Sarah that night. She appeared taller, thinner, towering over me in her heavy black boots. Her eyes were icy cold, the pupils small and dark. Pinpricks of night. She drifted around the library, the tassels of her grey poncho trailing behind her on the floor like lifeless tentacles. She was collecting books and stacking them at my feet, building a wall of titles which reached to my knees, my waist and then my chest. A slow incarceration. The final gap in front of my face was sealed with a copy of the Financial Services regulations, plunging me into darkness. I woke with a start.

I forced myself out of bed and did a few press-ups. This was where mental grit and character would show itself: in adversity, in enforced inactivity. Feeling irritable, I deliberately increased the pace of the workout, breaking into a sweat and struggling to catch my breath as I hung on to the bedroom doorframe with my fingers and heaved myself up and down.

I dressed in some of Dad's old clothes and breakfasted as if I were running late for a meeting – a couple of gulps of coffee and a slice of toast eaten while shrugging on my coat. 'When the going gets tough, the tough get going,' I muttered, slamming the front door, Elsie in tow.

I purposely walked in the opposite direction, away from the fields where I had seen Sarah and Bruce the previous day. It had rained steadily overnight. The ground was heavy and treacherous underfoot. My trainers were definitely taking a hammering, and my legs tired quickly as I slithered through the clods of sticky soil, the squish and suck of wet earth accompanying each slow footstep.

Climbing over a stile, I reached a wooded area surrounding a small lake. It was here I had learned to fish as a boy. There was a path around the edge. Several fishing platforms had been built from old railway sleepers and rubble. I had spent many hours at Elmsford Lake in my youth, not talking, not thinking, just watching the float at the end of the line. Hours would pass without movement or memory as I listened to the rush of wind through the leaves of the big oak tree and searched for a glimpse of a shadow or a ripple, the flick of a tail. In the summer, the sun would burn the tips of my ears and the back of my neck. Gangly insects would skate across the water. Midges would sting the warm sweaty parts of my body – armpits, elbows, knees, groin. Pebbles gleamed like jewels at the edge of the clear water, and I believed I possessed all the treasures of the world.

Now the pond smelt dank. The fisherman's path was slippery with mud. I peered into the stagnant waters, imagining catfish buried in the silt below and trying to spot the slow movement of koi, somnolent with cold, swimming through deep shadows. There was nothing there but my own wavering reflection.

On the way home I popped into the supermarket to pick up the newspapers. Elsie sulked outside, tied to a handrail. I wanted to read the business pages and the classified ads and treat myself to something from the bakery department. Lauren was stacking fresh loaves of bread on the shelves.

'You're still here, then?' She raised a well-plucked brow.

'I couldn't drag myself away.'

She eyed my muddy trainers and jeans. 'Rotten weather. Did you bring it with you?'

'I think it's brightening up nicely.' I winked and she giggled as I squeezed the loaf she was holding. 'Soft and fresh. Just how I like it.'

I passed my old primary school on the way home. The sports field which had looked enormous when I first learned to play football and cricket had shrunk with the passing years. The school building, once central to my world, was an unfamiliar collection of new extensions and playground equipment. Mum would be there now, tallying up the dinner money and photocopying handouts. Apart from a few vivid images of children jostling in line outside the classrooms, the smell of plimsolls and sitting crossed-legged in the assembly hall, I had little recall of my time at Elmsford Primary.

So many days of childhood had slipped down the stream of time with no memories attached, waters smoothly meandering, my life safe and uneventful. Now I had hit the rapids and recent memories cut through the surface like jagged rocks. The last couple of months contained enough painful recollections to last a decade, each one trailing unpleasant emotions – rejection, fear, failure, humiliation, rage.

I took several deep breaths. I wasn't going to let this get the better of me. I looked around to check if anyone had seen me loitering suspiciously at the school gates, and jumped when a middle-aged lady on the other side of the road stopped and waved. 'Vincent! Vincent Stevens! Coo-ee. Is that you? Well, well, well. Timothy and Heather will be surprised when I tell them I've seen you. It's Pat. Pat Hutchins.'

'Hello, Pat.' She was already crossing the road and hurrying towards me. There was no escape. 'How are you?'

'Very well. Very well indeed, dear. And you will be glad to know that Timothy and Heather are very well too. In fact, Timothy has just been promoted to be head of technical compliance in the bank where he works.' She was out of breath and talking very fast. 'He's married with two children. A girl and a boy. They're wonderful kids. Very bright.' She nodded towards the school gates behind us. 'I saw you standing there and wondered who it could be. You have to be so careful about men hanging about these days. I'm a member of the Neighbourhood Watch. No doubt you were remembering those happy schooldays with Timothy and Heather. Heather has done exceptionally well for herself. She's deputy head of a very good school. She was always a natural learner, as you probably remember. You were in the same class –'

'Yes we –'

'… and she was always on the top table. She's just the same now – her quest for knowledge is never satisfied! She excels at anything academic, but you probably remember that.' She stopped to draw breath. 'And what are you doing now? Stop that,' she said, pushing Elsie's nose away. 'Are you on a flying visit or staying a few days with your parents?'

'I've got some time off and thought it would be nice to spend some of it with Mum and Dad. And Elsie, of course.' I tugged at the lead. Elsie looked up at me, and then at Pat. 'It's been pretty hectic in the City recently.' Out of the corner of my eye I saw Elsie nudge the edge of Pat's skirt. I pulled her back before she explored any further.

'Yes indeed, you boys work too hard. Timothy is heavily involved in a regulatory project at the bank, which will result in a lot of changes to the financial rules. He doesn't get to visit very often. I have to suppress a mother's emotions and just accept that since he left home he's never looked back.'

I bet he hasn't, I thought. She droned on. Her grandchildren were musical, passing examinations with ease and winning academic awards and merits at their prestigious private school. Thankfully she didn't ask about my career. She looked at her watch.

'Anyway, it's lovely to see you. I'm running a bit late for an appointment, but do pop in for a cup of tea if you have a moment. I'm sure you remember where I live.'

I smiled and made some kind of vague affirmative gesture before saying goodbye and hurrying off as if I too had an important appointment to keep. What an obnoxious woman!

*****

As soon as I arrived home, I showered and changed into clean clothes. I brought my laptop down to the kitchen and unplugged the telephone. I had received a few emails from the job agencies I had contacted the day before, mostly acknowledging receipt of my CV and putting me on their books. I had also received an online application form from one of the big pension providers. I didn't have the necessary qualifications, but there was the opportunity to study for the exams. The starting salary was well below what I had been earning with Tony, but I decided to complete it anyway. There was always room for negotiation when they saw what I could bring to the table. I would 'think wild' as Tony would say, looking at any opportunity that could use my financial know-how – insurance companies, mortgage brokers, investment houses, banks, independent financial advisers. I had strong sales skills. I was well presented. I was good at explaining the details of financial packages to clients.

There was also an email from Chloe.

Guess what, Jake and Susie just got engaged! Can you believe it? What does he see in her? Had a great night on Saturday. You would have loved it. Sorry we didn't get the chance of a proper goodbye. Missing you. Chloe x

Jake and I had been friends for a long time. It hurt that he had not told me about the engagement himself. We had met at the gym and it was Jake who had introduced me to Chloe; she worked at the same PR agency as he did. He had been dating Susie for about six months. Behind her back, Chloe had been dismissive. We had been out together often as a foursome and Susie always struck me as being rather sweet, though she was nowhere near as bright or sophisticated as Chloe. I replied straight away.

Good to hear from you. I'm fine. Buzzing about Jake and Susie. I've got some good job leads. Pretty hectic here. Vinny xxx

I texted Jake.

Congratulations! You're off the shelf! I knew there must be someone stupid enough to have you. Vince.

I wasted a good part of the day watching funny YouTube clips and raunchy music videos. When I heard a key in the door, I quickly switched screen to a job-search site. Dad walked into the kitchen, unbuttoning his coat.

'What are you doing here?' I asked. 'The kettle's just boiled. Would you like a cup of tea?'

'Yes, thanks, that would be great. It's miserable out there.'

'You said it!' I muttered. I switched the kettle on and found a mug from the cupboard. Dad hung his coat up in the hall and came into the kitchen.

'I haven't been to work today. I saw Dr Robbins first thing. He suggested I have some blood tests. I thought I would get it over and done with. I've just been to the Path Lab at Bury Hospital. Don't tell your mother, though. She'll only worry. It's probably nothing.'

'When will you get the results?'

'In about a week.'

I poured hot water onto a teabag, gave it a quick stir and added the milk. We sat at the kitchen table. I pulled the lid off the biscuit barrel.

'Don't spoil your dinner,' Dad scolded.

'How old am I?' I asked biting into a digestive. 'Besides, it's ages until dinner.'

'I know, I know. But you'll always be our little boy, Vincent, however old you are. As your mother says, there's no such thing as men, just little boys, boys and old boys… and I'm one of the few people in the world who can ration your biscuit intake!' I grimaced and sipped my tea. 'I'm getting to feel like an old boy these days,' Dad continued, 'and as such I'm going to give you the benefit of my advice and experience.' I could feel a lecture coming on. 'Don't rush to go back to the life you had. You were working too hard and it was a lot of pressure, pressure to be someone you're not.'

'It's what I want.'

'There's more to life than a career and money. Don't get sucked into the whole success fallacy. As far as I'm concerned, you're successful if you have a full, balanced and mostly happy life. You don't have to impress us, you know. Take your time and have a good look around. This might be an opportunity for a career change, to get out of the rat race. Simon was serious about his offer to help you become a driving instructor.' Dad could see I was about to interrupt and he held his hands up. 'OK, OK. That's not what you want. I understand. And I think that's enough fatherly advice for one day, except to say that if you carry on eating all the biscuits, your mother will have your guts for garters!'

'I'll think about what you said, Dad, but I'm not moving back to the sticks. I want to live in the real world. The most important thing for me at the moment is to find a secure job with good career prospects to get me through this downturn. The big bucks can come later!'

*****

At dinner that evening I mentioned meeting Pat outside the school.

'Did she tell you all about Timothy and Heather?' Dad asked, raising his brows and peering over his glasses.

'Did she ever!'

'Now now, boys,' Mum said. 'Patricia has a heart of gold. She would do anything for anyone.'

'Yes,' Dad replied, 'except stop telling endless stories about her family.'

'Don't be unkind. I know she can be irritating. Lord knows, I've had to put up with it for years. It didn't help that Heather and Vincent were in the same class at junior school. I thought I'd never hear the end of it when Heather was Mary in the nativity play, and Vincent was a radiator. But she's quite a lonely woman since her husband died.'

'That's because she's unbearable,' I said.

'A radiator! Where does that feature in the Christmas story?'

'I was keeping the stockings warm, Dad. Don't you remember? It was a very important part. I had to gurgle.'

'It was a sweet story about a little boy who lived in a house without a chimney. He didn't know how Father Christmas was going to bring his presents,' Mum explained.

Dad grimaced and rubbed his chest. 'Are you OK?' I asked.

'I'm gurgling at the moment. It's my indigestion again.'

'It was snowy outside and a stray kitten sneaked in and curled up next to the radiator,' Mum continued, carrying the dirty plates into the kitchen. 'I can't believe you've forgotten this, Vincent,' she called.

'I can't believe you remembered,' I shouted back.

Mum poked her head round the door. 'Everybody loves a modern fairy tale. Even though the family was very poor and there were no presents that year, the boy found the kitten lying on his stocking on Christmas morning.'

'What's that to do with the nativity?' Dad grumbled.

'Gifts come in unexpected packages,' Mum replied. 'Life's like that. You think you know what you want and then something quite different comes along that's even better.'

'Only in fairy stories,' I said. 'Real life is about achieving success through hard graft, not receiving presents from fictitious men in red suits.'

'We'll see,' Mum said, putting a steaming chocolate sponge on the table. 'We'll see.'

Chapter 8

Wednesday passed uneventfully. I pored over the newspapers and scoured the internet for leads. I had walked the dog first thing. The sky was the colour of tarmac: unrelenting, solid, a vast unvarying grey. Apart from the occasional tree, a scrawl of black scratches in the distance, the line of the horizon was as flat as the edge of the ocean – or the edge of the world. It certainly felt like the end of the road.

By Thursday, the early morning routine was wearing thin. My alarm went off at seven o'clock. I lay in bed, reluctant to leave the warmth of the duvet. It was very dark outside. I could hear my parents preparing breakfast downstairs. It would be so easy to sink back and stay where I was… in bed… in Elmsford. All I had to do was nothing! The days were slowing down, the momentum of my life draining away. I had left Suffolk once. Now I was back I was beginning to wonder whether I would be able to extricate myself again. I pondered another morning searching the internet for leads. I had already emailed my CV to nearly 100 agencies, headhunters and financial institutions. With my track record, I had hoped to have some good responses to my enquiries by now, perhaps even a couple of interviews lined up.

I thought of my hectic London life, crammed full with late nights at the office and late nights down the pub. How I longed for the old frenetic existence, where I didn't have the luxury of reflecting deeply about life or pondering the kind of person I was becoming.

Having time to think had been an unpleasant shock. Without the next impossible deadline it was difficult to motivate myself, to set my own agenda, even to get up in the morning. My days were falling into a predictable pattern. I sent texts and emails. I made desultory small talk with Mum and Dad. I ate. I watched television. I contemplated my own misery, polishing it and viewing it from different angles. I didn't want to measure the hours by the number of cups of coffee I had drunk, or by my visits to the supermarket for chewing gum and chocolate. I was wasting time, wasting space, a waste of space. But walking Elsie was one of the few contributions I could make to the household, so I stumbled downstairs.

Once outside, I nodded to the neighbours and to other dog walkers. There always seemed to be someone who wanted to catch my eye and wish me 'good morning'. Their cheerfulness made me uneasy. I missed the anonymity of city life, where invisibility was always available. Once through the gate and in the fields, space opened up before me in all directions – a wide, flat world of brown fields and grey sky with me in the middle. Nowhere country.

I wandered into a field left fallow by the farmer. The long grass was neglected and yellowed by last year's sun. Dead stalks and the seed heads of forgotten wild flowers stuck up in all directions like bedtime hair. The landscape was sere, grey, as though I had stumbled into a sepia photograph from the distant past. I trudged on, my hands and feet numb, my mind blank.

On my way home, I visited the supermarket to buy the newspapers. There was no sign of Lauren. I had been toying with the idea of asking her out for a drink, but took her absence as an unpropitious omen. Perhaps the timing wasn't right. I wasn't in the mood for another knock-back. I hovered in the confectionary aisle. After a brief internal battle, I selected a bar of chocolate embedded with nuts and raisins, and a bag of toffees. As I approached the checkout, a door to my left marked 'Staff Only' swung open. Lauren hurried out with a pricing machine in her hand, narrowly avoiding a collision.

'Oops a daisy,' she laughed. 'That was a close encounter.'

'I don't mind,' I smiled.

'Listen to you, charmer!'

'When there's someone charming to be charming to, I can manage a compliment.'

'Get you!'

'And you're looking particularly pretty today, Lauren.'

'Am I?' She looked down at her uniform.

'Have you done something different?'

'Different! I wear the same thing every day, except on my days off, of course.'

'Your hair…?'

'I didn't have time to straighten it. We're a bit short-staffed. I had to come in early.' She patted her hair self-consciously.

'It's quality not quantity that counts.'

'What? Is that a reference to my hair? I hope that's not a reference to my weight!' she smoothed the nylon tabard over her hips and pouted.

'Certainly not! I mean... um... I meant it's the quality of the staff, not the quantity that counts. Better to have one good person than five who are incompetent.' I held my breath.

'Bless. We always appreciate positive customer feedback.'

I slowly exhaled. Here was my opportunity. 'Perhaps I could give you some more feedback later. Over dinner?'

She fiddled with the buttons on the pricing handset. 'Are you asking me out?'

'Yes, I am. Don't worry if you can't. I'll understand. You probably have a boyfriend. I won't take my custom elsewhere or anything. I just thought it would be nice. I'm here in the village for a few weeks and wanted to try that restaurant in Woolingham, the Tithe Barn.'

She jumped at the name of the restaurant. 'That would be lovely. I think I will.'

*****

Elsie gobbled her breakfast and settled down on her bed for a snooze. I made myself a coffee before logging onto the internet. I was feeling pretty pleased. The first girl I had asked out since Chloe had said yes. Result! I read the latest celebrity gossip and checked the Test Match score from the other side of the world. I made myself another cup of coffee and drank it watching the News Channel on the small kitchen TV before settling down to work.

There was an email from a well-regarded recruitment consultant. A job had just come up in the City. It sounded perfect. The person specification could have been written about me. The money was about the same as I had been earning previously. The agency offered to email my CV to the company. They would let me know the following week if I was shortlisted, with interviews scheduled to be held on Friday the week after next. I emailed back immediately then sent Chloe a text.

May have an interview in London Friday week. If so, could I sleep on your sofa? We could go out for dinner, perhaps to a club. No pressure. V x

Everything was going to work out for the best. This was the most positive lead so far. It had to be the one! To celebrate, I threw on my coat and jogged down to the Railway Tavern for a lunchtime pint and sandwich, taking the sports pages with me.

Walking to the pub would take me past the library. So what if Sarah saw me? I was feeling like my old self. I was on a roll. A date with Lauren, a potential new job, *and* the possibility of getting back with Chloe. In fact, I was tempted to glance through the glass library door to see if Sarah was as weird as I remembered. Somehow my overwrought imagination had transformed her into a combination of crazed spinster and unkempt shrew.

The library had a small front garden. I stepped onto the pathway, grass on either side. To my right, a lone bench had been planted by the garden wall, at a 90-degree angle to the library door. I mooched over. It was dedicated to Muriel, 'who loved books' and had died in 1998. I sat down and carefully unfolded my newspaper. From here I could see inside the library – the librarian's desk, the machines for borrowing and returning books, and the seating area. I couldn't see Sarah, but she might be hidden by the racks of shelving that criss-crossed the room.

My breath clouded the air. The seat was cold. The glow from the library lights was warm and inviting. What the hell! I would pop in with my new library card and take out a book. If I wanted I could ignore Sarah, make her feel as belittled and insignificant as she had made me feel. Or, if the opportunity arose, I could drop Lauren's name into the conversation or tell her about the interview the week after next. I was bursting to tell someone my good news. I wouldn't be her pity case. I wasn't going to feel awkward about meeting her. No more skulking behind lorries. It was time to take control of the peculiar emotional response she provoked.

I sauntered towards the business section. It had a small selection of titles: *Total Quality Management for Total Quality People*; *Economics Made Easy*; *Risky Business: Risk Management for Beginners* and *Understanding Cash Flow*. I skimmed through a few pages of *Risky Business* while secretly scanning the room. There was no sign of her.

Taking another book at random, I ambled to the queue at the checkout machines, glancing down the aisles as I passed. I joined the end of the line and casually surveyed the scene. A middle-aged librarian sat behind the help desk, flicking though a card index system and talking to a gentleman who was clearly well past retirement age and rather deaf. It was my turn.

I was relieved to remember how to scan the book. I borrowed *Total Quality Management for Total Quality People* and pocketed my receipt. Next, I walked at a leisurely pace up and down all the stacks, feigning an interest in their contents. Finally, I had to admit it. She wasn't there.

I had been in the library about ten minutes, a little too long for her to be on a loo break. It was only just coming up to midday, probably too early for her to be out at lunch. I toyed with the idea of casually asking where she was, but thought better of it. What if the librarian told her someone had been asking about her and then gave my description? I would look like a creep. Was I being a creep?

I walked slowly to the pub and ordered a pint and a ploughman's lunch. The TV was on in the corner and I watched the news. Half of Europe seemed to be bankrupt. The UK jobless figures had risen for the fourth successive month. The Arab world was in political turmoil. Footage of demonstrations and angry uprisings flickered across the screen. I thought it ironic that Muslims should envy Western democratic freedom just at the time when it had become apparent that our politicians had precious little control at all: the multinationals and the banks had all the power and they used it to pocket their bonuses and stuff the rest of us! I was beginning to realise capitalism was not all it was cracked up to be.

My bubble of excitement had burst. I tried to read my newspaper, but even news of Ipswich Town Football Club's progress in the league couldn't lift my spirits. I flicked through the library book I had taken out but couldn't concentrate on the contents.

As I made a move to go, I noticed Simon Addington sitting in the corner staring into an empty pint glass, his usual upbeat expression replaced by a look of despair. I assumed he had finished work for the day, as he was having a drink. I wasn't in the mood for small talk, nor a discussion about the bumpy economic road that lay ahead. Thankfully, I managed to leave without him noticing.

To my dismay, a familiar figure was sitting on the bench outside the library. Despite the cold, Sarah was eating a sandwich and reading a book, her face pale above the collar of her dark coat. She had draped a sludgy green scarf with bobbly tassels around her neck. It reminded me of damp seaweed. Her hair was clipped up in an old-fashioned knot. She was surrounded by an almost visible veil of stillness. I averted my eyes and tried to hurry past, hoping she was concentrating so hard on her book she wouldn't notice me. I couldn't conjure the elation and confidence I had felt earlier. I wasn't in the mood for an encounter now. At the last moment, she looked up. I stopped and adopted a surprised expression.

'Hello,' I ventured. 'How's your hand?'

'OK.'

She held it up and turned it over for me to see. One finger was almost totally black.

'Ouch!' Her expression was calm, serene even, as if our previous spats had never happened. 'It doesn't look OK.' I took a few steps closer. 'Did you get to A and E?'

'Yes. A friend ran me down to Bury hospital. It's a soft tissue injury. Nothing is broken. Apparently it happens to dog walkers quite often.'

I wondered what sort of a friend. A man friend? I saw her glance at the book in my hand.

'Yes, I've borrowed a book from you. I've been reading it in the pub. What are you reading?' She held up her book. It was the Highway Code. 'So, you're learning to drive after all.'

'Yes.'

'How long?'

'I've had my provisional licence for about 11 months now.'

'You must have had a lot of lessons.'

I had passed my driving test in under six months, but thought it tactless to brag.

'Not really. I haven't had any proper lessons yet. I'm working for my theory test at the moment.'

'Oh... well, if you want to know the name of a good driving instructor, my neighbour owns Addington's Autodrive. He's very good. He taught me to drive, and I passed the test first time.'

'I've heard of him. But I'm not ready for lessons yet. I need to master the theory side of things, get my head around the process. That's how I learn best.'

'You shouldn't worry too much about the theory at the start. Don't overthink things. Just get behind the wheel. You need the experience of driving first. Lots and lots of practice, that's the key. You can learn all the theory you like, but it won't really make sense until you get in that driver's seat and feel the engine running beneath you.'

'I don't have a car, so I don't have the opportunity for any informal practice outside of lessons... and I find meeting new people difficult. That's why I haven't got round to booking up a course yet.'

It seemed a rather lame excuse. I wondered if she was hiding something. Unexpectedly, I realised I was enjoying our conversation.

'Why don't you come and sit in my car and pick up the basics? You'll learn more in half an hour with me than a week of reading the Highway Code. It won't make sense until you see things from a driver's perspective.'

She looked away, faint colour stealing across her cheeks. Suddenly, I *really* wanted to persuade her to take up my offer. It was more than a casual suggestion. The salesman in me wanted the challenge of overcoming her resistance. I wanted to charm her and gain her trust. I would sell her the product – me!

'I couldn't...'

'Of course you could. I'm an excellent driver! Not being able to drive affects every part of your life. The job you can get, where you can shop, how much you can buy at a time, how you socialise. At the moment you're completely dependent on other people for lifts. And public transport here is a nightmare. Even if it wasn't, you would have to plan your route and check out the connections every time. What happens if services get cancelled or are late? You're stuffed! It's such a hassle. Driving means you can arrive safely, on time, in a warm, dry car. It's a no-brainer!'

'I know that! Not being able to drive is like having... I don't know... a hidden disability or something.' She chewed her fingernail.

'Then do something about it. Take control.'

'Have you ever taught someone to drive before?'

'No, but Simon, my friend who owns the driving school, suggested only last week that I have what it takes to become an instructor. It's a possibility, of course, but it would only be a stopgap. My real career is in the financial markets.'

She was wavering. I could feel it. Change her mind, and I wouldn't have lost my magic touch.

'I don't know...'

'There's really nothing to worry about. I assure you I'm not a pervert. You can have Bruce on the back seat as a chaperone if you are concerned about being on your own with me,' I joked. She seemed to consider this suggestion seriously.

'Why would you give up your time to teach me?'

'I have time on my hands at the moment. I like driving. It could be fun. I've had a big severance package from my previous employer so I can take my time to look around and find the right position.' Again, I was being fairly flexible with the truth. 'Mind you, there are quite a few opportunities in the pipeline, so you should take me up on my offer before it's too late. And when you're confident enough, I'll introduce you to my friend Simon. His business has been badly affected by the credit crunch. He appreciates every customer. I'll be doing him a big favour. It's a win–win situation.' Bizarrely my enthusiasm was genuine, but I remembered how perceptive she was and wondered whether she could spot I was selling her a line.

She chewed her lip, then straightened her back. 'OK. Just one lesson to see how we get on.'

'Great. What time would suit you? The afternoons are still quite short and it would be best to do it in daylight. You'll need a bit of practice before you tackle driving in the dark.'

'I can do Saturday morning, after I have walked Bruce.'

'Shall we say ten o'clock?' She nodded. 'Where shall I meet you?'

'I live at 28 Moon Rise. It's a small white bungalow with a black front door. There's a lilac tree on the left and –'

'I remember. Don't you have to work?' I asked, realising Saturday would be a busy day at the library.

'My shift starts at two o'clock this weekend.'

'Great, ten o'clock at 28 Moon Rise it is. I'll see you there.'

She responded by taking a bite out of her sandwich and studying her book with sudden intensity as though it contained the answers to life's imponderable questions – peace in the Middle East, the purpose of suffering, why it always rained on the days I gelled my hair. I felt her eyes on me as I walked away, but resisted the temptation to look back. After about 100 metres I needed to cross the road to reach my turning. I checked behind for traffic, glancing surreptitiously towards the library. The seat was empty. She had gone.

*****

Arriving home, I unplugged the phone and logged on to the internet. I had a reply from Blake's Recruitment Agency already. Shortlisting for the City job was taking place a week from Monday, with first interviews the following Friday. They suggested I keep the date free as they were confident I would make it through the first round. I texted Chloe with the details and asked again if I could sleep the night at her flat.

I saw a couple of possible jobs in the financial pages of the newspaper and printed copies of my CV together with covering letters. I was addressing the envelopes when my mobile rang.

'Hi, babe. It's Chloe.'

'This is a nice surprise.' My heart thumped. There was no way she could know I had asked Lauren out earlier in the day. Or that I had arranged to give a driving lesson to another woman barely an hour ago. But a little bubble of anxiety fluttered in my chest nonetheless.

'You sound squeaky. Have you got a cold?'

I cleared my throat. 'Maybe I'm coming down with something. How are you?'

'Stressy. I'm in a management meeting. This is my ciggie break. I have to be quick. I got your message.'

'I thought you'd given up smoking.'

'I have. Apart from a couple a day. That doesn't count. How are the yokels?'

'Pretty much inbred. Apart from my parents, of course.'

'Of course.'

'I'd forgotten how weird and small-minded people become when cut off from the real world. Talking of the real world, about me coming up for that interview…'

'You can stay at mine. Of course you can. I'm sure we can be civilised about things. I know *I* can be civilised about it. It will give us a chance to *really* talk things through.'

I groaned inwardly. Usually when Chloe wanted to talk things through it meant she would be doing all the talking and I would be doing all the listening. But it was a price worth paying for a free night's bed and breakfast. And perhaps something more.

'Great! I really appreciate it. I'm sorry about the way things ended. I was feeling depressed –'

'I can't talk about that now, babe,' she interrupted. 'You know I find it difficult when you get like that.'

'Like what?'

'It's not that I'm not sympathetic, but I can't get dragged down by all that negative stuff. Positive thinking! You need a more affirmative vibe, Vinny. Bad things happen; get over it already! I've got to fly. Talk to you later. Bye.'

*****

Over supper I told my parents about the possibility of an interview. They were pleased, but cautioned me not to take the first job offered.

'Make sure you check out the organisation thoroughly. There are a lot of "here today, gone tomorrow" businesses at the moment,' Dad said.

'I saw Simon in the pub this lunchtime, drowning his sorrows,' I remarked, wanting to avert another lecture.

'That's not like him. He's doesn't like to drink much, not even in the evenings, in case the alcohol's still in his blood the next day. You can't afford to drink and drive if you're a driving instructor. Things must be tough.' There was a pause. 'And what were you doing in the pub? I thought you were supposed to be job hunting.'

'I was celebrating the job lead, of course.'

I didn't tell them about my date with Lauren the following evening. It would raise Mum's hopes that I might be putting down roots in the area. Instead I told them I was meeting up with an old fishing friend in Stowmarket and wouldn't need dinner the next day. I didn't tell them about Sarah either, and the driving lesson on Saturday. I was self-conscious about the whole thing now that I had time to think about it. I couldn't bear the thought of their speculation or teasing. For some reason, Sarah was a sensitive subject.

Chapter 9

I woke early the next morning with a sense of expectation. For a moment I couldn't put my finger on why. I sat up amidst a jumble of bedclothes and half-remembered dreams. Then it hit me. I was having dinner with Lauren that evening. It was amazing how having something in the diary injected a sense of impetus and purpose. I jumped out of bed, dressed, and gulped my morning coffee standing in the middle of the kitchen.

'Come on, fetch your lead,' I ordered. Elsie stood up slowly, reluctant to leave her bed by the radiator.

'You need to lose a few pounds,' I scolded. She looked up at me with dark, liquid eyes, her head cocked to one side as if to say, 'You can talk!'

I nodded to a couple of other dog walkers out on the street before reaching the fields at the back of the village. There was no sign of Sarah or her enormous dog. I wondered what she was thinking this morning. Was she looking forward to seeing me tomorrow for our driving lesson? Did she even like me, or was she really as cool as she appeared? Perhaps she was shy. I hoped she wouldn't develop some kind of embarrassing crush. I hadn't thought through the implications yesterday. How would I extricate myself from the situation if the lesson proved a disaster or our acquaintance veered off course?

Having Lauren in the picture should be protection enough, I argued. There was no comparison between the two: one easy-going and flirtatious, the other awkward and uptight. I remembered how drab Sarah had looked the first time I had met her in the library, her body draped in some kind of crocheted knitwear that made her look as though she were caught in an enormous grey spider's web. Although the supermarket's uniform was unflattering, it suggested something of interest underneath. Dating Lauren could be a fun interlude in an otherwise dreary period of my life. And it would keep Sarah at a safe distance too.

Another band of high pressure had moved in overnight. The temperature had plummeted. The muddy fields had hardened to stone. The sun was creeping along the horizon, dazzling my eyes and tingeing the frozen landscape with a glow of gold. Ploughed fields stretched ahead of me, their frost-tipped peaks casting shadows into the furrows and transforming the clods into a choppy ocean of frozen earth. Each step was a tricky negotiation between the iron of the soil and the shards of ice in the crevices. I could have been walking across the surface of the moon.

I trudged past the copse where I had first seen Bruce galloping after his rabbit. The trees arched their arms to catch at the sun, which was whitening as it rose higher into the sky. I walked across the field where Sarah and I had finally caught up with Bruce and wrestled the rabbit from his jaws. Spiky, frosted tussocks crunched underfoot. The body of the rabbit had gone from the hawthorn tree, taken by crows or other scavengers. A bird in the hedgerow gave a sharp chirruping twitter as I passed by.

I would be offered an interview for the job in the City, I was sure. Up in town, Chloe and I would try to patch things up. Perhaps in the future I would remember my time in Elmsford as an oasis of tranquillity in the midst of a hectic and successful life, rather than an exercise in rejection and failure.

I was back home by 8.30, showered, shaved and breakfasted by nine o'clock. As I ate a slice of toast and peanut butter I watched Dad out of the kitchen window. He didn't need to be in the office for a meeting until later. Before leaving for school, Mum had instructed him to sweep a scattering of dead leaves and twigs from the patio. She liked it to look tidy from the French windows in the living room. He had developed a slow shuffle, as though raising his feet was an enormous effort. His head was bowed, his shoulders stooped as he pushed the few remaining withered leaves from last year onto the nearest flowerbed. In the past, he would have swept them into a dustpan and deposited them onto the compost heap at the bottom of the garden. As on other occasions recently, I noticed he was beginning to cut corners. He was getting old.

Unexpected tears pricked behind my eyes, tears for Dad and tears for myself. My earlier pragmatism vanished like the morning frost. However much we tried to protect ourselves against the unpredictability of events, the reality was that disaster could strike at any moment. Life insurance, health insurance, payment protection insurance and all the other policies

I had so eagerly promoted to clients – but omitted to take out myself – couldn't protect me from the advance of time. I was mortal.

I gave myself a shake. This was going to be a good day, after all. I wasn't going to let maudlin thoughts knock me off form before my big date. I would take a little holiday and give the job search a break for a few hours. I turned away from the view of the garden, unplugged the phone, switched on the laptop and Googled 'learning to drive'.

*****

I had booked a table at the Tithe Barn for eight o'clock. I needn't have bothered because it was almost empty when we arrived. The owners had converted the barn after I had left Elmsford 12 years ago. I hadn't eaten there on my previous visits home because Mum was always eager to cook for me, but I had heard it had a good reputation for reasonably priced home-cooked food. Lauren seemed pleased with my choice.

She was wearing a very tight red dress with very pale pink lipstick. Her dark hair was piled in a complicated updo, small tendrils curling on either side of her face – girlish yet seductive. The streak of blonde in her fringe had disappeared. I tried to keep my eyes fixed on her face, but I couldn't help noticing the goose bumps tumbling towards the dramatic slash of cleavage. I considered offering her my jacket, but thought better of it. In my experience, women did not appreciate their clothing choices being questioned, however chivalrously. Also, the fairer sex seemed to have a supernatural ability to tolerate the cold when going out on the town in something sexy.

'You're a Londoner, then?' she said.

'Not originally. I was born here… But I've been living in London for the last 12 years,' I added, seeing a flicker of disappointment on her face.

'I've never been to London.'

'No?'

'I've been to Norwich and Southend-on-Sea and King's Lynn. Once I went to Manchester with a friend who was thinking about going to college. She didn't get in.'

'I'll have to take you sometime.'

'To Manchester?'

'No, London.'

'Wow! I've always wanted to see the Queen.'

'I don't think she does private audiences…'

'No, silly. At Madame Tussauds. And Kylie Minogue.'

'It's just a quick train ride away. I'm surprised you haven't been.'

'We had a school trip to the British Museum in Year Nine. I had tonsillitis so I couldn't go. I don't think I missed much. Just a load of broken pots.'

She gazed around the restaurant. It was an impressive room, though not as intimate as I had hoped. The owners had compensated for the vast space and high ceilings of the barn by painting the walls a deep burgundy. Candles flickered on every table, but they couldn't distract from the empty, echoing space overhead.

'I haven't been here since my Auntie Jean's silver wedding anniversary last year. Bless. It's lovely, isn't it? Look at all the beams. It feels like a church.' I tried to catch the eye of a nearby waitress. 'This is where I would like my wedding reception... Don't look like that! I'm not with anyone at the moment, silly. What do you think I'm like?! I just think it would be a lovely place for a wedding. You can hire out the whole restaurant as a function room. It's nicer than the village hall, don't you think? That's where my sister had her reception.'

'You have a sister?' I asked, trying to get off the subject of weddings.

'Three. They're all older. I'm the baby! Two are married and one is engaged. The eldest has just had her second boy. I could eat him for dinner. Bless him, he's that tasty.' She picked up her white linen table napkin, gave it a shake and smoothed it carefully across her lap.

'You have two nephews?'

'No!' she exclaimed as if I should know better. 'I have four nephews and two nieces. My eldest sister has a girl followed by two boys. The next one has two boys, and the sister who is engaged has a little girl. She's two now.'

'Long engagement,' I said, still trying to signal that we were ready to order.

'Not really. The little girl isn't his. They only got together at Christmas. It's been a whirlwind romance. Really lovely. He can't do enough for her, bless his heart. Nothing's too much trouble. He buys her presents all the time and everything.'

At last a waitress brought our drinks. Lauren studied the menu and wrinkled her nose.

'I'm not having the rabbit. I couldn't eat a bunny. I had a white rabbit as a pet when I was younger. He was so sweet.' She took a sip of her port and lemon.

'Did you have him long?'

'No, the foxes got him. But I still couldn't eat a rabbit. Look!' She opened her handbag and brought out a key ring. A ball of white fur dangled amidst the keys. 'We found this in Scampy's cage the next day. It's all that was left. Dad treated the skin with some special stuff and Mum sewed it into this. It's a little parcel of bunny. Not quite a rabbit's foot, but it goes everywhere with me. I'm sure Scampy brings me luck. And dolphins, of course.' She pulled the neckline of her dress to display a small dolphin tattoo on her shoulder. 'Everybody loves dolphins. But I still love bunnies best. I have a toy rabbit on my bed and cuddle him to sleep every night. He's really soft.'

I knew then that it was going to be a very long evening.

'Lucky bunny,' I said, remembering the dead rabbit in the tree. I wondered how Lauren would have reacted if she had witnessed Bruce's kill. I began to see Sarah's unemotional response in a more positive light. After lengthy deliberation, we both ordered the salmon. Apparently Lauren had never owned a goldfish as a child.

The waiter brought over a bottle of white wine to go with our fish. I had selected the most expensive Chardonnay on the list.

'Excuse me,' Lauren called as he walked away. 'Could we have a bottle of lemonade for the table? I'd like to make mine into a spritzer.' She drank half her wine, leaving a pale lipstick stain on the edge of the glass. When the lemonade arrived, she topped up the glass with transparent fizz. 'Yummy!'

'How long have you been working at the supermarket?' I asked through gritted teeth.

'About eight months.' She cut the pink flesh on her plate into small pieces, checking for bones.

'And before that?'

'Bits and bobs. I did a Health and Social Care course at college. Level 2 and everything. If I'd managed to get it I could have done a Level 3 and then gone to uni to study nursing. I don't want you to think I'm stupid just because I work in a supermarket.'

'I don't think that at all.'

She chewed thoughtfully. 'There was a lot of coursework. I'm more a hands-on sort of person. To be fair, some people are. I really enjoyed the work placement. I worked at a care home in Stowmarket every Monday. Monday was the best day of the week for me, can you believe that? I just love old people. They didn't know which way was up half the time, but I'd give them a hug and a squeeze whether they knew who I was or not. Bless them. I don't know why the college moved me from there to a dental practice after the first term. Updating dental records isn't really me, to be fair. I need to be needed. Some people are like that. I've always been a mother hen – just wanting to cuddle people.'

I decided to order another bottle of wine for moral support, this time a house white. Alcohol was called for. I would phone for a taxi to take us home and collect my car early the next morning.

Chapter 10

I awoke the following morning with a pounding headache. I was meeting Sarah for our driving lesson at ten o'clock and time was tight. I jogged back to the Tithe Barn to collect the car, dragging Elsie behind me on the short cut across the fields – killing two birds with one stone, or one fat pug with overexertion.

Sarah was waiting for me at the end of her road when I pulled up at five past ten. I hoped I didn't look as dishevelled as I felt. We sat outside her bungalow, engine running, Sarah in the driver's seat and me in the passenger seat surreptitiously checking my hair in the wing mirror. After about five minutes of going over the controls, I decided to test her progress.

'What's the pedal on the right?'

'The accelerator.'

'Correct. What's the pedal on the left and what's it for?'

'It's the clutch and you use it to change gear.'

'That's right. So what's in the middle?'

'The brake.'

'Spot on. Now I want you to talk to you about routines. There are several very important routines you'll need to learn to enable you to become a safe driver.'

'I'm good at routines.'

'Excellent. The routine for moving off is called POM, which stands for Preparation, Observation, Manoeuvre. First we need to Prepare.'

I over emphasised the 'P' and a little daub of spit hit the walnut dashboard in front of me. Embarrassed, I swiped the spittle with the palm of my hand

'Push down on the clutch as far as it will go and put the gearstick into first.'

She didn't move. I looked across. Her mouth was tense, her cheeks flushed. I wasn't used to being this close to a woman who wasn't wearing make-up. I could see every pore, the downy fluff on her upper lip. Her face was unnaturally white. The delicate blue of a vein throbbed under the skin at her temple.

'It's all right, the handbrake's on. We aren't going anywhere yet.'

She pressed down with her left foot and placed her hand on the gearstick.

'First gear is straight ahead.'

'I know it is.'

'Come on. Do it, then.' I waited a few seconds. The glass was beginning to steam up. I wiped the passenger window with the sleeve of my coat and turned the cold air on to demist the windscreen. She jumped at the sound of the blower.

'I don't think I'm ready for first gear yet.'

'It's fine.' I put my hand over hers to push the gearstick forward, but she jerked away. A growl reverberated from the back of the car. Sarah had taken me literally when I said she could bring her dog.

'What?' I asked defensively.

Bruce leapt forward, the claws of his hind legs digging into the soft leather of the back seat, his front legs in the footwell, his enormous head thrust between us. He growled again. I moved as far away as possible from his hot, meaty breath, until my head was pressed up against the cold passenger window.

'I was just showing you how to get into first gear. What's his problem?'

'He isn't very tactile.'

'I wasn't touching him!'

'He gets jealous.'

'Back seat drivers!' I muttered, pulling the sun visor down and looking at Bruce in the vanity mirror. A long strand of drool dangled from his mouth. He turned his head towards me, his fleshy tongue lolling sideways over his teeth. The silver thread stretched, thinned and broke, landing from my shoulder to my elbow in a glistening line.

'He likes you,' Sarah said.

'How can you tell?'

'He hasn't tried to bite you.'

'Just beat me in a spitting contest,' I said nervously.

I wiped my jacket with a soft cloth from the glove compartment, usually reserved for polishing the interior. After a moment, Bruce flopped back onto the seat and stretched out with his head on his paws. It didn't take more than a glance in his direction to see that my seats were covered in russet hairs.

'Let's try again.'

Sarah pressed the clutch and selected first gear.

'That's great. However, you must remember to keep your other hand on the steering wheel. Stop biting your nails.' She grasped the wheel tightly with her right hand. 'If we were doing this for real, you would gently press the accelerator pedal and then smoothly bring your left foot up about halfway. When you are in that position, you are Prepared.' Once again I emphasised the P, but without the spit. 'Next you need to Observe by looking through every window and mirror in turn so you know if there's anything out there to prevent you from moving off safely. When it's safe to go, it's time to Manoeuvre. You release the handbrake and simultaneously ease off the clutch while pressing down on the accelerator, making sure you turn the steering wheel to guide the vehicle away from the kerb. That's POM. Simple!'

She took her hands off the wheel and reached up to the driver's window. I thought she was going to wipe it as I had wiped mine. Instead she drew a simple face in the condensation – two eyes, a nose and a down-turned mouth.

'What's that?'

'It's me.'

'You're doing fine.' As soon as I said it I knew I was wrong. She wasn't fine. There was an edginess to her body language, a hint of tears.

'Let's have a little break. It's a lot to take in all at once.'

'Perhaps I could read the car manual before we try again.'

'The manual! You don't need that.'

'I would feel happier if I knew what all these levers and buttons do. I learn better that way... from books.'

'It's completely unnecessary. I don't think I've ever looked at the owner's manual. I suppose I might have glanced at it once when one of the warning lights came up on the dashboard... But there's nothing in the manual that will help you learn to drive. It's all technical stuff.'

'How does the clutch link to the gearstick? Why do I need to press the pedal to push the stick forward?'

'It sort of… opens a channel.'

'Why can't I just press the accelerator to move forward?'

'Because you need to go through the gears.'

'Why?'

'It's to help you go faster. Each gear has its own limit. Once you've reached about five miles an hour you can change to second, then third when the car's at about 20 miles an hour, fourth at 30, fifth at 40.' I could tell from her expression I wasn't answering her question. 'I don't know the exact mechanics of it. I just take it as read.'

'But you haven't read the manual!'

'The car manual wouldn't explain how the gears work. You would need to read a book about engineering. Just trust me.'

She didn't look convinced, so I relented.

'All right, you can borrow the manual if it will help. But I have to have it back fairly shortly because it belongs with the car.'

'I understand the concept of borrowing and returning books. I work in a library. I will give it back tomorrow.'

'Tomorrow?'

'I'm available for another lesson at three o'clock.'

'Oh! Right… Three it is.'

'Are you sure it's OK for me to drive your car. The insurance –'

'Let me worry about that.'

I passed her the manual and changed the subject. 'How long have you been a librarian?'

'I'm not a librarian. I'm a part-time library assistant.'

'I didn't realise you worked part-time.'

'I do 20 hours a week. My shifts change depending on the rota.' She twisted a strand of hair around her finger. It was loose today, spilling around her face in unruly tangles.

'Do you want to be a qualified librarian?'

'No, I like my job. I like putting the books back in order.'

'Don't you find it boring?'

'Never. I love working in the library. It's quiet. There usually aren't that many customers. Everything is in order. The Dewey Decimal System is a marvellous arrangement. I like to think that one day I will have put all the books back and the library will be perfectly complete. Of course, that can never happen because people are constantly taking the books away again. It's like the tide. Books wash in and books wash out, all those words moving between different people, all those ideas sifting through people's brains, changing them, bringing them happiness... and sometimes sadness.' I hadn't heard her speak at such length and was a little taken aback. She really loved her job, not because it brought with it money, prestige, success or excitement, but for the job itself. I wondered if I had ever felt like that. I didn't think so.

'I like the patterns the books make. The way the same books keep going out and coming back over and over again. Children's books and crime novels are like that. And then there are the books that are hardly ever borrowed. When they're returned I like to think about the person who read them. Who would want to read *A History of Soap* or *Abattoirs Around the World*, for example? It's a mystery!'

As she spoke about the books she loved, I noticed the softness of her lower lip, the angular strength of her chin. Her eyebrows were darker than her hair, unplucked and pulled together in a little frown. She wore a dull, square-necked wool tunic, something a medieval serf might have chosen to wear. It fell in heavy folds around her body. She sat very straight, clutching her hands in her lap. She looked out of place on my plush seats, a relic from an earlier time. She smelt of fresh air and lavender.

'You should listen to people when they talk, even if they are becoming boring.'

'I was listening,' I said.

'What was I talking about, then?'

'Um... crime novels, abattoirs, soap? I was listening, honestly.'

'What was *your* job before you lost it?' she asked.

'Thanks for reminding me about that.' I turned my head away and stared out the windscreen at the road ahead. 'I worked for a firm of London brokers. Very niche stuff. Our clients were quality people who were looking for a bespoke personal service. We help organise their financial arrangements.'

'What are "quality people"?'

'At the top end we handle the financial affairs of celebrities, TV stars, footballers, rich Russians, those in the music business, etc. I can't tell you their names, of course, because we offer complete confidentiality. My boss, Tony, he tended to handle those clients himself. My demographic included bankers and City traders mostly, those with big bonuses but who were too busy making money for others to look after their own financial affairs. I once had a lottery winner.'

'So when you say "quality people", you mean rich people.'

'I mean the kind of people who don't always have the time or the know-how to deal with all the mundane details of life.'

'What details?'

'Life insurance, property insurance, mortgages, pensions, savings, stocks and shares, that kind of thing.'

'So you worked for rich people who weren't able to look after their own money.'

'Essentially... yes.'

'They don't sound like quality people. Why don't you work there any more?'

'Unfortunately, my particular client base – bankers and stockbrokers – were the ones most badly hit by the global economic downturn.'

'You mean the ones who caused the problem are suffering as a result.'

'I suppose so.'

'Have they lost their jobs as well?'

'Yes... no... I don't know. They're certainly having to economise. Their bonuses won't be what they were in the past. Instead of using our services they're having to manage their own affairs, or go somewhere cheaper. What's the point of taking out top-quality home insurance if your house is about to be repossessed?'

'Couldn't you cut your prices to keep their business?'

'We don't have much control over the price of the products we sell because we sell them on behalf of other companies and only get paid a commission. The financial products we recommend might be more expensive, but you get what you pay for. We only sell policies with the best cover and the safest rates of return. That's our unique selling point.'

'So the more you sell the more commission you make?'

'Yes. And I make a pretty decent living out of it.'

'If you get paid by commission, doesn't that mean you have a financial incentive to act against the interests of the client, to sell them something they don't need, for instance?'

'No... Technically speaking, I suppose, yes. But I like to think I've always acted in my clients' best interests.'

'Would you recommend a rival company if you thought they offered a better product?'

'Well...'

'I thought not,' she said.

'What exactly are you accusing me of?'

'I'm not accusing you of anything. I'm saying it's natural to want to act in your own best interests. Where money is concerned, human beings have a huge capacity to cheat each other and to lie to themselves.'

'We pride ourselves on our business ethics, you know. It's one of our unique selling points.'

'I thought your unique selling point was giving the best cover and the safest rates of return, though strictly speaking that's two points.'

'We do all of that.'

'You talk as if you are still working for them. In the present tense.'

'Do I? Old habits die hard, I guess. It's not beyond the bounds of possibility that I might get my old job back when the economy starts to improve. Anyway, let's get back to the driving.'

'About the driving...' she hesitated, and rubbed her palms against her knees. 'You will need to explain things very thoroughly to me. When someone gives me a direction and says, "You can't miss it," the reality is that I can miss it. I am an expert at missing it.'

'You'll be fine.'

'Maybe. But not today. I have to go. I've got a bit of a headache.'

I turned to look at her again. Her expression was strained.

'I'm sorry. You should have said earlier. Learning to drive takes a lot of concentration. In fact, I've got a bit of a headache as well.' I remembered the two bottles of wine that Lauren and I had consumed the night before.

'It's not that. It's your smell.'

I was aghast. 'My smell! I don't smell! I shower every day.' But that was a lie. I had overslept that morning, and in my rush to pick up the car I hadn't had time to shower or shave.

'It's a perfume smell. It's given me a headache.' She opened the car door.

'That's very expensive body spray!' I had dowsed myself with it after returning hot and sweaty to drop Elsie back in the kitchen before roaring round to Moon Rise.

'I'm sorry if I've upset you.' She stepped out of the car and opened the back door. Bruce jumped out. She held him by the collar close to her side. She bent down to face me through the open driver's door, keeping her eyes on the pavement. 'Perhaps we shouldn't have any more lessons. I think you may have bitten off more than you can chew with me. I'll contact your friend Simon.'

My exasperation instantly vanished. 'Don't do that. We've hardly started. I don't want to hand you over until you're confident you know the basics. I won't wear body spray or aftershave tomorrow. I'll come just as nature intended. Deal?'

She pushed a stray lock of hair behind her ear.

'Deal.' Without so much as a goodbye, she slammed the door, walked up the path with Bruce and disappeared into the bungalow.

Chapter 11

Mum and Dad were out when I returned. I kept out of their way for the rest of the day, not wanting to interfere with their Saturday afternoon routine of housework and *The Times* crossword. I had a long soak in the bath after tea to prepare for my night on the town with Jimmy. I went easy on the products – just soap, deodorant and mouthwash.

As arranged, we drove to Bury St Edmunds in Jimmy's battered Ford Fiesta. I was glad I'd left the BMW safely in Dad's garage when I saw where his friend lived. It looked like a student squat. Jimmy buzzed the bell and we were let in by a bloke called Spider, who didn't live there but was coming out with us and also staying the night. We dumped our sleeping bags on the dirty living room carpet. Our host, Dan, tossed us both a tin. Spider and Dan looked several years younger than us. They had already started drinking.

The plan for the evening seemed to be to drink as much cheap booze as possible at the flat before setting off for a curry, arriving at the nightclub around 11. Jimmy had spoken to his ex, Catrina, on the phone. She had arranged her shift at the bar so she could spend some time with us towards midnight. There didn't seem to be any hard feelings between the two of them; their school romance was a distant memory. Jimmy had already explained she was a single mother. Her seven-year-old daughter slept at Grandma's house when Catrina was working.

Jimmy, Dan and Spider worked together at the Bury sugar factory. I concentrated on the inane Saturday night quiz show on the telly, ducking their brutal banter. Theirs was a world away from my smart office in Newgate Street and the camaraderie with Tony and the team. I realised how much I missed the male bonding created by a high-stress environment, the excitement of following up new leads and the hard drinking sessions after sealing a deal or losing a quality client. I also missed talking to my customers, explaining the different financial packages on offer, reassuring them about the risks, winning them over.

I had enjoyed the driving lesson with Sarah for similar reasons. Teaching her the basic controls had been oddly satisfying. I liked being in charge, being the one to soothe her nerves. I was looking forward to our second lesson already. I would have slept off my late night by then. Determined not to have another hangover, I held on to my empty can until we left for the curry house. The others were too busy drinking and mucking about to notice I was lagging far behind.

We hit the nightclub on a high, carbed-up on chicken tikka masala, rice and chips. Spider knew the doorman and we were ushered in without having to queue. The noise and heat punched like a fist as we swaggered through the swing doors. I hadn't been to a dive like Strobes in years. Squinting through the flashing lights at the gyrating bodies, I realised Jimmy and I were the oldest by far. The dance floor was packed with a mixture of scruffy student types and girls wearing more make-up than clothes. We skirted round the edge looking for a table or somewhere to throw our jackets.

I found a couple of chairs and a small table in a corner. When I turned, the others had gone. Jimmy was shouting to a group of very young girls who were giggling at his wild gesticulations. Dan and Spider were already on the dance floor. A previous customer had left a half-finished beer on the table. I sat down self-consciously with my coat on my lap. At least it looked as though I was drinking.

Jimmy had planned the boys' night out to cheer me up after my run of bad luck, but I was beginning to feel depressed. It was obvious the others partied regularly on a Saturday night, either here or in Ipswich after a match, their raucous behaviour being a talking point at the factory for the rest of the week. They were proud of their laddish reputations, but I wondered how much longer Jimmy could pull it off. His waist was already thickening, his hair thinning to a widow's peak.

My mind wandered back to the driving lesson that morning. Sarah was annoying and pedantic, but her lack of artifice was strangely fascinating. Thankfully Mum and Dad hadn't realised I'd been out. I could do without the third degree. They had been at a fundraising committee in the village hall that morning and had left before I awoke and arrived home after I returned. The group was planning some kind of event in a couple of weeks' time to raise money for African children – an instant switch-off, as far as I was concerned. Mum had asked about the mouse over lunch. I didn't want to admit I'd forgotten to refill the poison trays and told her it was all under control.

Feeling stupid sitting by myself with somebody else's beer, I fished my phone out of my pocket and scrolled through my recent texts. There was a message from Chloe. I hadn't heard it arrive over the throbbing bass of the music.

Just found the Sorrento CD – you know the one! It brought back good memories. Do you want it back? C

I switched the settings to vibrate and texted back.

Keep it. I'll c u after my interview. Take u to dinner. Afterwards we can listen to sweet music. Can't wait. V x

I Googled the day's football results. Before I could find out about Ipswich Town, my phone vibrated.

Perhaps we could make a weekend of it? You're up late. I'm in bed, thinking of you. X

I wondered if she was telling the truth. Chloe was hardly ever in on a Saturday night. I texted back immediately:

In bed 2. Guess what I'm thinking bout? Don't know how I will get through the days. Kisses.

Jimmy rolled up to the table and shouted in my ear. 'Come on, Chubbs. Put that phone down. Oi didn't bring yer here to sit in the corner. Get on the dance floor, laughen boi, and let the East Anglian ladies see what they've been missen!'

I allowed myself to be dragged towards his flock of teenagers. I rocked from side to side, nodding my head in time with the music, wishing I was at home in bed. I bumped against a swaying body. I turned to gesture my apologies and saw it was Spider. He was passing something to one of the girls. He looked away when I caught his eye.

The music was mind-numbingly loud. I stared ahead, allowing my body to move to the beat while my mind floated back to Chloe. I imagined her in bed wearing something silky, two glasses of wine on the bedside table. She wouldn't be seen dead in a club like this, full of underage teenagers with forged identities. She was a grown-up with a career. She wanted more from life than binge-drinking and a quick bang. I thought of

Lauren, in bed with a stuffed rabbit. And then I thought of Sarah, so different from the girls in the nightclub and so different from Chloe that she might belong to another species altogether, with her clean skin and soft clothes. I imagined her striding silently across the fields, the air cold and bright, surrounded by space. Suddenly the darkness and the heat and the noise of the club were unbearably claustrophobic. I would have made my excuses and left if Catrina Pickard hadn't tapped Jimmy on the shoulder at that moment and given him a hug.

The music was too loud for us to speak. Jimmy and I moved towards the table with our coats and the half-finished beer. I mouthed a greeting and Catrina smiled. She shouted something I couldn't understand. Exasperated, she gestured we were to follow her and took us through a 'Staff Only' door into a dark corridor. The air immediately cooled. Once the door swung shut the music deadened to a recurrent thud. My ears felt thick and buzzed as we talked, but at least we could make ourselves understood. She led us to a dingy office with a kettle and small sink used by the staff on their breaks.

'Would you like a coffee?'

I nodded.

She switched on the kettle. 'So you're back in Elmsford.'

'The Chubbs is back in town,' Jimmy sang drunkenly.

'It's Vince.' I emphasised. 'I'm not Chubbs any more.'

'You'll always be Chubbs.'

'You can talk!' Catrina interrupted, patting his belly,

'Watch where you're putting your hands, darlin'.'

'I won't be here long,' I said. 'I have a job interview in London next Friday, so this is probably a flying visit. The recruitment agency hinted I was the best candidate they've put forward.'

'You never told me that!' Jimmy remonstrated. 'The old gang's jes getten back together! Don't tell me yer shoving off again. Look what you've been missing.' He stretched out his arms and swivelled his hips. I grimaced. Catrina laughed.

'Yeah, Jimmy. What's he been missing? Nothing's changed around here for years. You're still getting drunk every Saturday night. I'm still struggling to make ends meet and wishing I could find a decent bloke. Don't worry, Vince, you've not missed a thing. Get back to London as soon as you can, that's my advice.'

There were two chairs by the battered desk. Catrina passed us our coffees and Jimmy pulled her down onto his lap. We talked about the old times, teachers we remembered, our families. Catrina told us about her daughter and the man who had abandoned her just before the birth. Her appearance hadn't changed much. There were a few lines around her eyes. Motherhood had rounded her figure. Her expression was softer too, the edgy teenager long gone, replaced by a woman who had managed to salvage some humour and humanity from the debris of her dreams.

'Life didn't turn out like we thought, did it?' she said. 'Look at the three of us, drinking cheap coffee out of chipped mugs. A single mum, a jobless banker living back with mum and dad and an aging lager lout. That's you, Jimmy, by the way, in case you didn't recognise yourself.'

'Thanks, babe. Oi'll remember that.' He belched loudly.

'I can't believe I used to find you attractive!'

'I'm not a banker –'

'What's with the "used to"? Chemistry was never our problem, darlin'.' He nuzzled her neck.

'Get off, Jim.' She tried to wriggle away.

'Oi gotta hold on to you. If I don't hold on to somethen, Oi'm gonna fall off this chair.'

'Useless lout!'

'Pathetic lush!'

'Enough from the mutual admiration society,' I said, feeling like a gooseberry.

'We're not the only losers from our year at school, Cat. Chubbs met – who was it? – some drippy girl in the library.'

'Sarah Penny.'

'That's the one. Do you remember? She used to get right up your –'

'I remember.'

I leaned closer to hear what Catrina might have to say. There was a long pause.

'She dropped out in Year 11, just before GCSEs,' I prompted.

'You and the other girls did somethen to her in the changing rooms.'

'It wasn't like that.'

'Somethen happened. I know it did. You was a banterous babe back then, Ms Pickard. You wouldn't have been able to resist.'

'She had a go at *us*, more like it.'

'What!' I exclaimed.

'It's was a long time ago. Who cares about it now?'

'We do,' Jimmy and I said in unison.

After several minutes of polite pestering from me, and some inappropriate tickling from Jimmy, she agreed to talk. 'Just to shut you both up.'

She tried to stand, but Jimmy wrapped his arms tightly around her waist. 'No yer don't. You've got the morals of a bloke. If Oi let yer go, yer gonna do a runner.'

'It's no big deal. Just stupid girl stuff.' She did up a button on her white shirt that had become unfastened. 'We were all getting changed after netball. Things were said. But Sarah did most of the talking.'

'You lot was all giggling about it afterwards,' Jimmy said. 'The lads thought you girls had been up to somethen naughty. Somethen must have happened, and we want to know what!'

'I suppose we *were* going to gang up on her and give her a hard time, but it backfired. I can't remember exactly what we had been planning, I'm not sure we even knew, but Debbie Weaver, Hannah Naughton, Lauren Topp and Josie Jennings and me were all fed up with Miss Snooty Two Shoes and the way she swanned around as though she was better than everybody else. There was always something a bit odd about her, don't you remember? Something sly and calculating. It was difficult to put your finger on it, but it was ruddy irritating. That day, she was slow getting changed. We all kind of grouped around her, laughing and making stupid comments.' She paused.

'What happened?' I asked, a hard knot twisting in my gut.

'She didn't get upset or flustered. She just stood up and spoke to us. She wasn't frightened. She didn't seem to care what we thought of her. She told us a few home truths. Quietly, not shouting or anything. She asked why I was wasting my time with Jimmy when he was playing away with Debbie Weaver. I looked across at Debs to laugh it off, but she wouldn't look at me. I knew right then that you'd been up to something, Jim.' She turned round on his lap to look him in the face. He held up his hands in a gesture of innocence.

'Debbie stormed off, and then Sarah said some other stuff – how Lauren Topp had been the one who nicked Josie's history project, and how Hannah Naughton had a crush on Miss Taylor, the English teacher. She didn't say it in a horrible way, but everything she said hit home. She called me a gossip addict who wasn't able to think for myself. She asked us why we couldn't be in a group without creating a scapegoat or having an enemy to fight. By that time, other girls in the changing rooms were listening. It was embarrassing. And then she looked directly at me and told me I couldn't trust the others because they didn't understand themselves or their own motivations. One minute they would like me and the next they wouldn't. She said they would offer me advice when I didn't want it, and attack me if I didn't take it. And it was all true. It was like she was psychic or something. It's stuck with me right to this day.'

'You made me think it were somethen different,' Jimmy grumbled.

'I was ashamed of myself. Embarrassed. I'd met someone who couldn't be intimidated. She wasn't afraid to stand up to me and say what she thought. I didn't want to lose face.'

'So you lied!' Jimmy released her waist and leant back on the chair. She twisted round to face him.

'I didn't lie exactly. I wanted to laugh the whole thing off. What's with the inquisition, anyway? It was years ago. We were just kids. Sarah left the school a few weeks later.'

'You've just ruined one of my favourite teenage fantasies. Why didn't yer say anything about me and Debs? Was that why you dumped me?'

'Duh!'

'It were nothin' serious, darlin'. She fancied the pants off me. Oi had a moment of weakness.'

'I didn't want the argument. I didn't think you were worth it, to be honest, Jim.' She turned to me with a resigned expression. 'Honestly, Vince, what *is* he like?'

'He's a moron.' I smiled and took a swig of coffee.

'We had something special, Cat. Yer should have fought for me. I was heartbroken.'

'Heartbroken! You were a rat, Jimmy. Always were, always will be. I wasn't going to waste my time on a two-timing rodent then. And I won't be doing it now.'

'Hey! Oi 'ave got feelens, you know. I've got very tender memories of our time together. Proper cut up Oi was at the time. Sent me off the rails for a bit. But Oi'm a new man now. A metrosexual.'

I spluttered into my coffee.

'Oi let the ladies pay their way if they want to. That way they feel more respected. An' since I developed a shaving rash, I've been using moisturiser. Face Fuel, it's called. It works on cracked heels an' all.'

'You're a real catch, Jimmy,' Catrina said drily. 'Can't understand why you weren't snapped up years ago.'

'Any time you want to take me out to dinner to express your status as a liberated woman, let me know. Oi don't have a little lady at present. This could be your lucky day.'

'In your dreams!'

'Oh, you will be.' He kissed her neck. 'You will be.'

I thought of the girl he had spent last Friday night with who was currently visiting her sister in Birmingham, but said nothing.

Catrina laughed and pulled herself out of his arms. 'Come on, Vince, let's go and have a boogie.'

The three of us went back into the club and danced mindlessly for the next hour, Jimmy making regular trips to the bar and buying lagers for himself and expensive-looking cocktails for Catrina. I could tell he thought I was being a wimp, but I managed to make one beer last the rest of the evening. Jimmy's mates were still hanging out with the group of underage girls. I saw Spider groping the blonde he had slipped an ecstasy tablet to earlier. Eventually, we all staggered out into the cold night air.

Catrina was singing as she tottered down the road. Jimmy said he would see her safely home. Dan, Spider and I walked back to the flat in silence. I crashed on the sofa while Spider passed out in an armchair. If Jimmy arrived later, he would have to sleep on the floor. As I floated on the cusp of unconsciousness, I wondered if Dan had given him a door key. Nothing was going to rouse us, least of all the front doorbell.

*****

I awoke, stiff and cold, just after nine o'clock. Spider was snoring. There was no sign of Jimmy. I looked out of the window to see if his car was still parked in the road. It was gone. If Jimmy had rung the bell, no one had heard him. I made myself a black coffee. The milk in the fridge was off and the kitchen looked too unhygienic to risk toast. I left a note for Dan, thanking him for letting me sleep on his sofa, and let myself out, carrying my sleeping bag in my rucksack and wearing the previous day's clothes.

It was a fairly short walk to the station. I sat on the deserted platform and waited for about 45 minutes for the train to Elmsford. I was cold, tired, hungry and dirty. I had a painful crick in my neck from the armrest of Dan's settee. But I didn't have a hangover. When I eventually reached home, I ate a bowl of cereal while soaking in a hot bath. Mum and Dad were out – at church, I presumed – so I went back to bed for a couple of hours' sleep. I was eventually woken by Mum who shouted up the stairs that lunch was ready.

'I'd like to take your mother away for a weekend,' Dad announced between mouthfuls of roast beef. 'Looking after Nana has been quite a strain. I feel run-down too. We're going to book into a nice hotel in Dorset or Hampshire. It will do us both a power of good. Will you be able to keep an eye on Elsie and Nana while we're away?'

'What if I need to pop back to London? Looking after Elsie is one thing, but Nana is something else completely. It won't be 20 minutes of exercise and a scoop-the-poop.'

'You'd be surprised,' Dad replied caustically.

Mum gave him a filthy look. 'She'll have carers going in as well. You won't have to deal with anything like that.'

'Here's hoping!' he muttered.

'We just need to know you're here and available in case there are any problems. We won't relax otherwise.'

'Speak for yourself!'

'Derek! Stop being provocative. You know you won't relax either.' She turned to me. 'We put her in respite for a few days when we went to Scotland for Uncle Duncan's funeral. I don't think either of us can face that again. She cried for two whole days before going. She said I was dumping her in a death camp. I felt wretched leaving her, even though it was a lovely home.'

'It should be lovely at that price!' Dad said.

'Come on, Vincent,' Mum pleaded. 'Families have to rally round in difficult times. We're supporting you in your present situation. All we're asking is that you pop in once a day to check the carers are doing what they should be and that she's eating properly. I'll get all of her shopping before we go.'

'OK, OK, I'll do it. It's not that I don't love Nana. It's just I'm not very good at that sort of thing.'

'Who is?' Dad said. 'It'll be good practice for when your mother and I are going doolally. Think of it as an induction course. In-house training.'

Now they had my agreement, Mum changed the subject before I could change my mind. She cut me a large slice of lemon meringue pie. 'How was last night? Did you have fun?'

'I'm getting too old to be sleeping on a stranger's sofa.'

'At last, a little maturity,' Dad said.

'It was bound to come with time.' Mum smiled. 'Was it just you and the boys?'

I had already told her we had arranged to meet Catrina at the club, but I could tell she had something else on her mind.

'Why do you ask?'

'Just wondering. Pat Hutchins said she saw you in your car with a woman over on the Downswell Estate yesterday morning when she was running late for our committee meeting. She mentioned it after church this morning. I thought perhaps you might have made a new friend.'

She was fishing. I knew she would be ecstatic if I developed emotional ties in Elmsford. Pat Hutchins! I couldn't believe it! What was the chance Sarah and I would be spotted on our first lesson? Obviously quite high. I had forgotten how little privacy there was in a small village.

'You don't have to say if you don't want to.'

'Leave it alone, Gillian. He's not used to having his movements picked over by the local gossips.'

'It's OK, Dad,' I said, irritated but resigned. 'It was Sarah Penny. She's learning to drive and I was giving her some help. She doesn't have a car of her own to practise in.'

'Who's she having lessons with?' Dad asked. 'Is it Simon?'

'No. She hasn't had any proper lessons yet. She's too nervous. We just sat in the car and I explained the controls.'

'I think that's a bit much. There are driving instructors going out of business every week, and here you are giving free lessons to some girl you haven't seen in years. Are you being taken for a ride?'

Mum laughed nervously. 'That's a good one, Derek. Are you being taken for a ride? He was giving a driving lesson! Very funny, darling.'

'I wasn't trying to be funny. I'm just making the point that in these times of high unemployment, he shouldn't be taking work away from others. Honestly, bearing in mind your own position, I would have thought you would be a bit more sensitive to the economics of the situation.'

'I was planning to introduce her to Simon. I've already recommended him. But she's shy of new situations and new people. I said I would help acclimatise her to the car and then set up a meeting. She's a bit of a basket case, to be honest. I was doing her a favour. I'm sorry I bothered.'

'Calm down, both of you,' Mum said. 'I'm glad you're helping Sarah. It's a kind gesture, and I know Simon will appreciate the recommendation.'

'And as we're talking about my "position", Dad, I have an interview in London next Friday so things are starting to move in the right direction. Hopefully I'll get out of everyone's hair soon and won't be accused of taking work away from the locals.'

'That's marvellous, Vincent!' Mum exclaimed. 'Ignore your father. He's being a grumpy old man. Tell us all about it. Is it a reputable company?'

'I don't know much about the organisation at the moment. The recruitment consultant gave me a brief profile of the business. They sound the ticket. Bang on the money.'

Dad cleared his throat. 'I shouldn't have snapped at you, son. We're concerned about Simon at the moment, that's all. He has some fairly serious financial worries. He's not as upbeat as he seems. He won't mention it, of course, but Liz was telling your mother he's been to the doctor for some tablets. I wouldn't want him to hear from anyone else that you're giving private lessons to people in the village.'

'They're hardly private lessons and there are no "people". It's just Sarah. And it's been just the once. We didn't even leave the kerbside. I'm seeing her this afternoon, actually. I'll mention Simon's driving school again and encourage her to go for it. If yesterday's lack of progress is anything to go by, she'll make him an absolute fortune.'

'If you look after the pennies, the pounds will look after themselves,' Mum said.

'What?'

'Pennies. Sarah Penny. If Simon looks after the Penny, the pounds will look after themselves.'

I groaned.

'Penny for your thoughts,' Dad teased.

'Stop it!'

'In for a Penny, in for a pound,' Mum countered. I pushed back my chair.

'I've finished. I don't want any pudding thanks, Mum.' I pushed away my untouched pie. 'I'd better get going. Sarah will be waiting –'

'See a Penny, pick it up. All day long, you'll have good luck,' Dad called as I shrugged into my coat.

'I'm not picking anyone up,' I shouted back from the hall. But they were too busy laughing to hear.

Chapter 12

I drove Sarah to the next village where the roads were quiet. We parked in a neighbourhood I didn't know well and where I was pretty sure no one would recognise me.

'Do you remember the routine when you get in the car? Seat belt, seat position, check all the mirrors. Make sure you are comfortable and have a 360-degree view. On cold mornings, you might have to use a scraper or de-icer and the rear window heater. You can use the blower to get rid of condensation on the windscreen. You must be able to see everything to drive safely.'

'What about the blind spot?'

'Don't worry about that now. We will get to that in a minute.'

'It sounds like something I should be worried about. Where is the blind spot?'

'All in good time. We're not even moving yet. It only becomes relevant when pulling out or overtaking. Where was I? Once you are comfortable and can see out of all the mirrors and windows, you can put the key in the ignition. OK, Sarah, turn the key.'

'I'm not sure...'

'The handbrake's on. The car won't move.'

She chewed her lip. She looked calmer than yesterday, but only just. She was wearing a long-sleeved bottle-green dress. The sharp points of her knees poked up from beneath the floppy material. Over the top of the dress she wore a crocheted wool waistcoat made up of patterned squares in various muted colours: brown, grey, bluey-green. She reminded me of a tea cosy. She twisted the key and the engine turned over.

'Terrific! Now press lightly on the accelerator. That's the pedal on the right.' She pressed down and the engine roared into life. 'That's about 300 revs.'

'Is that good?'

'Tone it down a little. The engine should sound like a cat purring rather than a lion roaring.' She adjusted the pressure on the accelerator. 'Push down on the clutch until it touches the floor and put the car into first gear. Now, we need to remember the three magic words – Mirror, Signal, Manoeuvre.'

'I thought the words were Preparation, Observation, Manoeuvre.'

'Yes, we use those words too. Very good. As you've remembered them, let's start with POM. We've done the Preparation and now we're going to do the Observation. Look in your mirror. Can you see anything behind us?'

'There's a lady with a little boy on a bike.'

'Are they on the road?'

'No, on the pavement.'

'Sarah, we only have to worry about vehicles on the road. Cars, buses, bikes, etc. Is anything coming on the road now?' Even I could hear the impatience in my voice.

'No.'

'OK. Now signal that we're going to pull out.' Sarah pushed the lever down. I reached across and pushed it up to indicate right. My hand brushed her cold fingers. Bruce emitted a low growl.

'I knew that! Sometimes when I'm stressed I have difficulty with my right and left. That's all.'

I grimaced, but she was too busy concentrating on the steering wheel to see.

'Simon told me to think "upright" and "let down" to help me remember. To signal right you push the lever up. To signal left you push the lever down. "Upright"; "let down".'

'Shouldn't it be "left down"?'

'"Left down" isn't a familiar phrase. It's "I let down my parents," not "I left down my parents." If it doesn't help, just forget it.'

'OK.'

'Anyway, that's your Mirror and Signal. Let's do Manoeuvre.'

'I thought we were doing Preparation, Observation, Manoeuvre.'

'We are, but you also need to think Mirror, Signal, Manoeuvre, or MSM. You'll be using MSM whenever you change speed or direction. Don't look so worried. It will all click into place with practice. OK. This is crucial. Bring your foot up very slowly until you feel the car pulling forward but without actually moving, the way your dog strains against the lead while you're holding him. Excellent! Release the handbrake.'

The car jerked forward. Sarah screamed. Bruce jumped up from the back seat and barked.

'You stalled. That's all. Push the gearstick back to neutral. You need to restart the engine.'

Sarah didn't move. She gripped the wheel as though she had reached the crest of a roller coaster. Her bruised fingers were painfully red next to the white knuckles of her other hand.

'You need to raise your foot gently and hold it steady at the biting point.'

'Biting point! What's biting point?'

'That's the point when I bite you to stop you worrying about things that are never going to happen. We've gone over this. It's when you feel the car starting to pull forward but you're holding it stationary. It's important for hill starts... though I'm not sure where we are going to practise those because I can't think of any hills around here.' She wasn't listening.

'You never called it biting point.'

'Probably because I didn't want to give Bruce any ideas. That's a joke by the way.'

'Biting point! Blind spot! Let down! Why do you have to use these horrible phrases?'

'It's just what they're called. The blind spot's nothing to worry about, as long as you glance over your shoulder when pulling away to make absolutely certain nothing's coming.'

Bruce settled back onto Sarah's coat. She had laid it on the seat after I pointed out the hairs and claw marks he had left the previous day.

'Let's take a break. How did you get on with the owner's manual?'

'I finished it last night. It was fascinating.'

She twisted round and reached between our seats. She pulled her tote bag away from Bruce, who was using it as a pillow.

'Here it is.'

Her loosened hair brushed my face as she pulled back into a sitting position. It smelt of lemons.

'Perhaps I should give you a little test,' I teased, unnerved. 'How do you put the heated rear window on?' She pointed to the correct button.

'Air conditioning? ... Hazard lights? ... OK, clever dick, this is more difficult. Rear windscreen wipers.'

She pushed the lever down a couple of notches and the wipers swished across the rear window. I was determined to catch her out, and flicked through the manual.

'I've got a good one now. Which light comes on if the car experiences some kind of electrical fault and I need to contact the dealer?'

She instantly pointed to a light on the dashboard.

'You're amazing!'

'I have a very good memory for visual signs. It's a special interest of mine.'

'What is?' I put the manual back in the glove compartment.

'Signs, symbols, semiotics.'

'Semi-what?'

'Semiotics. It's the science of signs.'

'Is that why you were reading the Highway Code?'

'One of the reasons. For most people it would be pretty boring, but I like that kind of thing. Semiotics is more than just road signs. It can be anything: paintings, photographs, drawings, words, sounds...'

Her eyes were wide and bright. She radiated enthusiasm. With a sudden jolt, I realised she was beautiful. I had pushed a button and the electricity was on.

'That's interesting,' was the best I could manage.

'Semiotics is a science which crosses into all sorts of different academic subjects because it looks at the role of signs in all our social interactions.' She looked at me, waiting for a response.

I was out of my depth. I didn't know how to respond, but a warm glow was spreading through my body. For the first time she was happy and relaxed.

'Sounds heavy.'

'I like it because it *is* difficult, but at the same time it makes things clearer.'

Her cheeks were pink. The car had become a warm cocoon. The heater was whirring and the windows were misting as we talked. I watched a droplet swell, spill over and dribble crazily down the cold surface of the glass.

'I think we can turn this down,' I said, fiddling with the blower. 'It's getting hot. So... what's the point of semi-whatsits?'

'Semiotics. The point is to find meaning. Every sign means something. I see the signs, but sometimes I struggle to understand what they're saying. It's a bit like trying to put together a jigsaw puzzle which has no picture. It's difficult to put the pieces together without an image; difficult but not impossible. When there's something visual it's easier to understand how the meanings fit together.'

'I suppose it is.'

'It helps with the processing...'

'Uh-huh.'

'Words are tricky. They paint pictures which can be distracting. When I was a little girl, I thought I had to pull my socks up when the teacher said "pull your socks up". Of course, "pull your socks up" is a sign for "try harder". People can be very difficult.'

I hadn't understood most of what she had been saying, but I realised we had suddenly jumped rails and were travelling on a different track. I decided to hang on to side of the carriage and see where she was taking me.

'You can say that again.'

'People can be very difficult.' She paused dramatically. 'See! That's the perfect example of where the surface meaning of your words is at odds with the deep meaning. You didn't really want me to repeat myself when you said, "You can say that again." You were agreeing with what I said. Knowing what people mean underneath the words they say... well... I'm much better at that now. Most people like doing things they're good at, but I like to work at things I'm not so good at. It's a challenge, particularly when several people are talking at once. I can't take language for granted like you do. It's full of subtle meanings.'

'OK...'

'I don't rely on my instinct or emotions to tell me what's going on. In fact, they get in the way and often lead me in the wrong direction. I try and stand outside the system. I notice things other people take for granted. I've got into the habit of decoding the deep meanings behind what people are saying and doing. It's called deconstruction. That's how I knew when you said, "That's an unusual waistcoat. Did you make it?" you really meant, "That's dreadful. Surely you didn't pay good money for it."'

I squirmed in my seat because she was right, but she didn't appear to be offended.

'I'll be more careful what I say in future. It sounds a bit like psychoanalysis. You'll be telling me all about my traumatic childhood next.'

'School wasn't easy, was it?'

'Is it easy for anyone?' I deflected. She gazed for a moment out of the window, sucking her bottom lip.

'Do you remember that story we did in English about the little skunk? It was by John Updike.'

'No. I wasn't very good at English.'

'That's not true. I remember a poem you wrote about a fish. Miss Taylor read it out to the whole class.'

'Oh, that…' I had pored over the poem for days, trying different combinations of words to describe the ripples on Elmsford Lake. I had seen a pike pull a young cygnet under the water and had wanted to convey the beauty and terror of the enormous predator that lurked in the depths.

'I had trouble living that one down. In the end I told Jimmy I'd copied it out of one of my Dad's fishing magazines.'

'Had you?'

'No, but it got him off my back. Anyway, English wasn't my favourite subject. I preferred maths. What was that story you were talking about?'

'It was about a little skunk. None of the other woodland creatures would play with him because he smelled so bad.' She looked at me intently.

'I'm not wearing any aftershave, if that's what you're getting at.'

'No. You don't smell bad today. That wasn't what I meant. The story is a metaphor.'

'In that case it sounds a bit like everybody's secondary school experience, being left out and ridiculed.'

I remembered she had always been on the edge of the crowd. The other pupils made faces behind her back as though she was some kind of weirdo. It had upset me at the time, but I hadn't done anything about it because I didn't want to draw attention to myself. A wave of guilt lurched through my stomach, as though an elevator had unexpectedly plunged several floors. I wound my window down an inch and breathed in the cold air.

'Maybe… Anyway, I remember the story very well. There was a deep meaning trying to get out. Seeing you again all these years later has brought it back to me.'

She licked her lips. I had the feeling she was about to tell me something important, something personal. A sputter of excitement mingled with my earlier feeling of unease. She was going to say something that would make it impossible for us to continue as casual friends. We were at a turning point. Would we be accelerating forwards or reversing back the way we had come?

At that moment, a cat bounded over the picket fence next to Sarah's window. It streaked in front of the car and shot across the road. Bruce leapt up from the back seat, barking madly and throwing himself against the window. The cat looked over its shoulder at him, jumped onto the wall of the house opposite and delicately tiptoed across. Bruce's claws scraped on the window, each furious bark piercing my eardrums causing actual physical pain.

'Quiet!' Sarah commanded.

The cat disappeared over the wall. Sarah spent several minutes ordering Bruce to lie back down on the seat.

'Sorry, Vincent.'

'No worries.'

I waited for her to continue. She was catching her breath after wrestling with Bruce's lead through the gap in the front seats. I sat in silence, massaging my ear. After several minutes I realised the thread of our conversation had been irrevocably broken.

'Let's try to get this car on the road,' I suggested.

Avoiding all acronyms, I talked her slowly through the process. Ignition, clutch, first gear, biting point, mirror, signal, release handbrake, glance over shoulder, manoeuvre. The car very slowly eased out into the street.

'Straighten up.'

She didn't respond. A car was coming towards us in the opposite direction and we were headed straight for it.

'Straighten up!'

I looked across in panic. She was sitting very erect.

'You need to turn the steering wheel,' I yelled, grabbing it and guiding the car back to the left-hand side of the road. The other car passed safely. Bruce jumped up and started barking again.

'Indicate left. Pull back to the kerb. Press down slowly with your brake and clutch pedals so that they reach the floor at the same time.'

I held on to the wheel and the car hiccupped to the side of the road. When we were stationary, I put the handbrake on and wiped my brow.

'Straighten up means straighten the wheel, not sit up straight! You just said you were good at decoding words.'

'Not when I'm under pressure... there was no need to shout. Now you've upset Bruce.'

'Shut up, Bruce!' I snapped. 'He needs to go home. He's a distraction. It's too dangerous to have him in the back. I'm sure you can see the sense in that.'

'OK.' She unbuckled her seat belt. I opened my door and stepped onto the road. I assumed we were going to swap seats and I would drive her to her bungalow, but as I reached the driver's side she opened the back door. Bruce jumped out, wagging his tail.

'I'll drive you both home. We can drop Bruce off and continue with the lesson.'

'I think I'll walk. I've had enough driving for today. Besides, Bruce could do with the extra exercise.' She took her coat from the back seat.

'But it's miles back to your place. And it's freezing.'

'We'll be fine. I know a short cut to Elmsford across the fields.' She started to walk away.

'But I wanted to talk to you about Simon Addington, my friend the driving instructor, and whether you feel able to have proper lessons yet.'

She halted and turned back to look at me. 'Have you had enough of me, then?'

'No. Not at all. In fact, I've been enjoying myself.' The words surprised me as much as they surprised her. 'It's been a bit tedious these last few days, stuck at home filling out job applications. Being with you takes my mind off my own situation.'

'I would rather learn with you for a bit longer. Being with someone different will make me feel more stressed. I'm so useless...'

'No, you're not. We've all been beginners once. When would you like your next lesson? I'm free any time that suits.'

'I can make tomorrow after my shift finishes at two o'clock. Can you pick me up from the library?'

'It's a date... I mean, that's fine. I'll see you then.'

I jumped back into the car. I watched her walk away in the rear-view mirror. I turned the ignition and revved the engine, accelerating away with a roar and a cloud of carbon monoxide. Stupid to call it a date! I didn't want her to get the wrong idea. I didn't want anyone to get the wrong idea.

Chapter 13

Over the next few days, Sarah and I worked on the basics. She learned to pull away in first, change to second, turn left at a junction and stop. There had been a few false starts – stalling, kangaroo jumps, forgetting to turn off the indicator – but she was improving. Her movements were always deliberate, like a novice dancer marking steps while attempting to master some difficult choreography. Sometimes she completed the start-up routine only to find that the time lapse between first gear, biting point, backward glance and releasing the handbrake was too long; the road behind was no longer clear by the time she was ready to move off. Once I shouted at her to stop.

Despite the Learner plates, motorists would roar up behind, tailgating us until there was an opportunity to overtake. One bloke had sounded his horn when she was slow pulling out of a junction. I'd made a rude gesture through the window while Sarah was concentrating on the road. She continued to muddle her right and left and found it difficult to judge the speed and distance of other cars. Much to my embarrassment, we were once flashed and overtaken by a tractor. I prayed the farmer wouldn't recognise me.

'It's not your speed that's the difficulty,' I said diplomatically. 'The problem is the difference between your speed and the speed of everyone else.'

'I like my speed.'

'Twelve miles an hour isn't a speed.'

'Actually, it is.'

'Actually, it's not. It's a slow.'

After the fifth lesson she flatly refused to turn right.

'Now I know why it's called a crossroad.'

'Concentrate, Sarah. There's a gap coming.'

'It's a crossroad because it's making everybody cross.'

I glanced in the wing mirror at the queue of cars behind us. 'That's not the road; that's you. After this car you can go... go now, Sarah... GO!'

'I can't. There's another car coming.'

'It's miles away. Stop looking at the cars and start looking for the gaps.' A grey Citroën passed in front of us.

'How can you look for something that isn't there?'

'Stop being ridiculous. Just go! This is your chance. NOW!' Frantically looking in both directions, she eased the car on to the open road just as a car came into distant view on the left. She slammed on the breaks. The car behind hit our bumper with a loud crunch.

*****

Afterwards, I tried to reassure her that she wasn't to blame.

'It's always the fault of the driver who goes into the back of another car. It doesn't matter that you were dithering. He should have known better. He could see you're a learner.'

'But he was so horrible.'

'Yes, he was very rude. That's because he knows he was in the wrong and the damage will be on his insurance.'

'I'm sorry about your car.'

'Don't worry. It will soon be put right. There's a very good garage in Stowmarket that my father uses.'

I toyed again with the idea of introducing her to Simon, but having lost everything else in my life, a small dent in my bumper no longer seemed important. Previously I would have been furious. Now I was resigned to my run of bad luck. It wouldn't be fair to hand her over now. Simon wouldn't have the tolerance for her particular style of learning, I told myself, particularly if he were on antidepressants as Dad had suggested. Besides, I was enjoying each small success and didn't want to give up on her yet. Bruce now stayed at home. She trusted me. I couldn't let her down.

After the crash, I conducted our lessons on a circuit, making sure we only turned left, to avoid crossing two streams of traffic. I told her roundabouts would be easier because everybody was going in the same direction. Ironically, the first time we tackled one she turned right when I told her to. Literally. Thankfully we were the only vehicle on the roundabout when we went the wrong way.

'So whichever way I want to go, I have to turn left. If I want to turn left, I turn left. If I want to go straight on, I turn left. If I want to turn right, I turn left. Why not make it easy and have a crossroad?'

'You don't like crossroads, remember. At least with a roundabout you only have to look in one direction to see if there's a car coming. A roundabout keeps the flow of traffic moving better. As you slow down on the approach, you have time to see if there's a gap. The key is to keep moving if at all possible, no matter how slowly, and slot in with the other drivers.'

'Slotting in has never been my strong point.'

I made a mental note to avoid roundabouts as well. I would leave those to a professional, someone with dual controls.

My life was falling into a predictable routine. I walked Elsie. I taught Sarah. I searched for jobs and played games on my computer. Mum was leaving instructions in the kitchen so I could get a start on the dinner before she came home. The three of us spent the evening watching the television with the dog lying in front of the gas fire. I read the book I borrowed from the library.

'What's it about?' Dad asked as I finished the last page of *Total Quality Management* and tossed it onto the coffee table. 'Is it any good?'

'It's about being the best and motivating your staff to be the best too. It talks about getting things right first time, every time. The author suggests a constant drive towards perfection by reviewing everything you do to see how it could be done better.'

'Sounds exhausting.'

'I don't think these self-help books do much good,' Mum said. 'If there really were seven steps to happiness or ten steps for a successful marriage, don't you think all of us would have discovered them by now? Bookshops are jam-packed with this stuff but the world is full of misery just the same.'

'Modern businesses are constantly evolving. It's important to learn new ways of working that take into account digital technologies and emerging markets. China and India, for example, are forging ahead. Britain is going to get left behind unless we buck up our ideas and change attitudes towards working life. Elmsford, for example. It's not exactly a hive of entrepreneurial business activity, is it?'

'Are you saying that we don't have total quality people here?' Dad said, flicking through the pages of the book.

'Of course not. You two live here, for one thing. Total quality management is not a judgement about the kind of person you are; it's about your attitude in the workplace, and the kind of commitment that today's companies require from their staff. The author uses an agricultural metaphor in one chapter, so even the good folk of Elmsford should be able to understand it. He illustrates the dedication he expects from his staff by asking how committed a chicken and a pig are to the full English breakfast. Of course, the chicken is committed. She lays a beautiful egg. But the pig shows real commitment because when he contributes the rasher of bacon he gives his all. Total quality people give everything. They hold nothing back.'

'But the pig dies!' Mum said.

'That's not the point.'

'That's exactly the point. The chicken can lay eggs every morning for breakfast, but the pig can only contribute once. Then he's dead. Fat lot of good he is in the long term. He's burned out... or rather sliced up and grilled!'

'The metaphor can only be extended so far. The real point of the story is to show the difference in the degree of commitment that is expected...'

'You mean the difference in stupidity between an animal that knows when to stop and one that doesn't,' Dad said. 'That's exactly the point I've been making, son. You don't have to rejoin the rat race. We know you better than anyone else. You're forcing yourself to be a round peg when you're a square one. If you keep trying to force yourself into a round hole, bits of you will be broken off.'

'I'm not forcing anything anywhere! This is me, or haven't you realised it? I was living the dream in London...'

'There's no need to raise your voice,' Mum said. 'We're on your side, you know. We don't like to see you neglecting your best qualities. There's room for kindness and sensitivity and imagination in business, I'm sure.'

'Not if you want to succeed!'

'Perhaps that's enough talk about pigs and hens and rats,' Mum continued. 'The main thing is that the Elmsford hens know how to produce total quality eggs and our pig farmers breed total quality pigs. You can buy their chops down at the farm shop. I get them for Elsie every now and then.'

'You spoil that dog, Gillian.'

119

'A tomato is a fruit but it doesn't go in a fruit salad,' she replied. She looked at the two of us and repeated herself slowly. 'A tomato is a fruit. That's knowledge. But you don't put it in a fruit salad. That's wisdom. Wisdom is an infinitely more complex thing. For that you need to know the rules, but you also need to know when they can be broken. You won't learn about wisdom from a self-help book. You don't need technique, Vincent, what you need is life!'

*****

Even though I hadn't received confirmation about my interview for the City job, I knew these things often came together at the last minute. I kept the whole of that Friday free in my diary and allowed myself a little breathing space, glancing only briefly at the job adverts on the internet.

I was spending more and more time with Sarah, either in the car or out in the fields. I was getting used to the pattern of her shifts and could fairly accurately predict when I might bump into her walking the dog. She rarely initiated a conversation, but her responses were intelligent, intriguing, unfailingly honest and occasionally bizarre. She was content to listen without offering opinions or advice. She wasn't impressed by any of the things that impressed me: money, status, success. She accepted people as they were and expected to be treated in the same way. I found myself telling her about my redundancy and the loss of my flat. If she had been overly sympathetic I might have allowed myself to wallow in self-pity, but her matter-of-fact manner made me realise there were worse things in life than living back home with Mum and Dad at the grand old age of 30. I'd even mentioned my break-up with Chloe. She asked why we had argued.

'She thought I was being pathetic. I know I didn't behave well. A couple of times I had too much to drink. I thought she could have been more understanding. Chloe's a very get-up-and-go sort of person. She liked to tell me what to do, and would have a go if I didn't take her advice. It felt like she was kicking me when I was down. We're talking again now. You never know...' Sarah didn't comment and we walked on.

She rarely divulged anything about her own past. I thought it might be tactless to bring the subject up. Her childhood had obviously been unhappy, and in my own small way I might have contributed to that. I hoped we might return to our previous conversation, the one that had been abruptly cut off by the cat when I was sure she was about to share something important, but the moment of intimacy had passed.

120

After a tedious weekend, I dragged Elsie out for a second walk on Monday afternoon, hoping I would bump into Sarah walking Bruce after her shift finished at midday. My hunch paid off. I no longer bothered with small talk. I knew she hated it. I asked where she would like to drive to first after she had passed her test.

'Cambridge. I used to go to Cambridge a lot with Mum. I would love to be able to drive there myself.'

'Then you shall!' I promised with a flourish. 'The world will be your oyster. Holidays! Weekends away! Nights out! You won't have to be stuck doing a part-time job in Elmsford. Think of the libraries in Cambridge, or Ipswich, or Bury. You could get a full-time job.'

'I like working part-time.'

'As a stopgap, maybe –'

'I don't want to be working all the time.'

'Nobody does, but we all have to earn a crust. What if everybody wanted a cushy little number? Where would we be? The economy would crash. There wouldn't be enough taxes to pay for our public services, including our libraries...'

She stopped walking and faced me. 'But I'm not everybody, and everybody doesn't think like that. What's the problem?'

'I'm just saying it's no way to manage your career. If you want to get on, you have to put in the hours to be noticed. Plus, the money would be better. Are you able to save anything on what you earn at the moment?' She stared at the ground. 'Sorry. It was rude to ask. It's just that I'm used to talking to people about their financial situation and giving them advice.'

'I don't really have any savings. But then, what am I saving for?'

'A car, for starters! And perhaps some new clothes to go with the new car and the new job.'

She looked down at her body. 'What's wrong with what I'm wearing?'

'Dress to be the best, that's my motto.'

'Dress to be comfortable, that's mine.'

I thought of the girls queuing to get into Strobes at the weekend, the way they folded their arms across their shivering bodies and pulled their microscopic skirts down over their thighs, their bare legs mottled with the cold. 'Image is everything.'

'That's obviously nonsense. Image isn't everything. It isn't reality, for starters. Image is something you project to cover up your own insecurities.'

My feet were getting cold standing still. I started to walk and she fell into step by my side.

'Let's forget about clothes for a minute. Let's get back to the savings issue. It's really important that you think about your long-term financial security.'

'My mum left me the bungalow. I don't have to worry about anything except the bills. '

'But you shouldn't just be thinking about your immediate commitments. For example, it would make financial sense to sell the bungalow and buy a small flat that's easy to maintain. You might even be able to sell to a developer. Those bungalows in Moon Rise have good-sized gardens. Have you noticed that a few of them have sold their plots and two or three small houses have been built in their place?'

'I don't want to move. And Bruce wouldn't like a flat.'

'No... that's true.' I patted Bruce, whose head came up to my waist. 'But it's an option. You need to think about maximising your potential.'

'What *are* you talking about?'

'You know, making the most of your assets. You're bright, intelligent, reliable, mostly polite,' I laughed, remembering a few of our conversations. 'Mum says you're very helpful in the library. Once you've learned to drive you could find a much better job, maybe even one in an office, and get some kind of savings plan going. A personal pension or life insurance, perhaps.'

I thought of the mess I had made of my own finances and silently vowed to take my own advice once I found a new job.

'A good character is the best insurance.'

'Are you kidding? Is that one of your mother's famous sayings?'

'No. I just said it. A good character *is* the best insurance.'

'Let's get back to the real world. People have to earn money to live. Economics for Beginners, Lesson One.'

'Don't be patronising. Of course we all have to earn a living, but it doesn't have to be all about the money. You don't *have* to be the flash guy with the flash car, you know.'

'I like being the flash guy with the flash car. Oh, wait. I'm the guy with the flash car with a dent in the bumper.'

An awkward silence descended the moment the words left my mouth. 'I'm sorry, I didn't mean to rub it in. The car will be fine.' We reached the end of the field. I opened the gate and let her pass through ahead of me.

'I've booked it into the garage for next week. The bloke is settling privately to save going through his insurance and losing his no-claims bonus.'

She turned to face me as I fastened the gate behind us. 'I *really am* sorry about your car.'

'And I'm sorry for bringing it up. All I'm saying is that it's important to have some kind of savings plan so you can build a better life for yourself.'

'I *have* built a life for myself. I have a home and a job. I have Bruce and I have these beautiful fields to walk in every day. That's more than you can say.'

'But you could do so much more than stamping books in the library.'

'We don't stamp books any more.'

I took a deep breath and softened my tone. 'You know what I mean. Don't you have any ambitions, any dreams? Wouldn't you like a really satisfying career where you could meet exciting people and be proud of your work, where people respect you for what you have achieved? I know what a good salary can bring. It can change your life, change the sort of people you meet, the sort of restaurants you eat in. Wouldn't you like to go to the theatre, see your favourite musician in concert, have a holiday somewhere hot?'

'I like the sort of people I meet here in Elmsford, and I don't like the heat. You're confusing me with yourself. I don't need all those things. It's no good lecturing me about my life. Think about your own. Think about the sort of a person you are becoming. Don't put yourself in a box just because that's what society says you should be doing. You don't have to enslave yourself to earn money you don't have the time to spend. I don't know anything about the world of finance –'

'No, you don't,' I interrupted.

'… but I do know you don't have to swallow the lie that the more money you have the happier you will be. Consumerism breeds anxiety. Money makes people cautious. They get scared of losing it. They lose their authenticity. What did you ever get out of the rat race, Vincent? Making money for someone else, and then being dumped at the first sign of trouble.'

'It's easy for you to say that money doesn't make you happy. You've just inherited a nice bungalow! For the rest of us, it's *not* having money that makes us anxious. For your information, it won't be long before I'm back on top again. I have an interview next Friday. I'm not going to sit and wait for someone to hand me success on a plate. I'm going to make it happen! Surely you don't want to coast through life and get to the end feeling you've achieved nothing? As my boss used to say, "Don't take care, take risks!"'

'If you try to be someone you're not, you murder your own truth. What's left? A nice outside with fancy lettering. An empty packet and a few crumbs. That's not me. That's you.'

Her criticism sliced my heart like a surgeon's knife. Unexpected tears pricked my eyes. I shielded my hand against the low winter sun to cover my distress. 'I like working hard and playing hard. We can't all float around on our own private planets doing just what we like, not planning for the future, being a drain on the welfare state in our old age. Yes, there are moments when I'm sure we would all like to have a little part-time job and spend our days picking daisies, but we need to make a contribution to the economy. Part of that is earning a good wage and paying taxes.'

'You're just frightened to be yourself. Don't you want to be free from all that pressure? Free to breathe the air?'

'What? Drop out and become some kind of free spirit, like you? I don't think so. You thumbed your nose at school and the chance to get any qualifications. Now you're stuck with a job any teenager could do on a Saturday morning for a little extra pocket money.'

'Things happen for a reason,' she whispered. She cleared her throat and said in a stronger voice, 'Take your situation, for example. Sometimes you have to lose everything to find out who you really are.'

'Well, I don't like losing,' I snapped.

'You can learn a lot from losing.'

'Yes. You learn that winning is better!'

'Haven't you noticed that it's the people who suffer who make things better for other people? It's the parents of children who have terminal illness and the families and friends of those who have died of cancer who are raising money for hospices and medical charities. Those who are in pain find meaning through helping others. It's the ones who don't have much who are willing to share. People who are comfortable will never change the world for the better. You can't learn patience, perspective, understanding and sympathy for others if you're always winning.'

'Maybe I don't want to learn those things,' I replied petulantly. 'It's a dog-eat-dog world out there – or maybe a dog-eat-rabbit world, in Bruce's case.'

'But if you live in a world of winners and losers, the strong will always be winning and the weak will always be losing. Do you want to live in a world like that?'

'Wake up, Sarah. We *do* live in a world like that!'

'Well, I don't want to live in that kind of world, and I won't! That's what it was like at school for me. I was one of the losers, as our classmates were so fond of telling me. But Mum took me out of that hellish place and taught me at home. She could see I was learning nothing except rejection and despair. She took me out of the arena where you either sink or swim, and showed me another way. She allowed me to be me.'

My earlier dismay now turned to anger on her behalf. 'Yes, and look at you now! Your mum didn't do you any favours by taking you out of school. It didn't help you get on the career ladder, did it? You're a part-time dogsbody in a village library that will probably be closed down in the next round of government cuts. She should have protected you better, made sure you were prepared to face the world. What will you do if you lose your job? I have first-hand experience of *that* situation. Believe me, it's not easy to find work, particularly if you lack qualifications and experience. It's even worse in the public sector. I'm only trying to help, Sarah. Don't fritter your life away. Regret is a terrible thing –'

'Don't worry about me!' she exclaimed, her eyes flashing. 'When people reach the end of their life I think they regret the things they *did* do rather than the things they didn't.'

I was already feeling sensitive, but I thought I detected a personal reproach in the way she looked me directly in the eye.

'What's that supposed to mean?' The sense of unease that lingered around my teenage memories of Sarah suddenly reasserted itself. Was she hinting I had done something wrong in the past?

'All I'm saying is that Mum wasn't worrying that she never went to fancy restaurants or had holidays abroad when she was dying. She was regretting she had cut all ties with my dad's family after he passed away. They never liked her and had disapproved of their marriage. She was sad I didn't have the opportunity to get to know my paternal grandparents.'

'Did she regret letting you waste your life like this? Sometimes it's easier to give up than fight for what's important.'

'She loved me and –'

'Maybe she couldn't face up to the realities of life…' I remembered what Mum had said about Eleanor Penny's mysterious death. 'Maybe that's why she ended up in a cupboard. Just because she was a quitter, it doesn't mean you have to be.'

From her expression, I realised I had gone too far.

'I'm sorry... I don't know why I said that. It was unforgiveable. I'm sure it wasn't like that at all.'

She turned her face away and stared at the horizon, tight-lipped. Had I really suggested her mother might have contributed to her own death?

'I'm sorry.' I took a step towards her but she shrank back, her hands clenched at her sides. The dogs sniffed the hedgerow, apparently unconcerned at our disagreement. I didn't know how we had managed to get ourselves into this impasse. It had been the last thing I wanted to happen.

'I don't know why we're arguing, Sarah. I didn't mean to upset you. I just wanted to help.' She didn't reply. 'It's just, if you need any advice... about financial matters, I'd be glad to help. I know it can be very confusing. I'm good at analysing different products and working out what would be best for your personal circumstances, ways to pay less tax, for example, to get the best personal pension...' I trailed off.

'I think I'm OK, thanks.'

'Well, the offer's always there... I guess we'd better be getting back.' We turned around and began to retrace our steps. Dark clouds had blown across the sky and were bunching like clenched fists over the village, their purple bellies flecked with gold from the setting sun. I was desperate to think of something to say to break the tension.

'Didn't you miss being with all the kids at school?'

'No. No one ever spoke to me, apart from you, anyway. When you started hanging out with Jimmy Hodges even that stopped.' I felt myself reddening. I hadn't realised it had been that obvious. 'He still lives in the village, you know.'

'Does he? I didn't realise...'

'He hasn't changed much.'

'Hopefully you don't have to bump into him too often.'

'I don't think he recognises me, anyway. Either that or he's ignoring me.'

We put the dogs on their leads. I waited while she pushed open the kissing gate that led to the road.

'Can you forgive me, Sarah? I'm an idiot.'

126

She walked through with Bruce and turned to face me with the gate shut between us. 'Yes.'

'Yes you forgive me, or yes I'm an idiot?'

We were standing so close to each other I could feel her breath on my cheek.

'Just yes.'

'Are you still OK for a lesson tomorrow?'

'If the flash guy with the flash car wants to spend time with a daisy picker like me, who am I to argue?' An expression of sadness fell across her face. 'I can't change the way I am, Vincent. I wish I could.'

I had to fight the urge to touch her, to reassure myself that everything was all right between us, but Elsie's lead had become twisted in the gate. Bruce tried to nudge his way back to our side. Sarah stepped back to let the two dogs pass. The gate clanged shut behind us.

'Anyone can change,' I replied.

'Yes, you could, Vincent... but only if you want it badly enough.'

Chapter 14

The Railway Tavern was quiet on Monday nights. Tuesday night was curry night. Wednesday had big-screen football. Thursday was quiz night. Fridays were crowded with karaoke clones. At the weekend the pub was heaving with Elmsford youth. But on Mondays there was no loud music or TV. Consequently that was the night the old boys of the village met up for a quick pint and a game of darts.

Jimmy and I were the youngest punters by about 30 years. It had been more than a week since I had seen him and he was eager to fill me in on what had happened with Catrina after they had left the nightclub together. She had been sick on the pavement. He had helped her into a taxi and taken her home. Nothing else had happened.

'She was well wasted. Oi've got principles, yer know. Tipsy is fair game. Hammered is 50–50, depending on how fit she is. Proper trashed is off limits. Oi don't want a repeat of the trouble I had after Auntie Beryl's funeral.'

Besides, Jimmy wanted to see her again. He had staggered back to his car just after five in the morning and driven home to bed, seemingly unbothered that he was over the limit and had abandoned me to his friends.

The heavy door of the pub swung open. A blast of cold air blew in from the street. From where we were sitting – in a dark booth at the back of the pub created by high-backed settles arranged in a square – it looked as though the door had mysteriously opened and closed by itself. I was just going to ask Jimmy if stories of the pub's resident ghost were still circulating around the village when a very small man with a disproportionately large head walked into view from behind the back of the settle in front of us. He waddled to the bar.

'Here comes Dopey, or is it Grumpy?' Jimmy smirked. The man climbed up onto a stool so that he was tall enough for the barman to see. 'Where's Snow White, mate?' Jimmy said a little too loudly.

'Shut it, Jim,' I hissed.

Another icy breeze blew through the pub. I turned to see the door swing shut. Standing just inside the pub was a skinny man with hunched shoulders and a scruffy beard. Next to him stood Sarah.

'I spoke too soon,' Jimmy laughed as the two made their way over to the dwarf. 'Here she is!' I instinctively shrank back into the shadows cast by the wooden settles and prayed she wouldn't see me. Mortification swept through every inch of my body. Just my luck that she would see me with Jimmy, someone she hated and thought had been a bad influence on me, the very day I had feigned ignorance of his whereabouts.

As much as I didn't want Sarah to see me with Jimmy, I was frantic not to let Jimmy know I was teaching Sarah to drive. I'd been on the receiving end of his horrible banter enough times to know I'd never hear the last of it. Of course, they might not recognise each other in the darkness of the pub. Jimmy didn't seem to remember who she was, in any case, but I didn't want to take the chance. What if he said something unforgiveable and I was blackened by association? After the argument that afternoon, I was already on thin very ice with Sarah. My number one priority was to extract myself from the situation without Sarah seeing me and Jimmy, or Jimmy seeing Sarah.

The unlikely threesome at the bar ordered their drinks and made their way towards us. I held my breath, waiting to be spotted. Just at the last minute they stopped at a table on the other side of the tall settle opposite. Sarah and the dwarf sat with their backs to us; the thin man sat in profile. They shrugged off their coats and sipped their drinks.

The thin man was doing most of the talking. His cheekbones jutted sharply above his bearded jaw. He had a nervous habit of ramming his glasses up his nose every time he paused for breath. Even from this distance I could hear his monotonous drone. Half-listening to Jimmy's tirade against the government's immigration policy, I concentrated on the snatches of conversation from the table in front. The man was telling Sarah and the dwarf about his journey to the pub. There had been a last-minute alteration to his plans. He had changed buses... one bus had broken down... he had taken a more circuitous route. Sarah murmured intermittently, but I couldn't distinguish what she said because she had her back to me.

'Are you listening, mate, or am I speaking to the fresh air?'

'Sorry, Jimmy... go on.' I tore my eyes away from Sarah and her friends. Jimmy changed topic. He filled me in on Spider's drug habits. I mentioned he had slipped a girl a tab at Strobes. It was only a matter of time, Jimmy said, before their supervisor suspected the real reason for his erratic mood swings.

'Brainless junkhead. He'll end up losing everything if carries on as he is.'

I wasn't interested in Spider's recreational pursuits. I was more concerned about my current predicament. I was trapped in a corner – literally – and couldn't see a way out without walking in front of Sarah. Jimmy was sure to make a loud, inappropriate comment, particularly as he had downed several pints in quick succession. The other option would be to stay put. But if we waited until they were ready to leave, there was a good chance Sarah would need the Ladies at some point; just to our right was a door marked 'Toilets'.

'Your round,' Jimmy said, slamming his glass down on the table and smacking his lips.

This was a more imminent problem. To reach the bar I would have to walk past Sarah's table, stand in full view until I was served, and walk back to my seat. Sarah was bound to recognise me, if she had not already done so. Thinking furiously, I reached in my wallet and took out a £20 note.

'I need a slash. Here.' I pushed the money across the table. 'I'll have the same again, Jimbo.'

Jimmy willingly picked up the cash and walked to the bar. I slipped through the door to the toilets. There was a short corridor with a door to the Ladies on the left and a door to the Gents on the right. I desperately needed a way out of the pub, a fire escape or window, but the corridor was a modern extension, a dead end.

I went into the Gents. There were two cubicles, both of them empty. I went into the first one, shut the toilet lid and sat down. Why did it bother me what Jimmy thought about my friendship with Sarah? I was ashamed to admit it, but I was embarrassed. She was odd and a bit of a mess. She wouldn't add to my credibility, and Jimmy would torment me mercilessly. And why was I bothered that Sarah might think less of me for having a drink with Jimmy? Did her opinion matter? I'd be gone from Elmsford in a few weeks. I was ashamed I hadn't mentioned my drink with Jimmy when I had had the perfect opportunity that afternoon. It made me look weak and easily swayed. I leaned forward, head in hands.

Why couldn't I be open about my friendships, and stuff the consequences? If they thought any the less of me, then maybe they weren't the people I should be mixing with. Maybe I was blowing the whole thing out of proportion. Maybe neither of them would be bothered either way... Who was I kidding? I knew what would happen. Neither of them would keep their thoughts to themselves. Both could be blunt and outspoken in their different ways. If I didn't avert the inevitable confrontation, there would be carnage.

I raked through my hair in misery. The door to the toilets opened and swung shut. Footsteps crossed the tiling floor. Silence. I guessed it wasn't Jimmy because he knew I was here and would have shouted something crude. I couldn't sit on the toilet lid all night. Jimmy would be phoning me or flushing me out in person. Grimacing at my unintended pun, I flushed the toilet and unlocked the door.

Standing at the urinals was the dwarf. I studiously avoided looking at him, firstly because he was a dwarf and must hate being stared at, and secondly because men don't watch each other pee – not unless they want their faces smashed in... or kneecaps in this instance. I finished washing my hands and activated the hand dryer.

All of a sudden, I was shoved hard in the back. I toppled forward onto the dryer and banged my head on the wall above. I turned to see the dwarf standing next to me, shouting.

'What's your problem?' I yelled above the sound of the hot air.

'Leave... alone... answer to me,' was all I could catch.

'I can't hear you.'

'ARE YOU TEACHING SARAH PENNY TO DRIVE?'

'What's it to you?' I shouted, frantically shaking my wet hands dry in case they were needed for self-defence.

'ARE YOU A QUALIFIED INSTRUCTOR?' he screamed.

'NO, SHE'S A FRIEND.' The hand dryer switched off and my voice echoed around the cubicles.

'I don't think so.'

'What business is it of yours?'

'I'm making it my business. If you try anything on with her you'll have me to answer to. What are you after? She wouldn't be able to spot a scammer from 20 paces, but I can. And I'll know what to do about it.'

I was incredulous. I was being threatened by a dwarf.

'Sarah's a grown woman. She can spend time with who she wants.'

'When Sarah told me you were giving her driving lessons, I was suspicious. Now you're offering financial advice. My alarm bells are really ringing, matey. I've checked you out. You're unemployed and living with your parents, but somehow you manage to drive a tasty-looking motor. It doesn't add up. What could someone like you, with your designer jeans and expensive aftershave, possibly see in a girl like Sarah? She's a meal ticket, that's what! She's inherited a property. She's all alone in the world. Just the sort of woman a conman like you dreams of bumping into. Well, I'm here to tell you to BACK OFF!'

I couldn't believe he had pried into my private business, let alone accused me of trying to steal Sarah's money. 'You back off before I push you over, you little squirt!'

Before I could register the movement, his leg shot up. His boot caught me in the groin. I gasped and staggered backwards until I was leaning against the sink, doubled over with pain.

'What the hell is your problem?' I shouted.

'You're my problem! If you're really Sarah's friend, where have you been the last few years? Where were you when her mother died and she was left all alone, brokenhearted, with all the paperwork to sort out? Now she's beginning to recover, you suddenly turn up. She doesn't look such a bad prospect now, does she? Why else would you be offering to help a vulnerable girl like her? Out of the goodness of your heart? Give me a break, I know your type. We all know Jimmy Hodges. Any friend of his is no friend of ours!'

'Vulnerable!' I spluttered, straightening up at last. 'Vulnerable! Have you ever had a conversation with her? She's as tough as old boots. She's not going to let anyone get close to her in a hurry.'

Before I could continue the dwarf interrupted. 'Just remember, the Specials are watching you and we won't hesitate to act!' He pushed open the door to leave, but I grabbed him by the arm.

'Does she know I'm in the pub?' I could hear the fear in my voice and despised myself for it.

'Of course she does. She pointed you out to me. Haven't you realised yet? Sarah notices everything.'

'And does she know we're having this little chat?' I spat.

'No. She doesn't have any suspicions that you're not what you appear to be, an old schoolfriend. I don't want her to know you're after her money any more than you do.'

'I'm not after her money!'

'She's been through a bad couple of years. She's only just getting her confidence back. It makes her happy to think you're her friend. I don't want to be the one to disillusion her. Do us all a favour, go back to London as soon as you can. If you stir up trouble, I'll tell everyone I kicked you in the nuts. Do you want people to know you were bested by someone half your size? Thought not.' The door swung shut behind him.

I stood huffing and puffing in the toilets for a good five minutes until the pain in my groin had subsided. What should I do next? Should I return to Jimmy and pretend nothing had happened? Or should I tell him I had been assaulted, and unleash him on the dwarf? He would probably crack up laughing. Perhaps I should approach Sarah privately and tell her about the dwarf's suspicions, convince her of my innocence. But what if she believed him?

It was unbearable. It was libel – or was it slander? How dare he say those things about me! What if he spread his malicious lies around the village? My parents and their friends would be bound to hear about it. Looking at it from one angle, I could see his point. It did look a bit strange that I would strike up a friendship after all these years, and after she had just come into an inheritance. Why, oh why, had I offered to give her financial advice?

The door opened, and Jimmy poked his head around the door. 'Alright, Chubbs? Planning on being here all night? Looking for a hot date or somethen? Shift it. The beer's getting warm.'

'I'm not feeling too good, Jim. I think it's something I ate.'

I splashed my face with water and followed him back to our table, keeping my eyes on the highly patterned carpet.

Droplets had condensed invitingly on the pint glasses. We both took a long swig. There was no sign of the change from my £20 note, and I was too stressed ask.

My situation was as bad as before... No, worse! Sarah knew I was here with Jimmy. At any moment she could walk over and confront me. If

Jimmy recognised her he would either blow her off or blow her out of the water. Sarah disliked Jimmy; her friends disliked us both. And who the hell were the Specials? It was a sure-fire recipe for a punch up.

I wondered how much longer I could sit there not looking at the other group, pretending everything was all right. I could stand it no longer. I quickly glanced up at the table opposite. It took me a moment to focus. They had gone.

Chapter 15

Jimmy and I made a night of it; as sure as chickens come from eggs I awoke the next morning with a hangover. Mum and Dad had left for work by the time I staggered downstairs. There was a note stuck to the fridge – a shopping list of groceries and a reminder to replenish the stock of mouse poison. Elsie looked up expectantly. She had her own agenda as to how I should be spending the next hour. I drank a strong black coffee with a couple of painkillers and pulled on my dog-walking clothes.

As I walked, I turned over the events of the previous night. I remembered the encounter in the toilets with painful clarity. Much of the latter part of the evening was a blur. Jimmy sang a smutty football song, even though it wasn't karaoke night. I was sick in the car park, but that might have been a bad dream.

Back home I had opened my bedroom curtains and stood at the window, breathing in the cold night air from an open fanlight, hoping my stomach would stop churning. My pyjamas were on inside out but I was too drunk to care. Shadowy clouds had scudded across the sky on a cold east wind, obliterating the stars. The moon was nothing more than a pale haze behind a bank of cloud.

My bedroom faced front. Most of the houses opposite were in darkness, with only the occasional bedroom light glowing through pulled curtains. Shivering, I had fumbled with the latch to secure the window slightly ajar. Two houses down from ours, a street lamp was casting a circle of artificial light onto the pavement. A bicycle was leaning against the post, its angular spokes and handlebars clearly visible.

I began to worry about my pyjamas. I had yanked the top off that morning without undoing the buttons and without turning it back the right way round. Now that the buttons were on the inside, I wondered how I would get it off again. I tugged drunkenly at the front for several minutes before giving up. If necessary I would cut myself free in the morning.

I looked out of the window again. A smooth bulbous shape jutted from the ragged outline of a bush in next door's garden. I hadn't remembered seeing it there a minute ago when I was looking at the bike. I stared at the rounded shape as a drunken man might stare at the bottom his glass: blankly bewildered, expecting something more. It just looked odd.

To my surprise, the curve suddenly moved. The silhouette of the bush had split in two. The outline of a stranger wearing a cycle helmet had stepped out of the darkness and into the puddle of light. I backed away from the window, glad that my bedroom light was off, hoping I hadn't been seen.

In the cold light of day, I couldn't understand why I had recoiled from the appearance of the solitary figure on the pavement below our house. After all, we were in a Neighbourhood Watch area. I had had a perfect right to be looking out of my bedroom window in the middle of the night. But I had stepped back instinctively all the same. A minute had passed. I had gently pulled the corner of the curtain, leaning to one side so I couldn't be seen, and looked on to the street below.

Under the light, next to the bike, stood a motionless figure. From the stranger's height I had concluded it was a man, though the shoulders and hips were as narrow as a girl's. His head had appeared huge, rounded at the front and tapering into a streamlined point at the back. Because of the shape of his helmet, it was clear he was facing towards me. I had the uncomfortable feeling he was watching our house. He had remained unmoved for several minutes before taking hold of the handlebars of the bike and guiding it away from the lamppost. He flung a thin leg over the crossbar. Wobbling dangerously, he pushed off from the kerb with a squeak, regained his balance and then cycled off down the road. I had climbed into bed, suddenly sober and very cold. Now I wondered whether I had imagined it all.

I chose to walk as far away from Sarah's usual haunts as possible. I didn't want to meet her until I had decided what to do about the dwarf's accusations. How could I possibly disprove something I hadn't done and had no intention of doing? How much time would need to elapse before it became obvious I had no evil intentions towards her? I could back off, say I was too busy for driving lessons and walk Elsie in the next village, but that might create the appearance of guilt and give validity to the dwarf's allegation that I was after Sarah's inheritance. I was too proud to be frightened off by a stunted idiot like him. In any case, why should I change my behaviour? I had done nothing wrong.

I worried about the problem as I trudged across the fields, head pounding with every step. I didn't like the idea that Sarah had been repeating our private conversations, but perhaps I shouldn't have been surprised. She never seemed to be on the same page as everyone else when it came to social conventions, when to speak and when to keep quiet. Perhaps I should tell her about the incident in the pub toilets and take the wind out of the dwarf's sails. Then again, Sarah had obviously been talking about me. Was she suspicious? Had she asked him for advice? The thought was strangely painful. I thought we had built up a measure of trust. However much I turned the matter over in my mind, I was unable to come up with a strategy. I returned home frustrated and depressed.

I pulled off my muddy trainers in the porch and wiped Elsie's paws with an old towel. By the time I showered, had something to eat and picked up the groceries, another morning would be gone. It was taking me longer each day to get down to my emails and phone calls. First there had been simple requests to empty or fill the dishwasher or buy a pint of milk. Next Mum's list of jobs included hoovering and hanging the washing on the line. The days were flashing by; I wondered how I ever had time to go to work and keep on top of my own shopping and laundry, let alone go the gym and see my friends.

My vigorous daily workout of press-ups and weights had fallen by the wayside. My pace had slowed in direct proportion to the amount of time expanding around me. I no longer walked briskly around the village. I had adjusted to the gentle stroll of the locals, stretching each small excursion into a meaningful event. Consequently, I had put on a few pounds since returning home.

Rather than avoiding the neighbours, I now made every crumb of small talk last as long as I could, extracting every scrap of nourishment possible from the brief human contact. When I was alone, a fog-like sensation filled my head. I was finding it difficult to think or be motivated, or even think about being motivated. Although I told my parents I was far too busy to visit Nana, I had begun to take little naps in the afternoon. There was nothing in the diary for the rest of the day: no driving lesson, no snooker with Jimmy, just hour after empty hour to fill with mundane chores, the television and the internet. But I still felt under pressure.

Elsie and I walked into the kitchen. Before I knew what was happening, she lunged forward. From the corner of my eye, I sensed rather than saw a flick of brown brushing along the skirting board. Elsie's plump frame was jumping around the kitchen, pushing the breakfast stools aside as she forced her way under the counter, bottom waggling like a puppy. It took a moment to process what was taking place before my eyes. A mouse was skimming the floor tiles, running back and forth along the wall with Elsie trying to match it move for move but far too slow to catch the flash of silky fur. I slammed the kitchen door shut to stop it escaping into the hall. When I turned back to the room, I was just in time to see a tail disappear down the side of a short pine bookshelf housing Mum's recipe books.

Quivering with excitement, Elsie plunged her flat nose as far as it would go into the inch-wide gap between the bookcase and the wall, her bottom in the air. I approached and peered along the narrow gully formed by the wooden shelves and the corner of the room. Sitting right at the end, up on the rim of the skirting board, its tail hanging to the floor and its eye glistening black as a glass bead, was a mouse.

That was it! If there was a mouse in the house, there were bound to be several in the garage. I had let the situation slip. A small irritation was about to explode into a massive problem – I was thinking about my mother rather than the rodent. She would go absolutely ballistic!

Leaving Elsie standing guard, I marched from the house and reversed the car out of the drive. A soldier manoeuvring a tank through a battle zone would not have been more determined than I was at that moment. I sped to the hardware shop in the next village (I couldn't face Lauren in the supermarket) and stocked up on an extra-large box of mouse poison and three traps: two for the garage and a pet-friendly trap for the kitchen. The latter was sealed in a white plastic box to prevent dogs and children touching the bait and getting hurt. As I paid, the shopkeeper gave a wry smile.

'This is war!' I announced.

Driving back to Elmsford, I noticed a familiar figure standing at a bus stop outside the hairdresser's on the high street. Sarah was at the back of a short queue consisting of a couple of elderly ladies with shopping bags on their arms and a tall man wearing an anorak. I recognised the man as the friend she and the dwarf had been with in the pub the night before. He was holding Sarah under the elbow. As I drove past, she pulled slightly away from him with an expression of panic on her face. I looked in my rear-view mirror. To my annoyance, the car behind was too close for me to brake without warning. I indicated left and pulled over into the first available parking space and leapt from the car.

Sarah was a short distance away on the other side of the road, still resisting the grasp of the thin man. I attempted to cross the road but had to stop to let a bus pass. Grinding my teeth in frustration, I jogged along the pavement before darting between the back of the bus and the car that followed. Hangover forgotten, I quickened my pace as the bus indicated it was pulling over. The automatic doors opened with a hiss.

A noisy crowd of teenagers poured onto the pavement, fanning out across my path, laughing and jostling each other. I moved left to a gap between the teenagers and a low wall belonging to a terrace of cottages. It was quickly blocked by a man in a suit hurrying to overtake the meandering group. I moved impatiently to the middle of the pavement, hoping they would part to let me through, but they were oblivious to my approach. At the last moment I stepped off the pavement and into the road. My view cleared just in time to see Sarah being yanked onto the bus.

Almost immediately the doors swished shut and the bus pulled away. With a final spurt of energy I sprinted forward, drawing parallel with the passenger windows in a desperate attempt to reach the door at the front of the vehicle in the hope the driver would see me and stop. As I looked up, I glimpsed Sarah being guided along the aisle and pushed into an empty window seat. The man sat beside her, blocking her escape. She stared out of the window. For a moment our eyes locked. Fear and panic shifted to surprise when she recognised me. In a second she was gone. I was left on the pavement with a mouthful of diesel fumes and a heart full of rage.

Without thinking, I spun round and raced back the way I had come. I pushed through the gang of teenagers, ignoring the expletives, and dashed back across the road, fumbling in my jacket pocket for my keys. I was forced to let three cars pass before pulling out and executing a U-turn at speed. Swearing loudly, I drove up the road in pursuit of the bus, catching up with a small tailback of cars. The vehicle two cars in front displayed the Addington's Autodrive sign on its roof. I braked heavily, reducing my speed to 15 miles an hour. After five minutes or so, the two cars in between had turned off at a junction and I was immediately behind the learner driver.

I remembered the times that Sarah had been flustered by impatient drivers tailgating and overtaking on dangerous bends. The irony of the situation was obvious, but there was nothing I could do. By the time Simon and his pupil had indicated, slowed and turned into a side road, the bus had disappeared.

I reached a roundabout. The bus could have taken any of the other three exits. I cursed myself for not having noticed the number of the bus. It probably wouldn't have helped, because my knowledge of the local bus routes had vanished along with my interest in skateboards and prawn cocktail-flavoured crisps, but I was frustrated none the less. Where had she been going? All three routes would take her away from her bungalow and the library. Why wasn't she at work? I turned the car round despondently and drove home.

Elsie was lying on the floor, her nose still by the gap between the bookshelf and the wall. The mouse hadn't moved.

'Outstanding job, old girl!' Elsie's tail, curling like a Danish pastry, rocked gently on her bottom in response.

I read the instructions on the traps. They recommended using peanut butter or chocolate spread as bait. I rummaged around the cupboards and managed to locate an out-of-date jar of chocolate spread. I smeared a teaspoonful on each of the traps and gently pulled back the springs, checking that they clicked into place before I released the levers. Once primed, I set the pet-friendly trap at the entrance to the crack between the bookshelf and the wall. To get out of the crevice, the mouse would have to go into the hole in the side of the box, and snap! Target destroyed.

I refilled the trays in the garage with bright blue pellets and set a trap by the up-and-over door and one by the freezer. I also filled the new trays which had come in the box I had just bought, hiding them strategically around the kitchen where Elsie couldn't reach them and where Mum wouldn't see – one under the sink behind the bleach bottles, another in a little-used cupboard full of sandwich boxes and flasks that were only ever brought out for picnics in summer. I would secretly monitor these trays over the next few days to check for other unwanted visitors in the house.

It was nearly ten o'clock. I was exhausted, more exhausted than if I had done a full day's work. I realised I hadn't had breakfast. I boiled the kettle and sat down at the kitchen table with a coffee and a bowl of sugary cereal, my ears straining to hear the snap of a trap coming from the bookcase or the garage.

Except for Elsie's gentle snoring, the house was silent. Now I was home, she was happy to relinquish her post. I could wait. I had all day – at least until half-past three, when there was a chance Mum might return home early from the school office. The stand-off with the mouse had to be resolved by then.

I thought about Sarah. I hoped she was OK. I had overreacted, of course. She must be wondering what the hell I was doing, chasing her bus. What *had* I been doing? Why had I jumped to the conclusion she was in trouble? I wondered how much alcohol was still in my system from last night's bender. What would I say at our driving lesson tomorrow? This was another layer of complication on top of the close encounter in the pub.

I plugged my laptop into the phone jack and Googled the local bus timetable. After poring over maps and routes, I was no nearer to finding out where she might have been going or why. I began to formulate a cover story. From her stop, I might have been trying to catch a bus to Bury St Edmunds. I could say I wanted to do a bit of shopping there but didn't want the hassle of parking. Maybe my car was at the garage for a service. I would keep these options up my sleeve and see if she asked for an explanation. If not, I would pretend the whole incident had never occurred, and carry on as normal. The key to overcoming awkward incidents or delivering tricky cover stories was an impression of complete self-confidence.

I ate my lunch in the sitting room with Elsie at my feet. Our presence in the kitchen was probably deterring the mouse from investigating the sweet aroma of the chocolate spread. With the smelly pug out of the way, I was hoping to lull my enemy into a false sense of security.

I thought again about the cyclist standing outside our house. He had probably been answering a call of nature. That stupid dwarf with his threats! He had me seeing things that weren't there. My paranoia dissipated along with the fog in my head. Nobody was watching me. There was no dark cloud of danger hovering over the Elmsford assistant librarian. I wondered if the mouse was capable of experiencing unwarranted anxiety. Then again, it wasn't paranoia in his case; he really was being stalked!

By three o'clock there was still no progress. The mouse – quite happy perched up on the narrow ledge of the skirting board – was craftier and more self-restrained than I had given him credit for. He had to be ejected before Mum returned. Otherwise I would be dealing with a hysterical female and receive another chalk mark on my parents' board of shame.

I rummaged in the garage for an appropriate implement and discovered a long garden cane propped up in a corner. Armed with my weapon, I returned to the kitchen and moved cautiously to the bookcase. The last thing I wanted was to botch the whole exercise and have the mouse disappear behind the shelves or get past the trap somehow and into the rest of the house. Better to know the whereabouts of one's opponent; ignorance would be a strategic disaster.

Standing at the other end of the low bookcase, out of sight of the mouse, I carefully inserted the cane down the back and moved it gently along the wall towards the corner. I held my breath. Time expanded; my heartbeat quickened. Suddenly, a quick scuffle and the plastic box jolted a couple of inches across the kitchen floor. The mouse was in the trap. Without hesitating, I pushed it against the wall, sealing off the hole.

Panting slightly with excitement, I waited for the trap to spring. An eternity passed. Through the opaque white plastic I saw a dark shape skirting around the metal mechanism. Then 'BANG', the box leapt up from the floor, landing with a clatter. Elsie barked from the living room. I pulled the cane from behind the bookcase and held it aloft, an end in each hand. Legs astride, head flung back, I let out a deep roar of triumph. 'Yes!' Superiority had been established. The victory was mine.

Wildly elated, I pushed the box with my toe. A slight movement inside. The little pest was still alive. I picked up the trap and placed it on the kitchen table, tentatively easing the lid free. There was my quarry. Velvet-soft with oversized, petal-pink ears, its torso pinned beneath a merciless metal spring, its nose a few millimetres from the chocolate spread. Surprisingly there was no blood. As he lay in what must have been agony, he stretched forward as far as he could, but not far enough to reach the sweet brown treat. I watched the minute tragedy unfold: the futility of greed, the insatiable desire, the inability to comprehend one's own mortality.

I walked to the kitchen sink and extracted Mum's yellow rubber gloves from the cupboard underneath. Picking up the box, I closed the lid respectfully and opened the back door. I needed to dispose of the body. I walked to the bottom of the garden, deciding the best thing would be to throw it over the fence and into the fields beyond. No doubt it would make a tasty treat for a bird or a colony of ants.

I opened the lid again to look at the small creature. Its eyes were still open, but the bright gleam had faded. Its paws were beginning to stiffen and curl. I pulled it free from the trap and lobbed it over the fence.

I was wiping my feet on the doormat when the front door slammed. I shoved the trap into the carrier bag from the hardware shop and straightened up as Dad, looking very pale, walked into the kitchen. His eyes dropped to the yellow rubber gloves on my hands. 'Honey, I'm home,' he drawled in a fake American accent.

'Very funny!' I pulled them off with a snap and threw them under the sink, breathing a sigh of relief. Mum need never know.

Chapter 16

By the following morning, I still hadn't decided whether or not to talk to Sarah about the dwarf's suspicions. She had seen me with Jimmy in the pub; that was bad enough. I braced myself for a difficult conversation, some grovelling and a few excuses. Our lesson had started ten minutes earlier. On the surface everything was as it had always been.

Perhaps none of it mattered to her. Either she didn't like me enough to care about my friends, or she liked me so much she would overlook Jimmy as a minor inconvenience. Similarly, if she knew the dwarf thought I was after her money, keeping quiet could mean she didn't believe it or she wasn't worried about my motives because I had no emotional hold over her. Alternatively, she might like me so much she was willing to risk being fleeced.

I watched her closely, looking for any sign she might be developing feelings for me – moistening her lips too often or flicking her hair, smoothing her clothes down over her body, leaning a fraction too close. Unflatteringly, there was no sustained eye contact or flirtatious smile. She was giving nothing away. *Had she ever even been in a relationship?* A ludicrous thought about someone of her age, but there was something so childlike about her manner I was beginning to wonder. She was certainly clueless about the rules of male–female interaction. Maybe she just didn't find me attractive, I chided. I pushed the thought away. By any objective standards I was way out of her league.

The most important thing from my point of view was that she made absolutely no reference to the encounter in the pub. I began to relax.

'OK, now you have mastered the nine-point turn,' I said, 'let's see if we can try and get it down to eight.'

The street was empty as she began the manoeuvre. She put the car into reverse, turned the wheel hard left and backed to the other side of the road. Straightening up, and with the car straddling the road, she pushed the gearstick forward into first.

'Damn!' She jerked and waggled the lever. I looked down to see the tassels of her grey poncho entangled at the base of the gearstick.

'Let me,' I said, but somehow the poncho was knotted tight, caught in a small gap at the base of the lever. We fumbled for a few minutes, me moving the stick and Sarah pulling at the threads while frantically looking out of the window.

'There's a car coming!' she cried, her voice rising with a note of hysteria.

'Keep calm. They will have to stop and wait. They can see we've stalled.'

I yanked hard at the threads of wool, which stretched but were surprisingly strong. The approaching car stopped.

'It's not budging!'

'Take if off!' I ordered.

'What?'

'Take if off!' I reached over and pulled at the knitted material around her waist.

'What are you doing?' she shouted, slapping my hands away.

'We have to take it off.'

'Move it, idiot. Go and get a hotel room!' the driver of the other car shouted out of his window, clearly misunderstanding the situation.

Finally realising my intentions, Sarah yanked the poncho over her head. She flung open the car door and stepped onto the road, tears streaming down her cheeks. A horn sounded impatiently as I jumped out and ran round to the driver's side. Although the tassels were still knotted around the base of the gearstick, I forced the car into first and pulled away to park on the other side of the road. The driver sped past, shouting obscenities.

I switched off the ignition and jogged across to where Sarah was standing, her arms wrapped tightly round her waist, her body shuddering and racked with spasms. Instinctively, I reached out and touched both arms, running my hands up and down from her shoulders to her elbows in a gesture of comfort. Tears spilled over her eyelashes and splashed down her cheeks. I took a step closer, my heart constricting at her distress.

'It's OK. Everything's OK. It's nothing to worry about. It was an unfortunate incident. These things happen... and with your wardrobe, *anything* can happen!'

I fumbled through my pockets trying to find a handkerchief. She wiped her cheeks with her hand and sniffed. I pulled her towards me again and hugged her tight. 'Don't worry. He was an idiot.'

I felt her body, surprisingly small and fragile, through the fabric of her shapeless dress. Her wet eyelashes were as soft as feathers against my skin. She stood completely still while I ran my hands up and down her back.

A yearning as ancient as time moved in the deepest part of my being. Shocked by the unexpected ache in my heart I pulled back and gazed down into her grey eyes. We looked at each other for a long moment. For once she didn't glance away. I swallowed nervously, suddenly frightened. She stepped back, shivering. I looked away first.

'Let's get you back in the car. You must be freezing without that ridiculous poncho.'

We walked side by side across the road. I held the door open as she climbed into the passenger seat. I jogged around the front of the car and climbed in next to her. After a few minutes of tugging at the poncho, I managed to untangle the tassels. She pulled the offending garment awkwardly back over her head.

'Perhaps that's enough driving for one day,' I said, in what I hoped was a comforting voice. She nodded. I started the engine but remained stationary. I reached across and took her hand.

'That's my hand you're holding.'

'I know it is.'

'Why are you holding it?'

'Because it's the hand I want to hold.'

There was a heartbeat, before she replied. 'I can hold my own hand… thank you.' She extracted her fingers and grasped her hands in her lap. I put the car in gear and pulled away.

'Are you all right now?' She nodded. 'Perhaps you would like to go for a drink. You deserve a nice glass of wine.'

'No, thank you. I don't drink.'

'You could have an orange juice. That's what you were drinking when I saw you in the Railway Tavern the other night, wasn't it?'

'Yes.'

'Why did you ignore me?' I asked, suddenly sick of my unanswered questions.

'Why did you ignore me?'

'You were with your friends.'

146

'You were with Jimmy!' she flashed.

'Yes. It was all a bit... awkward. Is that why you left?'

'No. Gavin hadn't eaten. He was hungry. We went to get fish and chips and then we went back to his house.'

'Oh! You go into *their* houses, then,' I grumbled. She looked confused. 'You wouldn't come back to my place for a cup of tea, remember? The day you hurt your hand and called me a stranger.' Irritation from that day begin to re-emerge.

'I've known them for years.'

'You've known *me* longer.' Remembering the shifty body language of the thin man and my hostile conversation with the dwarf, I pressed on. 'Admit it. I'm not as strange as they are.'

'Just because a computer doesn't run Windows, it doesn't mean it's broken.'

I thought about that for a moment.

'No. But it will cause compatibility issues.'

'What *is* normal, anyway?' she snapped. 'Besides, Gavin lives with his mother. I wasn't on my own with them, not that it would have worried me if I had been.'

'That just about says it all, doesn't it? He lives with his mother!'

'You live with your mother.'

'That's different. I'm just visiting. It's not a permanent arrangement. But your friends... don't you think they're...' I searched for the right word, '... funny?' If they were going to blacken my reputation, I wasn't going to take it lying down. I would sow a few seeds of doubt about them first.

'I don't think either of them has much of a sense of humour.'

'I meant funny peculiar. Can't you tell?'

'I don't want to tell.'

I glanced across, confused. She sat stiffly looking out of the window, still holding her hands tightly in her lap. Had she misunderstood my line of questioning? Was she being deliberately obtuse and evasive, or had that been a Freudian slip? Was there a secret about her friends she didn't want to tell?

'If you can't say anything nice, you shouldn't say anything at all,' she said, before continuing in a softer voice: 'Of course, I know I don't always stick to that rule myself.' She sounded sad. 'It's not that I don't want to.

The trouble is, I don't always know whether the things I say are nice or not.'

'It would be nice if you said you would come out for a drink with me.'

'I can't. Gavin is coming round to watch a DVD tonight. I need to get home... but thank you for asking.'

Disappointment was instantly followed by an intense sensation of rejection. She didn't want to have a drink with me and was making some lame excuse, embarrassed by the moment of intimacy that had passed between us. What if seeing me with Jimmy had made her reassess our friendship? What if the dwarf had been unable to keep his suspicions to himself after all, and she had been put on her guard?

Then I remembered she didn't tell lies. She was unrelentingly honest and would not have hesitated to tell me to take a running jump if that was how she felt. As much as I didn't want to accept it, she had a date with 'Gavin' – either the dwarf or the drip.

After mumbling a quick farewell, I left her standing on the pavement outside her bungalow. My hurt melted into fury. One of her friends was trying to blacken my name to keep me away from her, and the other reminded me of the kind of bloke you might see in a homeless shelter or on *Britain's Most Wanted*. Neither of them looked like they had much success with the ladies, yet Sarah seemed to prefer their company to mine. I was hardly aware of the rest of the journey home. It took until I turned into our road to identify the reason for my sudden anger. I was intensely and inexplicably jealous.

Chapter 17

I parked on the drive and slammed the front door behind me. The incident had popped the pustule of rage which had been growing unseen ever since I had returned to Elmsford. Rage at the unfairness of it all; rage that I had been helpless to prevent the disaster that had overtaken me; dented pride and grief at the loss of my comparatively sophisticated lifestyle.

Now I was going to spend the evening stuck at home in my bedroom like a sulky teenager, while some sad woman I had taken pity on was enjoying a semblance of a social life. Why should I care if she had a boyfriend? Maybe I should mind my own business! I didn't know why this woman was getting under my skin, but I didn't like it. I had to get a grip while I still had some control over my emotions. I breathed hard and tried to calm down, attempting to smooth out the scrunched-up feeling in my head and regain my equilibrium.

I was hoping to be able to let myself into the house and escape to my bedroom until dinner, but Dad was sitting at the kitchen table with a cup of tea, reading the paper.

'You're home early again,' I snapped.

Dad looked up. 'Yes. The surgery phoned this morning and said I needed to make an appointment with Dr Robson to discuss my blood test results. He had a slot just after lunch so I booked in straight away. I've just got back.'

'Not bad news, I hope,' I said, experiencing a sudden twist in my gut.

'He doesn't know. My blood levels are a bit haywire. I'm anaemic, that's probably why I've been tired recently. He thinks I might not be absorbing my food properly. I've lost about half a stone in six weeks without trying. In fact, I've been very hungry in between feeling nauseous and having a touch of diarrhoea. My stool sample didn't show up any sign of an infection, though.'

I picked up the kettle to hide the expression of panic on my face. 'What does he suggest?'

'He wants me to see a consultant. I'll probably have to have an endoscopy and a colonoscopy.'

'That sounds serious.' I had been so wrapped up in my own problems I hadn't seen how sallow and gaunt he had begun to look beneath his beard.

'It's just exploratory. They put a small camera down your throat and up your backside to see if there's anything sinister in there. They take biopsies too, I think.'

My heart thudded. 'So, they're looking for cancer.'

'Not necessarily. It might be colitis, Crohn's disease or even a tapeworm. Your mother and I did go to Greece last September. The good news is that it's not diabetes.'

I grimaced. Some comfort! 'Mum's going to be beside herself,' I commented. I put a teabag in my mug.

'Yes,' Dad replied, 'and that's why we're not going to tell her, not before we know something definite. It might be nothing at all, just a horrible virus I've been unable to shake.'

'And just how do you think you're going to keep this from Mum?'

'I've been on the phone to my private health provider. They're going to let me have a date with the consultant as soon as possible. After that, we'll see if I need these camera thingies. If I do, it will be just a day procedure under local anaesthetic. I'll take the day off work. I thought you could take me to hospital and collect me afterwards. Mum will be at work. She'll be none the wiser.'

'She has a right to know.' I poured boiling water into the mug, stirred and added milk.

'Yes, once we know what we're dealing with. I don't want her to be worrying unnecessarily. You know what she's like – tears, sleepless nights, talking about it endlessly with the neighbours. She won't be able to keep it to herself.'

'I suppose you're right. But she'll go ballistic when she finds out.'

'We'll cross that bridge when we come to it.' Dad smiled. 'If I can face a camera being stuck up my bottom, I think I can deal with your mother!'

I sat with Dad and drank my tea, my earlier anger forgotten. I had never thought seriously about my parents' mortality. They had always been there, like the sun and the moon: predictable, ageless, warming me with their love, guiding me by their light, generally unnoticed unless a passing cloud temporarily hid them from view. Now the situation was reversed; I needed to be strong for them.

I winced away from the intensity of the pain the future held, if not now then a few years hence. Watching Dad, then Mum, crumble into nothingness, followed by the slow process of degeneration myself. Accepting the mortality of my parents would be the final blow to a childish faith, so stubbornly held, that real tragedies only happened to other people. I knew it wasn't true. Hadn't the last few weeks of my own life taught me that? But this was a different order of disaster.

I found myself pondering the most simplistic of questions. How was death possible? How could all the thoughts and feelings and memories of a person solidify, liquefy and finally disintegrate into dust? How could a warm, mobile body – my own breathing, pumping, sweating, digesting, defecating body, for example – harden, congeal and rot? How could I bear to see my father deteriorate and watch my mother worry and suffer by his side? With no brothers or sisters or wife to share the coming pain, how I could face it alone?

Dinner was excruciating. Mum kept up a constant stream of chatter. Dad and I tried to respond normally, but all the time the secret hung heavily between us. I tried not to think about what a bad diagnosis would mean for us as a family, would mean for me, and reprimanded myself for being so selfish when it was Dad who was going through the ordeal. When Mum commented that Dad looked particularly tired, he managed to steer the conversation to the charity fundraiser taking place soon. Would I be able to be on the car-washing team in the village hall car park, raising £5 a time to help replace the roof of a disability school in Africa? I quickly hedged.

'I don't know if I'll even be in Elmsford then. If this interview goes well, I might need to start right away, in which case I'll be flat-hunting almost immediately, though I have some friends who might let me sleep at their place for a few weeks until I get myself sorted.'

Dad looked at me sharply. Suddenly I realised what I was saying – I might not be around to drive him to and from the hospital if the consultant decided that further investigations were required. I might not be there for him when he needed me.

'Don't say that!' Mum exclaimed. 'We've only just got you back.'

'You knew this was only going to be short-term arrangement. I thought you were pleased that things are starting to move in the right direction.'

'Of course I am, darling. I just like having my family all together, that's all.'

I swallowed back a hard lump. How would Mum cope if Dad were no longer around? I knew the answer. She wouldn't! He had always been the quiet strength in their marriage, the gravitational pull that allowed Mum's planet to spin. I would have to be back in London if, God forbid, anything happened to Dad. Living with my widowed mother was not part of my game plan.

I was beginning to catastrophise the situation. I needed to get away from the dinner table – and quickly – if I was to hide my distress from Mum. I pushed my plate away and stood up.

'I'm too full for pudding. I need to fill my car with petrol. I think I'll treat myself to one of those takeaway cappuccinos from the garage. Do you want me to get you anything?'

They both shook their heads. Before they had a chance to waylay me, I grabbed my jacket and keys and left the house. I drove around the village for a few minutes feeling wretched, my thoughts full of my own misery. No job, no flat, no girl, and now Dad was ill, just when I thought things couldn't get any worse. Recent events were chipping away with excruciating precision at the foundations of my life, stripping away layer after layer of the protective coatings I had developed to indemnify myself against pain of any kind. How much more could I lose? How much more could be exposed? How small could I become before I disappeared completely into a black hole of despair?

Before I knew it, I found myself driving towards the northern end of the village and turning into Moon Rise, Sarah's street. It was a dark night. I parked as far from the nearest lamp post as possible, on the opposite side of the road from Sarah's bungalow.

A ripple of nostalgia for the easy days of childhood radiated from my punctured heart. Several times I had walked Sarah home from the train station on the days when Jimmy had been elsewhere. We had sat on her front wall in our school uniforms talking about music and books and the teachers we had in common. Her bungalow was just as I remembered: pale walls with mock Tudor beams and a heavy wooden door inset with glass.

The lights at the front were on but the curtains on the left-hand side were closed. I guessed this must be her bedroom because the window on the right looked into her living room. Bookshelves lined the back wall. A framed picture hung over the fireplace. Without getting out of the car and walking past, I wouldn't be able to see any further into the room. A shadow moved behind the closed bedroom curtains. She was getting ready for her visitor, I surmised bitterly. The light snapped off. I watched the living room intently but she didn't appear. Perhaps she was at the back of the bungalow in the kitchen or bathroom.

Snow had been forecast. I turned off the engine, and the car heater automatically cut out. The warm interior quickly cooled. I pulled my beanie hat down over my ears and tried not to look suspicious. A notice on a nearby lamp post declared this to be a Neighbourhood Watch area. I put my phone to my ear when a man walked past, hoping he would think I had pulled over to take a call and wasn't a burglar casing the joint. The reality of the matter was probably worse. I was spying on a woman alone in her home, some kind of crazed prowler showing complete disregard for her privacy. Had my fall into unemployment, homelessness and relative poverty opened up a dark space which could only be filled by a voyeuristic thrill – watching the only female in the village I could loosely call my friend? Why was I here? I should be at home with my parents, sharing a meal before the shadow of illness fell upon our lives.

What was it about Sarah? She was unlike any girl I had ever met. She could have come from an alien planet for all we had in common. She was both a challenge to be conquered and a test of my choices and lifestyle. My past was entangled with hers, and I didn't know how to release myself. She held the answer to the mystery of how I had become the person I was today. She was a secret I needed to unwrap, the hidden meaning behind a baffling sign.

A bus approached on the opposite side of the street. It indicated and pulled into a stop. Several people disembarked and splayed out in different directions. A man, bundled up against the cold, walked towards me on the other side of the pavement, his eyes on the ground and his hands deep inside his pockets. He had a rucksack on his back.

The bus exhaled a breath; its engine revved and it moved slowly away from the kerb. The man stopped and turned back to look at the bus as it passed him. He continued to stare at it as it disappeared down the street. He checked his watch and jotted something down in a small notebook, nodding with satisfaction. He carried on walking until he reached number 28, unlatched Sarah's gate and walked up the short path.

Instantly, Bruce's face appeared at the living room window. From across the street I could hear his furious barking. The hall light came on and a warm glow spilled onto the porch through the panes of glass in the front door. I saw the man's profile clearly. He was thin, almost gaunt, with a straggly beard, his shoulders hunched against the cold. Gavin!

I watched as a shadow approached through the glass pane. Sarah opened the door. They greeted each other briefly. I noted with satisfaction that they didn't exchange a hug or a kiss. She stood to one side to let him pass. For an instant I saw her slender frame silhouetted against the light, the soft folds of her dust-brown skirt falling almost to the floor. The man shuffled inside; the door slammed shut.

Bruce's head spun round and disappeared from the living room window in an instant. Sarah and the man came into view. They were framed by the bay, a perfect tableau, the man with his hands jerking up and down, spinning left and right to avoid Bruce's boisterous welcome, and Sarah obviously remonstrating and pulling Bruce into the hall. She reappeared alone a few seconds later. They spoke briefly before Sarah walked out of the room. The man disappeared from view, presumably because he had sat down. After about five minutes Sarah returned with two mugs in her hands. She bent to set them down. Then she disappeared too.

Light snowflakes drifted across the glow of light from the nearest lamp post like motes of white dust. The car was freezing. There was no point sitting there any longer. Either I should drive home now or pluck up my courage and walk past the bungalow to try to see what was happening inside. Were they on the sofa together? Were they watching TV, or talking? Feeling guiltier than before, but justifying my behaviour with the thought that the quicker I got on with it the quicker it would be over and I would be back home, I opened the car door.

I strolled casually across the road and along the pavement. As I approached her gate, I took out my mobile and pretended to text. My steps slowed in feigned concentration until I stopped by her wall. Angling my phone towards the light spilling from her window, I pretended to get a better view of the screen, while surreptitiously glancing to my right.

The small front garden was simply kept – paving stones and a few shrubs in pots. A terracotta tub of bulbs stood beside her door. Crystal flakes glimmered on the spiky leaves and on a tight snowdrop bud that was just beginning to swell. I leaned on the garden wall and peered into her lounge, confident that Bruce was at the back of the house and the night was too dark for Sarah and her friend to see anything out of the window.

The snow was heavier now, swirling on invisible currents, settling on the paving stones like icy scales. I blinked away the flakes. Sarah's room was small and lined with dark wood bookcases. The furniture was heavy and old-fashioned, presumably because it had belonged to her mother. A deep red settee and mismatched armchair, a dining table with a plant in the middle, a couple of Tiffany-style table lamps shining like multifaceted jewels. The man, Gavin, was sitting stiffly on the armchair, his hands twisting together on his lap, still wearing his coat, hat and scarf. Sarah sat opposite, on the sofa, drinking from her mug. The TV at the back of the room shed a bluish light as images flickered on the screen.

My phone rang shrilly. I jumped and walked swiftly away from the bungalow. Sarah probably wouldn't be able to hear the ring tone from inside and with her television switched on, but my heart thumped with fear and guilt all the same.

'Vincent. It's Mum. Where are you?'

'I told you. I'm getting a coffee at the garage.'

'You've been gone a long time. It's started to snow. I was worried. The roads will be slippy.'

'OK, OK.'

'Are you still at the garage?'

It hadn't taken long for our relationship to regress to the days when I had to account for my whereabouts. I replied tersely. 'I'll be back soon. I've been talking to one of the staff. We both support Ipswich.'

'So does everyone else around here. Were you talking to Pete, the tall one, or Jerome? He's the older man who's usually on the till.'

I didn't want to get into specifics so I grunted that the snow was getting heavier and hung up before she could ask any more questions. I crossed the road and jumped back into the car, shivering. I looked over again at the lighted window. The whole exercise had been futile. I was even more frustrated than before. I started the engine and turned the heat up high.

155

Chapter 18

By morning, snow had enveloped Elmsford like a straightjacket. I borrowed Dad's wellington boots and strapped Elsie into her winter coat. Together we stepped into whiteness. Elsie's low-hanging stomach grazed the cold surface; she wrinkled her nose reproachfully, panting clouds of vapour like a squat steam engine. Grey streets and roofs were overwhelmed by the dazzling purity of the snowfall. The trees were weighed down by thick ridges of white. The branches of a neighbour's fir tree were drooping with exhaustion under their load. The thick silence was broken by the small plopping sounds of melting snow which left little pits in the drifts below. Occasionally a small avalanche cascaded through the foliage.

The views beyond the village were perfect, the muddy fields transfigured. A smooth white expanse stretched to the horizon, broken occasionally by a frosted hedge. Each step was accompanied by a satisfying crunch and the knowledge that I was the first person to mark the pristine surface. I had brought my ski sticks with me and I jabbed each pole firmly into the snow before wading forward. Elsie plodded by my side, unimpressed.

I turned through a gap in the fence into what had been the overgrown field left fallow by the farmer. The brown tussocks of last year's dead grass poked through the layer of snow like blond stubble. Two sets of prints marked their way around the perimeter, small boots and large paw prints. I quickened my pace and hurried round the field in the opposite direction, shivering with anticipation. I might be able to bump into Sarah on her way back. After about five minutes, I saw her familiar figure approaching, Bruce loping in front.

'Hello,' I said. 'Do you like the snow?'

'Yes, it's beautiful. I don't mind the cold. I would rather be too cold than too hot.'

'I agree,' I replied, remembering several fabulous holidays where I spent every day on the beach baking myself in the sun.

'No, you don't!'

'Well, perhaps not... but if it's cold you can put more layers on. In hot weather there's a limit to the number of layers you can take off.'

'Yes. You can't take your skin off.'

I nodded and turned to walk back in the direction she was taking. Bruce trotted confidently in front, his head held high, decisive leadership in every step. He glanced back intermittently to check we were following. Elsie trailed behind.

'Did you have a good time last night?' I said, before mentally kicking myself for letting my curiosity get the better of me.

'Yes.'

'What film did you watch? Anything good?'

'We watched the Highway Code Theory Test DVD.'

'You're joking!' At least it wasn't a romantic movie, but I didn't like anyone else muscling in on my territory.

'No, I'm not. We did.'

'Is your friend learning to drive as well?'

'No. Gavin's dead-set against the use of private cars because of the damage to the environment. He goes everywhere by public transport. He's a bit of a railway and bus timetable buff.' That sounded about right. The geek!

'Is he trying to dissuade you from learning to drive?' I asked, ready to defend our lessons against any criticism.

'Something like that, though he really enjoyed the DVD. Sometimes he notes down car registration numbers if he thinks the drivers are doing something careless or illegal. He writes a report for the police with full details. The DVD gave him a whole new set of ideas.'

'The Elmsford constabulary must love him!'

'They think he's a pest, actually.'

'I was being sarcastic,' but I smiled into my scarf.

'Oh!'

We walked on, the deep drifts slowing our progress. Bruce tried to play tug of war with one of my ski sticks. After a swift, 'Leave,' from Sarah he walked away disdainfully.

I had blown everything out of proportion. There was no indication that she and this Gavin were anything but friends. She was probably just being kind, though a little naïve to let some obsessive-compulsive trainspotter type into her home. I had become distracted by things that were unimportant in terms of my grand comeback plan. I had too much time to think, and too little to do. 'Get a life!' I told myself. But that was just the problem. I didn't have much of a life to speak of at the moment, and it was getting more and more difficult to maintain a sense of perspective. I needed to drag myself out of my general dejection, where Sarah was the only high point in my routine, and focus on the real world – my career, Chloe, getting another flat.

I looked across at her face. Her scarf was draped around her neck. Her green knitted bobble hat had been pulled firmly over her ears. She looked very young and vulnerable, her cheeks pink with the cold, her eyes bright. Gavin was probably just the sort of bloke to get the wrong idea and make a nuisance of himself. Then I remembered it had been me sitting in the dark watching her bungalow last night. A hot surge of shame warmed my cheeks. It was time to regain some sort of control over my behaviour.

'I don't think we can have a lesson while this snow is on the ground. Driving in slippery conditions is a skill you'll need to learn once you've got the basics mastered.'

'OK.' She hadn't disagreed. A wave of disappointment washed over me, despite my resolution to get a grip of my emotions.

'I'll let you know when I think the conditions are suitable.'

I didn't have her phone number. We had always arranged our next driving lesson in person, either when I dropped her back home or while walking the dogs.

'Can I have your mobile number so I can give you a call?'

'I don't have a mobile.'

I was surprised. Who under the age of 80 doesn't have a mobile?

'You can call me at home,' she said. 'If I'm out you can leave a message on my answering machine.'

'OK,' I pulled off my gloves and inputted her name into my phone's address book. She reeled off her number and I typed it in.

'Don't you find it inconvenient that people can't reach you when you're out and about?'

'They might find it inconvenient, but I don't want to be at everybody's beck and call. I don't feel I am so indispensable that I have to be available 24–7 like the emergency services. I like the freedom of coming out here, for example, and getting away from everything and everybody. I like silence. It helps me think.' She looked across the landscape, squinting against the dazzling brightness. 'See how empty it is!' she exclaimed in elation.

'I'm sorry. I didn't realise you liked to walk alone.' The increasingly familiar sting of rejection punctured my fragile self-esteem.

'Don't worry. I've got used to walking with you now. You don't talk too much, not lately anyway... since you stopped trying to impress everyone.'

I looked across the snowy fields so that she couldn't see the smile that was spreading across my face. Obviously we were still friends. If she had heard any accusations against me, she didn't believe them. If she disliked Jimmy, she was choosing to overlook my friendship with him. She took long easy strides through the snow, coincidentally matching my own pace perfectly, arms swinging in a relaxed rhythm. She belonged out in these fields, I decided, with her dog running ahead like a royal protection officer, Sarah following like a queen.

'Life's so much easier out here,' she continued. 'There are nobody else's rules to worry about. No paths, no traffic signs or lane discipline to abide by. We can just step forward and go wherever we want, though it's a bit more difficult today in the snow,' she laughed as she slithered towards me. I grabbed her elbow to catch her before she fell.

'I thought you liked rules.'

'Not like, exactly. If they're there I have to obey them. Much nicer if there are none at all.' She regained her balance.

'What about the countryside rules? Shut the gate behind you! Don't drop litter!'

'Those aren't really restrictions. That's just about being considerate to the animals and the environment. It's common sense.'

'You would think so!' I replied, throwing a snowball at an empty can of cola perched coincidentally on a nearby gatepost, iced like a cake with a circle of snow on top. 'The Highway Code is common sense too, if you break it right down.'

'Modern life is complicated.' She picked up the empty can and put it into a deep pocket in her winter coat. 'Everything seems to run too fast. Sometimes I wish I had been born in an earlier era when there were fewer expectations. The world today seems full of false people with veneered teeth living impossible lives and thinking they can have it all. Society wants to put us in a box from the day we are born – school, exams, career, mortgage. The media tells us what we should buy, what we should think, who we should look like and how we should live. And worst of all, there's the virtual world where reality becomes a kind of dream and people live a fantasy life in chat rooms and computer games, with TV anaesthetising them against the meaninglessness of their lives. Death by entertainment!'

'But we couldn't go back to the days without computers or television, could we?' I was thinking of the daily reality show I had become addicted to in recent weeks.

'I could.'

'But you have a TV?'

'Yes, but I don't use it as a TV. I don't pay the TV licence. The aerial has been disconnected in case the TV licence van comes round and wants to check. I only use the TV to watch DVDs.'

'And the best you can do is the Highway Code,' I mocked.

'No! I like nature programmes, and anything to do with history, but I prefer reading and listening to the radio. Then there's my semiotics. I like to read a book or article and do a semiotic analysis of it.'

'As you do!' I said dryly.

'Do you?' She turned to me in surprise.

'No, of course I don't!'

'I don't meet many people with similar interests to me,' she said sadly. 'What about you? Do you still collect stamps? I expect you're glad to be back here near the fishing lake.'

'You remembered! No. I don't do that stuff any more.'

'What do you do, then?'

'When I was in London I had to work late a lot of the time. Chloe and I liked eating out, going to wine bars, clubs…' I trailed off lamely.

My social life didn't sound so great when I described it to Sarah. I had visited the places other people had wanted to visit. I did things because they sounded impressive, not because I necessarily liked them. I had been to exclusive clubs, drunk in the newest wine bars, taken holidays in exotic places – a weekend in New York, white water rafting in France. If I had had any doubts about how I was spending my time and money, I'd quickly quashed them because everybody else was telling me what a great time I was having. I hated the white water rafting, I remembered, longing instead to be standing by a slowly meandering river trying to bag a trout.

At that moment I realised I had created a social curriculum vitae, a list of things I had done, places I had visited, people I had met. I had turned myself into the sort of person I wanted as a friend: handsome, successful, popular, rich. It was an identity to be proud of, except knowing Sarah as I did I knew she wouldn't be impressed. My life had been a snowy landscape, smooth and shining on the top, frozen mud underneath. Now it was melting into dirty slush and I was scared there would be nothing left at the end of the thaw.

'What do you do in the evenings *now*, here in Elmsford?' she said, interrupting my train of thought. A suspicion flashed across my mind that she somehow knew I had been sitting outside her house the previous evening. I pushed it aside.

'Well, there's always the Railway Tavern... and I go clubbing in Bury sometimes...' She wrinkled her nose. 'Well, once anyway. But mostly I've been staying in and watching TV with my parents. Sometimes I watch a DVD in my room or work on my computer, looking for jobs or social networking.'

I felt guilty for spying on her and found myself babbling to try to change the subject. 'I'm doing a lot around the house, visiting my nan, who's quite frail now. Dad's quite unwell at the moment so I've taken over some of his chores – taking out the rubbish, emptying the dishwasher, walking Elsie. There's been a mouse in the garage. I've been putting out poison and setting traps and...'

'He's not going to die, is he?'

'It's already taken care of. I killed him the other day.'

'Oh!' Her hand flew to her mouth.

'I know you love animals, but Mum won't tolerate vermin.'

'I was talking about your father. Is he going to die?'

It was my turn to be shocked. 'No, of course not! At least, I hope not... I don't know.'

'That was tactless. I shouldn't have asked. I'm sorry. It's just that when my mum was dying I needed to talk about it, and nobody would discuss it with me. People kept telling me everything would be alright. Death makes people uncomfortable, even doctors. They don't like telling people they don't have much time left. They talk about medicine and surgery, even though they know it only delays the inevitable, and the side effects are worse than the illness itself.'

We were back at the gap in the fence where I had first seen her footprints in the snow. We would be parting company soon. She would be going to the library later. I would have a lonely day in an empty house, both parents having struggled into work despite the weather.

'I'm sorry about your father,' she said, as we paused before going our separate ways. 'It's horrible watching someone suffer. I was glad when it stopped.'

'How long was your mum ill?'

'A couple of years, on and off. She had a lot of different treatments. Sometimes it looked as though she was getting better. In the end, I wanted her to be put out of her misery.' She stamped her feet in the snow, trampling it into hard ice. Her face was frozen too. 'You wouldn't let an animal suffer like that... but in the end it was quick. It was right.'

'If you ever want to talk about it, I'd be happy to listen.'

'There's nothing more to say. She doesn't suffer any more. Please let me know when it's safe for me to have another driving lesson.'

'Yes, of course. I'll give you a call.'

She walked away, her long coat dark against the snow.

On the way home, my thoughts turned to Dad. Was this the beginning of the end? Would the doctors tell us the real prognosis, or would they try to protect us in the same way he was protecting Mum? Would we be able to talk about it as a family, or would it be a subject shrouded in secrecy and fear? I rubbed my hands together to increase the circulation, mentally chastising myself for getting caught up in yet another cycle of negative thinking. I needed to plan for the future instead of worrying about things that might never happen.

As I approached the house, I noticed a white van parked halfway across the entrance to our drive. I wondered if it had slid there on the ice or if it had broken down. It would be extremely inconvenient if it didn't move before Mum and Dad returned and wanted access to the drive. I didn't relish the thought of having to help some hapless driver dig it out of the snow. When I drew level, the engine started and the van began to move slowly away, its tyres spinning and spraying wet snow onto my trousers. I cursed loudly. The van accelerated harder and pulled away too fast for me to see who was in the driver's seat.

Once in the house, I changed my trousers and decided to check the mousetraps while Mum was out of the way. Two of the three traps in the garage contained small, stiff bodies. All the trays of poison were empty. It would have taken more than a couple of mice to have eaten that amount of blue pellets. I wondered where they were nesting and how many pink, naked babies were squirming behind the paint pots.

I refilled the trays and reset the traps. Perhaps Mum's hysterical overreaction hadn't been misplaced after all. If I didn't manage to eradicate the problem, as far as my parents were concerned it would be another failure in a long line of disappointments. I checked the trays I had hidden in the kitchen cupboards. They were untouched. Hopefully that meant there were no more unwelcome guests in the house.

The following day was the day of the interview. I hoped the snowfall wouldn't disrupt the trains into London. The weather forecaster said that milder air was on the way. The thaw was already beginning. Hopefully the snow was a one-day wonder, though frozen slush and black ice could still cause travel delays.

I hadn't received confirmation of the timings yet, or any indication from Blake's as to the format of the interview. It really wasn't good enough! Would I be required to give a presentation, for instance? Would I have to do one of those psychometric personality tests? I had mentally blocked out the rest of the day for preparation, but I wasn't nervous. I knew my stuff and felt confident I would be able to pull it out of the bag. I checked my email account on my phone. Nothing! I punched in the speed dial for the recruitment consultant's direct line, determined to ask him what the hell was going on. I was connected after the first ring.

'Carl, this is Vincent Stevens. I'm still waiting to hear the time of my interview tomorrow.'

'Interview?'

'Yes, the financial adviser's post in the City. You told me to hold tomorrow in the diary for an interview.'

'Let me have a look on my screen…' There was a long pause. I heard Carl clearing his throat. 'There appears to have been a mistake. I'm sorry. My assistant should have emailed you earlier in the week to say that you weren't shortlisted.'

'What!'

'I apologise that we have kept you hanging on to hear. I'll have a word with Kiera, find out how you slipped through the system.'

'Did they say why?'

'No. I must admit I was surprised by their decision because you looked an ideal candidate. But we've got your details on our database and will be in contact as soon as anything else suitable comes up.'

I tossed my mobile onto the table, inarticulate with disappointment and rage. I couldn't believe it! I had told everyone I had an interview – my parents, Chloe, Jimmy, Sarah. It had been the light at the end of my personal dark tunnel. Chloe was expecting me to stay the night. She had probably changed the sheets in expectation. How could I face the mortification of telling her that even at this initial stage I wasn't wanted?

Chapter 19

It was my most expensive suit, steel grey, sharp as a knife, tailor-made by a little man in Savile Row. I hoisted up the trousers and tucked in the shirt I had ironed the previous night. Its crisp fragrance was cool against my hot skin but the collar was stiff and uncomfortable. The trousers were a little tight, but with the jacket buttoned up you couldn't tell. The mirror in front of me reacted with surprise at the businessman checking his tie. I hadn't worn a suit in a while. Somewhere along the line I had lost the knack. The care and attention I had paid to shaving and styling my hair had almost made me forget this whole thing was a charade. I rehearsed the conversations I planned to have that day.

I hadn't told a soul that the interview was off, and I had no intention of doing so. Instead, I would spend the day in London visiting recruitment agencies, perhaps doing a little shopping, before staying with Chloe overnight. I also planned to drop in unannounced on my old boss, Tony. He might offer to take me out to lunch. It wouldn't do any harm to remind him of my existence, show him how much he missed and needed me. It's not easy to replace your right-hand man.

I walked to the train station, carefully avoiding the slush that had been shovelled to the edges of the path. I didn't want water marks on my polished leather shoes. I bought an off-peak ticket to Liverpool Street station. The train was only ten minutes later than scheduled.

After the quiet of the countryside and its wide open spaces, London felt noisy and cramped. Too many people were squashed into too small a space, and all were fighting for air. The city showed no sign that it might have snowed the previous day. I knew that warmth from the street lights and office central heating systems hovered over London like an invisible cloud, the hot air generated by its inhabitants creating an unnatural micro-climate with the power to turn snowflakes into sleet.

Everyone was walking quickly. In Elmsford, there was no reason to rush and I didn't hurry now, choosing to saunter along the familiar streets, past St Paul's and across Paternoster Square with its cafés and of out-of-season tourists.

I pushed open the glass doors to my old office building and walked into Reception. A rush of hot air greeted me from the heating vent above. There was no sign of Stella, the usual receptionist. A much younger girl with bleached hair sat behind her desk. Two smartly dressed young men and an older woman sat in the waiting area, checking their phones and flicking through magazines, avoiding each other's eyes. I approached the receptionist.

'If you're here for the interviews, take a seat over there,' she said. I was taken aback. The firm was supposed to be reducing its staffing levels, not taking people on.

'No… I've just popped in to see some old colleagues. I used to work here. Where's Stella, by the way?'

'She phoned in sick. She's been off all week. I'm a temp.' She had a list of names and times on a sheet in front of her. If this was the interview list, it looked as though there were about half a dozen candidates. Even upside down, I could clearly see the logo at the top of the sheet – Blake's Recruitment – the agency that had told me about the position in the City, the job that had interviews today!

I gave the girl my most charming smile. 'So what's it like working for Morgan Phillips Barnes?'

'It's OK.'

'You certainly bring a bit of glamour to the old place. Who's left the organisation? What's the job they're interviewing for?'

She looked down at the diary. 'It says here: "Financial Adviser, Assistant to Tony Barnes".'

I swallowed hard. I had applied for my old job without realising it and hadn't been shortlisted!

'Oh, Tony… that was who I was hoping to bump into. I can see he's very busy today. Looking at the interview times, do you think he'll be free for lunch?'

'I don't know. There's a gap in his schedule between 12.30 and 1.30pm, but he might be working right through or discussing the candidates with Human Resources.'

'I'll give him a ring. Don't disturb him now. I've got an appointment round the corner. I only came in on the off-chance I might be able to take Tony out to lunch later. I can see it's not great timing. Nice to meet you...?' I hesitated, inviting her to tell me her name.

'Chantelle.'

'A pleasure to meet you, Chantelle. I hope you've enjoyed working here...' I turned and walked towards the door, '... with this bunch of conniving crooks,' I muttered under my breath.

'Excuse me!' Chantelle called out. I turned slowly. 'Do you want to leave your name?'

'No, thanks. I'll surprise Tony later!'

I made my way to the nearest coffee shop. I remembered some of the staff, but they showed no sign of recognising me. I ordered a large black coffee and sat near the window watching the passers-by, mentally dismembering Tony 'Backstabber' Barnes.

Perhaps I had a case for unfair dismissal. Could they make someone redundant and fill the post a couple of months later? I would have to Google that question when I got home. How could he do it to me? We were the A Team. Butch Cassidy and the Sundance Kid. We made it happen! I remembered his face when he broke the news that the bosses upstairs were axing my job. He had been devastated. I had ended up reassuring him. Don't worry, Tony. It will fine... The hypocrisy made me want to vomit.

There was an hour to kill before Tony would be out of the interviews and I could ring him on his lunch break. I jotted down a few pithy words on the edge of my napkin as ammunition. I had originally planned to visit some recruitment agencies in the area but I wasn't in the right frame of mind now. My well-groomed assurance had been replaced by burning rage. I thumped my cardboard coffee cup down on the table. Hot liquid splashed over my hand. I swore and had to apologise to a mum with a toddler sitting at the table next door. My phone bleeped. I checked my messages.

Good luck. Do your best. We are so proud of you. Mum

I felt sick. No... I felt like a drink. Something stronger than coffee. I shoved my way past the tables and chairs and exited to the street. There was a pub round the corner. If I went there now I could get ahead of the lunchtime crush.

*****

I had arranged to meet Chloe outside Bank tube station at five that afternoon. The winter sun had slipped below the city skyline and was shining by proxy in the office block windows. Light ricocheted from glass to aluminium, streaking the afternoon with cold, polluted rays. I missed the horizon.

I knew I needed to cross the road. I looked up and watched a plane draw a line on the sky. Impatient Londoners pushed past as I stood like a statue on the kerb. Somehow I had missed the green man. The torrent of traffic rushed before my eyes, deafening my ears, confusing my senses. The lights changed again. Both streams of traffic momentarily stopped. The roar of buses and the putter-putter of taxis quietened to a drone. A pause. The city held its breath. I held my breath too until the persistent bleep of a green man unleashed another flood of people across the tarmac. I was carried with the flow, buffeted by briefcases, weaving between the equal and opposite flood of humanity from the other side of the street. The lights changed. A vast tide of traffic broke across the junction. I lurched along the pavement, wincing at the sound and smell of the engines rumbling past.

Chloe was already waiting, looking impatiently at her watch. I was only 15 minutes late, I rationalised, as I waved to her and stumbled forwards. Grabbing her round the waist, I kissed her firmly on the lips.

'You're late!'

'I was held up.' I hugged her tightly.

She struggled backwards to look at my face. 'Have you been drinking? It's a bit early.'

'I had a quick half. What of it?'

'It looks like more than that to me. Are you celebrating? Or drowning your sorrows?'

'A little of both.'

'What does that mean?' We started to walk down the steps to the Underground.

'I'm celebrating because I'm seeing you.'

'And you're drowning your sorrows because you didn't get the job?'

'I wouldn't touch that job with a bargepole. They couldn't pay me enough. They can stick it where the sun don't shine!'

'Interview went well then! Sorry you had a wasted journey.'

'Not wasted if I'm spending time with you, babe.'

We caught the tube to Euston, changing at Tottenham Court Road. We had to stand, Chloe clinging to a handle in the ceiling, and me with my legs astride, trying to ride the sway of the carriage without holding a rail. More and more commuters crammed into the carriage. The train rattled through blackness, Chloe smiling tightly as our bodies brushed together. I studied the faces of the lucky ones with seats. Their minds were numb, their eyes blind. My own reflection in the black window was distorted by the curve of the glass – a sinister man leaning over a woman, her face hidden by the fall of my coat.

I thought back to my phone call with Tony. I had heard the surprise in his voice when he answered my call. 'Vince, mate! How's it hanging?'

'Great! I've been learning a lot about friendship. Who you can turn to when things get tough.'

'I knew you'd be fine. You're the kind of bloke who'll always land on his feet. People like you. You've got charisma. How's the job hunt?'

'I'm back in London now.'

'Epic! Let's schedule a drink.'

'How about today?'

'Diary's squeezed to the limit. Sorry, buddy. Big client. Brown-nosing time.'

'Business is picking up, then?'

'Ticking over, ticking over… Look, can I call you next week?'

'Not sure about that, Tony. You might be too busy training up your *new Assistant.*' There was silence on the other end of the phone. 'Did you really think I wouldn't find out that you're filling my old post?

'Vince, mate, I –' but I cut him off.

'I do have contacts, you know! I could slap you with an unfair dismissal lawsuit. I threw my hat into the ring just to see how you would react, to see if you had the decency to pick up the phone and explain what the hell you're playing at! If you had a problem with my work, why didn't you speak to me? What was all that gab about taking me back as soon as the economy turned around?'

'Desperate times call for desperate measures. You're a solid bloke, Vince. You're great with the clients. They trust you. You sell the product that's best for them. But I need more. You haven't got that ruthless streak. No guts, no glory. I want people who are prioritising the business… and sometimes that means screwing the client!'

'You're so full of it. What about "Good business is good for business"? You know, the whole integrity lecture you trot out to the team?'

'I have to say that. It's expected. But the bright boys read between the lines. You never were that sharp, were you, Vince?'

'I thought we were mates, Tony.' Even I could hear the hurt in my voice.

'Yeah, well I'm not in the business of making friends. I'm in the business of making money.' I heard a click. He was gone.

'Don't you think so?' Chloe shouted above the rattle and boom of the train, her tone challenging. I realised with a start she had been talking to me, probably about office politics. She always wore that patronising expression when criticising her colleagues.

'Of course,' I nodded, not knowing what I was agreeing with, but knowing what was expected.

'I knew you'd take my side.' She revealed a row of sharp, unnaturally white teeth.

We reached our station. We pushed against the eddy of people trying to board the train. Even if I hadn't been tipsy, it would have been impossible to walk steadily along the crushed platform. Big steps, little steps. I followed Chloe to the exit. Little steps, big steps, weaving through the small gaps between trolley cases and buggies. Down long corridors lined with dirty tiles; floating up the escalators and leaving behind the hot breath of the Tube. Posters advertising a multitude of destinations and events accompanied our upward journey: art exhibitions, West End shows, blockbuster films I hadn't seen. I tried to read each one as I passed, hungry for each bite of civilisation, but they merged into a multicoloured blur.

Once we were out on the street and walking side by side, I babbled the news from Elmsford, filling her in about my concern for Dad and Nana's bizarre behaviour.

'I don't like thinking about sickness and old age, Vinny. It's so depressing. It's important to think about positive things. Don't get dragged into other people's problems or you'll never get out of the negative rut you're in.'

'This isn't other people's problems! It's my family I'm talking about.'

'I know that. But your nana has lived her life. She's not your responsibility. You need to concentrate on getting yourself back on your feet. It's what she would want.'

'Perhaps...'

'You know I'm right. The quicker you get back in the saddle the better.'

We arrived at the wine bar just before six o'clock. It was modern and impersonal with glass tables and chrome-legged chairs. I assumed we would be alone and was disappointed that our friends Jake and Susie were already at a table. Chloe waved, obviously expecting to see them.

After the usual round of kissing and slaps on the back we settled down, the girls complimenting one another on their clothes and hair while Jake and I smiled stupidly at each other. I congratulated the pair on their engagement and admired the ring. After a few minutes of general wedding talk, Jake and I split away from the girls' conversation to discuss his favourite subject, Arsenal's progress in the league. My heart wasn't really in it. I ordered a couple of expensive bottles of red wine for the table and some tapas to cheer myself up.

'What did you think of the caterers last weekend?' I overheard Susie ask Chloe. 'We're thinking of using them for the wedding.'

'They were OK for an engagement party, but I'm not sure they're right for a wedding. The canapés were sweet, but the desserts were a bit of a cliché. I mean, *Black Forest gâteau*...?'

'It's my mum's favourite. We asked for it to be put on the menu.'

'Oh. Well, I suppose it did bring a kind of retro feel to the occasion, along with the coronation chicken...'

'You had an engagement party!' I exclaimed, interrupting Jake, who was taking a long time to say not very much about Arsenal's injury list.

'Yes,' Susie replied. 'It was a spur of the moment thing, really.'

'Just a few friends having a drink,' Jake clarified.

'With caterers?'

'You can get people at very short notice since the downturn,' Chloe said.

'How long have we known each other, Jake? Five, six years now?'

'I know. It's not that I didn't want to ask you. We thought you might feel awkward, after you and Chloe...' he trailed off. 'But you're invited to the wedding. You'll come to the wedding, won't you, mate?'

I gulped back the rest of my wine and topped up the glass. 'Yeah, yeah. Of course I will, mate. Whatever!'

'Great. How did the interview go?' he asked, anxious to change the subject. Chloe was no longer listening. She and Susie were whispering and giving each other knowing looks, the way women do when they talk about their relationships, or manage to avert a toddler tantrum. I gave a more reasonable reply to the question than I had given to Chloe earlier.

'It wasn't really my bag. They liked my presentation, but if they offer it to me I'll be turning it down. Not enough money for what they would want me to do. I'm not giving myself away that cheap. There's a more senior position in the pipeline. It's all good.'

The lies came easily. Jake took them at face value. No one seemed interested in asking more or finding out what I had been up to in Elmsford. They were too busy talking about themselves and several ongoing dramas at work I didn't know about. Other than sarcastic comments and innuendo, they didn't seem to be saying very much. I wondered whether I had enjoyed this kind of conversation in the past, or whether I'd been kidding myself.

I watched Chloe closely as I poured myself another drink. She looked tough and business-like, make-up immaculate, hair sprayed ruthlessly into place. She was wearing a tailored jacket with an acid-green blouse underneath. Her narrow skirt was tight and creased across her stomach. Sitting on the high chrome stool, her hem had hitched high above her knees. She caught me looking, smiled, and crossed one leg provocatively over the other. Her thighs looked like plastic in her high-sheen tights.

Did I want to confide in her about Tony and the job interview? Could I admit I was struggling and hurt and angry? Would she listen quietly without bombarding me with advice or criticism? Would she calmly tell me the truth?

The wine was taking effect. On top of my lunchtime beers, my blood alcohol level was snowballing down the hill and gathering speed. I loosened my tie. I talked loudly and expansively about mice and dogs, the state of the Suffolk bus service and the inherent creepiness of men with beards. I ordered a double Scotch. Nobody wanted to listen to my thoughts on the beauty of roundabouts. I stared morosely at my empty glass. I couldn't follow the conversation which echoed distantly on the other side of the table. Their mouths were moving, but I couldn't catch the words. Jake tossed his head and laughed, lips wide, tongue and teeth shiny with spit. The women responded with brittle glee and the restless click of acrylic nails against the glass table top. I was stranded on the wrong side of a dark chasm: alienated, alone and unable to speak.

With a blinding, drunken flash of insight, I realised I didn't know them at all. And they didn't know me. I understood what Sarah had said when we had first met in the library. I didn't go beyond the surface of things. To an outsider, our little group would have appeared to be the best of friends. In reality, I didn't like any of them. I wondered who the real Chloe was beneath the confident exterior. Was she scared and empty like me, frightened of not being able to keep up with the pack, terrified of failure and obscurity? What would it be like not to be frightened any more, not to have to keep up appearances, not to worry about what anyone else thought of you?

Unexpectedly, I wondered what it was like to be Sarah. Was that freedom? I could see her in my mind's eye, walking quietly into empty spaces with Bruce at her side. In that instant, I knew I didn't want to be in the wine bar any longer. I wanted to go home. I stood up unsteadily.

'I haz to go.'

'Toilets are at the back, mate,' Jake said.

'I haz to go home.'

'I thought you were coming back to my place tonight,' Chloe exclaimed. 'I've got a surprise waiting. I've bought that extra special muesli mix from the health food shop you like so much, and...' she paused suggestively, '... some scented candles.'

'I should have said before. I haz to be somewhere furz thing tomorrow... an appointment.' I thought of Sarah and Bruce walking across the fields. 'It's been great. Fablus. Epic and all that. Thanks for the offer of yourz bed... maybe next time.'

'Or maybe not!'

I kissed her cheek, noticing the scent of her perfume, the slight chemical taste of her skin. *If I'm quick, I can make the 2035 from Liverpool Street station.* I stood up too quickly, and without warning vomited a stream of red liquid into Chloe's lap.

Chapter 20

I had informed my parents I was staying overnight in London. They wouldn't be expecting me home until the following day. I couldn't face telling any more lies about my non-existent interview; I knew I was too intoxicated to make a good job of it. They would draw their own conclusions about the state of my relationship with Chloe if I returned home drunk as a skunk a day earlier than planned.

I stood outside Elmsford station with my overnight bag in hand, considering my options. I could spend the rest of the evening in the pub, creeping home in the early hours when they were both asleep. With any luck, Mum and Dad would leave for work the next day without realising I was asleep in my room. Then I remembered the following day was Saturday. They would both be at home. Alternatively, I could ask Jimmy to put me up on his sofa. I called his number. He didn't pick up for several rings. I was preparing to leave a message when his voice exploded down the line.

'What!'

'Jimmy. Iz me.'

'Who?'

'Vince… You know. Chubz.'

'Chubbs! Are yer bladdered? Can't talk now, mate. Oi'm in the middle of somethen.'

'Don't hang up, Jimboes. We're frenz, aren't we? I fink I need a bed for the night. Can I come round to yourz?'

'Shove off!'

I heard a woman's voice in the background. 'Is everything all right, Jimmy?'

'You've got female company… you, you rascal you.'

'Yeah. It's not a good time.' He lowered his voice to a whisper. 'Catrina's come round, and it's going well, if yer know what I mean.'

'Trina! Thas fablus.'

'Yeah, well, Oi've always had a soft spot for her. She was my first... you know... Oi never should have done the dirty on her back then. Oi'm not going to blot me copy book now.'

'Too right you won't!' she shouted. 'Who's that you're talking to?'

'It's Chubbs,' Jimmy yelled back. He lowered his voice. 'I've still got the old magic. See yer later.'

'No! Wait... I'll be quiet as a tiny, tiny mouse. A tiny dead mouse. I luvs yer, man. Tell Trina I luvz her too. You won't know I'm there.'

'That's because yer won't be here.' He hung up.

I walked away from the station, partly because I didn't know what else to do, and partly to keep warm. The cold country air was clearing the fog in my head. What an idiot I'd been! I should have stayed in London. I could have been having the kind of night Jimmy was having. Did it really matter that I didn't fancy Chloe any more? I was a good liar, after all.

Then again, if I hadn't lied about the interview this whole disastrous day wouldn't have happened. I could have stayed at home and walked the dog with Sarah. We would have talked – or not talked – it wouldn't have mattered. Her cheeks would have blushed with the cold. Her eyes would have watched for the movement of a bird in the hedgerow. I could have picked her up after work for another driving lesson, secretly smiling at whatever outrageous clothing combination she had decided to wear.

I walked with my eyes fixed on the pavement, deep in thought, oblivious to my whereabouts. I stopped at a kerb and looked up to get my bearings. Directly opposite and over the road was the turning to Moon Rise. Once again my subconscious had drawn me to Sarah's house.

My first instinct was to panic. What if I bumped into her taking Bruce for a bedtime stroll? What would she think if she saw me in my present state of intoxication? I thought about this for a few minutes. Out of all the people I knew, she was the one who was the least judgemental. Ironically, although she never hesitated to question my beliefs and values, I felt less of a failure with her than with anyone else. I crossed the road and walked up Moon Rise.

The light was on in her living room. This time, the curtains were closed. I shuffled up the short path and stood by the terracotta pot, deliberating whether to knock. Should I take the chance she was alone and would be pleased to see me? I didn't want to face the kind of embarrassment I would have felt if I had turned up unannounced on

Jimmy's doorstep and had the door slammed in my face. I pulled up her number from my contacts list. After a couple of rings she answered.

'Hello?'

'It's Chubbz.'

'I think you've got the wrong number.'

'Sorry. I mean iz Vincent.'

'Oh. Hello.'

'I had an interview today.'

'I know. You told me.'

'Aren't... you... going... to... ask... me... how... it... went?'

'How did it go?'

'Not very well.'

'I'm sorry.'

'Yeah, well, theze thingz happen.'

'You sound different.'

'I'm a bit down... I jus' wanted to hear your voice.'

'Oh.'

'And I've split up with Chloe.'

'I thought you had already split up.'

'We had. We might have made it up today... but we didn't.'

'So it was a hypothetical split. After a hypothetical reunion.'

'I fink it woz worse than that.'

'Are you still in London?'

'No.'

'Where are you?' Her tone was wary.

'I'm outside your front door.'

The line went dead. A shadow approached through the glazed pane. Then she was standing in the porch, the light from the hall shining through her loosened hair in a golden haze. I took an unsteady step forward.

'There was no need to get drunk. It was only an interview.'

'I'm not as thunk as you drink. Can I come in?'

'Why?'

'Because... I... would... like... to... talk... to... you.'

Realising he was missing all the action, Bruce suddenly shot through the living room door, barking, and jumped around my legs in excitement, his tail whipping the air like a rapier.

'Steady, boy,' Sarah commanded. I patted him on the head. 'You had better come in before the neighbours complain about the noise.'

I closed the front door behind me and lumbered into the lounge. I dumped my bag on the floor and looked around stupidly. Books and files were neatly stacked on the dining table. A tall chair had been pushed back as though recently vacated. A jar of pens stood guard over a pile of papers covered in neat handwriting.

'I'm sorry if I disturbz you. If you're busy –'

'I *am* busy.' I was used to her matter-of-fact manner and didn't jump to the conclusion she wanted me to leave. 'I'm doing some research into the Paris School of Semiotics. It's fascinating.'

'It soundz fablus.' I slumped into the large armchair, my arms on the armrests, my legs stretched wide in front of me, head flung back. I closed my eyes and sighed deeply. Complete exhaustion flooded every cell of my body.

'You don't look good.'

'I don' feel good.' My head was beginning to throb. I rubbed my temples.

'What's the matter?'

'It'z a washout –'

'What exactly has been washed out?'

'An tellum you I didn't get the job. Ha ha ha! It didn't exzizt! I found out I wozn't any good at my job in the firzt plaze. The girl I thought I loved iz…' I struggled to find the right words, '… hideouz troll… No one luvz me. I have no frenz, no money, no job… I've drunk a whole bodle of wine. And some beerz. And a large whisky. I can't go home to Mum and Dad…' Bruce flopped down onto a thick oriental rug with a sigh. 'Coz they ask toooo many questions.'

'I don't understand. What do you mean the job didn't exist?' She was standing in the middle of the room staring down at me.

'I told a teenzy tiny porky pie. I didn't have an interview. Tony stole it from me. It'z all his fault. Now I knowz… everything.' I tapped the side of my nose. 'Then, I saw Chloe. Split up with her… not split up… she wozn't my girlfriend… split up wiv someone who woz my girlfriend and could have been my girlfriend again. But it'z all over now.'

'Why?'

'We woz wrong together. Don't think we even liked each other! An tellum you we never talked about thingz the way you and I talk about thingz… and I puked in her lap.'

'No, I meant why did you lie about the interview?'

'Oh… that. I was overcondifence. I thort it woz in the bag. I wazn't shortlisted an' I had gonnan told everyone I woz going to London. I didn't want you to know I'd failed in that too… I'm a good salesman. I… don't… understand… why… this… iz… happening to me.'

'Yes, you are a good salesman.' She sat down at the table and twirled a pen between her fingers. 'After all, you've been selling yourself a lie ever since you left Elmsford 12 years ago.'

I blinked, not understanding. The warmth of the room and the alcohol in my system were pulling heavy covers over my consciousness.

'Are youz calling me a liar?' I said, struggling to get out of the chair and failing.

'Yes, of course. You've just admitted to lying about the interview. But I'm not talking about that.'

'What, then?'

'Perhaps "lying" is too strong a word. You put on a façade.'

'What iz this? Whack Vinzent day?' I sank petulantly into the cushions.

'I'm not attacking you. I'm saying you are more than the things you own and the job you do. You don't have to perform for me. I already know who you are.'

'You don' know anything!' I shouted. Bruce looked up, startled.

'Truthfully, why did you come here?'

'I told you. I didn't have anywhere elze to go. I'm sorry. Pleez can I sleep in this chair? I can't move. I'll leave firz thing in the morning.'

'Stay here?'

'Pleez,' I begged. 'I jus' want ta go ta sleep. I won' make a nuisance of myself. You won't know I'm here.'

*****

After agreeing to let me stay, Sarah continued with her work as if she really didn't know I was there. I shrugged out of my coat, loosened my tie and kicked off my shoes. She picked up a large book and began to make notes on a pad. Despite our earlier spat, an atmosphere of peace settled over the room. I closed my eyes and listened to the wooden clock on the mantelpiece.

We hadn't observed any of the social niceties associated with visitors. I hadn't been offered anything to eat or drink. I hadn't been shown the bathroom. She hadn't found any pillows or blankets for me to use. She had accepted my presence without any sense of social obligation. Instead of making me feel unwelcome, this made me feel completely at home.

I must have fallen asleep. I vaguely remember her placing a throw on my legs and turning the light off. I heard Bruce's claws on the kitchen floor as he was taken to bed. I heard a tap running, the sound of brushing teeth, a toilet flush, silence.

I awoke in the small hours, stiff with cold. The throw had slipped to the floor. My back ached, my head pounded, my mouth was dry. I stumbled into the moonlit kitchen at the back of the bungalow and found a glass in the cupboard above the sink. Bruce was curled in his basket by the back door, his head tucked into his shoulder. He looked up when I entered but didn't bark, accepting my presence with the indifference of his mistress. I gulped down the water and edged back into the hall to find the toilet.

I tried to remember the direction of the bathroom, based on the sounds I had heard earlier. I gently pushed a door and peered inside. The curtains were open. Light from the moon sifted through a pair of lacy nets. I sensed immediately that the room was empty. It had a cold, unused smell. My eyes slowly adjusted to the shadows. A double bed stood against the wall opposite. The counterpane was as flat and smooth as a sheet of ice.

Carefully closing the door behind me, I turned and pushed open another door. This room was much smaller and faced on to the road. The curtains were closed, but light from the lamp post outside spilled through a chink. A segment of lighter grey thrust through the darkness, cutting an angle across a single bed. There was an outline of a body beneath the duvet.

A low growl rumbled behind me. I spun round to see Bruce's eyes gleaming in the darkness. I quickly closed the door and pushed open the remaining door in the hall. The bathroom at last! I switched on the light and emptied my bladder as quietly as I could. While waiting for the apparently endless stream to stop, I examined the contents of the bathroom shelves. A glass with a toothbrush. A tube of toothpaste. A bottle of lemon-scented shampoo. A bar of soap in a dish. I had never seen so few toiletries in a woman's bathroom before. I had more beauty products than she did! Glimpsing my haggard face in the bathroom cabinet mirror I was under no illusion why.

Without flushing, I returned to the living room and pulled my pyjamas out of my overnight bag. My interview suit was sadly crumpled and smelled of booze and sweat. I changed quickly and stretched out on the sofa, pulling the throw up to my neck and covering myself with my coat. Bruce had followed me and thrown himself down on the rug. Sleeping companion or guard? I didn't know and I didn't care. I listened as the bungalow settled down for the night, then fell headlong back into oblivion.

*****

Apart from the sound of blood pounding at my temples, the bungalow was in silence when I awoke the next morning. There was no sign of Sarah or Bruce. I assumed they had left for an early morning walk. It was Saturday. I couldn't remember whether she was working at the library from 9.30 until 2.00 or 12.30 until closing time this week, but I assumed the former.

I rummaged around the kitchen and managed to make myself a coffee and a slice of gluten-free toast. I could only find soya milk; I left the coffee black, which was probably just as well because I was in dire need of a caffeine hit. On a typical day, Chloe's fridge would have contained several ready meals, a bottle of wine, blueberries, celery, skimmed milk, Greek yoghurt, perhaps a little pot of olives from the delicatessen. Sarah's fridge was practically empty apart from margarine, vegetables and a tube of tomato puree.

The kitchen was very tidy. White mugs and plates were lined up neatly in the cupboards. Bags of rice and lentils had been arranged in order of size. One cupboard was completely filled with tinned tuna. I wondered if she fed them to Bruce or had some weird fish compulsion.

I carried my breakfast back to the living room and sat at the dining table. Sarah's papers and books had been swept into an organised pile. I opened a notebook and glanced at the first page. Her writing was small and childish, belying the complete incomprehensibility of the subject matter. I read the first paragraph, chewing a mouthful of cardboard-flavoured toast.

One of the foremost principles of structural organisation acknowledged by Greimas is the fundamental role of binary

180

oppositions. He argues that the primary organising principle of narrative is that it always moves from an opening scenario to a conclusion which is the exact opposite. This takes place through a transforming event, or transformation. Therefore, a narrative programme is a semantic axis which articulates an opposition. A transformation cannot take place without narrative operators to facilitate the change.

I flicked through the rest of the notebook, my eyes resting momentarily on different passages. I couldn't understand any of it. I placed it back on the top of the pile and finished my coffee.

Sarah's bookshelves were stacked to overflowing. Gold lettering gleamed on red, green and brown leather spines. Faded paperbacks were squeezed next to hardbacks in dust jackets. Small pamphlets had been slipped between large illustrated volumes. I noticed that each of the deep shelves housed a double layer of titles, whole rows hiding behind those that were on show. At first sight, the books looked untidy, randomly jumbled together, at variance with the austere neatness of the kitchen and bathroom. I stood up for a closer look.

Poetry, ancient religions, mythology, codes, maps, literary theory, volumes of natural history with hand-drawn coloured plates, fiction, philosophy, science... After a few moments scrutinising the chaos, I realised the books were arranged in distinct sections, in alphabetical order by author rather than by size of book. No doubt Sarah or her mother had adapted the Dewey Decimal System in some form or another for their own personal use.

I carried my toilet bag into the bathroom, showered, cleaned my teeth and helped myself to a couple of painkillers from the bathroom cabinet. As I emerged into the hall wearing nothing but a pair of clean boxers, the front door opened. Bruce bounded into the passage, followed by Sarah wearing her long coat and wide-brimmed hat. She stopped abruptly when she saw me. Cold air blasted through the open door. My wet hair dripped onto the wood floor. I smiled apologetically, shivering, and rubbed my head with one of her pink towels.

'Morning, Sarah... Bruce.'

'Hello.'

She stared down at her feet. Her cheeks were flushed, but whether from the cold or from the sight of a half-naked man standing in her hall I couldn't tell. She turned and closed the front door behind her. I darted into the living room and pulled on a pair of jeans and a grey sweater. The front door opened and closed again. I hurried into the hall. Bruce was standing on his back legs, his front paws resting on the glazed door, looking down the garden path, wagging his tail dejectedly. Sarah had gone.

I spent the next ten minutes frantically wondering why she had left without a word. Had I upset her? Frightened her? Embarrassed her? I looked at my watch. It was after nine o'clock. Then the penny dropped. She was running late. On foot she would only just make it to the library for the early shift.

I paced round the living room in frustration. We needed to talk. I wanted to thank her for letting me stay. I wanted to apologise for turning up drunk and uninvited last night. I needed to make sure everything was OK between us. I hoped I hadn't alienated my only friend. I decided to try to catch her during her lunch break.

I spent the next 20 minutes clearing up after myself, washing my plate and cup, hanging the wet towels on the towel rail, folding up the throw, plumping the cushions and packing my overnight bag. A framed photograph on the wall caught my attention. It was a close-up of a house spider. To achieve that angle, the photographer must have been lying on the floor staring directly into the creature's many eyes. I recognised the rug as the one I was standing on. I tried to imagine Sarah stretched out, focusing her camera on the spider sitting in front of her like a clawed hand. Its jointed legs reminded me of scaffolding or something angular I might have made out of Meccano as a boy. An unusual picture for a woman to take and keep, I concluded. She certainly had peculiar tastes.

I wondered if she had found my earlier nakedness to her taste. I knew I wasn't the best-looking bloke in the world, but I was certainly more attractive than Gavin or the dwarf – her only other male companions of whom I was aware.

The Victorian clock on the mantelpiece chimed the half-hour. She would be starting her shift in the library. My parents wouldn't be expecting me home for some hours yet, if at all today. I needed to lie low. I hoped Sarah wouldn't mind if I took advantage of her hospitality a little while longer.

I didn't want to think about the previous day, but Tony's voice kept returning. 'You haven't got that ruthless streak… Sometimes that means screwing the client… You were never that sharp, were you? … I'm not in the business of making friends. I'm in the business of making money.'

I needed a distraction. I pressed the switch to the TV. The screen filled with static. Of course, the aerial wasn't connected! I switched the DVD player on and the credits for *The Official DLA Theory Test for Car Drivers* came on the screen. I looked around to see if there were any other DVDs I could watch, but before I could find one, my mobile bleeped. It was a text from Chloe.

I'm so over U!

I didn't bother to respond.

I wandered into the hall, looking for a magazine or a newspaper to read. Sarah's bedroom door was slightly ajar. Through the crack I glimpsed a neatly made bed and a tall chest of drawers. I gently pushed the door with my foot and peered inside. It seemed too intrusive to step across the threshold, and I was worried that Bruce might take offence if I entered his mistress' private domain. At a glance I noticed that the decor was plain – not a pattern, flower or frill to be seen. Sarah's grey poncho was draped across a wooden rocking chair in the corner. There was a pile of books on the bedside table next to a large photograph of an emaciated woman. It looked as though she was sitting at a desk writing a letter. Her grey hair was cropped close to her head; her eyes were luminous with pain.

I opened the door to the double bedroom next door. In daylight, I could see it had been emptied of all personal possessions except for some framed photographs of a man and a little girl, presumably Sarah and her father. As I had observed the night before, the bed was unnaturally flat. I guessed the counterpane had been placed directly on top of the mattress. Considering the fairly recent loss of her mother, I was surprised that Sarah had stripped the room so thoroughly of keepsakes. It had the unused atmosphere of spare bedrooms everywhere. Curious, I felt no hesitation in entering.

A soft veneer of dust coated the dressing table. I opened the wardrobe which stood to the right of the bed. Neatly folded sheets and pillowcases were stored on the top shelf. Several empty coat hangers dangled from the rail. A double duvet in a black plastic sack had been shoved to the back of the cupboard. Apart from the bedding, the wardrobe was empty. There were no shoes or clothes to give a clue to her mother's character. It crossed my mind that this might have been the cupboard where Eleanor Penny's body had been found. It was certainly big enough. But there were no ghosts here, just a resonance of absence and loss. I felt a bit miffed that Sarah hadn't offered me this room for the night, preferring instead that I should sleep on the sofa. Perhaps she hadn't been able to eradicate her mother's presence entirely from the room after all. Or perhaps she didn't want the hassle of making up the bed.

I returned to the hall and opened a door I hadn't seen the night before. Several coats and jackets of various thicknesses hung on the pegs. A vacuum cleaner and a large umbrella leaned against the back wall. Small boots and shoes were lined up on the floor, a pair of newly muddied wellingtons at the front. This didn't look the kind of cupboard that could comfortably house a body.

I returned to the kitchen. The cupboards here were too small for anyone to crawl inside. Next to the back door was another door. This led to a small utility room containing a sink, a washing machine and what I presumed to be a larder or coal bunker because the entrance was a little lower than a normal-sized door. It had a round brass knob and a large, empty keyhole. I slowly turned the door knob, felt the latch release with a click, and pushed.

Bending my head to peer inside, I realised the space was larger than I had thought, more of an old-fashioned pantry with shelves on either side. Greenish light from the back garden filtered through a fanlight window at the top of the wall opposite. A bare light bulb dangled from a wire in ceiling. Groping the inside wall I located a switch and snapped on the light.

Stringy cobwebs wafted on the draught I had created by opening the door. They clung to high corners and stretched dustily across the window. The glass was thick with grime. Black mould stained the metal frame and speckled the wall beneath. I stepped down onto a red tiled floor, stooping to enter but standing upright once inside. The temperature dropped several degrees. There was a strong smell of damp… and something else. Alcohol.

A stool with a set of foldaway steps underneath stood in the middle of the pantry. The square seat was splashed with white paint and I guessed it had been used for decorating at some point. By unfolding the steps it would be just the right height to paint a ceiling or reach the topmost shelf. There was no need for the steps today: the shelves were empty and greying with dust. A half-full bottle of sherry stood by the foot of the stool; they were the only items in the pantry apart from a small tray of bright blue pellets in the corner and a packet of rat poison.

I turned to leave, noticing from the corner of my eye a heavy key sticking out of the keyhole on the inside of the door. Why would the key be on the inside? I turned the lock. It clicked smoothly into place. I was locked in. I stepped back and sat down on the stool, pondering the question.

Shut inside, the pantry seemed to contract in upon itself. A wave of dizziness washed through my body. My stomach churned and I tasted again the bitter flavour of the coffee I had drunk earlier. The damp walls and low ceiling pressed closer; my skin prickled with icy sweat. I felt as though the available air was shrinking and I heard rather than felt my breathing quicken in panic. I jumped up, terrified, and rattled at the key. It was stuck in the lock. As I frantically twisted it back and forth, the face from the photograph on Sarah's beside table flashed into my mind – the hollow cheeks, the eyes hungry with pain, the shadow of death in her smile. The key turned. I flung open the door and stumbled up the step, slamming the door behind me.

I decided to leave right away. There was nothing to occupy me in the bungalow except curiosity and the ridiculous suspicions of an overactive imagination. I needed fresh air to blow away my hangover, which was worse than I had thought. I would take a brisk walk across the recreation ground and spend the rest of the morning in the Railway Tavern testing the hair of the dog. I would catch up with Sarah later to check she was OK in herself and OK with me. Somehow I would think of a way to ask her more questions about her mother's death without letting slip I had been searching the bungalow for clues.

I picked up my overnight bag from the living room. As I was leaving, the telephone rang in the hall. I hesitated, unsure whether to pick it up or not, but deciding it would be difficult to explain my presence. After several rings, the answerphone switched on.

'Sarah. Big Micky here. I'm going to be away on a job for the next few days. The Specials will be coming round next Wednesday night, the 20th. Make sure you're in and have the stuff ready. Don't try and wriggle out of your obligations. I want you there early, Saturday week, or I'll be sending Gavin round…' There was a sinister pause, '… and you know what that means!' Click and silence.

Whatever the message was about, it didn't sound good. The man's voice was harsh and abrupt, and his concluding words seemed to contain a threat of some sort. 'I'll be sending Gavin round… you know what that means!' However much she insisted Gavin was a friend, he still looked creepy and suspicious to me. There was definitely something funny going on. Question marks over her mother's death, a substantial inheritance, intimidating phone calls, threats to me. I didn't like the look of it at all.

I considered erasing the message but thought better of it. If Sarah didn't respond, Big Micky might send Gavin round before Wednesday, or come round himself. I had one big advantage: I knew when the Specials would be visiting, and I would be waiting outside.

Chapter 21

I ate a sandwich and a packet of crisps in the pub and waited for Sarah's lunch break at 12 o'clock. The news channel was on the television. The Chancellor of the Exchequer was being questioned about the possibility of a double-dip recession.

'The current financial climate will last longer than was first expected,' he told the interviewer. 'We need to work our way through problems that have built up over many years.' The politician looked straight at the camera, his face smoothed into a cultivated expression of sincerity. For a few seconds it seemed as though he was addressing me personally, gazing out of the lighted rectangular box in the corner of the room with a secret message for my ears only.

'There are still some dangers ahead. We need to be vigilant if we are to come through this crisis without causing further damage. This is not the time to sit back and do nothing!'

Either my blood alcohol levels were still dodgy or I was beginning to develop one of those obscure mental health conditions where everything around me, any incident or throwaway remark, spoke directly to my personal situation.

Unable to wait any longer, I finished my beer and hurried to the library. I knew I was being irrational, but I needed to see for myself that Sarah was safe and had no regrets about letting me sleep over. I wanted to find out more about the pantry with the key on the wrong side of the door without revealing I had been snooping around her home. I needed to get to the bottom of the telephone message. My imagination was running wild. Had she been duped or threatened into doing something illegal for the Specials, whoever they were? What was the 'stuff' they were going to collect? The more I thought about it, the more sinister the whole thing appeared. Had she become entangled in some kind of secret society or religious cult? And why was I being watched – the cyclist under my window, the white van parked outside our house – and warned to stay away?

I pushed open the glass doors to the library. I saw her almost immediately. She was standing on a step, returning a book to the top shelf. I strode towards her and called her name. She turned, surprised, and almost fell into my arms. I steadied her and helped her down.

'You're dressed, then!'

'About last night... thank you for letting me stay over. You were wonderful... it really meant a lot.'

Pat Hutchins walked round the corner of the aisle and stopped in her tracks.

'Great,' I muttered under my breath, knowing she had probably overheard everything.

'Vincent! Sarah! I didn't know you two knew each other.' Her eyes darted between us.

'We were at school together,' Sarah said.

'You went to school together? That's nice. And you've kept in touch all these years?'

Realisation dawned. Her knowing smile told me she recognised Sarah as the girl she had seen in my car on our first driving lesson together. It would be all round the village now!

'My two went to a private school in Bunton. Do you know my children, Timothy and Heather? Of course, they're grown up now, and Timothy has a family of his own.'

I pulled an exasperated expression when Pat turned to Sarah. Sarah ignored me.

'Heather is the reason we are having our fundraiser, Sarah. She set up the charity here in the UK. I told her I would do my bit. How are the contributions for the bookstall coming along?'

'OK, I think,' Sarah replied with a stiff smile. 'I've put a box at the back of the library for donations of second-hand books –'

'Oh, no dear. You must move the box forward. It must be more prominent.'

'The librarian said it has to be out of the way of the library books. She doesn't want any of our books to be returned to the donation box by mistake... Or for customers to try and borrow a donated book.'

'Nonsense! I'm sure you could put the box and notice right by the front door, dear, so people can see it as they walk in. Vincent, help me carry the box to the foyer.'

I was hurried to the back of the library where the photocopier was humming and blinking and collating papers for a teenage boy. Sarah trailed behind, nodding helplessly that I should pick up the box as directed. Frustrated that our conversation had been so comprehensively hijacked, I carried the cardboard box to the foyer and dropped it down with a heavy thump. Pat asked me to adjust the position to be sure it was as prominently placed as possible. She sent Sarah to get a pen and paper. Sarah stuck a notice on the wall above which read, 'Second-hand Book Donations in Aid of African Children'.

'Your parents have been absolutely marvellous on the organisational committee,' Pat said, turning back to me. 'Timothy is the treasurer of the charity.' *He would be*, I thought. Pat touched Sarah's arm to keep her attention. 'My son, Timothy, works in London. I don't know if you knew that, dear. He's the vice-president of technical compliance for an American bank so he can't be as hands-on with the fundraising as he would like, but he's hoping to drop in on the day. I haven't seen him for ages. It will be a real treat.' She laughed with delight.

Sarah's mouth was tight. I could tell she didn't like Pat holding on to her arm.

'Although Timmy does his bit, it's really Heather's pet project. She wants to replace the roof of a school for disabled children somewhere out in Africa... I forget the name. It's a funny name, as they all are out there. We must support her all we can, mustn't we? In the rainy season the school has to close because everything gets wet. I do hope you can come along on Saturday, Vincent.'

'I don't know. I'll try. Sarah, can I speak to you for a moment?' I grasped her by the other elbow and led her towards the lending machines, letting go as soon as we were a couple of paces away from Pat.

Pat called after us. 'You've probably got some books and bric-a-brac to donate, Vincent, as you've just downsized. Every little helps!'

'That was tactful,' I said, thinking of the boxes of my belongings in the loft at home.

'No, it wasn't,' Sarah said.

'You're right. It wasn't. I didn't realise you were involved in this fundraiser.'

'I'm running the second-hand bookstall.'

'That's appropriate!'

'Pat thought so.'

I wanted to get back to the subject of the previous night. I guessed it wouldn't be long before my parents found out I had spent the night at Sarah's place. I swallowed hard and looked at the floor.

'I think Pat overheard what I said. I think she might have misunderstood... she's not very discreet. We might find that there are rumours about us.'

'Don't worry,' Sarah said. 'People have always talked about me behind my back. I take no notice. You should do the same. If people ask, we can just tell them the truth.'

'And what is the truth?'

'That we are friends.' Her face was a mask. 'Anything else would be out of the question.'

*****

Mum and Dad didn't show any surprise when I arrived home earlier than expected. I decided to be completely honest; well, not completely honest, but as honest as the situation warranted. I told them the interview had gone badly, and I didn't like the job in any case. I told them Chloe and I had both moved on. The relationship was definitely over. Trying to avert any rumours started by Pat Hutchins, I mentioned I had gone into the library to arrange the next driving lesson with Sarah, and Pat had overheard and misunderstood the conversation.

'I thought you were going to give Sarah a couple of lessons and then pass her on to Simon?' Dad sighed in exasperation.

'That was the plan. But it's been more difficult to disentangle myself than I thought.'

'Bit of a sticky toffee paper, is she?' Mum asked. 'Hard to shake off?'

'You really are too soft-hearted,' Dad said. 'People will take advantage of your good nature if you let them. You don't want a girl like Sarah getting the wrong idea. You shouldn't get yourself too involved.'

'Don't be so hard on him, Derek,' Mum interrupted. 'I'm sure Vincent knows what he's doing.'

'I'm not so sure. He has a knack of getting involved with the wrong types of people. Look at Jimmy!'

'What's wrong with Jimmy? What do you mean "the wrong types of people"? You're such a snob, Dad!'

'I'm not talking about class. I'm talking about values.'

'What do you know about Sarah's values?'

'I don't know anything about them, but we all know about Jimmy's. I'm probably doing the poor girl an injustice. I'm just going from your past record. I never did like the look of that boss of yours, for example. What was his name?'

'Tony,' I said bitterly.

'Yes. If it hadn't been for Tony, you wouldn't have persuaded us to get an endowment mortgage for the extension. Now it's not going to pay off the loan. Tony told us we were going to have money in the bank at the end of the payment period. Not just a bit of money – telephone numbers! If I hadn't taken out another savings plan to cover it, we would have been left with an outstanding debt in a few years' time. We would have needed another mortgage. Not so easy to get at our time of life.'

'But everyone was recommending endowment mortgages back then. We weren't to know what would happen to the stock market.'

'If it looks too good to be true, it is too good to be true!' Mum said.

'Your mother and I wanted a repayment mortgage. We only went along with your endowment idea because you were young and we wanted to help your career, and we wanted you to have the commission.'

I looked down at the floor miserably.

'Come on,' Mum said kindly. 'That's all water under the bridge. We can't do anything about that now. You did your best, and that's all we've ever asked of you. Nobody can get things right all the time.'

'But I don't seem to be getting anything right, any of the time,' I muttered.

'It will turn around. You'll see.' She patted me on the back. 'You can't avoid the storms of life. Everyone experiences a little rain now and then. Try to keep singing whatever the weather.' Dad grunted. 'It's true, Derek, you know it is. We have to embrace life's storms; we can't run away from them. The reason you're in the shadows at the moment, Vinny, is because you're standing in the way of your own sunlight. Have you ever thought about that?'

I didn't reply. What Mum said was all very well and good, but I wondered if she would feel the same if she knew about the dark cloud hanging over Dad.

Whether he was thinking the same as me, or whether he was just feeling guilty for his earlier outburst, Dad went into the kitchen and made us all a cup of tea.

'We're all overtired and irritable,' Mum said. 'We're really looking forward to our mini-break next week. Simon and Liz didn't leave until quite late last night. We shouldn't complain about our problems. Simon might lose his business the way things are going, and that might mean they'll lose the house too. Let's talk about something a bit more positive. Don't you think your father has been looking a bit better lately?'

I looked at Dad as he passed me my tea. He nodded his head imperceptibly.

'Yes, he does.'

*****

Mum asked me to pop out and buy a few bits and pieces at the supermarket later that day. I didn't feel I could refuse. It was obvious I had been a massive disappointment to them. While the general layout of the store was now familiar to me – in particular where to find bread, milk, biscuits and sweets – I had to walk around the aisles several times to locate vanilla essence, freezer bags and black shoe polish.

A disabled lady on a mobility scooter was making her way up and down the aisles. We passed each other a couple of times. Because of the size of her electric scooter and the awkwardness of my wire basket, I had to stand with my back against the shelves, holding the basket to my side, to allow her to pass. The first time I smiled politely. She was younger than I first thought, maybe in her late teens or early twenties, with brown shoulder-length hair. She didn't look at me. I imagined she felt awkward, practically forcing me out of the way. The second time we passed each other, I tried to lighten the mood.

'We must stop meeting like this.'

Her mouth was set in a hard line. Obviously she had lost her sense of humour along with the use of her legs. I let her pass without another word, turning at the far end of the shop to walk down an adjacent aisle, leading to the checkout. Unbelievably, as I was about halfway down, the scooter appeared around the corner. She was in front of me again.

She must have rocketed down the shop, far exceeding the speed limit for mobility vehicles, to have reached the end of her row and turned into mine so quickly. She looked intently at the rows of tinned soup to her left, maintaining her speed. I moved towards the dried pasta and rice on the other side of the aisle. Almost immediately she swerved in my direction. I stepped swiftly to the right, inwardly cursing women drivers, only to hear the whine of the electric motor rise to an even higher pitch as she charged towards me, apparently oblivious to anything but the dried goods on the shelves.

In a panic I made a last-minute dive across the aisle, holding my basket above my head and pressing my back against the rattling jars of bolognese sauce. She passed without an apology or a backward glance. I stood for a few minutes, breathing fast, aghast at the near miss. Did her disability include blindness as well? Perhaps I should be giving *her* driving lessons!

Lauren was on the checkout. Since our date, I had been buying my newspapers at the petrol station. I recognised that this was both cowardly and inconvenient, but justified my change of shopping habits by convincing myself each time that I fancied a takeaway cappuccino at the garage.

'Hello,' I said. 'How are you?'

'I'm fine. I wondered when I would see you again.' She grimaced as she scanned a packet of bathroom air freshener through the till.

'I've been tied up with business these last few days. But we must do that again sometime. I'll give you a call.'

'Do you have my number?'

'Oh… perhaps not.'

She grabbed my hand and wrote it on the bare skin with a biro. 'Now your turn.' She passed me the pen and pushed her hand towards me. I took her moist palm and reluctantly wrote my number on the back of her hand. I transposed two of the digits, congratulating myself on my quick thinking. A lady behind me in the queue tutted at the delay. I gave Lauren an apologetic smile and hurried to pack my purchases into a plastic bag.

The woman on the scooter drew up at the next till. She had bought one item, a pint of milk. I wondered why she had needed to criss-cross the entire shop to find it. A memory stirred, the memory of a lady on a scooter talking with Sarah while I dodged behind a lorry. Could this be the same girl? How many disability scooters were there in Elmsford? Passing her so many times no longer felt such a coincidence. I remembered what the dwarf had told me: 'The Specials are watching you.' I was beginning to think it hadn't been an empty threat.

On the way out, my eye was caught by an advertisement on the customer noticeboard: 'Pest Control. Rats, Mice, Cockroaches, Wasps, Bees, Moths. All pests quickly and humanely eradicated. Ring Harry on Elmsford 336510.' I made a mental note of the number and rang as soon as I got home. I told him the mice were getting through packets of poison, with no sign of the infestation petering out. He agreed to call round after lunch on Monday, once Mum and Dad had left for their mini-break in Dorset. He promised to be discreet.

Sunday passed uneventfully. I hadn't scheduled a driving lesson because originally I was hoping to be with Chloe in London. Sarah's words to me in the library had brought a shutter down on our conversation. 'We are friends. Anything else would be out of the question.' I couldn't see how I could bring up my concerns about Gavin or the message I had overheard after that.

Mum had made a list of things I needed to do while they were away. Check what time the carer and cleaner visited; check that Nana was taking her medication and tick if off on the chart to avoid any omissions or duplications; check Nana was turning off taps, electrical appliances and the gas hob; check that the doors and windows were locked at night. She also gave me a list of numbers I could call in an emergency. I waved them off after breakfast on Monday morning, deciding to visit Nana in the early evening before returning home with a pizza, beer and an action DVD from the garage. For once I would have my parents' flat-screen TV and sofa to myself.

Harry the pest controller rang the bell promptly at half-past one. He was a small grey man with an over-officious manner. He inspected the garage thoroughly, sniffing at the corners like a bloodhound.

'Urine! Mouse urine. It's not rats. That'd be stronger.' He poked behind a pile of flowerpots with a stick. 'You've got a definite infestation here.' He bent down and picked up a small black dropping the size of a match head. 'Your rat, now, he produces a turd about half an inch long, not so evenly shaped.' He flicked the poo away. Discomfited by his smug expertise, I explained the measures I had already taken.

'I've killed at least four now, but they're still eating the poison and it's been over a week.'

'They don't fall ill straight away. The stuff you've been using takes a while. It's the accumulation. The little monsters don't realise they're eating poison. The trick is to keep giving it to them regular. Every day. As soon as the trays is empty. To be fair, my guess is you've let things slide.'

I didn't reply.

'If used correctly, the stuff stops their blood from clotting. It damages the capillaries. The packet says it's humane, but effectively they're bleeding into their muscles and joints. That's got to hurt! They die from shock or anaemia.'

I began to feel a little queasy.

'These vermin you've got here, well, they haven't eaten enough of it over several days. They've gawn an' developed a tolerance. What you buy in the shops isn't strong enough to kick 'em into touch. You have to be licensed to get your hands on the kind of stuff I use. It's five times stronger. If you've got enough of it, and I've got bagfuls in my shed, you could kill a horse.'

I feigned surprise. 'A horse!'

'An elephant maybe. With mice and rats, you've got to hit them hard with the good stuff. Otherwise you start off with one of the little brutes and before you know it you've got hundreds. Like I said, the stuff you've been giving them probably makes them feel a bit poorly. It'll kill off the old and the weak but the others, well, they get used to it. The next thing you know, you've bred supermice. They're the ones that have become resistant, like the superbugs in hospitals.'

He delivered the final sentence with an air of accusation, as though I were personally responsible for breeding the world's next great catastrophe.

'This stuff here is magic.' He pulled a box of pellets from his bag. 'One dose is enough. It increases their calcium absorption. Basically, their innards get calcified. Straight up! Kidneys, stomach, lungs. They all fill up with calcium crystals. Sorted!' He poured some pellets into the trays I had positioned around the garage.

'What doesn't kill them only makes them stronger. This stuff here…' he said, proudly shaking the half-empty box of pellets, '… this'll do the job. This'll put them out of their misery, like I said. It's an overdose of mouse heroine. They'll have a happy despatch. Mark my words. A happy despatch. Swift and painless.'

A sensation of déjà vu distracted me from Harry's lecture. Where had I heard that phrase before? I recollected Tony sitting on the corner of my desk as I cleared out my drawers, assuring me that redundancy – if it didn't kill me – would only make me stronger. But there was something else. I watched Harry as he set out more trays of the 'good stuff'. Then it came to me. I remembered Sarah talking about her mother's death, how relieved she had been once she was out of her misery. A happy despatch. I hated the way Harry had said it. It sounded as though he was doing the mouse a favour, but it was killing just the same.

'I'd never heard the phrase "happy despatch" before. It's strange but I've heard it a couple of times in the village recently.'

'It's one of my sayings and I'm well known hereabouts. I'm in the business of death. Why not make it happy?' He laughed. 'It makes me happy to be ridding the world of those who are not wanted. Hopefully you and your mum will be happy once I've finished here.'

I recalled the mouse poison in the pantry in Sarah's bungalow. If it was as dangerous as Harry suggested, I wondered if it could kill a human being, one who was already seriously ill and weak from months of medical treatment. Had Sarah's mother poisoned herself? I remembered the stool in the pantry, the half-finished bottle of sherry, the box of poison, the key on the inside of the door. Would a mother choose to leave an only child in that way?

Sarah had been unemotional, evasive even, when discussing her grief. Could she have been involved in an assisted suicide, or even taken it upon herself to help matters along? I could hear her words now: 'Mum suffered a great deal at the end. I wouldn't want her back like that. I was glad when she was put out of her misery.'

Euthanasia! It was a terrible word. I immediately recoiled. Of course Sarah wouldn't do a thing like that – would she? I thought of my own father. If he were to be diagnosed with cancer, how would Mum and I cope? Would we offer comfort and unwavering support, or would we fall to pieces in the face of his pain? Chemotherapy was a toxic cocktail of drugs. It could destroy a tumour, but in the process would also poison the patient. And if it didn't work? If Dad faced a hopeless future of agony and degeneration, could I stand by and watch?

Chapter 22

After Harry left, I grabbed my coat and jumped in the car. I had arranged to collect Sarah from the library when her shift finished at three o'clock. We would have an hour's daylight to practise manoeuvres on the quiet village roads.

There were so many things I wanted to ask, but all my questions would be intrusive, crazy or downright rude. How could I ask about the telephone call I shouldn't have overheard? How could I question her about the rumours surrounding her mother's death, or why the key was on the inside of the pantry door? How could I enquire about the 'Specials' without letting on about the dwarf's accusations and his warning that I should stay away? To elicit the information I wanted, I would need to practise some manoeuvres of my own.

'What are we doing here?' Sarah asked, as I pulled up outside my parents' house.

'I thought it would be good to work on the theory test for a change.'

'I could have done that on the library computer.'

'It's less distracting here. At the library, people would interrupt and ask for your help. Here we can work undisturbed.'

'What about your parents?'

'They've gone away for a few days. It'll be just you and me. That won't be a problem, will it? You said yesterday we are friends... and good friends can be trusted.'

'Oh! So I did.'

I climbed out of the car and walked round to the passenger side. I opened the door and waited for her to climb out. 'Elsie will be glad to see you,' I said, keeping my tone light.

'I don't like tests.'

'All the more reason to practise them and increase your confidence.' I escorted her up the path and ushered her through the front door. 'Besides, you'll pass with flying colours. You know you will. For a girl with no education, you're extremely bright.'

'I had an education!' she exclaimed. Bingo! I'd touched a nerve.

'Maybe... but not the kind of education you deserved. Just at the crucial stage, you stopped interacting with people your own age and missed out on structured lessons and assessments.' I helped her off with her coat and she followed me into the kitchen.

'There's more to education than exams. People shouldn't *just* be judged on their performance,' she replied defensively.

'Why not?'

'Because it can lead to low self-esteem.'

'That's total —'

'No, it's not. Think about it. If people are judged only by how they perform, or on how much they produce, they're not being valued for who they are. If you base your self-esteem entirely on your performance, you're going to doubt yourself when you've had a bad day. You worry that people won't value you any more. That's what happens when people are disabled or get ill or when people get older. They lose their sense of worth because they can't perform as well as other people.'

'In the real world people are judged by their outputs.' I switched on the kettle. 'That's what the job market is all about. You put a value on a person's performance and pay them accordingly.'

'And who decides what's valuable?'

'The market decides. Put in the effort, and you'll get paid more.'

'But it doesn't work like that, does it? Why should a professional footballer earn more than a nurse, for example?'

'Because of the footballer's skills.'

'So the market values the skill of kicking a ball more than the ability to ease suffering or save someone's life?'

I made us both a cup of tea and put the biscuit tin on the kitchen table. 'I'm not saying that at all. We all love our nurses — that goes without saying — but a Premier League footballer contributes more to the economy than a nurse through ticket sales, television rights, sponsorship and all that stuff. You've chosen an unfair example. Generally the more skilled and productive you are, the more valuable you are to the economy.' I tried to steer the conversation back to her past. 'What did you get up to at home all day after you left school? Didn't your mum have to go to work?'

'Yes. She worked in the library too. I was old enough to be in the bungalow on my own. I was probably about 15. She always left me something to do.'

'Such as?'

'Sometimes she would leave me a passage in French and tell me to translate it into German.'

'That sounds fun!'

'Yes. I did enjoy that. Sometimes she would leave out a recipe and I would have to shop for the ingredients and make dinner that night. There would always be a novel for me to read. Some days, though, she would just leave me with a Rubik's Cube or the cryptic crossword from *The Times*. I would go for long walks by myself...'

'Sounds lonely.'

'Lonely?' She was genuinely surprised. 'I was never lonely. I used to feel lonely at school, among all those people, but I never feel lonely when I'm on my own... Why are you unplugging the telephone, Vincent?'

'We don't have broadband. I'm going to plug my laptop in so we can do the test online. Don't look so worried.'

'I'm not worried,' she said, nervously sipping her tea.

'You can't just take a child out of school without providing them with a proper education,' I continued, taking my laptop out of the bag. 'What sort of syllabus did your mother use? How did she teach you?'

'She taught me by telling me stories.'

'Telling you stories! At 15! Weren't you a little old for that?'

'You're never too old to hear a good story. My mother had a great belief in the power of fiction. A story gives the reader an opportunity to experience an imaginary scenario and consider how they might deal with it themselves, without having all the inconvenience or pain of going through the reality. It's a simulation – a test drive, if you like. When I was little, stories helped me to know what would happen when I went to the dentist and the hairdressers.'

'I don't believe I'm hearing this. What about the national curriculum?' I searched the internet for the online test.

'You can cover the curriculum through stories. History is a collection of stories, some of which are true... though that depends on your perspective. Geography is the narrative of our planet. Science is the

199

account of people who are questioning and testing and discovering. It's self-evident that art and music are all about storytelling. Even a mathematical equation has a beginning, a middle and an end, just like a story.' I must have looked puzzled for she explained in more detail. 'You begin with a number. You end up with a solution. In the middle something happens to the first number, it has to jump through a few hoops with other numbers before it reaches a resolution. Isn't that what a story is all about?'

'We live in the real world, Sarah. Not some make-believe fairyland.'

'Stories may not be true, but a good story will always contain truth. Stories tell us who we are, where we have come from and why we are here. Don't you remember the first time you became lost in a really good book? It's a leap of faith. You suspend disbelief and put yourself entirely in the hands of the author. I love that. Bursting the bonds, forgetting my worries, escaping the concerns of my ego and touching something transcendent. It's the first step towards the spiritual life, I think.'

'I must have been reading the wrong books,' I replied drily. 'I enjoy the occasional crime thriller. One thing's for sure, I know the difference between fact and fiction.'

'Do you?'

'Of course.'

'Then why are you always telling stories about yourself?'

'I don't!'

'When we first met you talked about yourself as if you were the hero of your own adventure. Lately you seem to be recasting yourself as the victim of the tale.'

'I am not!'

'You can't turn black into white, however much you try.'

'What's that supposed to mean?'

'Why can't you just accept yourself?'

Once again, the tables were turned. I had brought Sarah home to find out more about her life and here she was scrutinising mine.

'Although Mum had a funny way of showing it at times, I always knew she loved me. More important than that, I knew she accepted me. That helped me to accept myself.'

'Isn't love and acceptance the same thing?'

I pushed the laptop over to her side of the table and turned the screen round to face her.

'Not at all.'

'Here's the test. The first part is on the Highway Code and the second part is all about hazard perception. For that there'll be some short video clips. You need to click as soon as you see the hazard on the screen. The quicker you spot the hazard, the more points you get. You have to pass both parts of the test.'

Sarah started the program, immediately focusing on the questions before her. I was smarting from her jibe that I had been telling myself stories, living a fantasy rather than seeing things the way they really were. Things were not going to plan. I watched as she worked efficiently through the screens, answering the multiple-choice questions at breakneck speed. Once she began the hazard perception test, however, her progress slowed. She chewed her lip and twisted a strand of hair as she watched several scenarios involving cyclists, lorries, sharp bends and hump-backed bridges. By the end she had scored 100 per cent on the Highway Code, and dismally failed the second test.

'I'm not very good at spotting hazards.'

'I noticed. How did you not see the lorry overtaking on the bend?'

'I did see it. It just took me a while to work out what it meant… what the implications might be.'

'You need to anticipate the other driver's intentions. However good the system is, there will always be those who break the rules.'

'Why would they do that? It's dangerous.'

'People are unpredictable, irrational. They make mistakes. You need to think of the worst case scenario, what might happen if you're not ready to take evasive action. It's an important lesson in life, not just in driving. We live in a dangerous world. People can't always be trusted.' I was thinking about Gavin and the dwarf. I hoped she was picking up the hint.

'I have to go.' She stood up and put her dirty cup in the sink.

'Don't you want to try another test?'

'It's getting dark.'

'That's OK. I'll run you home. We have time to go again.'

'I'm not sure that's going to help.' She walked into the hall and picked up her coat. I followed her out. 'I can walk from here.'

'I won't hear of it! I've got to visit my grandmother, in any case. I'll drop you off on the way.' She nodded glumly. 'Don't be despondent. You did very well. During our next lesson, I'll point out potential hazards every time I see them, to get you into the swing of things. Will that help?'

'It might. On the other hand, it might just turn me into a nervous wreck.'

Chapter 23

I rang Nana's bell. The living room light was on behind the closed curtains, but there was no answer. I used Mum's key. The door opened a crack, then stuck. The security chain was on the door. Despite ringing and knocking and calling through the letter box, there was no response from inside. Beginning to feel seriously concerned, I climbed over the side gate and peered through the kitchen window.

The door to the living room was partly open. Nana's slippered feet, crossed at the ankle and sticking out into the middle of the room, were clearly visible. The television flickered in the corner, audible from where I was standing in the flowerbed. I tried the back door, but it was firmly locked. I pulled my mobile from my pocket and dialled Nana's number. If she didn't answer, I would have to break a window.

'Hello?'

'Hello, Nana. It's Vincent.'

'Who?'

'Vincent. Turn the television down, Nana.'

'I'm sorry, I can't hear you. I'll just turn the television off.' There was a rustling sound, followed by silence.

'Hello?' she said again. 'Are you still there?'

'Nana, it's Vincent. I'm in your back garden. Can you come and unlock the kitchen door for me?'

'What are you doing in the garden? Have you forgotten your key?'

'No. You've put the chain on the front door. I can't get in.'

'Have I? Oh, yes… I remember now. I put it on to stop those women coming back.'

'What women?'

'The ones who want to steal my handbag.'

'Nana, those are your carers. You need to let them in. They're not going to steal from you. They're being paid to help you.'

'I caught one of them with my handbag. I told your mother, but she wouldn't believe me. Now she's gone away and left me all alone with them.'

'You're not alone. I'm here.'

'I'm not letting them in. I don't need them.' I knocked on the kitchen window. 'And now they're banging on the back door!' she cried.

'That's me, Nana. Please open the door so I can talk to you properly. It's cold out here.' I saw her ankles uncross. Her feet move backwards until they were planted firmly side by side. Then she was standing, bent over at first but slowly straightening as she leaned on her stick. She shuffled into the kitchen and switched on the light. After a few minutes fumbling in a drawer, I heard the key in the lock. The door swung open. I stepped inside and shut the door behind me.

'Don't you forget to wipe your feet,' Nana said sharply, looking at the mud on my designer crocodile-skin shoes.

*****

After I had made us both a cup of tea, I rang the carer to find out what had happened. She should have arrived an hour or so earlier to help Nana wash and get ready for bed. Reluctant to retire for the night at the ridiculously early hour of half-past six, Nana would usually stay downstairs in her nightie and dressing gown and take herself up on the stairlift at around ten o'clock.

The carer *had* visited earlier but left, she said, because she couldn't gain access. I asked why she hadn't telephoned me immediately. At first she was evasive. When I pressed for a satisfactory explanation, she became angry. She was highly offended Nana should think she was a thief and wouldn't take that kind of disrespect from anyone. After a tense conversation I hung up.

'It's just you and me tonight, Nana, and probably for the rest of the week until Mum gets back and sorts this mess out.'

Anxious to get home to my pizza and beer as quickly as possible, I helped Nana onto the stairlift and followed behind with her stick. While she was in the bathroom, I perched on her bed. It was covered with a pink candlewick counterpane. The headboard was deeply padded with pink velour and studded with buttons. In two places the plush material was faded, rubbed thin where Nana and Grandpa's heads had rested when they sat up in bed with their morning tea.

I looked at my reflection in the full-length mirror and sucked in my stomach. A hairbrush full of white hairs lay on the dressing table next to a bottle of indigestion medicine. A small clock, an embroidered handkerchief and a macramé coaster were cluttered together on one of the bedside cabinets. On the other side of the bed, a man's wristwatch and spectacle case had been reverently placed next to a photograph of my grandfather. These small personal objects, ugly and utilitarian as they were, tugged at my heart in a way I wouldn't have thought possible three months ago. The beloved grandparents of my childhood, dead and now dying, had become reduced to trivial possessions on bedside cabinets. I blinked and breathed deeply to steady the sudden rush of despair, and noticed a familiar odour.

The bed had been made by the cleaner that morning. I sniffed the counterpane and pulled it back to investigate. There was a yellow patch in the middle of the undersheet. The cleaner must have tucked in the bedding without checking the condition of the bed. I stripped the sheets and wiped down the plastic mattress cover with a tissue. I would certainly mention this to Mum on her return. I guessed fresh sheets would be in the airing cupboard in the bathroom. I knocked on the door.

'Are you all right, Nana? Can I come in?' She opened the door. 'Have you cleaned your teeth yet?'

'No, not yet.'

I carried the soiled sheets behind my back. 'Where's your toothbrush, then?'

She turned towards the sink. I opened the laundry basket behind her and threw in the sheets. She shuffled round to face me again, holding an electric toothbrush in a trembling hand. I squeezed a small amount of toothpaste onto the brush.

'Off you go!' I surreptitiously opened the airing cupboard, liberating the clean bedding without her noticing.

I remade the bed and waited. Silence from the bathroom. 'Is everything all right?'

I gently pushed open the door. Nana stood exactly where I had left her, in front of the sink, staring at the toothbrush in her hand. The globule of toothpaste was still upon the bristles.

'I don't know what to do,' Nan said, tears welling up in her eyes.

'Do you usually take your false teeth out?' I asked.

She lifted her free hand to her mouth, spat a denture plate into her palm and offered it to me. I looked around the bathroom, located an empty glass and held it out to her. She dropped the dentures in.

'That's the way to do it, Nan.'

I opened the bathroom cabinet and found a tube of denture-cleaning tablets. I filled the glass with water and dropped a tablet in with a plink.

'Your teeth are like stars... they come out at night!' I wasn't expecting laughter. The joke was prehistoric, after all, but I had hoped for a smile. 'Time to clean the rest of your teeth.' When she didn't move, I gently took the electric toothbrush from her hand and switched it on. 'Open wide.'

I cleaned her teeth as if she were a child. When I finished, she stood with a mouth full of foam and an expression of panic on her face.

'Spit, Nana, spit.'

She dutifully bent down and spat into the sink. Before I could pass her a towel, she took hold of the bottom of her jumper, lifted it up over her bra to her face and wiped her mouth on the soft pink wool.

'All done.' She mumbled, smiling in triumph. She lowered the edge of the jumper back down to her waist.

I took her flannel and held it under the hot tap, squeezing out the excess before gently wiping her upturned face.

Back in her bedroom we gazed at each other wordlessly. I knew what needed to be done, which was more than she did. I stood behind her with my eyes closed and pulled her jumper quickly over her head. Eyes still shut, I fumbled on the bed for her nightdress and pulled it over her head. With the nightgown falling to her knees, I managed to pull her skirt and tights down from underneath. For one night, she would have to sleep in her bra and knickers. There are some things a grandson should never have to do. Whatever it took, I would get a carer for the remainder of my parents' holiday. And I knew just the person to ask.

*****

First thing the next morning I popped into the supermarket. I waited my turn in the checkout queue with a small basket of groceries. Lauren ignored me, her eyes on the packet she was scanning.

'Hello. I'm sorry I haven't been in touch. I've been busy.'

'Haven't we all! Lose my number, did you?' She scanned my newspaper. 'Did you bring your own bags?'

'No. Can I have one, please?' She rummaged under the checkout and made a big performance of slapping a carrier on the conveyor belt, an expression of disdain on her face which plainly said, 'This man is personally responsible for the destruction of the planet.'

'I haven't been able to get out much recently. I've been looking after my grandmother. I wanted to thank you again for coming out with me the other week. It was great to get a change of scene.'

'I thought you were staying with your parents.'

'I am. But they're away at the moment. Mum usually cares for Nana. I said I would take over while she gets a break. It's been a bit more challenging than I anticipated.' I lowered my voice. 'She's suffering from dementia.'

Lauren's expression instantly changed. 'Bless! And bless you for stepping in like that. There aren't many men who would do that for their grans.'

I packed my milk, biscuits and chewing gum into the carrier bag. 'It's nothing, really. I wanted to help. She has a carer going in mornings and evenings to help her get up and to put her back to bed, but she's taken against her. She's now putting the chain on the door and won't let the carer or cleaner into the house. She doesn't trust them.'

'Oh dear! Does she let you in?'

'Yes. I'm family. But it's a bit difficult, helping her wash and dress...'

'Bless your heart, of course it is. That'll be £6.37. Is she incontinent?'

'No,' I lied, reaching for my wallet. I was a desperate man. I didn't want to lose my one possibility of help.

'You've probably got that still to come. You should have said something earlier, struggling on your own like that. I've worked in an old people's home. I know what it's like.'

'I thought you'd think less of me, doing that kind of thing. It's not exactly... manly.'

'Don't be silly. I think more of you, not less. I can help you out around my shifts, if you want. I've done it for others in the village before.'

'Are you sure? That's very good of you.' I couldn't believe my luck.

'What are friends for?' She squeezed my hand as she gave me my change.

*****

207

'Hello Nana?' I shouted, opening the back door just after six o'clock. I had left the side gate open and confiscated the kitchen door key in case I couldn't gain entry at the front.

'Is that you, Derek?'

'It's Vincent.'

'Who's that?' she asked. Before I had the opportunity to introduce Lauren, she pushed past, bent down and kissed Nana on the cheek.

'I'm Lauren. Your grandson has told me so much about you. I hope you don't mind us popping round like this.'

'Not at all, dear. You never told me you had a lady friend, Vincent.'

'Well, I –'

'Why don't you put the kettle on,' Lauren interrupted, 'and give us ladies a chance to get to know each other? I've bought a packet of chocolate digestives, Nana. I hope you like them.'

'Lovely. Would you like a toffee, dear?'

'Bless your heart. I think I will.'

I retreated into the kitchen, feeling wretched and relieved. The bedtime routine was sorted.

*****

Lauren and I visited early on Wednesday morning. She helped Nana wash and dress while I made breakfast. Once Nana was settled in her armchair, with the TV remote control and a plate of sandwiches covered in the fridge, Lauren grabbed her coat from the hook in the hall. I was going to drop her off at the supermarket and would pick her up after work that evening; we would put Nana to bed together.

'It's a bit like having kids, isn't it?' she giggled.

'Yes, all work and no sex,' I blurted. 'Or that's what I've heard.' I regretted my light-hearted comment immediately. It didn't take a detective to see which way Lauren's mind was working. Flirting with a girl from the provinces was quite different from the sophisticated sexual allusions casually thrown around in London.

'What are you like, cheeky! We'll have to see what we can do about that. I'm on a late shift tomorrow. I'll be around up until three o'clock but I won't be able to help you in the evening. I'll be working, more's the pity, because everybody else wanted *tomorrow night* off. It's rather a special day, after all.' She winked saucily. Lauren pulled on a pair of sparkly pink gloves. 'Perhaps you would like to come round to my place for your lunch tomorrow, after we've sorted Nana out.'

I was anxious to get back home to take Elsie for her walk, and wasn't really listening. I hadn't seen Sarah since Monday. The previous day I had camped out at the library, hogging one of their computers to surf the internet for jobs, but Sarah hadn't appeared. I was hoping to catch up with her in the fields. My mind was still buzzing with unanswered questions.

'I'm otherwise engaged,' I lied, not wanting to get embroiled any further. 'Thanks all the same. Nana and I have plans for lunch tomorrow,' I raised my voice. 'Don't we, Nana?'

'Plans?' Nana queried, unexpectedly roused from her quiz show.

'Yes, you remember. I'm taking you out for lunch.'

'Are you?'

I rolled my eyes at Lauren. 'Yes. It's your... wedding anniversary. We're going to that restaurant in Bury St Edmunds that Grandpa used to take you to.'

'It's my anniversary tomorrow?' Nana asked uncertainly.

'Bless her heart. And aren't you a good grandson to remember!'

Nana's focus wavered; she returned to staring at the TV screen. I lowered my voice.

'Well, it's a family tradition, since Grandpa died. Mum and Dad usually take her out and make a fuss of her, but as they're away I thought...'

Lauren leaned towards me. 'It's a lovely thought,' she whispered, smiling up into my eyes. 'And on Valentine's Day too. Isn't it romantic that your grandparents were married on the 14th February?'

*****

I caught a glimpse of Sarah and Bruce in the distance and quickened my pace across the field. The cool air was a welcome antidote to the heat of Nana's living room and Lauren's suffocating helpfulness. Dragging Elsie behind me, I mulled over the last few weeks.

Emotionally I had been all over the place. Despair, anger, hopes awakened, hopes dashed. There had been that peculiar night when I had felt insanely jealous of Gavin and sat outside Sarah's house like a crazed stalker, no doubt a weird aberration brought on by the stress I had been under. I had become overly sensitive to the thought of rejection in any form, even from someone I didn't want a relationship with.

She was right! Of course anything more than friendship between us was impossible. At least *she* hadn't misunderstood our time together. The good thing was I wouldn't have to have that awkward conversation when one party has to let the other down. No one was going to get hurt. I had to admit my ego had been a little dented at first. No man likes to discover they are *not* secretly desired. But now we could continue with our walks and our driving lessons, free from the threat of emotional entanglement. We were friends. She might have a low opinion of me, think me a fantasist, even, but I would prove I could be trusted. I didn't care what Jimmy or the Specials thought.

When I managed to catch up with her, I commented as usual on the general dreariness of the weather and landscape.

'You seem determined to see ugliness instead of the beauty in front of you,' she replied. I looked at the dark fields spreading like a stain to the line of the horizon. The sky was overcast; a pale glow was the only break in the monotony – the sun held captive by the clouds.

'I see grey sky and a lot of mud, dead weeds and bare trees. It's depressing.'

'You're not looking closely enough.'

'It's flat; it's cold. What else is there?'

'When you come here every day, like I do, in all seasons and in all weathers, you begin to appreciate how much everything is constantly changing – the light, the colours, the smells. If you breathe deeply now you can sense the North Sea. Can you smell it?' she asked.

'No.'

'It's a tang, very faint. If the wind is coming from the north-east you can almost taste the waves and the spray and the brine. If the wind is coming from the west, you can smell the sugar beets and the pigs.'

'Fascinating!'

'And it's not all grey out here, either. See those trees? If you look closely, in the middle, near the trunk, the branches are a kind of pale yellowish-green.'

'I think you mean grey.'

'No. Look closely. You need to retrain your brain to *really* see what's in front of you instead of assuming you know what a tree in winter looks like. The pale green colour is lichen. Then there's the outline of the trees. Do you see the bronze haze where the twigs are at their smallest? It gives the impression of a glow or halo at the tip of the branches.'

'You notice all these little details about the landscape, but you can't see danger ahead when it's staring you in the face.' I was referring to the hazard perception test she had taken at my parents' house.

'People are more difficult to read than trees.'

'I suppose so. What did you mean when you said love and acceptance were not the same thing?' Her comment had been niggling away at the back of my mind ever since.

'Most children know they are loved by their parents, but there are lots of people who don't think their parents accept them for who they are. They feel they have to be good, or to be high achievers, or to look a certain way to be acceptable. I didn't have to earn Mum's love. It was a gift. She allowed me to be me, even though it was highly inconvenient at times.'

'In what way?'

'I was a challenging child. I didn't see the need to conform. It must have been difficult, particularly after Dad died. Mum used to shut herself away when it became too much. "Time out" I think they call it, except *she* would be having the time out rather than me.'

'All children can be naughty.'

'I wasn't naughty in the usual way. I didn't mean to be disobedient. There were just so many things I found stupid and pointless. At primary school, for example, I wanted to spell words the way I wanted to spell them. My teacher told me that nobody would be able to read what I had written unless I followed the spelling rules. It didn't matter to me that nobody could read my work. *I* knew what I had written. Mum was always having meetings with the head teacher. It used to drive her to distraction.'

'What did she do when you didn't cooperate?' I was edging closer to the nub of their relationship. Perhaps Sarah would reveal some deep-seated resentment that would explain her emotional detachment when discussing her mother's demise.

'Nothing. That was the point. She would sit in the dark and think things through, process stuff that was difficult. It was her safety valve. She would never lose her temper with me, or smack me, or blame me, or anything like that. She would just take herself away. She said she was frustrated with her own limitations rather than mine. That's how I knew she really accepted me.'

'I can't imagine how terrible it must have been to see her suffer at the end. If I ever become seriously ill like that, I'd want someone to hit me on the head with a hammer.'

'No, you wouldn't. That's a horrible thing to say.'

'If you're in pain and there's no possibility of it lessening, only the knowledge that it's going to get worse, why not end it all? You wouldn't let an animal suffer like that. You said yourself you hated to see her in pain and it was better that she died quickly.'

'Did I say that? I suppose I did.'

'So did you ever want to... ease her suffering?'

'Of course. I wanted her to be as comfortable as possible. I arranged for a carer to come in every day, remember. She was very good.'

'No, I mean, didn't you ever think about helping her... on her way?'

There was a brief pause, then a look of shock as she realised what I had been implying. 'No! Why do you ask? Do you think I had something to do with my mother's death?'

'Of course not!' I denied. 'I'm just thinking out loud. I'm just trying to put myself in your shoes and see things from your point of view.'

'You can stay out of my shoes in future!' she cried. 'Life is precious, even when it's unpleasant and painful. We were both glad we had the time to say everything we wanted to say to each other. Some days were very bad, but there were good days too. If we had meddled with fate or predestination or whatever you want to call it, we would have lost something priceless – her time, her opportunity to think and speak and love. She could still do those things even when she was unable to do anything else.'

'I'm sorry. I'm being tactless. I'm not myself today. I'm feeling a bit low at the moment. My imagination seems to be going into overdrive... negative thoughts, that sort of thing. I'm just worried about the job situation... my dad... Nana. They're both going downhill at the moment. Just ignore me. I'm sorry if I caused any offence.'

'You really make me angry, Vincent.'

'Sarah, please...' I grabbed her hand. 'I'm so stupid.'

'Yes, you are,' she murmured, but she didn't pull her hand away.

'I've been worrying about lots of things lately. And worrying about you too. You're all alone and...'

'I'm not alone.' I bit back a disparaging remark about her friends. This was not the time. 'There's no need to worry about me.' Her tone had softened. 'I'd tell you to stop worrying about the other things too,' she continued, 'but I know from my own experience that telling someone not to worry is a waste of time.' We had stopped walking, and stood opposite each other, her hand still in mine. I gave it a little squeeze.

'If telling someone not to worry doesn't work, what's the answer?'

She thought for a moment.

'Love.'

****

When Elsie and I returned home, I was surprised to see two small suitcases in the hall. Dad was lying on the sofa.

'What's happened?' I asked.

'I was sick last night. I couldn't face eating anything this morning. It's probably a 24-hour bug, but we decided to come home in any case. There was no point staying with me feeling like this. Your mother's gone round to check on Nana. You've just missed her. Did you manage everything OK?'

'Of course. Nana decided she didn't want the carers any more and kept the chain on the door. But I managed to get in and sort her out. Mum will have to give her a good telling off. We'll probably have to get a new carer. I had a bit of an argument with her...'

'And you managed all on your own, did you?' Dad raised himself onto his elbow, a look of surprise in his eyes. The light from the window fell onto his face. His skin had a yellow, waxy appearance.

'Are you sure it's just a bug, Dad? You look like hell.'

'No, but that's the story we're going to tell your mother. I managed to get a last-minute cancellation with the consultant while you were up in London for your interview.'

'You should have said something.'

'You were a bit upset about your break-up with Chloe when you got back. I didn't want to burden you.'

'What did he say?'

'He agreed with the GP. I need to have a colonoscopy and endoscopy as soon as possible. He is going to try and fit me in this week.'

I swallowed hard, sick to the pit of my stomach. What was the point of anything if the people you loved were suffering and you could do nothing but stand by and watch? I looked at the familiar face, lined and increasingly emaciated. His skin had taken on a strange, papery quality, sere, fragile, dry. There seemed to be so many things I should be saying to him at a time like this, words of support, words of comfort, words of

213

appreciation for all he had done for me over the years, but my mind was numb and my lips stayed silent.

I waited for Mum to return, anxious to know if she approved of my efforts with Nana. Dad dozed. I found myself comparing his life with mine. He was not yet 60, not yet twice my age. I had to admit he looked older than his years. A horrible thought struck me. If Dad was dying now, then when he was my age he was more than halfway through his life. Yet he had been responsible for a wife, a young son and a mortgage on their first flat.

For my generation, a mortgage was an impossible dream. Lenders were cruelly cautious after the near-collapse of the banking system. Property prices in the south of England were unattainably high. The time left for me to pay off any mortgage shrank with each passing year. I imagined myself white-haired and decrepit, still having to endure the daily commute to work in my seventies in order to pay the bills. One day I would inherit from my parents, but I didn't want to think about that at the moment, particularly with Dad's health problems. In any case, they might live for another 40 years and spend it all on nursing home fees.

All my life I had been climbing to reach something better – to grow taller, to grow into the hand-me-down clothes passed on by an admired older cousin, to catch a bigger fish in the local pond, to see Ipswich Town reach the FA Cup Final, to pass my A levels, to get a job, a car, a better-looking girlfriend, a promotion... always climbing upwards, trying to meet deadlines, reach targets, achieve goals. But perhaps I'd already peaked, passed the half waymark and was sliding down the other side.

What a thought! Were the best years behind me already? Was the future a long crumbling descent into oblivion, a struggle against the inevitable gravitational pull of old age and death? What was the point of life if it was so short and unrewarding, so apparently random? With so many days wasted, the thought of starting again from scratch filled me with dread. I had frittered away my time, not investing in the things that really mattered – friends, family, decent qualifications. I had put in long hours at work, surfing a wave of adrenaline, taking risks with other people's money, pinning all my hopes on a fat commission, trusting my annual bonus. All for nothing.

In a blinding flash I realised everything I held dear was built on an illusion. Confidence in the stock market. Belief that our political masters could run the economy effectively. Financial transactions which took place in a virtual world. What was the intrinsic worth of the money in my pocket? It was just pieces of paper with a picture of the Queen and a promise to pay. But what were those promises worth when we lived in a world of variable rates of exchange, fluctuating inflation and rising interest rates? Everything was relative, all was shifting sand.

The front door slammed shut. Mum hurried into the living room, her cheeks pink from the cold.

'We're going to have to get Nana another appointment at the memory clinic, or increase her tablets or something. She's getting worse.'

My stomach sank. I had only left her a few hours ago. Usually she would spend the day watching television and dozing in her chair. Lauren had made her a sandwich for lunch and left it wrapped in silver foil in the fridge, with a jug of lemon squash on the small coffee table within easy reach.. What could have happened?

'You'll never guess, Vincent,' Mum declared, hands on her hips. 'She only thinks you're gone and got yourself a wife!'

*****

After lunch, I popped over to the supermarket to explain to Lauren that my parents had returned early and I wouldn't be requiring her help any more.

'Would your mum like me to give her a hand?' she asked. 'I've done it before. I used to look after the village librarian when she was ill.'

My heart lurched. Lauren had been Eleanor Penny's carer. She might have been the one who discovered the body. Sarah and Lauren knew each other. I prayed I had never been a topic of conversation between them.

'That's very kind of you to offer. No doubt Mum will make sure that Nana stops this silly nonsense with the carer. Thankfully, she listens to Mum. Once the carer can access the house again, it will be business as usual. But you've been a real Godsend. I couldn't have managed without you. I can't thank you enough.'

'I'm sure I can think of some way you can thank me properly,' she replied, smiling. I beat a hasty retreat.

Chapter 24

It was Thursday 14th February. Valentine's Day! It had crept up upon me unexpectedly. If Lauren hadn't mentioned it the day before, it would have passed me by completely.

The wind direction had changed, blowing an aroma of pig from the west. The last vestiges of snow, frost and ice had vanished. As I walked Elsie around the fields, I found myself relaxing into milder air rather than tensing against the cold. The ground was soft underfoot and the breeze, though cool, was sweet and refreshing.

The coppice of trees at the end of the field was undergoing a transformation. Whether this had happened overnight or whether I had only just noticed, minute leaf buds were forcing their way through the crusty twigs, spreading a sour yellowish-green haze across the branches. Shafts of sunlight pierced the gloom, splashing the trees and undergrowth with light, illuminating a whole universe of particles which spun and danced between the mossy trunks. A soft mist clung to the tree roots, evaporating in the delicate sunlight. Thick green shoots had pushed through the previous autumn's fallen leaves, promising bluebells in the spring. For the first time that winter I sensed an awakening. The worst of the winter was behind us; the days would now lengthen and warm. Surely I had hit rock bottom and things would start to turn my way. I had precious little left to lose; surprisingly, I was feeling more liberated than I had for years.

There was no sign of Sarah. We had a driving lesson scheduled for two o'clock that afternoon. I remembered our conversation the previous day. I hoped she had forgiven me for blundering in with stupid insinuations about her mother's death. My imagination had definitely been in overdrive, seeing sinister motivations and plots at every turn. I could not doubt Sarah's sincerity or her horror when I suggested something untoward might have taken place.

I had tried to justify my tactlessness by blaming it on the stress and worry of Dad and Nana. Like a child with a scab, I couldn't leave it alone, picking at the things that worried me about her situation. I recalled her words vividly: 'I'd tell you to stop worrying but I know from my own experience that telling someone not to worry is a waste of time.'

'If telling someone not to worry doesn't work, what's the answer?' I had asked.

'Love.'

'Love! I didn't have you down as a romantic.'

'I'm not talking about romance. I'm talking about real love, the love that is more than just an emotion, the love that is an act of will. Loving when it's difficult and when there's nothing in it for you. Not those commodified relationships where you only invest in someone if you think you're going to get a good return.'

'Why are you looking at me like that?'

'I'm not looking at you like anything. I'm just saying that love is the antidote to anxiety. Act in a loving way towards others, let them love you, and learn to love yourself. That helps to get things in perspective. It's easier to accept what you cannot change if you know you are loved.'

As a result of our conversation, I had cleared the air with my parents. I told them everything that had happened since I first lost my job, crying like a little boy when I described Tony's betrayal. I told them it would take me longer than I thought to get back on my feet. Mum had hugged me hard and said I could stay with them as long as I needed.

She had been right all along. The stars did shine brightest on the darkest nights, but only if you lifted your head to look. I had a roof over my head and people who loved me. My dream of picking up my career in London and getting back together with Chloe might have been shattered, but I could change my dreams.

I had got a lot of things wrong recently. Perhaps I had misjudged Lauren too. She had a kind heart, and was attractive in a kittenish kind of way. Maybe I would ask her out for a drink later this week, to thank her for her help with Nana. Sarah was right: relationships were about giving. Lauren had proved she was generous with her time and liked to do things for others. It was a win–win situation. By some miracle I hadn't lost Sarah's friendship, and I was still free to date other girls.

I would try to be less selfish in future. Friends helped each other out in difficult situations. I wasn't going to turn a blind eye to the pressure being exerted on Sarah by the Specials. I would get to the bottom of it, call in the police if necessary. I would be there looking out for her next Wednesday night. A small thrill of excitement rippled through my chest as I thought about the secrecy of my mission and the possible danger I might face. Perhaps, after all, I could recast myself as the hero.

I dropped Elsie back home and popped into the supermarket, grabbing a large box of chocolates from the shelf. Before I had time to overthink the gesture, I selected an expensive bouquet of red roses from a bucket of water by the checkout queue. There was nothing more low key – chrysanthemums or carnations – so, despite the expense, they would have to do. Lauren was on the till. She raised an eyebrow at the flowers. After paying for the chocolates I gave her the box with a flourish.

'For you, Lauren. For all your help.'

'Bless your heart. You'll have to help me eat these or I'll be losing my figure.'

'Nana's favourite,' I said, gesturing to the roses. It wasn't a lie.

'Ahhh. Aren't you lovely!' she sighed. 'You're one in a million.'

I drove to Nana's house, hoping she had let the carer in that morning after Mum's lecture the previous day, but also hoping she had forgotten about our lunch date. I could grab a quick sandwich at her place; she would have forgotten my promise of a restaurant. I left the flowers in the boot of the car and let myself in. Mum had solved the problem with the security lock by unscrewing the chain from the door and leaving it on the telephone table in the hall.

I walked into the lounge, and jumped with shock. Nana was standing in the middle of the room, leaning on her stick, already wearing her coat. A mauve woolly hat had been pulled down over her grey curls. Still wearing her slippers and smiling proudly, she shifted her weight from foot to foot like a cat on a hot tin roof.

'You're ready, Nana?' I exclaimed.

'Of course I'm ready!'

'We're not in any hurry. We don't have to be there yet.' I frantically ran through the list of restaurants and pubs I knew in the area, wondering if any of them would have a table free for lunch on Valentine's Day.

'The weather's cold for August, isn't it?' she observed.

'August?'

'Yes. I married your grandfather on 29th August 1956. It was beautiful. The sun shone all day long. I didn't need a coat and hat then.'

'Climate change has a lot to answer for,' I replied, steering her towards a chair at the dining table and frantically thinking how I could distract her from the idea of a meal out. I walked into the kitchen and shouted, 'Would you like a cup of tea?'

Everything was suspiciously tidy for 10.30 in the morning. I touched the kettle. It was cold. I walked back into the living room. Nana had stood up again, clutching her handbag to her chest.

'Have you had breakfast, Nana?'

'Oh…' She thought for a moment. 'That's the one thing I *have* forgotten to do.'

'Don't worry, I'll put the kettle on and make you some toast and marmalade. Let's take off your hat and coat. We have plenty of time before lunch.' I guided Nana to the small dining table in the living room.

'Are you sure we have time?' she asked, her voice wavering, her earlier excited confidence beginning to diminish.

'It's fine, Nan. I came early just in case you needed help. But you've done very well to get ready all by yourself.'

'I'm not taking off my coat,' she replied petulantly. She sat heavily on the upright chair.

I returned to the kitchen and set out a tray of tea and toast. I noticed a bottle of pills on the kitchen top. I looked at the checklist of medication on the fridge door. That morning's dose had not been ticked off.

'Have you taken your medicine today, Nana?' When she didn't respond I popped my head around the door. 'Nana, have you taken your pills?'

'Oh… that's the one thing I *have* forgotten to do.'

I returned to the kitchen, filled a glass of water and brought her a couple of tablets which she obediently swallowed. I ticked off the day's date on the sheet and carried the tray through to the living room.

The aroma of brewing tea and hot toast mingled with the smell of mothballs from Nana's best coat. With a pang, I was reminded of the afternoons I had spent with Nana and Grandpa after school while waiting for Mum to collect me from work.

'Lovely cup of tea, Reggie,' Nana sighed.

'I'm not…' I began, but thought better of it. 'Thanks. You can't beat a good cuppa.'

I washed up the crockery and left it to drain. When I returned to the living room, she had taken off her coat and laid it over the back of the dining chair. Her hat was on the table. She was sitting back in her armchair, searching down the side of the cushion. She located the remote control and eased herself into the depths, shifting her weight on either buttock until she was perfectly positioned.

With a sigh, all tension left her body. Everything shifted downwards; shoulders, breasts, mouth, and pendulous cheeks all relaxed and sank into stillness. The TV screen flickered to life. She stared ahead, expressionless, her eyes glazing like those of an infant about to fall into a deep and dreamless sleep. I noticed the buttons of her cardigan had been fastened to the wrong holes. I quietly closed the front door behind me.

I picked Sarah up from outside the library just after two o'clock. I drove to a quiet road and parked. We swapped seats. On my way round to the passenger side, I opened the boot and took out the bouquet. I wondered whether she had ever received a Valentine's Day gift before. The cellophane crackled as I climbed back into the car. She looked up, startled.

'Happy Valentine's Day! I thought the occasion warranted some flowers. I never thanked you properly for letting me sleep at your place last week.'

She stared at the flowers, looked across at me and then down at her hands. My heart sank.

'I didn't mean to embarrass you.'

'No, it's not that.'

'What's the matter, then?'

'Nothing, really. They're lovely. Thank you.' She took them from me and gazed absentmindedly at the lush blooms.

'You can tell me what's bothering you. I won't be offended, honestly. You're usually a pretty straight-talking person. I've got used to it. I'm wearing my tin helmet...' I knocked on the side of my head. '... So don't worry if you want to take a pop at me. I suppose your silence means that I've crossed a line.'

'It's not that.'

'What, then?'

'It's the flowers.'

'Don't you like roses?'

'I love roses. I just don't like dead ones.'

'Dead!' I looked closely at each of the beautiful blooms, their deep red petals curling sensually around a tight central whorl. 'They don't look dead to me.'

'That's just because the decomposition hasn't set in yet. They've been severed from their roots. Over the next few days they'll shrivel and go brown at the edges. Every day I look at them they will look a little sadder. Their petals will fall and leave a sticky residue on my furniture. The water will stink and turn green...'

'OK, OK,' I said. 'Don't worry about it. I'll give them to Mum, if it makes you feel better.'

'Thank you for the thought. Perhaps I could press one in kitchen paper between the pages of a big book. Then it would last forever, a kind of ghost...'

My phone rang so I didn't have to respond. 'Hello.'

'Chubbs! It's Jimbo!'

'Hi!' I moved my phone to my left hand, furthest away from Sarah, and leaned into the passenger window.

'Oi've got an emergency, mate. Oi've broken down. Need yer help as soon as yer can get here. Can't go into details, but Oi wouldn't ask unless I were desperate. Are yer able to come and pick me up on the A14?'

'I'm a bit busy.'

'Come on, Chubbs. Oi need yer. This isn't some wind-up.' There was a note of desperation in his voice. I remembered the night after my trip to London when he hadn't responded to my request for a bed, then decided I was bigger than that. I was turning over a new leaf.

'OK, OK. Where exactly are you?' Jimmy explained he was stranded just before the westbound junction into Bury St Edmunds. 'I can be there in about 40 minutes.'

'Forty minutes! Oi can't wait that long. This is a dire emergency. Where the hell are yer, anyway?'

'If I put my foot down, I can make it in 20.'

'Then do it!' He hung up.

'Is there a problem?' Sarah asked.

'Yes. That was Jimmy... Jimmy Hodges.'

'Oh!'

'He's broken down on the A14 and needs rescuing. There's obviously some kind of complication because he sounded pretty panicked. I'm sorry, but we're not going to be able to have a lesson now. I've got to drive over there and get him. If I drop you back home, the round trip will add another 20 minutes on the journey. He seems to think that's too long. I can drop you off at the nearest bus stop, or you can come along for the ride and we might be able to get a bit of driving practice in later, once we have rescued him.'

'Let's do that.'

'I'll understand if you don't want to see him.'

'I'll manage.'

We swapped sides again. I took the flowers from her hands and gently placed the bouquet on the back seat.

On the way there, I decided to help her practise her hazard perception, building slowly on the basics.

'When you see a hazard ahead, you should use your mirrors. Why?'

'Because things that are behind you can affect how you react to what is ahead.' She seemed distracted, as though thinking about something else.

'Yes. You need to assess how your actions affect the following traffic.' I wasn't convinced she had really understood how my answer differed from hers. It was more specific and took into account the impact of her actions on other road users rather than the impact of the hazard on her. I tried a slightly different question to check if she understood the point. 'Before you perform a U-turn, what should you do?'

'You need to look backwards to know what is behind you before you commit to a new path. Otherwise you might have a disaster.'

'Mmmm. Yes. You need to look over your shoulder for a final check before indicating.' Again, her answer was slightly off-key. I had the feeling that she was talking about something other than the Highway Code, but we were close to the rendezvous point so I let the matter drop.

Jimmy's car was easy to spot. It was parked on the hard shoulder with its hazard lights flashing, next to a pig farm. A concentration camp of corrugated iron pig sties stretched across the field as far as the eye could see. Huge mother pigs, dirty and pendulous, stomped through the mud, pestered by groups of persistent piglets.

'Phew, smell that!' I exclaimed, as we pulled over. Jimmy was perched on a concrete bollard randomly set into the grass verge, smoking and gazing aimlessly at the pigs.

'Who's this?' he shouted over the roar of passing traffic as we walked towards him.

'Sarah, you remember Jimmy. Jimmy, this is Sarah Penny.'

'Gordon Bennett!' He spat out his cigarette and squashed it into the mud with his foot. 'Alright?' He nodded dismissively in her direction.

'Yes, thank you. How are you?'

'In it up to me armpits, darling!'

Sarah winced at his tone of voice and moved a little further away from us so we could talk.

'What's she doin' here?' Jimmy whispered angrily. 'Oi've got a serious problem and Oi don't need an audience.' We both glanced up but she had turned away, buttoning her coat against the cold and breathing out clouds of vapour.

'She was with me when you rang. It would have added another 20 minutes to your waiting time if I had dropped her off home first. What's the big drama?'

'Oi've got a flat tyre.'

'You've dragged me all the way out here to help you change a tyre? Jimmy, couldn't you manage that by yourself?'

'Shut up and keep your voice down,' he spat. 'Changing the tyre's not the difficulty. The spare's flat too. That's the problem.'

'You stupid…'

'Oi know, Oi know,' He raised the palms of his hands defensively. 'Oi got a flat just before Christmas. Drove over some broken glass in a pub car park. It was late. Oi meant to replace it, but the festivities took over, if yer know what I mean. I didn't regain consciousness until New Year,' he grinned. 'By then, Oi forgot.'

'It's illegal to drive without a spare tyre,' I hissed under my breath. 'You could lose your licence.'

'You don't have to point out the obvious, Einstein. Oi'm not thick, yer know. Oi've got to get it sorted before a police car comes along and stops to see what the trouble is. Can you drive me into Bury? We can pick up a spare at a garage Oi know. Oi've already rung ahead and they've got one in stock in case this one can't be mended.'

'OK. But just so you know, I don't appreciate getting involved with your stupid dramas. Next time leave me well out of it. Ring Dan or Spider or one of your other loony friends.'

'Let's go. Get your little dog in the car.'

'I heard that,' Sarah called across. 'And just so you know, I like dogs so I'll take that as a compliment.'

'You do that, love,' Jimmy shouted back.

'Shut it, Jim, or so help me I'll leave you here stranded.'

Jimmy took the damaged spare wheel out of his boot and put it in mine. Without looking at Sarah, he flung open the front passenger door and climbed in.

'Great!' I exhaled under my breath.

Sarah walked slowly towards the car. I could tell by her face she was aware of the snub. She slipped in the back. Jimmy glanced behind, took one look at the bouquet on the seat next to her and laughed.

'Ruddy Norah, Chubbs, what *do* you think you're doing?'

'You're pushing me too far… just… just… Get out of the car –' Before I could say more, Sarah interrupted calmly.

'You might think Vincent's stupid for giving me flowers, but he's a greater idiot for giving you a lift.'

'Thanks a lot!' I exclaimed. 'Why am *I* getting it in the neck?'

'Because you allow yourself to be manipulated,' she replied.

'Sorry, mate,' Jimmy cut in. 'I was well out of order. I'm a complete jerk. I can't help myself sometimes.'

'He's doing it again,' Sarah said.

'Doing what?' Jimmy asked, a picture of hurt innocence.

'Trying to get round you.'

'Shut up, you stupid –'

'You shut it, Jim!' I spat, turning the key in the ignition.

I indicated to pull out onto the dual carriageway. As I eased forward, looking over my shoulder at the oncoming traffic, Jimmy suddenly slammed his hand on the dashboard and shouted.

'Stop. Oi've left me phone in me car.' We jolted to a halt. He flung open the door and ran to his car. He was back in a matter of seconds, phone in hand. 'Thanks, mate,' he panted. We set off again and drove in silence to the garage.

Sarah and I waited in the car. She sat hunched on the back seat, staring out of her window. The atmosphere was thick with humiliation and annoyance.

'I'm sorry,' I ventured. She closed her eyes. 'Jimmy's a scoundrel, I know.'

'Then why are you friends?'

'I don't know. We go back a long way. It's difficult to disentangle those kinds of ties.'

Jimmy jogged onto the forecourt and approached my side of the car. I wound down the window. He leaned in.

'You couldn't lend me 50 quid, could you? Oi'm a bit short.'

I let out a loud exasperated breath, flung open the door and stormed into the grimy office with my wallet in my hand.

*****

When Jimmy and I returned to the car with the new wheel, Sarah was sitting in the front passenger seat with the roses in her lap. I grinned. She gave a tight smile in return. Jimmy climbed in the back without a word. We set off on our return journey in silence.

When we were about five minutes away from his car, my mobile rang. I reached into my jacket pocket and passed it to Sarah.

'Answer that for me, please, will you?' She gazed at the handset. 'Just press the little green telephone.' She located the button and pressed.

'Hello? Hello? No... Yes... I'm with him now... He's driving at the moment and can't speak on the phone. Yes. We're just on our way there. We should arrive in a couple of minutes. OK. Thank you.'

'Who was that?' I asked.

'The police.'

'The police!' Jimmy sat bolt upright and leaned forward.

'What did they want?' I asked.

'They wanted to know if I was the owner of a silver BMW...' She reeled off my car registration number and model.

'How did you know that was my registration?'

'I've been in your car enough times. I remember details like that. Anyway, I said "no".' Jimmy relaxed back in his seat. 'Then they asked if I was with you and I said, "yes". I told them you were driving and couldn't speak on the phone.'

'We got all that. But what did they want? You were on the phone for several minutes.'

'They wanted to know if we knew the owner of a blue Ford Fiesta because it had been found abandoned on the A14. I told them, "yes".'

'You what!' Jimmy exploded, leaning forward between our seats. 'Why did you say that?'

'Because it's the truth.'

'You stupid cow!'

'Stop it, Jimmy. What else, Sarah?' We were approaching the stretch of dual carriageway by the pig farm. We would have to pass by on the other side of the road, take the next exit and double back on the westbound carriageway to reach Jimmy's car.

'They said they would see us in a couple of minutes.'

'Why did they say that?'

'Because they're with Jimmy's car. Look!'

We all looked across the road. Parked behind Jimmy's car, lights flashing, was a black and white police car.

'Drive past, drive past,' Jimmy shouted.

'No way, Jimmy. I'm not going to get into trouble for you. They know my number plate. I can't cover up for you any longer. You're only getting what's coming to you.' I pulled off at the next exit and immediately turned and rejoined the road in the opposite direction, Jimmy cursing from the back seat. I stopped behind the police car. A tall officer sauntered over. I wound down my window.

'Would you turn your ignition off please, sir, and step out of the car?' I did as I was told. He put his hand under my arm and guided me away onto the grass verge.

'Is that gentleman in the back seat the owner of this vehicle?' he asked, indicating Jimmy's car. I nodded. 'Then would you mind telling me what has occurred here this afternoon?'

'My friend... Jimmy... rang to say he had broken down. He asked if I could come and pick him up. My friend and I drove over and agreed to take him to a garage in Bury.'

'And why were you going to a garage in Bury, exactly?'

'Because he had a flat tyre. When he went to get the spare out of the boot he found that that one was also flat. We've just picked up a new tyre and are about to fit it. I do hope there's no problem, officer.' He stood, scratching his chin thoughtfully for a moment. A thought suddenly occurred to me. 'How did you get my mobile number, and how did you know I had picked Jimmy up?' I looked along the road, searching for a CCTV camera or anything that might explain the apparent omniscience of the local constabulary.

'That's not too difficult. When we found this car apparently abandoned on the roadside, we ran a check on the tax disc and found that it belongs to your car. It only took a matter of minutes to get your details from the DVLA database.'

I stared at him, stunned. How had my tax disc turned up in Jimmy's car? Then I remembered Jimmy had been sitting in my passenger seat. He had suddenly jumped out and returned to his car saying that he had forgotten his mobile phone. He must have pinched my disc while I was looking over my shoulder to pull out. Not only was he driving without a spare tyre, he was driving without road tax. He had wanted to cover up that fact in case a police car pulled over. But his stunt had gone spectacularly wrong.

'If you don't mind, I'll just ask your... er... friend, Jimmy, to step out of the car and accompany me to the station. I will arrange for his car to be towed away.' The officer reached into his pocket. 'Here's your tax disc, sir. Take better care of it in future.'

We both walked back towards my car. The policeman opened the back door. Jimmy peered out.

'Everything all right, Chubbs?'

'Yes, you can get out now. I've explained everything.'

He smiled with relief and climbed out of the car. As he straightened up, I punched him as hard as I could on the chin.

Chapter 25

Although Jimmy decided not to press assault charges, it was after ten o'clock before Sarah and I left Bury St Edmunds' police station. At first the police were suspicious I might have been in on the tax disc swap. But the duty sergeant recognised Sarah as a friend of Gavin's, and when she affirmed my innocence he believed her straight away. I was a bit miffed he had taken her word rather than mine. I thought I had a pretty honest-looking face.

We didn't know how Jimmy was going to get home, or even if he would be allowed home that night. To be honest, we didn't care. Sarah's roses were beginning to wilt by the time I parked outside her bungalow. Bruce had been left alone for more than eight hours. After putting the flowers in water, she clipped on his lead to take him on a short walk around the block. I had been hovering by the front door, scratching Bruce behind the ears and hoping to be invited in. When I realised she was going out again, I fell into step beside her.

The moon had risen in a haze of white. The night was bright and silent as we walked along the empty pavements. There didn't seem to be anything to say. The embarrassment and anger of earlier in the day had passed. My punching Jimmy had placed us both firmly on the same side of the fence and we walked in companionable silence. Bruce sniffed and marked the lamp posts, happy to be out in the world of invisible aromas. I breathed the sharp clear air deeply into my lungs.

I had probably lost one of my oldest friends today; I had been betrayed by someone I should have been able to trust. But I had also stood up for myself – not soon enough, probably, and certainly not soon enough for

Sarah. As Jimmy had been led to the waiting police car, I thought I saw a grudging respect in his eyes and a note of regret in his parting comment.

'No hard feelings, Vinny?'

I looked across at Sarah. She was staring at the pavement, her expression masked and perfectly calm. It was impossible to tell what she was thinking. As I gazed at her face, pale in the darkness, with bedraggled hair sticking out from underneath her grotesque green knitted hat, I realised I was looking at the face of my best friend.

Everything became very clear. *She* was the kind of person I should have in my life, not people like Tony and Jimmy and Chloe. She was the most honest person I had ever met, honest with others and honest with herself. She was someone I could trust, perhaps the only person other than my parents who would tell me what they really thought. It was as though my vision, impaired by the bright imprint of the sun, was adjusting to the gloom and now registered the subtlety of her beauty, the pale skin, the soft hair, the simple subdued clothes which swung from her slender frame.

How could I have found the strident artificiality of Chloe's hair and make-up attractive? How could I compare Lauren's crushing common sense, her heavy mascara and garish lipstick, with Sarah's quiet words and delicate mouth? She was beautiful, natural and uncomplicated. She didn't need to flirt or adorn herself. Being herself was enough! I plunged in.

'What do you think of the newest Ben Affleck film?'

'I don't know. I haven't seen it.'

'I'm thinking of going on Saturday.' I rubbed my hands together to dispel the adrenaline coursing through my system.

'You can tell me what it's like, then.'

Was she being dense, or was she giving me the brush-off? I tried a different tack.

'OK... Even though you said you didn't like the roses, I'm glad you didn't have a problem with me.'

'I don't.'

'Does that mean you like me?'

'Yes. We're friends now.'

I hesitated, weighing my words carefully.

'I really like you, Sarah. In fact, I've found myself liking you more each time I see you. I don't have to pretend when I'm with you because you see right through me. You're always completely yourself. You never put on an act or try to be something you're not. You don't play games.'

'I don't know how to play games.'

'Exactly. That's what I mean. You're completely truthful. I found it hard at first but I like it now. I know where I am. I can be a different person, a better person, when I'm with you.'

'Vincent, you will always find it difficult to be really honest because other people's opinions matter too much.' Her words cut deep. She was right. I was shallow and hypocritical!

'I know I've been weak and spent too many years following the crowd. I don't know why. When I think about people like my old boss and Jimmy and Chloe, I'm not sure what I saw in them in the first place. I liked what they represented, confidence and a kind of ruthlessness that I don't have. I thought that was what I needed to be a success. I'm not sure I want to be a success any more. I want to be honest with myself... I want a fresh start... I want you.'

We stopped walking and looked at each other.

'You don't mean that.'

'I do.'

'I shouldn't have agreed to the driving lessons. It would have been better if we had never become friends again.' She rung her hands together, deep distress on her face.

'Don't say that. Don't ever say that! Your friendship has been one of the most meaningful things in my life. You've made me see how shallow my world is. You've made me reassess the things I want. I've been chasing dreams, I see that now... desires that can never be satisfied because the more I get the more I want. Now I know what's real. I want to be with you.'

She refused to look me in the eye. 'You might think you do, but people like you can never be with people like me.'

'What does that mean?'

She glanced at me briefly. 'You know what I'm talking about.'

'No, I don't... Honestly.'

'I'm fundamentally different from you.'

'Yes. I'm a man and you're a woman! Isn't that what this conversation is all about?'

'It goes deeper than that. I've dropped enough hints. We're very different people. You think you like me romantically but that's just because you've lost pretty much everything else in your life right now. You're clutching at sticks – or is it straws? Once you get back on your feet, you'll be only too glad to leave Elmsford. I'm a novelty at the moment. That will wear off...' she looked sad, '... it always does.' She started to walk away.

'That's not true,' I said, catching her up. 'It isn't like that. I've been fighting my feelings for you right from the word go. I didn't want this, but I can't help myself any more. I have nothing to recommend me, except that I care for you. I'm a total waste of space. I have no job, no home, no friends. Your friends think that I'm after your money, by the way, even though I'm not. All I have are some gadgets, a receding hairline and some extra weight. Not much to show for 12 years of hard work. I know now that all I really need is you.'

'I don't need to be needed.'

'Well, what *do* you need?' I asked, exasperated.

'I would like us to be friends. I don't want to get hurt.'

My heart thudded. Was I being turned down, or had she just revealed I was in a position to hurt her, that she had feelings that were more than friendship, feelings which went deep and would wound her if I let her down?

'I would never hurt you.'

'It's inevitable. People like me can't be with people like you, not without the kind of compromises I don't think you would be able to make.'

'What do you mean, "people like you and people like me"? I can compromise! I compromised all the time with Chloe, believe you me!'

'I can't live the kind of life you want to live. Your friends wouldn't want to be my friends.'

'That's no problem. I don't have any friends!'

'We're just not compatible, Vincent. You have to accept that.'

'I can't. We are compatible... and I'll prove it!' I pulled her close, gathering the thick material of her coat in my hands and gazing down into her startled eyes. My breathing quickened, clouding the air between us. 'I've got under your skin, just as you've got under mine. Admit it! I could only hurt you if you had some feelings for me. You don't have to be frightened. This isn't some stupid crush. I'm not going to let you down.' With one hand I pulled her closer, with the other I stroked her cheek.

'Don't...'

But I was no longer listening. I bent my head and kissed her full on the lips, her skin cold and fresh next to mine. A bolt of electricity shot through my chest and flooded my body with desire. I ignored the warning growl reverberating from Bruce's throat.

For several minutes I held her cheeks and kissed her repeatedly on the lips, on her face and eyelids, in the hollow of her neck. I pulled her to me, holding her tenderly and burying my face in her hair. She didn't struggle, but her body was rigid. I could have been holding a plank of wood. Bruce stopped growling. He must have interpreted her stillness as consent. He became restless and began to circle, winding the lead around our legs.

'Tell me you feel the same,' I whispered.

She pulled her head away and looked up into my eyes. I continued to hold her close, both arms encircling her body, my hands resting on the small of her back.

'My personal space limit is about three feet.'

'Oh…' I released her immediately and stepped back. She brushed her hands down the front of her coat as though brushing away my touch.

'Do you remember that story I was telling you about; the one about the little skunk?'

I was taken completely by surprise. Of all the things she could have said, this had to be the most off the wall. A slap to the face would have been more understandable in the circumstances. I didn't know where she was going with this, but I did remember the last time she mentioned that story she had been trying to tell me something important.

'Yes. The one where none of the other woodland creatures would play with the skunk because he smelled so bad. You were remembering our schooldays.' The words tumbled out in my eagerness to understand the point she was making. 'I'm so sorry I made things worse for you at school. I guess I was like one of those creatures who wouldn't play with the skunk. But I've changed, I promise. I will never stand by and let you be ostracised again. I want to care for you, share myself with you…'

'I never got to tell you the rest of the story.' She fiddled with the buttons of her coat. 'Little skunk went to a wizard and asked for help. The wizard cast a spell and suddenly the skunk smelled of roses. When he went back into the woods, the other creatures let him join in their games.'

'So your story has a happy ending. Is that what you're saying?' I reached for her hand again, holding it tightly so that she couldn't pull away. Bruce growled softly, but I ignored him.

'That's not what I'm saying. Little skunk isn't meant to represent me. He has always reminded me of you.'

'What!' I was aghast.

'He changed something essential about himself to become something different, so he would be accepted by the others. Jimmy was your wizard. You allowed yourself to be changed because you were frightened to be an outsider. I saw it happen and it broke my heart.'

'I can change back.' Even I could hear the pleading in my voice.

'Can you? In the story the little skunk goes back home. His family is horrified. They don't like the smell of roses. His mother marches him back to the wizard and demands his natural smell back.' There was a long silence, as though she was waiting for me to ask the obvious question.

'What happened?' I had the feeling I didn't really want to know.

'He changed back.'

'That's good, isn't it?' I said with relief.

'Not according to the story. The skunk is angry with his mother. Now he has nothing. He has lost his friends and his new life. Plus, his relationship with those who loved and accepted him for who he was is spoiled forever. He can never forgive them for changing him back – and that's how it would be with us. We had our chance years ago. Maybe we could have been together then. But if you wear a mask for long enough, ultimately your face will mould to fit it. Now you know what it's like to smell of roses, can you go back to smelling of skunk?'

I didn't know what to say. Was that how she had seen me? An outsider like herself? Had I had my chance back at school and blown it without even knowing? But I had known! Of course I had known. I had felt the chemistry even then. That was why I experienced those strange feelings of disquiet and guilt when I first saw her in the library. At some deep level I knew I had hurt and disappointed her. I had turned my back on her to be popular, chosen to tag along with a bully like Jimmy because I was weak and scared.

'I *can* change,' I pleaded.

Bruce was tugging at the lead, eager to be in his bed. We had reached her garden gate. She turned and looked at me.

'I know you can change. I remember the changes you made when you were a teenager. You were determined to lose weight. You used to jog round the village after dark, do you remember? And then you began to hang out with Jimmy and Catrina and the rest of the cool kids. You had aspirations. That's what made you fearful. You didn't want someone like me dragging you back into outer darkness. You were happy to tag along with Jimmy, hoping some of his popularity would rub off on you. And it did! I don't know if you can change back again. Or if you did, whether you would always resent me.' I caught the glimmer of a tear in the corner of her eye. 'Goodnight, Vincent. Think about what I said. We can only be friends.'

She walked away quickly. Before I could reply, Bruce had pulled her into the bungalow. Without a backward glance, she shut the door firmly behind her.

Chapter 26

Days passed in a blur of misery. I walked Elsie around the fisherman's pond, avoiding the fields. I slumped in front of the television when my parents were out, only going through the motions of job hunting when they were around. I didn't want to lose my grip on things, to sink into lethargy, to give up, but it was happening just the same.

I measured the hours by the number of coffees I had drunk. Small domestic chores became enormous obstacles to overcome. Expeditions to the petrol station for chewing gum or biscuits triggered a wall of exhaustion, but I couldn't face the obligatory flirting that shorter jaunts to the supermarket would involve. Mum had spoken to Lauren. They had come to an informal arrangement until new carers could be found. With her flexible shifts, she would help Nana for an hour at both ends of the day.

It was time to pass Sarah over to Simon for proper lessons. She was ready. We hadn't spoken since Valentine's Day, and I knew she wouldn't approach me first. She had made her position clear. But I procrastinated.

Simon and Liz had come round to play Scrabble on Saturday night. I excused myself and hid in my room. I stripped down to my boxers and lifted some weights for ten minutes. I had lost all the progress I'd made at the gym. I looked at my reflection in the full-length mirror inside the wardrobe door. 'You're as good as you look,' Tony always said. An unshaven, dark-eyed, overweight slob gazed back, confirming what I already knew. I looked as bad as I felt.

We can only be friends. Sarah's words and the sadness in her eyes as she left me standing on the path played over and over in my mind. I thought back over the last weeks. Had she ever given me any encouragement? No! Then again, I hadn't given her any indication of my feelings either, probably because I hadn't recognised them for what they were myself until the crashing realisation after Jimmy's betrayal. Perhaps I had moved too fast and scared her off. Or was there something else standing between us other than the possibility she just didn't like me in that way? Why did she insist we were incompatible? I couldn't shake the impression there was something I had missed.

I toyed with the idea of ringing her to arrange another driving lesson, acting as if nothing had happened. But to spend more time with her in the close proximity of the car would be unbearable now I had held her in my arms. But there was one thing I *could* do. If we could only be friends, I would be a *good* friend. I would watch over her when the Specials came to call.

*****

Wednesday night found me parked a few houses down on the other side of the road from Sarah's bungalow. I had persuaded Dad to lend me his Ford Focus so she wouldn't recognise the car. Feeling guilty for breaking my honesty resolution, I told him my BMW had a slow puncture and I would be taking it down to the garage in daylight to check the air pressure. Mum and Dad were left with the impression I was playing snooker with Jimmy in a pub in Stowmarket.

A packet of biscuits and a bottle of orange juice were in a carrier bag on the back seat. A map book was open on the passenger side, waiting to be studied intently when any passers-by approached. I also had my favourite prop, my mobile phone, which I could pretend to use to justify my presence in the street. All I needed was a fedora hat and a pair of sunglasses, and my disguise as an amateur detective would be complete.

I had no idea what Big Micky had meant by 'Wednesday night'. It could be as early as six o'clock or as late as midnight. I was prepared to wait it out. I switched on the radio. Listeners were phoning in to discuss the rumour that the government was about to abolish the 50 pence tax rate in the Budget. The show was polarised between those who argued calmly and rationally that the 50 pence tax rate was stifling entrepreneurialism in the UK and driving away the best business minds. In their view, the revenue raised would not justify the damage to the economy. These were the voices of the educated and rich. And then there were the shouters, ranting that the poor were getting poorer and the weak were suffering the most from the cuts. Why should the rich benefit from the Budget? If you earned enough to pay the highest rate of tax, you could afford to pay it! These were the voices of the angry and desperate. After about half an hour, and irritated with both sides of the argument, I switched over to a music channel playing eighties pop. I began to feel drowsy. I hadn't slept well the previous night.

At 21:27 on the digital clock in the car, an unmarked white van drew up outside Sarah's bungalow. Suddenly I was wide awake. I switched off the radio. I heard the driver open his door and slam it behind him. I couldn't see what he looked like because the van was blocking my view of the garden path and Sarah's front door.

I unwound my window, straining to hear the sound of voices. Frantic barking. Another door closed. I switched on the ignition and slowly reversed a few feet so I was parked with a better view of the front of bungalow. All the curtains were closed. I waited.

After about ten minutes the door opened and Sarah stepped out onto the path, a bulky black sack in either hand. She was followed by a pair of legs staggering under the weight of a large cardboard box. It was obvious the box was being carried by someone very small. All that could be seen of their head was a mop of hair poking over the top.

They walked to the back of the van and placed their burdens on the pavement. The dwarf from the toilets at the Railway Tavern unlocked the double doors and began to load up the box and bags, climbing into the van to push them further inside. In the meantime, Sarah returned to the bungalow and came back with a couple of large carrier bags. The dwarf collected another box. These were loaded into the van. Then they carried a particularly bulky box between them. After lifting it into the van, the dwarf slammed the door shut. It looked as though their transaction was complete. The dwarf opened the driver's door but paused before climbing in to say a few words to Sarah. I strained to hear.

At that moment, a cyclist came tearing along Moon Rise towards them and stopped in front of the van. Throwing the bike onto the pavement, the cyclist ran towards Sarah and the dwarf, shouting and gesticulating. There was an animated conversation between the three. The cyclist's voice rose higher. He stamped his feet. Even from where I was sitting I could see he was working himself into a complete frenzy. Sarah spoke but I couldn't catch the words. She stretched out her hand as if to placate him.

Meanwhile, the dwarf reopened the van and lifted one of the boxes down onto the pavement, and staggered with it to the nearest street lamp. He opened the top and began unloading the contents. Sarah had taken the cyclist's arm. He shrugged her rudely away.

The dwarf had not been able to find what he was looking for. He retrieved another box from the van. By now the pavement was covered with dark shapes. If he was transporting something dodgy, he didn't seem too concerned about concealing his load. I glanced back at Sarah and the cyclist. He was sitting on the kerb, rocking back and forth, his hands holding either side of his cycle helmet. Whatever it was they were looking for was clearly important.

The dwarf took the last box out of the van and began piling its contents onto the pavement. Sarah had her arm around the cyclist's shoulder. With my window open I could hear the calming rhythm of her voice above the man's distressed sobs. Bruce's frantic barks could be heard from inside the bungalow.

The dwarf stood up, his search obviously complete. He walked back towards the cyclist, his hands held out in front of him, shrugging. Immediately the cyclist sprang to his feet and furiously kicked out at the objects on the pavement, scattering the piles into the road and screaming in incoherent rage. The dwarf shouted back, his voice stern and authoritative, the kind of tone a schoolteacher or a father would use when reprimanding an unreasonable child. Sarah tried to grab the cyclist's arm again as he stepped menacingly towards the dwarf. He pushed her roughly away. She fell to the ground. That was it!

I leapt from the car and charged across the road. Sarah gave a little shriek when she saw me racing towards her in the dark, her fear turning to shock when she recognised me. I knelt down beside her and took her in my arms.

'I'm alright,' she said, pushing me away.

'Are you hurt?' I asked breathlessly.

'No, no. I've got to help Gavin. He's having a meltdown.' I turned to the cyclist, who was wrestling with the dwarf. Helping Sarah to her feet, I held her tightly round the waist as she tried to reach the struggling pair. Unexpectedly, the dwarf knocked Gavin's legs from under him. He tumbled to the ground. In a flash, the dwarf had him in a headlock. I couldn't believe my eyes. Either Gavin was particularly feeble, or the dwarf exceptionally strong, using his lowered centre of gravity to gain the advantage.

It was a good thing the cyclist was wearing protective headgear because he went down with an audible crack onto the paving slabs. I lessened my grip on Sarah and allowed her to pull me forward. The dwarf was murmuring something over and over. What was he saying? His tone reminded me of an occult incantation or magic spell. Holding Sarah firmly by the arm, I took another step forward to catch his words.

'I'm going to hold you until you can hold yourself. I'm going to hold you until you can hold yourself.'

The dwarf whispered the phrase repeatedly, still pinning Gavin's neck to the ground with his thigh. The stricken man begin to relax. His arms and legs twitched and stilled. I heard the sound of sobbing. The dwarf shifted his body away and cradled Gavin's head in his lap. Sarah shook herself free of my grasp and ran to the pair. She knelt on the pavement and gently unclipped the cycle helmet.

In the yellow glow of the lamp light, Gavin's face looked sallow and distorted. I could see he was crying. Mucus had collected in his straggly moustache and his cheeks were wet with tears. I looked at the ground around us. It was littered with paperback books, some of them battered and creased, some of them open and face down on the pavement, their pages smeared and torn. So this was what was in the boxes. In that moment I remembered the box of donated books in the library. The Specials must be collecting items for Saturday's fundraiser.

Feeling ashamed, I began to pick up the books, dusting them down and stacking them back into the boxes. After a few minutes, the dwarf stood up, reassured that the drama was over and it was safe to leave Gavin in Sarah's care. She was sitting next to him on the edge of the kerb, wiping his face with her handkerchief.

'What are you doing here?' the dwarf demanded.

'I've come to see Sarah,' I replied belligerently. 'What the hell is going on?'

'It's none of your business!'

'I'm making it my business. I'm quite happy to call the police. Your friend has been disturbing the peace, not to mention assaulting Sarah.' I folded my arms across my chest and tried to look tough.

'Stop arguing, Micky,' Sarah said. 'It's not helping Gavin.'

'What's his problem?' I asked nodding towards the cyclist. Neither Micky nor Sarah answered, but Gavin turned to me with an intense expression on his face

'My brother has given away my book. It's called *Railway Journeys through East Anglia*. He shouldn't have done that. It was my book! It was signed by the author.'

239

'I'm sure it's all a mistake, Gavin,' Sarah replied. 'Your mother is very careful with your things.'

'No, he took it from my bedroom.'

'I am sure it's at home somewhere. Stuart would never do that to you. He knows how upset you get. When I unpack these boxes at the village hall I will keep my eye open for it. We can't look properly here in the dark. We won't sell it, I promise.'

'As if anybody would want to buy it!' Micky muttered under his breath. The others didn't hear.

'Come on,' Sarah continued. 'Let's put everything back in the van.'

Micky and I worked in silence for a few minutes. Gavin stood to one side, trembling and flapping his hands like a flustered penguin. When all the boxes were back in the van and pushed against a toolbox and a couple of stepladders, Micky loaded Gavin's bike into the back without asking. He escorted Gavin to the passenger seat.

I wondered what adaptations had been made to enable Micky to drive the van. Then I wondered why he needed a van rather than a car in the first place. Suddenly the thought that he had a job, that he might be a tradesman, filled me with furious envy. Why was I unemployed when a jumped-up little jerk like him had a job?

'Let's take you home,' he said to Gavin. 'Will you be alright?' he asked Sarah, glancing at me meaningfully.

'Of course she will!' I spat. '*I'm* not about to throw her down on the pavement.' Ignoring me completely, Micky continued to talk to Sarah.

'I suggest you say goodnight to your... friend... and get an early night. You're looking tired.'

'Who do you think you are?' I spluttered.

'Thanks. I will. Feel better soon, Gav,' she called as Micky clambered into the driver's seat.

'I'm warning you,' I shouted. 'I don't like the way you operate. You don't intimidate me. I won't let you and your friends upset Sarah!' but the van pulled away and we were left standing on the pavement.

'He's a bit of a nutcase!' I exclaimed, thinking of Micky but realising immediately that the term could more aptly be applied to Gavin.

'I don't want to talk about it. And I'm not upset,' she replied.

'Aren't you? I was worried back then. It was turning nasty.'

'I was fine.'

'He was completely out of control. Couldn't you see the signs? You shouldn't approach people who are very angry. They can lash out unexpectedly. His body language should have told you to keep well away until he had calmed down.'

'I don't speak body language,' she replied stubbornly. 'My friend was upset. I wanted to help.' The distance between the two of us was growing.

'It sounds like Bruce needs some calming down too,' I said, trying to move the conversation on to less contentious ground.

We looked at the window and saw Bruce barking at us, his head thrust up from underneath the living room curtains.

'I'd better go in. The neighbours will complain.'

'Do you want me to stay with you for a while?'

'No thanks, I'm fine.'

'If you're sure...'

She looked at me directly, a puzzled expression on her face. 'Why are you here?' she asked, as though the thought only just occurred to her. 'Are you stalking me?'

'Oh... um...' I had no rational explanation for my presence. I made a sudden decision to be completely honest. 'Just as I was leaving your house the other day – after I had stayed the night – you had a telephone call. I didn't mean to listen to it. I wasn't spying on you or anything. I was collecting my things together. Micky left a message. He said the Specials were coming round to your house to pick up the stuff, and that he was sending Gavin round if you didn't come on Saturday. It sounded like a threat.'

'So you *were* spying on me.'

'It's been playing on my mind ever since. I decided to drive by, just to check you were OK. And I'm glad I did!' I said defensively.

'We were OK.'

'It didn't look like it to me. What did your friend... Micky... mean by threatening to send Gavin round?'

'He meant if I backed out of the fundraiser on Saturday, he'd send Gavin round to collect me. He knows I don't like crowded places and I'd try to wriggle out of it if I could. Micky thinks it would be good for me to go, help me get used to being with lots of people. If Gavin came for me I would have to travel on the bus with him. I have a bit of a phobia about buses. That's partly why I'm so keen to learn to drive. Also, Gavin goes on and on about the different bus routes and the specification of the

241

particular bus he's on. He tells people off if they put their feet on the seats or drop litter or ring the bell too early or too late or too often. It's a bit awkward.'

'I see.'

It was all becoming clear. I had jumped to the wrong conclusion again. I had seen for myself Sarah's reluctance to get on a bus, but had put that down to a fear of Gavin rather than a dislike of public transport. She began to walk up the garden path.

'Perhaps I could give you a lift to the village hall on Saturday, then.' I made a split second decision to help Dad in the car park. 'I'm on the car-washing team.' She hesitated and I pressed my advantage. 'What time should I pick you up? You could even drive there yourself to give yourself some more road experience.'

We stood under her porch by the large terracotta pot. The snowdrop buds had swelled since I had last been outside her door, one flower opening its stiff waxy petals and glowing like a dropped pearl in the moonlight.

'I'm supposed to be there by nine o'clock to help set up the bookstall.'

'I'll be here at 8.45.'

'I meant what I said yesterday. We can only be friends.' She looked at her shoes and fidgeted anxiously with a button on her coat.

'No strings attached,' I replied, but I was determined to change her mind, however long it took.

'OK… if you're sure. Thanks.'

'My pleasure.'

I leaned towards her, in the way I would to kiss any female friend on the cheek goodbye, though we had never been quite on those terms before. She was taken by surprise. She took a swift step backwards and turned towards her front door. She had left it on the latch and she pushed it open easily.

'I'm not going to give up,' I blurted out. 'I realise you don't feel the same, but I can't just switch my feelings off. I'm here tonight because I care about you. I'm worried about the influence your friends are having over you.' As soon as the words were out of my mouth I realised I should have played it cool. She needed space to discover her own feelings. I was behaving like a lovesick fool. She stepped into the hall and turned to face me.

'Vincent! You wouldn't be good for me. However hard you tried, you would want to change me. You wouldn't be able to help yourself. I need to stay with my own kind.'

'What do you mean, "your own kind"? You keep talking as though you are some sort of space alien.'

'I am an alien… in a way. I am one of the Specials…'

'What *is* that?' I interrupted. 'Some kind of secret society, a religious cult? If Micky and Gavin are your Specials, I'm not impressed. A bunch of nutters, if you ask me.'

'They are good friends; they don't judge.'

'I think you should know that they've been following me, and threatening me and telling me to leave you alone. What the hell are you mixed up in? Did Micky tell you I'm some kind of confidence trickster, that I'm after your money? It's a complete lie!'

'Of course I don't think that, and I'm not mixed up in anything funny. It's what I am… I'm special because… Look! You know why I'm special.'

'Of course I know you're special. That's what I've been trying to tell you.'

'Let me finish. I have special needs. I'm on the spectrum.'

I must have looked as stupid as I felt. She took another deep breath and started again. 'Deep down you've always known. You've just never wanted to accept it. But it's there. It always will be there. We're not kids any more. You've got no excuses now. If you can't handle it, just tell me. Go back to London. Pick up where you left off. I'm not stopping you. But don't tell me you love me and then ignore the biggest part of me.'

Everything clicked into place. I felt as though I'd been punched in the stomach. I rubbed my hand across my mouth and chin and lowered my eyes.

'Do you want me to spell it out for you? I'm autistic; high functioning, but autistic all the same. The Specials are a support group in Elmsford for people with disabilities.'

I didn't want her to guess the images that were floating across my mind: pictures of screaming children, drooling adults, geniuses locked in their own world, rocking, spinning, refusing to talk but able to work out what day of the week it would be on 2nd June 2109. I was gripped with despair. Nothing had been what I thought it was. She wasn't the girl I had fallen in love with. She was somebody else.

'Goodnight, Vincent.' She was resigned.

'I… I…'

'It's OK, you know. I understand. That's how most people feel.'

'I don't know what to say…'

'You don't have to say anything… or continue with the lessons if you don't want to. I appreciate the time you have given me. I think I can speak to your friend now and book a proper driving course.'

'Sarah…'

'I won't forget your help.' It seemed as though she was saying a permanent goodbye. She looked over my shoulder, gazing up at the starry sky, and sighed. 'If it's any consolation, I've always liked you. But I lost your friendship once and I can't face being rejected again. That's what would happen if I allowed this to continue.'

She shut the door in my face. I was left speechless on the path.

Chapter 27

By the time I stumbled into the house, Mum and Dad were asleep. I was wide awake, more awake than I had been for years. Thoughts and emotions whirled in a confusion of disbelief, fury and despair. How had this happened? Was there some malign power hovering over my life, some evil entity who enjoyed my suffering and had decided to trick me into falling in love with an invalid? I'd been lured like a mouse to a trap, only to discover that the sweet reward on offer was incomplete, deficient, lacking in some fundamental way? In-valid. What had I done to deserve another kick in the teeth? Hadn't I had a bellyful of misery already?

Memories of our walks together, our arguments, the feel of her lips on mine came tumbling through my frantic thoughts. How could she be autistic? She was so consistent, real and true. Her strange ways were as familiar to me now as breathing. There must be a mistake. I crept to my room and retrieved my laptop. I carried it quietly back to the shadowy kitchen and plugged it into the phone jack. I Googled 'autism', and began to scroll through the hundreds of different websites.

There was a confusing array of categories: Kanner's autism, Asperger's syndrome, Pathological Demand Avoidance, Pervasive Development Disorder... Most of the characteristics sounded nothing like Sarah. After all, she could talk and hold an intelligent conversation. She lived independently and held down a job. She didn't flap or spin. She wasn't suffering from the kind of catastrophic disability being described on the screen that glowed in front of me. My hopes began to rise. Maybe she was under a misapprehension. Perhaps she had been misdiagnosed as a troubled teenager.

But as I scrolled through the pages, a few characteristics began to resonate. Her shyness, her quirkiness, our strange misunderstandings. She became stressed when under pressure, but didn't we all freak out at times? She liked places that were quiet and empty – the library and the fields for instance, but that was hardly a crime. She took things literally and always told the truth. From our conversations, I imagined her IQ was off the scale. But surely these were strengths rather than weaknesses! She enjoyed theoretical pursuits that other people would find completely tedious... She had narrow, focused interests... She didn't like to be touched... She found it difficult to share her emotions... She could appear distant, cold and inexpressive... My heart sank to my boots.

I considered my options. The first was to walk away. It was what Sarah expected, what everyone else would expect me to do in the circumstances. It was what I would advise myself to do. A stab of pain shot through my chest as I considered this possibility.

My second option was to act as though nothing had happened, to carry on with the driving lessons and dog walks, and remain friends. For this to work, I would have to stifle my feelings and pretend she had never told me that she liked me. There would be moments of awkwardness, topics of conversation we would avoid, but perhaps that was better than the gaping void that would open up before me if I walked away.

My third option was to step into the unknown, to leave the neurotypical world as it was called and join Sarah in her world of theory and logic, a world of honesty and wide, quiet spaces. My friends and family would be shocked and disapproving. My life would change forever. I would be sacrificing any possibility of a return to my frenetic former life in London. She could never join me in my pursuit of money and success, luxury and prestige. Could I do it? Did I want to do it?

I Googled 'John Updike Little Skunk'. The story was in a collection entitled *Pigeon Feathers: And Other Stories*. I decided to buy the book online rather than borrow or order it from the library. I didn't want Sarah to know that I was reading it. It would be with me in a couple of days.

By now the night was nearly over. I slumped forward, resting my head on my arms, too tired to think any more. The next thing I knew, Dad was switching on the kitchen light.

'You're up early!' he exclaimed. I lifted my head and held it between my hands, elbows on the table for support. He stood opposite, tying the belt of his dressing gown. 'What's the matter? Are you still upset about the job interview? There'll be other opportunities.'

'I'm not upset about that any more.' I muttered. I looked at my watch. It was just coming up to 6.30. The sky was grey, the stars fading. 'You're up early too.'

'Yes, I couldn't sleep. Worrying about the tests today.'

Of course! It was the day of Dad's endoscopy and colonoscopy. I had completely forgotten. 'How are you feeling?'

'Don't change the subject, Vincent. What's the matter? I know there's something wrong. Have you even been to bed?'

'No,' I replied dully. A weight of exhaustion pressed down on my head and shoulders. 'I've been up all night.'

'I hope you've not been worrying about me. I can do enough of that for the two of us.'

I dragged myself from my chair and put the kettle on. A strong black coffee was on the cards. I looked across at Dad. He looked dreadful.

'Obviously I'm extremely concerned about you, Dad. I hate seeing you look so thin and tired. And I'm worried for Mum...' Dad stiffened at the thought I might have told her about his hospital appointment. '... though she doesn't know anything about it, of course. But it's something else.'

'What is it, son?'

'Women trouble!' I grimaced, trying to belittle the strength of my feelings.

'Women. There's trouble with them... and trouble without them. Is it that girl in London?'

'No. It's someone here in Elmsford.'

Dad looked surprised. 'Not Lauren Podmore?'

'No . . . How did you know about her?'

'We shop in the supermarket too, you know.'

'Oh! Right!'

'It's a good thing it's not Lauren,' Dad said. 'You've only got to sneeze on one of those Podmore girls and they're pregnant.' He looked thoughtful. 'So it's somebody else in Elmsford. Gracious me, Vincent, you've only been here a few weeks. I thought you were working hard to find a job. It sounds as though you've been keeping yourself busy in another direction entirely.'

'Honestly, Dad, it's not been like that. I haven't spent all my time playing the field, far from it. It's someone I didn't think I really liked... but in fact I've found myself thinking about her almost against my will. She's not my usual type. She's not any kind of type. She's a one-off, completely unique, the kind you either love or loathe...'

'And you've discovered that you care for her.'

'Something like that. She's shown me I need to be more honest about things, more honest with myself. She can see right through all my pretences. She's not impressed by me. I have nothing to offer her that she wants. She's head and shoulders above me in terms of intellect and integrity. You and Mum will think she's completely unsuitable...'

'It doesn't matter what your mother and I think. What matters is what you think and what she thinks. What does she think?'

'She thinks we're incompatible.'

'You've got a problem, then.'

'Yes... And I know she's right. I know it can't work. She's too different from me. There's a kind of fatal flaw in the whole relationship. Whatever I do, I'm stuffed. Life would be difficult with her, maybe impossible, but now I can't bear the thought of living without her.'

'Maybe it would be good for you to have a bit of a challenge for a change. You've always gone for the easy option. I had to fight for your mother, you know. Then again, I was completely certain we were right for each other. Is that the case here?'

'I'm not sure.'

'So what are you going to do?'

I shook my head. 'I don't know. I'm too tired to think straight. I have to walk Elsie and then drive you to the hospital in a couple of hours. We have to make Mum think it's just another ordinary day.'

The kettle boiled and I made myself a drink. Dad wasn't allowed anything but water. By now the sky was turning white and a few brave birds were beginning to chirrup into the frosty dawn.

Chapter 28

I dropped Dad off at the private hospital at half past nine. The Reception was like a swish hotel. The receptionist looked like one of those girls behind the make-up counter of a department store: white uniform, thick foundation, hair sprayed to rigor mortis. Dad agreed to ring me as soon as he was ready to be collected. We shook hands and hugged. I realised again just how thin he had become. I watched as he followed a nurse through a pair of double swing doors. He looked calm but underneath he must have been as scared as me.

I walked slowly back to the car park and called Sarah's home number on my mobile. Her answerphone picked up after a few rings. I hung up, then thought better of it and rang back.

'Hello, Sarah. It's me, Vincent. I really need to speak to you. Please ring back.' I left my mobile number, just in case she didn't have it. She had always been strangely evasive about swapping numbers and I couldn't recall if she had ever written it down.

The caffeine from my morning coffee was wearing off. I put the car seat in the recline position and lay back. It would be irresponsible to drive back to Elmsford in this condition, particularly without Dad keeping me awake from the passenger seat with a constant stream of relationship advice. Physically, mentally and emotionally exhausted, I closed my eyes.

When I awoke it was after 12. My stomach was rumbling and I drove the short distance to the town centre in search of a café. The white tower of St Edmundsbury Cathedral dazzled bright against the blue of the sky. I found my steps drawn through the Abbey Gardens, where as a boy I had fed the ducks along the river and played among the cloister ruins. I followed the signs to the Refectory. I might as well buy a sandwich here as anywhere. I ate a tuna salad sandwich on wholemeal bread, denying myself a slice of coffee walnut sponge. The cloistered air felt too holy for cake.

When I finished my lunch, I wandered into the gift shop. It was packed with stout, grey-haired ladies examining mugs and tea towels. It was impossible to move further forward than the first display table where a collection of cookery books, Sudoku puzzles, tourist guides, poetry anthologies and children's picture books were heaped in colourful piles. I guessed a coach party had just arrived. I restlessly flicked through a glossy coffee table book entitled *The Big Book of Answers*. It had more than 500 pages. On every one there was an answer. Some were negative, some affirmative, all were in different colours and fonts. The blurb dared the reader to ask a question and open the book at random for a response. I thought of Sarah and opened the book. In large red letters the page shouted, 'There will be regrets.' I slammed the book shut and strode into the cathedral, hoping its quiet coldness would clear my troubled thoughts.

I hadn't been inside a church in years. My parents still attended the Anglican church in the village, more out of habit and a sense of social duty, I thought, than any real belief. My footsteps echoed on the stone floor. Embarrassed, I sat in a pew. I looked up at the elaborately painted wooden ceiling, marvelling that simple men had devoted their lives to the construction of such an impractical and costly edifice. Daylight glowed brilliantly through the stained-glass windows. I didn't understand the stories depicted on the coloured facets. The only recognisable person was Christ, pale and humble, outlandishly blond, suffering and dying. Were there any answers for me here? If God had something to say, how would He begin?

I jumped as a man in dark robes swished past the end of the pew. *His* footsteps made no sound as he hurried down the aisle. He looked like a member of staff so I stood up and walked quickly after him.

'Excuse me,' I whispered loudly. He swung round. 'I wonder if you could help. My father's in hospital...' My voice caught and I was unable to continue. The man took my elbow and guided me back to a pew. We sat down next to each other. 'I'm sorry. I didn't mean to take up any of your time. You probably should be doing something...'

'Yes. I should be talking to you. It's Paul, by the way.' He held out his hand.

'Vincent.'

He shook my hand firmly. 'I'm sorry to hear your father's unwell.'

'He's having tests.'

'That must be difficult.'

'Yes.'

I found myself telling him about Mum and Dad and how I had been living with them since losing my job.

'When I was made redundant, everything else went wrong too. And then I met this girl. She started to make me question what I've been doing with my life. At first I found her damned annoying... sorry, I shouldn't have said that.'

'God doesn't have a problem with honesty.'

'She's like an itch you really want to scratch. Do you know that kind of person?'

'I think so.'

'And because of her I can't go back to being the person I was previously, not if I want her in my life. I had a pretty great life, you know, before it all went belly-up. Holidays, fancy restaurants, designer gear...' I put my head in my hands and gazed at the floor. He was wearing a pair of battered trainers under his robes. He must have seen me looking.

'I cycled in this morning. Stupidly forgot to pack my Jesus sandals and socks.'

I glanced up. There was a mischievous smile in his eyes.

'I don't know what's the matter with me. I'm always looking for something more than ordinary life can give. I wouldn't have admitted it then, but even when I was living the dream I found myself asking, "Is this it?"'

'And what is *it*, exactly?'

'It! You know. It! What we all want. Something that's going to make me happy. Something that isn't going to let me down. I thought I'd found it... found her, Sarah... but she isn't what I thought either.'

'Why did you come here, Vincent?'

'I don't like the place my head's in at the moment. I don't know which way to turn. I feel as though I'm going to explode if I don't get some help, some answers.'

'And what is the question?'

'I don't know. I don't know anything any more.'

'Have you thought of telling all this to God?'

'I thought telling you would be the same thing.'

'Not at all. God is always willing to listen, and always ready to speak.'

'I'm not sure I even believe...'

'The problem isn't that God doesn't speak to us. He speaks all the time.'

'Not to me He doesn't.'

'If you speak to Him the way you have spoken to me, He'll say something back. And when He does, wham! You'll know it. The problem is, we often don't want to listen. It's been great talking to you, Vincent.' He stood up. 'You don't realise it, but you are in a very good place indeed. It's not often we come to a point where we see our lives as clearly as you are seeing yours. Your longings are higher than anything this material world can provide. Use that dissatisfaction to search for something that will give your life true meaning and purpose.' We shook hands. 'I hope we can meet again.' He walked down the aisle, bowed briefly before the altar and disappeared through a side door.

Was that it? I was fuming. How often did someone just walk in off the street, go into a church and ask a priest for help? Surely he should have told me what to do? Wasn't that the church's job, to tell people how to live their lives? The guy had completely blown it! There had to be some kind of complaints procedure, someone higher up the ecclesial ladder I could speak to about the way I'd been treated. I ranted inside my head for some minutes, before realising I was doing what the priest had suggested. I was talking to God.

The words were coming out all wrong, more a monologue of anger and worries and longings, a desperate belief that if I wished for something hard enough it had to come true.

Phrases came back from my Sunday school days, a vague memory about asking and seeking and knocking. I hadn't bothered God recently, not about my job, nor about my flat or Chloe. Perhaps He owed me a favour. I wanted Dad to be well and that the doctors wouldn't find anything horrible growing inside him. Images from the past flashed across my mind, memories of when he had been young and clean-shaven, his hair brown rather than white, his eyes alight with laughter as we played football together or sat on the riverbank waiting for a fish to bite.

My mind wandered to Sarah. Sarah in the library, Sarah in the fields with Bruce, Sarah talking intensely about the possibility of a better world if only people could overcome their addiction to consumerism. I wanted her to be normal, whatever that meant, and to love me.

I raised my head from my hands. I had put my case. Now it was time for God to answer. I watched as the coach party of elderly ladies shuffled around the edge of the building, reading the memorial plaques and consulting their newly purchased guidebooks. I smiled inwardly at their enthusiasm. Libraries and churches were alike in many ways, places where the elderly, the unemployed, the dispossessed could search for truth and a sense of community. I shuffled my feet. Libraries might be somewhere warm to sit on a cold afternoon, but the same couldn't be said for St Edmundsbury Cathedral. The enormity of the space above my head was chilling in itself. The sun was now descending. My breath left a faint trace of vapour on the air, like incense, like a prayer.

I stood up, disappointed. On my way out I passed the gift shop. This time it was empty. *The Big Book of Answers* called to me from the display table. What would happen if I opened the pages again? Would I receive the same answer as before? The risk was too great. Another book caught my eye. It was called *The Message*, and claimed to be the Bible in contemporary language. Eyes closed, I opened it and placed my finger on a page. When I opened my eyes my finger was on a passage entitled 'The Very Tree of Life'. I read it eagerly.

You're blessed when you meet Lady Wisdom,
when you make friends with Madame Insight.
She's worth far more than money in the bank;
her friendship is better than a big salary.
Her value exceeds all the trappings of wealth;
nothing you could wish for holds a candle to her.
With one hand she gives long life,
with the other she confers recognition.
Her manner is beautiful
her life wonderfully complete.
She's the very Tree of Life to those who embrace her.
Hold her tight – and be blessed!

A great peace settled upon me. I had made my decision.

Chapter 29

Dad looked washed out and wobbly when I collected him from the hospital. He sat in the front passenger seat, his eyes closed, not talking until we reached the dual carriageway and I no longer had to concentrate on the afternoon school traffic. He filled me in briefly with details of the procedure. They hadn't found anything sinister, he reported. He would be told the results of the biopsies and blood tests in about ten days' time.

'Dad, do you accept me for who I am?'

'Where did that suddenly come from? Of course I do.' He cleared his throat. 'You know I love you. Perhaps I don't say it enough.'

'I know you love me, but that's different to accepting someone. Parents can love their children but still want to change them.'

'What's the matter?'

'I think I've been a bit of a disappointment to you, not just since the redundancy thing but for a few years now.'

'Your mother and I are very proud of you...'

'But?' I asked, sensing a hesitation.

'We've been worried... but not disappointed.'

'Why worried?'

'We never doubted that you worked very hard at your job. You seemed to be doing well in your career before this spot of bother. But we were concerned about your motives.'

'My motives for working hard? Surely that's obvious – to get on in life and earn good money. Isn't that what everybody wants?'

'Yes... and no. You didn't seem to be enjoying the pressure, and you weren't building a future for yourself. To us it looked as though you were trying too hard to impress other people. All those extravagant presents you used to give to your girlfriends, that last one in particular. You asked whether I accept you. Perhaps the better question is, "Do you accept yourself?"'

'You're not the first person who's asked me that.'

'Really? Who else has said it? Was it this girl you like?'

'Yes.' I told him about my day in Bury and, with a little embarrassment, mentioned the incident with the Bible.

'It's not good practice to take passages of Scripture out of context like that,' he warned. 'The Bible's not a giant fortune cookie or a horoscope. I'm certain whatever passage you read had absolutely nothing to do with this woman friend of yours. It was talking about the wisdom of God. You were reading into it what you wanted to see. It confirmed what you already wanted.'

'Isn't that a good enough answer? I didn't know what I wanted before then. I was confused. Now I'm going to talk to her, make her see that I accept and love her for who she is.'

'You can't force someone to love you, son. I don't want to see you get hurt. If I remember rightly you felt pretty strongly about Chloe a few months back. Are you sure it's your heart that's telling you this girl's the one and not another part of your anatomy?'

'OK. I admit I've fallen physically for women in the past.' I shifted uncomfortably in my seat. 'That's not the case here. I've only become… attracted to her since I've begun to value her as a friend.'

'Obviously friendship is a very good basis for a relationship. That's what's kept your mother and I together all these years. But you do need to make sure you're not on the rebound. This all seems to have happened rather quickly. Who is this girl? Do I know her? Did you meet her in that nightclub when you went out with Jimmy?'

'No, I didn't meet her there. I just bumped into her, really, and it went from there.' I wasn't ready to tell him it was the odd girl from the library. 'My relationship with Chloe cooled a while ago. I wasn't willing to admit it, not with losing my job and flat and everything. It was all too much to take in at once.'

'What will you do if she doesn't feel the same about you?'

'I can't think about that.'

'I guess you had better talk to her,' Dad concluded. 'Good luck.'

'Thanks. I'll need it.'

Once I had dropped him back home, I drove past the bungalow. All the lights were off. I knocked on the door but there was no sign of Bruce. Perhaps they were on a walk. Perhaps she had been out all day and hadn't bothered to listen to her telephone messages yet. I sat outside in the car for about half an hour before deciding I was becoming a little obsessive, particularly as this wasn't the first time I had camped outside her door. I needed to get home for dinner. I didn't want Mum asking questions. I knew Dad would keep our conversation to himself, but he needed moral support and some diversionary tactics if he were to keep his hospital visit a secret from Mum.

My phone remained stubbornly silent throughout dinner. I covered my restlessness and Dad's sickly pallor as much as I could by keeping Mum engaged in a lengthy discussion about Saturday's fundraiser.

'Goodness, Vincent, what's brought on all this interest? What's the matter, Derek? Do you feel sick again?'

Dad pushed his food slowly around the plate. 'I'm fine. I just haven't got my appetite back since that tummy bug.'

'Perhaps I should ring the doctor again.'

'I'm interested because Pat filled me in on what's going on,' I interrupted, 'and because it's for a good cause. It sounds like you and Dad have worked very hard. I didn't realise it would be such a big event. Pat's son Timothy is involved too, so the charity must be professionally run. What does it do, exactly?'

'It's a small charity set up to raise money for children in Togo. Heather Hutchins spent a year there as part of her French language degree, working for a relief agency. They speak French in Togo, you know. She was so struck by the plight of the children, particularly disabled children, that she came back to the UK and started fundraising among her friends.'

'She's been sending money out there for years, particularly to help with a disability school,' Dad said.

'They have kids out there with cerebral palsy, Down's syndrome, autism, learning disabilities… terrible physical and behavioural conditions. They get practically no support from the authorities. Of course, there's the stigma and enormous ignorance. The parents often think it's some kind of curse on the family, or that the child is possessed by demons. Others think the parents have sold the child's soul for money.'

I nodded. No wonder Sarah was helping with the fundraiser. The plight of autistic children in Africa must hit her particularly hard.

'Pat organised a quiz night last year,' Mum continued. 'It was great fun. We raised more than £300. Simon and Liz did the questions and Simon was the quiz master. We brought our own drinks and nibbles and paid £5 a head. Liz and I got together a kickboxing team, and your Dad was on the Gardener's Club team. Even some of the lads from the local football team came, dressed up in their football strips. Everyone agreed it was a great success.'

'Yes,' Dad said his voice heavy with irony, 'shame about the typing mistakes on the anagram question sheet!'

'Liz was mortified,' Mum admitted, 'but nobody else minded.'

'The team from the Scrabble Club were pretty hacked off,' Dad reminded her.

'Anyway, that's in the past. We need all the help we can get at *this* fundraiser. Are you going to be able to help your father on the car-washing team? Looking at him, he needs all the help he can get!' She laughed, but glancing across at Dad's strained face she became serious again. 'Are you sure you're all right?'

'Just a little tired. I think I'll go to bed. It's been a long day.'

'You do look peaky. You get in your pyjamas, and I'll bring you up a cut of tea once I've cleared the supper things.'

Mum helped him upstairs and then busied herself in the kitchen. Suddenly I wasn't seeing them as my parents any more but as two people, separate and distinct from me, who were clinging to each other as the darkness approached. What looked so stifling in my late teens and early twenties now appeared to be a small but resilient shelter in the face of a relentless storm. But I was on the outside… an outsider, as Sarah pointed out. I could see clearly what I had been unable to see before. The central relationship in this home had been between Mum and Dad; it hadn't been about me. I was part of the family, but I could detach and reattach myself as I pleased. They, on the other hand, would remain here facing the endless necessary boredoms and duties of life, then illness and death. I had chosen glamour and fun and sex, sniffing disparagingly at their provincial commitments. Mum and Dad had invested their time and energy in things that were real and lasting – a steady marriage and constant friendships. We might all be suffering in our different ways, but I was suffering alone, reaping a harvest of self-centredness… self-interestedness… self-absorption… my own personal brand of autism.

I went up to my room and flopped on the bed. I was physically and emotionally exhausted. So much had happened since Valentine's Day. My argument with Jimmy. The realisation that I loved Sarah. My discovery of her autism. My decision to love her whatever the consequences. In a matter of weeks my life had undergone a complete reversal. I no longer worked for a ruthless rip-off merchant. I'd split from a girl with whom I had no real sympathy or affection. I'd moved from London to live with the people who knew and loved me best. I now had the opportunity of a completely fresh start. I was beginning to think the positives outweighed the negatives.

But what was the point of a fresh start without Sarah? Why hadn't she rung me back? Where was she? I remembered the look on her face when she had told me about her autism. She assumed I would walk away from her, yet there wasn't a trace of defensiveness or resentment in her sad expression. She had probably been down this path many times before – labelled and judged, ridiculed and avoided. How much more difficult her life had been than mine. Tomorrow I would sit outside her bungalow for as long as it took to speak to her. I would bombard her with messages until she returned my calls. I had to convince her that I accepted her unconditionally, as she accepted me. With her face before me, I fell into an exhausted and dreamless sleep.

*****

Even though I lingered longer than Elsie appreciated, there wasn't a sign of Sarah in the fields the next morning. I was removing Dad's muddy wellington boots when the front doorbell rang. It was the postman with a package addressed to me. I tore open the protective cardboard case to find my copy of *Pigeon Feathers: And Other Stories* by John Updike. I carried it through to the kitchen and sat down at the table with a cup of coffee, and started to read 'Should Wizard Hit Mommy?'

It was a disquieting story, filled with suppressed rage and tension. It seemed as though everyone was being controlled and judged by everyone else. The little skunk longed to be popular, but was punished for wanting to smell of roses and forced by his mother to return to being a proper skunk. The ending was ambiguous. Though there was a suggestion that his friends accepted him eventually, he was left in an ugly middle position unable to please both family and friends. I couldn't turn back the clock and become that overweight adolescent again, even if I wanted to. There had to be another way, somewhere between the smell of skunk and the smell of roses.

I plugged in my laptop and went through the motions of checking my emails, Facebook page, Twitter account and the usual job sites, but my heart wasn't in it. I was caught in the middle of a plot I didn't like, desperate for a happy ending. What would smelling like a skunk look like? Surely I didn't have to become a pig farmer or quantity surveyor to be true to my roots.

The latest edition of the *Bury Free Press* was in a pile of papers on the kitchen table. I pulled it towards me and turned to the back. In between the cars for sale and the personal advertisements was a small jobs section. I ran my eye down the page. Office assistant, clinical nurse, clerk to the parish council, Children's Services worker, casual drivers, care assistant, midday supervisor at the primary school in the next village, sheet metal worker, optical assistant. Apart from the casual drivers wanted by a local car rental office, I was hopelessly unqualified for any of the positions. I threw the paper on the floor, disheartened.

Until I got a new job, I would have to start by making small manageable changes to my life. Eleanor Penny's saying, 'Always tell the truth, but don't always be telling the truth' would be a good start. I would try to be honest in future, and examine my motives. I would do my best to be courteous to everyone, not just those who could be useful to me. I would stop projecting a false image to impress others. Dad had told me long ago that a man's character is built brick by brick through the small decisions he makes in life; integrity, like muscles, must be exercised every day. I would use Sarah and my family as yardsticks. I no longer trusted my own instincts. I would judge the rightness of my actions by imagining whether they would be proud of me, or ashamed.

Ultimately I wouldn't be changing for my parents, for Sarah or for any future employer. That would be to make the same mistake again, becoming somebody else to please others. I needed to be more me. I hoped Sarah would give me a second chance. My longing to see her gnawed at me from the inside. I wanted to tell her what I had decided about myself and admit the feelings she had begun to arouse in me. I imagined myself holding her in my arms, kissing her and hearing her sigh my name. I wanted to tell her that she was beautiful and unique and mysterious. I wanted to spend the rest of my life discovering everything about her. I imagined the long walks we would take and the life of intimacy we could build together.

But she hadn't rung back. I had moved too quickly. I needed to make her feel comfortable again. I would make myself indispensable. I would learn all I could about autism. I would join the Specials, I would study semiwhatsits if that was what it took. I would put her first. I would be her friend.

I gritted my teeth and opened a new document on my laptop. I began to draft out a new CV, one that presented a different Vincent Stevens. First, an inventory of my strengths and weaknesses. Instead of trying to fit myself to a job, I would find a job that fitted me, even if I ended up stacking shelves in the supermarket. What was I good at? What did I enjoy?

I was good at explaining things and I liked helping people. Teaching Sarah to drive had taught me that much. I wasn't good with confrontation unless my back was to the wall. I was a bit of a pleaser. I liked sales and I understood a balance sheet. I preferred to be out and about meeting new people rather than sitting in an office all day. Although I hated to admit it, I had begun to enjoy the peace and quiet of village life and the domestic jobs around the house.

The front doorbell rang again. To my surprise, Harry the mouse man was standing on the front step. I had forgotten we had arranged a second appointment. His fixed price for two visits had been £110. He would throw in a third for free if the situation hadn't been resolved. He was confident this would not be unnecessary. We went into the garage to check the traps and bait trays.

'Let's see what the little monsters have been up to, shall we?' he said. The trays were all empty. There was a small body in one of the traps.

'If they've eaten all that stuff, they're well and truly stuffed!' He poked behind a few old pots with the garden cane I had used to flush out that first mouse in the kitchen. 'You'll probably never find the bodies. They just disappear... crumble to dust.'

'How will we know if they've finally gone?'

'You could always put a tasty morsel out tonight, a bit of cheese or bread, and see if it's gone in the morning. I think you'll find my stuff will have done the trick.' He tapped the side of his nose with his finger. 'And you can trust me to be discreet. Your mum will never know what's gone on here between the two of us. I've not been working with vermin all my life without learning to be discreet. You'd be surprised what some people in this village have lurking in their cupboards. Lauren will be discreet an' all. My girl knows how to keep a secret.'

'Lauren!' I exclaimed. 'Lauren from the supermarket is your daughter?'

'Of course she is,' he replied. 'Didn't she tell you?'

'No.' My mind frantically thought back to our date at the Tithe Barn. She had talked about her sisters, but not her parents.

'I'm not surprised. She doesn't like what I do for a living. Doesn't like anything unpleasant. She dresses everything up in pink bows and white fluff, bless her.' He winked. 'And don't think I don't know you took her out for dinner! Not much goes on in that girl's life without me knowing. If you want me to pass on your best wishes or anything else, I'd be glad to do it. Like I've always said, she'll be a good catch for someone one of these days. If you're interested, you'd better hurry.'

'I think there's been a...'

'She'll cheer you up, will Lauren. Both my other girls' blokes are on benefits. You've nothing to feel ashamed of, not with the government we've got at the moment. Any son-in-law of mine is welcome to come into the business with me, if he's got the stomach for it. Like death and taxes, there'll always be vermin. It's a recession-proof industry.'

Alarm bells were ringing. My mind was racing ahead. Sarah's mother had died unexpectedly. Her body had been found in a cupboard. Lauren had been her carer. Lauren's father had large quantities of mouse and rat poison in his shed. Lauren had used the phrase 'happy despatch' to Sarah. Worst of all, Lauren had been in my nana's house!

'Don't look so worried. You've got yourself all in a sweat over these mice for nothing. You can always trust a Podmore to get rid of your problems for you. We knock 'em dead!'

'I've just remembered, Mr Podmore – Harry – I've got to be somewhere in five minutes...'

'I've about finished anyway. Keep your dog out of the garage, in case there are any traces of poison left. We don't want a tragic accident, do we?'

'No, we don't,' I whispered.

*****

I raced round to Nana's place. I found her sitting in her chair, sucking toffees and watching an American made-for-TV movie. I quickly scanned the kitchen for anything suspicious, looking in all the packets and jars for the familiar blue pellets. I checked Nana's pills against Mum's checklist stuck on the fridge door. She was up to date; there were neither too many nor too few in the bottle. I opened drawers and cupboards, feeling increasingly stupid. Nothing!

'What are you doing in there, Reggie?' Nana called from her chair.

'Nothing, Nana. Just making sure you have everything you need. Are you going to the fundraiser tomorrow?' I asked as a distraction.

'Going? Going where?'

'To the village hall. Mum and Dad said they would collect you. They're raising money for children in Africa. '

'I am *not* going to Africa! *Dancing on Ice* will be on the telly.'

'No, Nana... the village hall. It will be a nice little outing for you, and there's a cake stall. Mum's baking a banana cake and one of her fruit loaves.'

'I've got too much to do here to go out gallivanting with you. There's the hoovering for a start...'

Reassured there was nothing poisonous in the kitchen, and excusing myself to go to the toilet, I bounded upstairs and checked the bathroom, even looking inside the tube of denture-cleaning tablets. In the bedroom, I unscrewed the bottle of indigestion medicine by Nana's bed, put the end of my finger inside and tasted the chalky peppermint mixture. Again, all seemed fine. I breathed a sigh of relief. Lauren wouldn't be setting foot in Nana's home again if I had any say in the matter. I poked my head around the living room door.

'If you're OK, Nana, I'd better be off.'

'All right then, lovey, and make sure you bring your beautiful bride with you next time,' she called as I let myself out of the front door.

Chapter 30

On arriving at the fundraiser, I discovered there were two teams of car washers. Simon Addington had taken Dad's place at the last minute. His partner was the barman from the Railway Tavern. To my horror I had been teamed up with the dwarf. He was introduced as Big Micky without a trace of sarcasm. I turned my back on him and started on the first vehicle.

There was a steady stream of cars into the car park. We were charging £5 a wash. Each car took about 15 minutes. After an hour we had washed four cars and I had concluded it was the hardest £20 I had ever earned. If I could have turned the clocks back, I would have donated the £20 and cut out all the aggravation.

The warm soapy liquid soon cooled. My hands turned red and raw in the icy wind whistling across the car park. Micky worked on the other side of the vehicle, silent and out of sight. An appropriate demarcation of work would have been for him to tackle the wheels and doors, and for me to wash the windows and roof. I didn't want to make any concessions, but unless I wanted to carry on doing my side plus half of his I would have to work on our communication issues. Unfortunately, working as a team meant we were sometimes on the same side of the car.

'Sarah's told you about herself?' he said at last.

'Yes.'

'It doesn't bother you?'

'No!'

'That makes me all the more suspicious of your motives.'

'You can think what you like. All that matters is what Sarah thinks.'

'She doesn't know what she thinks!'

'Don't be so patronising. Who put you in charge of things, anyway?'

'I'm the chairperson of the Specials. That means I take a close interest in my members. I've been battling ignorance, discrimination and worse all my life. I'm not scared of anything any more, least of all a pretty boy like you. I'm quite prepared to behave as outrageously as necessary to show you up for what you are.' He rubbed the wheel arch vigorously.

'I'm not the bad guy here, all right?'

'If you really cared about Sarah, you would realise the best thing you can do for her is leave her alone. She's taken a long time to reach a place of equilibrium. Don't spoil it now!'

'I'm not spoiling anything. I want to make things better.'

'Better for who?'

'For Sarah… for both of us.'

'You're a slick operator. Nothing else. You're thinking only of yourself. What makes you think you would be any good for her?'

'Because I love her. That must count for something. Surely it's better to be loved than not loved.'

'It depends how conditional your love is… and what you expect in return.'

'I'm not expecting anything at this point in time. But I know I can help her. She's an intelligent woman. With the right support she could get some National Vocational Qualifications or something, get a more satisfying job.'

'What are you talking about?' he spluttered in disgust. 'NVQs! That shows how much you know about Sarah. She's got a First from Cambridge in English Literature and Linguistics. She has no problem learning. It's real life that's the difficulty.' He laughed at the expression on my face. 'You didn't know that, did you?'

I sloshed my sponge back into the bucket and wiped the windscreen of a Nissan Micra. Suddenly her desire to drive to Cambridge became clear. It was her old stomping ground. Dropping out of school at 15 hadn't held her back academically at all. Why hadn't she mentioned her university days? Was she being deliberately secretive? Perhaps she didn't set much store by the plaudits and honours of this world. Certainly if I had been to Cambridge I would have been dropping that fact into every other conversation, particularly if I had gained a First. Her autism had been a difficult pill to swallow. This made her even more unattainable.

'I don't know why we're even discussing Sarah,' I growled. 'Being in charge of some kind of support group doesn't give you the right to poke your nose into the private lives of your members…' A thought occurred to me, '… unless your interest is a little more personal too.'

His face turned red. A vein throbbed in his neck. 'My only concern is Sarah's well-being. We'll be the ones to pick up the pieces when you move on. The Specials are much more than a support group for Sarah. We're the only family she's got.' Angry white spittle collected at the corners of his mouth.

'She has me now. And I'm not going anywhere. I won't be bullied or intimidated by your gang of misfits. Stop following me. Keep out of my way. You're just a jumped-up little twerp on a power trip.'

'I'm already on the edge. Don't push me over!' he shouted. 'I could have you in a lockdown position in 30 seconds.'

'You and whose army? Talk about overcompensating!' I sneered. He took a step towards me, his face suffused with rage.

'What did you say?'

'You heard me,' I said. 'Talk about over compensating.'" He took another menacing step forwards, his hands clenched into fists at his side. I remembered how easily he had felled Gavin. Without thinking, I upturned my bucket of dirty water on his head.

*****

My shift at the car wash ended at 11.30. I went into the toilets to run my hands under the hot tap, regaining some feeling in my fingers. Big Micky had gone home to change. I had washed the last few cars on my own.

The village hall was crowded. People were shuffling down narrow aisles between the rows of stalls. I would have to weave down the whole length of the room to reach the hatch where the teas and coffees were being served. I recognised the girl sitting behind the toy stall as the driver of the mobility scooter. Liz Addington was sorting through a pile of second-hand clothes. I spotted the bookstall, but there was no sign of Sarah. Instead, Gavin was scratching his beard and shifting from side to side behind the table.

Suddenly Sarah stood up. She must have been rummaging underneath. She handed a paperback book to a woman waiting on the other side of the table with her purse in her hand. I edged towards her, my progress hampered by the people browsing in front.

The room was noisy. People were talking and laughing. Children were shrieking and pushing between the adults. Somewhere a baby was crying. When I eventually reached the bookstall I had to shout for Sarah to hear me.

'Can you recommend any good books?'

'What do you like to read?' she replied, expressionless.

'Thrillers, action adventure, that sort of thing.'

She pointed towards a box at the end of the table. The spines were black and grey and scarlet, completely unlike the books in the box the lady next to me was looking at with their pastel colours and pictures of flowers and sunsets on the front. Gavin stood behind a large box of factual titles: cookery books, encyclopaedias, books about planes and cars, a tatty copy of *Fowler's Modern English Usage*. I wondered if he had found his railway book, but decided it would be undiplomatic to ask. I saw the box of books I had donated. The adventure books from the bottom of my wardrobe.

It wasn't possible to talk to Sarah further. The crush of people forced me forward. I quickly bought a book and continued the slow shuffle towards the hatch, where I purchased a cup of coffee and a jam doughnut. I sat down at a table covered with a white paper tablecloth. A bowl of sugar sachets and a cup of plastic teaspoons had been laid in the middle. I pushed a used paper plate and half-finished cup of tea to one side.

I sipped my drink slowly. The door to a smaller side room swung open. Several hot and sweaty people emerged amidst a swirl of pulsing Latin American music. As the door thudded shut, I noticed the sign advertising Zumba taster sessions every half hour for £2 a time. Mum would be in there with her teacher, showing the novices how it was done.

My eyes turned back to the stalls in front of me. With a shock I recognised Jimmy and Catrina easing down an aisle with a young girl between them. They stopped by the toy stall. Jimmy put his hand in his pocket and bought the child some kind of stuffed animal.

I hadn't spoken to Jimmy since the night of the flat tyre. I had ignored his phone calls and text messages. I discovered he had been driving without insurance or a valid MOT as well as without a tax disc and spare tyre. His case would be up before the magistrates' court in a few weeks' time. I felt little sympathy.

Any minute now he would reach the bookstall and would be face to face with Sarah. There was nothing I could do to stop the encounter. In any case, intervention on my part might only make matters worse. With any luck, they would ignore each other. I gulped down the rest of my coffee and stuffed the last piece of doughnut in my mouth, hoping to avoid an encounter with Jimmy if at all possible. As I pushed back my chair, Pat Hutchins approached my table, clipboard in hand.

'Vincent! I'm so glad you could make it. I saw your name on the car-washing rota. Good boy!' She gave a sly smile. 'I'm glad you've made a new friend in the village. She's a sweet girl, you know... often misunderstood, but very sweet all the same. She's had some *terrible* tragedies in her life, of course, losing both parents.' She lowered her voice. 'She doesn't like to talk about it, which is quite understandable, but her mother passed away in strange circumstances. There had to be an inquest! At the time we were all very shocked. Elmsford doesn't go in for inquests as a general rule. But that was Eleanor all over, doing things the unconventional way.'

'Was there an autopsy?' I replied disingenuously. This was too good an opportunity to miss. How else was I to discover what had happened without causing Sarah further distress? And if I were deep in conversation with Pat, Jimmy would be less likely to approach.

'Gracious me! I hope not. What a horrible thought! There was no need for any of *that*. She only banged her head, after all. There was no question of foul play.' She stepped forward, standing very close, her eyes darting from left to right, before whispering, 'It was just the strange way it happened. The coroner said it was accidental death. We were all very relieved. Though what she was doing sitting in the larder in the first place, I really don't know!'

'She was in the larder?' I asked, anxious to squeeze as much information as I could from the conversation.

'Yes. Can you believe it? Lauren Podmore, her carer – a very nice girl, by the way, you probably know her, she works in the supermarket – Lauren told me that Eleanor used to sit in the old larder, with the radio on and a blanket wrapped around her when the pain got very bad. Personally I would have preferred a nice warm bed. She would take a bottle of sherry in with her.' She grasped the collar of my coat and pulled me down to her level. 'Eleanor was very fond of a glass of sherry. I remember *that* from the Women's Institute Turkey and Tinsel Supper the year before last. The coroner decided she had tripped on the blanket when getting off the stool – it was one of those high, wobbly ones – and cracked her head on the door. By the time they found her she had been on the floor for some hours. They took her to hospital, but it was too late. She never regained consciousness. Sarah was heartbroken.'

My head was spinning. There was a logical explanation for everything. I had been worrying about Sarah's innocence and Nana's safety for nothing. There was no dark angel promising care but delivering death. There had been no suicide, assisted or not. Just a frail woman tripping in the darkness, returning from an interlude of private agony and wanting to show a brave face to her daughter. I felt guilty and ashamed.

'Anyway, it's very nice she has a friend now,' Pat released me from her grasp. 'I wouldn't have thought she was your type. But that's none of my business. You must talk to Timothy. I'm sure he will remember you. Timothy!' she shouted, waving frantically at a balding man with spectacles standing awkwardly by the Guess the Weight of the Cake table. He turned after her third call and started to make his way over.

So this was the whizz-kid from Canary Wharf! He looked nothing like the boy I remembered from primary school; older than me by a couple of years, he had been football-mad and a bit of a practical joker.

'Timothy, you remember Vincent Stevens. He was in the same class as Heather at Elmsford Primary.' We shook hands. 'I've told Timothy all about you, and how lucky your parents are to have you living at home with them. Such a treat!'

'Mum!' he chided wearily. No doubt this was a sore point. 'I heard you were back in the village, Vincent. I understand you've been let go. What field of work are you in?'

'Financial sales,' I replied grudgingly, not at all pleased he knew my business.

'Really!' he began, but I was distracted by the sight of Jimmy, Catrina and the girl standing at the bookstall and talking to Sarah. It looked as though Jimmy was introducing Catrina. Sarah bent down to the little girl and pointed to some books at one end of the stall. I wished I could hear what they were saying. Unexpectedly the three adults began to laugh.

'... so email your CV to me and I'll see what I can do.'

I was brought back to the present by Timothy holding out his hand to me. I looked down. He was offering a small white card.

'Great... that's... thanks,' I said, trying to hide my surprise. He sat down at the table. My wish to escape Jimmy had now turned into a longing to return to the bookstall to find out what was going on; social protocol forced me to sit down and continue the conversation with Timothy.

We talked a little of my previous job. I didn't try to big up my experience or qualifications. I kept everything brief and to the point, which I think he appreciated. I also talked about the need for integrity and the importance of making sure that financial products were right for the

268

client. And I believed every word I said. He nodded now and then and asked intelligent questions. I gradually found myself warming to him.

Simon Addington sat at a neighbouring table, clutching a hot drink. The front of his anorak was covered in dark splashes from washing the cars. His moustache hadn't been trimmed for a while, and there was a day's stubble on his chin. Mum, Dad and Nana joined him almost immediately, Mum mopping her flushed face with a towel and carrying a large glass of water to help cool her down after her Zumba session. Dad parked Nana's lightweight wheelchair by their table. Mum gave me a little wave.

I introduced Timothy to Simon across the tables. He remembered my parents so no formal introductions were necessary there. Nana gazed around the room, confused amazement on her face. Dad, Simon and Timothy struck up a conversation about Timothy's Porsche, newly washed and gleaming in the car park. My thoughts returned to Sarah.

I had spoken to her earlier that morning as we drove together to the village hall. She had been surprised to see me waiting outside her bungalow as previously arranged. In fact, I had been sitting outside her house since eight o'clock in case she decided to walk or take the bus rather than hang around for me. Now I knew about her autism, she probably thought I would renege on my offer of a lift.

Acute anxiety had gripped me as I waited for her to open the door. Even though I told myself I accepted her for who she was, I dreaded the possibility I might react differently towards her now I knew the truth. Would we feel awkward with each other? If so, would she misinterpret any embarrassment on my part as a lessening of my feelings, or a prejudice against her condition? Should I refer to her disclosure or pretend it never happened? My heart was stuttering even before she appeared in the porch at 8.20.

It was obvious she had decided to make her own way to the fundraiser. So much for her opinion of me! She fumbled with her keys as she double-locked the front door and shouted something through the letter box to Bruce, who was objecting loudly to her departure. My heart did another flip as she walked down the path, putting her keys into an inner pocket of her large floppy tote bag.

She was wearing her long black winter coat, heavy boots and the green bobble hat with matching seaweed scarf. I couldn't control the smile which stretched across my face. My chest swelled with a cascade of emotions – hope, fear, excitement, and an uncharacteristic and overwhelming desire to protect her from anything that might cause her anxiety or harm.

Why had it taken so long for me to appreciate her subtle beauty? If I hadn't been so blinded by stereotypes of women in magazines and on TV, I might have been able to see immediately the loveliness beneath the bizarre clothing and tousled hair.

She stopped in her tracks when she saw me getting out of the car. Her forehead wrinkled and her eyes flitted from my face to her feet. Any last doubts disappeared as I strode towards her. Remembering her personal space rule, I planted myself three feet away, blocking her path.

'Good morning,' I breathed. 'You look lovely.'

'What!' she exclaimed, glancing up.

'I'm complimenting you on your appearance.'

She looked down at her coat and boots. 'Oh!'

'Let's get going.' I ushered her forward before she had time to think. 'Do you want to drive, or shall I?'

'You.' I noticed her hands were shaking. I walked round to the passenger side and opened the door, helping her in as though she were a fragile and priceless treasure.

'I'm autistic, not incapable!' she exclaimed.

Our conversation on the way to the village hall had not been easy. I told her I cared for her and that her autism wasn't an issue. I had decided to stay in Elmsford. Her reply had been stinging.

'It might not be an issue for you, but my autism is an issue for me! It's not all about you and what you would be sacrificing by staying here. I don't want you to feel sorry for me. I'm one of the lucky ones. There are plenty of women on the spectrum who haven't been diagnosed because the so called "experts" think it only affects men. Autistic women present differently. We are more sociable and less likely to have obsessive interests, in the same way "normal" women differ from men. At least I understand myself and can manage my anxieties. Who knows where I would be without the support I received from my mother and the Specials? Probably suffering mental health issues such as anorexia or depression, or self-harming like so many autistic girls.' She drew in a deep breath. I was just about to say something when she said, 'You must have known.'

'I didn't know.'

'How could you not know? I've been dropping enough hints. Surely you knew back in school I was different? I thought you found out and that was why you stopped wanting to be my friend.'

'I didn't know. Well, maybe on some deep level I knew. But I had big plans back then. I wanted to get out of Elmsford. Make a success of my life. If I had allowed myself to fall in love with you, none of that could have happened. I would have stayed here and probably resented you for it. I squashed the feelings I had and blanked out the reason for squashing them. But I can't do that any longer. Now I know there's nothing in the world that I want more than you.'

'You think you are doing me a favour by staying. Deep down you think I should be grateful you care. I'm difficult and annoying. Probably no one else would have me. But you can be difficult and annoying too.'

'I know that.'

'Neurotypicals are exhausting to be with. They are unreliable, unpredictable, illogical, manipulative and overly emotional. They appear charming but have very underdeveloped consciences. They see nothing wrong with white lies, believing the means justifies the end. They will often choose the expedient path over the right path and congratulate themselves on their choices! They don't speak in a straightforward, clearly understood way. Their motives are often hidden, from themselves as well as from others. They are dishonest about who they are and what they want. They care too much about appearances. They want to be touching and pushing and holding all the time, with no regard for other people's personal space. They are too loud and too fast and…'

'OK, OK, that's enough. I get the picture.' I was hurt by the vehemence of her argument. But she didn't stop.

'… and yet we are supposed to be the ones to change, to fit into your world, because we are in the minority. But we can't stop being what we are. It's impossible. That's why we are labelled disabled. But tell me, what is more valuable, being able to chat sporadically about nothing in particular, or being able to talk with a high degree of accuracy and expertise on a particular subject, like Gavin telling us about the local bus timetable? Neither group is right or wrong, and yet the latter are considered inferior or lacking in some way. I am only disabled because I am not like you.'

'I don't want you to be like me. I don't like me very much. I never want you to change.'

271

The sweet lemon scent of her hair reminded me of our kiss. As I glanced across at her hands twisting in her lap, I wanted nothing more than to take one of them in mine. But I was driving and she continued with her train of thought as if I hadn't spoken.

'I don't *feel* disabled. Just because I'm different doesn't make me deficient or impaired. When I was younger I was told I wouldn't ever be able to hold down a job or live independently or have satisfactory friendships. They were all wrong.'

'Of course they were wrong. You *can* have relationships, I know you can. Look at us! Our friendship is so special. I know we can make it work.'

'I don't have much experience when it comes to relationships, but I would imagine you have to have things in common, have the same goals and values...'

'Let me prove to you that we can be good together. Give me the chance to show you. I will never let you down. You said you cared for me when we were at school.'

'Yes. I liked you then because you had a kind, sensitive heart. But sometimes having a kind heart isn't enough. Kind deeds are required too. It's not necessary to *be* strong. Sometimes it's enough just to *feel* strong, to face things head-on even if you know you can't fight them. Sometimes you have to stand alone, with nothing to help you but your own head and your own heart...'

'But you don't have to be alone. We're 30 years of age –'

'I'm 31,' she interrupted.

'OK, OK, you're 31!' The convention of keeping one's age secret obviously didn't apply in her case. 'What I'm trying to say is that we're not spring chickens any more. This could be a real chance for both of us for happiness. I don't want to invest in another emotionally draining relationship like the one I had with Chloe. I want to be with you. If this doesn't work, then I think I'll give up and spend my life alone. I think you might be the same.'

She snorted. 'You could never be on your own.'

'Why can't you give us a chance... just try? I'm not asking for a lifelong commitment at this point, I'm just asking you to try!'

'Why should I have to try? See, you are placing demands on me already. I don't want a relationship. That whole area causes me more anxiety than any other area of my life. I've seen what neurotypical relationships are like. Take more than you give, that's a bargain. Give back more than you receive, that's a bad affair. Ditch it. That's not love. I don't want the stress and pressure involved, however much I might care for you.'

'Then you do care!' I cried, a note of triumph in my voice. I didn't get a chance to hear her reply. We had pulled into the car park. She swiftly stepped out of the car and scurried into the village hall. Whatever she was feeling, I knew this conversation wasn't over yet. I was prepared to bide my time and wait.

I was roused from my reverie by something Simon was saying to Timothy.

'The road I've been driving on has been pretty rough and steep lately. Business has been bad, coming to an almost complete stop at the moment. Liz keeps telling me I'll see light at the end of the tunnel, but all I can see are the headlights of a juggernaut thundering towards me – bankruptcy! I can't keep swerving out of its way. It's only a matter of time. It's been bad for you as well, hasn't it, Vincent? It's a lot easier to roll down the hill than accelerate back up again!'

'I'm hoping my downward spiral is coming to an end,' I replied. 'I've had my ups and downs but I think I've reached a plateau now. It's been a challenge, but I'll reach my destination eventually. I'm not sure what that might be, exactly, but I'm feeling more hopeful. Going somewhere is better than going nowhere, right?'

'That's the spirit,' Dad said.

I heard the sound of scraping chairs, and turned to see Jimmy and Catrina setting their coffees down on the other side of my table. Catrina's daughter was having her face painted at a stall nearby.

'Hello, mate,' Jimmy said.

'Hello, Catrina,' I replied.

'Oh, don't be like that, Chu… Vincent. I've said I'm sorry.'

'But not often enough.'

'My car's been crushed, if that makes it better.'

'It doesn't.'

To my horror, I saw Sarah and Gavin approach. Was there some kind conspiracy abroad to cause me the greatest amount of anxiety and embarrassment? Flies around roadkill could not have been more unwelcome at that moment. Here was a mix of completely incompatible, combustible personalities, the perfect ingredients for a collective meltdown, with Timothy Hutchins – a man I now wanted to impress – sitting next to me.

Sarah and Gavin had been relieved from their stint on the bookstall; she was holding a jacket potato and a bottle of water and he carried a hot dog and a cola. They sat on the only available chairs, against the wall, awkwardly positioned at right angles to our two adjoining tables, one seating Mum, Dad, Nana and Simon and the other seating Timothy, Jimmy Catrina and myself. I noticed Mum and Dad were holding hands under the table.

Timothy was responding to the comments Simon and I had made earlier. He raised his voice so that everyone in the circle could hear what he was saying.

'It's important to remember that however bad things are for us – the economic downturn, cuts to services, rising unemployment – life is much more difficult in other countries. I'm sure it must be challenging to be in your position Simon, and for you too, Vincent, but coming here today and remembering the children of Africa, the poorest and most marginalised citizens of the earth, helps to put our own troubles in perspective.'

'Sanctimonious twit,' Jimmy murmured under his breath. 'It will take more than a bring-and-buy sale to solve the problem of poverty in Africa, mate,' he said loudly.

'Of course. In many ways you are right. What's needed is a roots and branch reform of the way Western governments distribute their aid, and the way banks and multinationals do business with the poorer economies. But Heather, my sister – she set up the charity Togo Disability Support, by the way – she thinks it's better to have small initiatives with low administrative costs. She'd rather provide one small drop in an ocean than do nothing at all. I asked her once who she could realistically help with so few resources and so much need. She pulled out her photo album and showed me pictures of the children she had met on her visits. "I can help this one, and this one and this one," she said.' He laughed indulgently. 'I support her in her endeavours, of course, but she can be a little naïve. At the bank we realise more needs to be done than just putting a sticking plaster on a continent. The banks have been getting a bad press recently, but we're not all about greed, despite what the media is saying. Banks are responsible, well-run organisations. Sure, we need to make a good return for our shareholders, but we also provide thousands of jobs for our employees and have an absolutely crucial role in helping businesses across the country.'

'Yeah right!' Jimmy muttered.

'We're looking at better ways of doing business – social responsibility, lower interest rates for developing countries, developing self-sustaining capital projects, that kind of thing. We need to work with governments to rethink trading practices and improve Third World debt and aid packages.'

'Make poverty history. We've heard it all before, but nothing changes, does it?' Jimmy slammed the polystyrene cup down on the table, splashing the paper cloth.

Sarah and Gavin were both quiet. I remembered what she had said about the difficulties she experienced in group conversations. She appeared to be listening as the argument went back and forth, concentrating hard.

'I think I can safely say we've learned our lesson.' Timothy smiled at those around him, obviously used to an audience. 'This is a once-in-a-lifetime opportunity to change the global economic environment for the better. The banks recognise the need for more transparency. We have to adjust the bonus culture and embrace ethical business practices. I'm part of a team looking at ways to ensure that nothing like the credit crunch can ever happen again. Banks are here to provide a public service as well as make profits.'

Jimmy snorted. Sarah leaned forward. 'You can't set up systems and controls and think you are going to make the world a better place.' I held my breath, feeling anxious for her. Were we about to have a scene? 'You need to deal with the root causes of the problem – greedy and grasping people! I don't understand why people can't be nice to each other. We should share our money.'

'That's a very simplistic point of view, if I may say so,' Timothy replied. Had I really started to like him only a few minutes ago? Now he appeared stupid and pompous.

'Those who benefit from the current inequalities are not going to change the system in favour of those who have been suffering under those very inequalities. The banks can't be trusted to put their own house in order. It's all just talk and public relations.' Her eyes were flashing.

'That's a ridiculous accusation. Corporate governance is extremely important to the banking industry. For example, our bank will match any funding raised here today. All of our employees can apply for matched funding for any charitable work they are involved with, providing they meet certain criteria –'

'You're all enjoying the affluent lifestyle too much to instigate fairness,' Sarah interrupted. 'We all are. We all like our cheap clothes and cheap coffee. We don't want to think about the poor souls who produce them and the conditions in which they are living and working. We won't sacrifice our own comfort to improve theirs.'

'If you'll let me finish what I was saying, young lady... We're overhauling all our procedures. What this banking crisis has taught us is that we need more checks and balances in future. What we don't need is more government control – politicians interfering with the freedom of the markets and stifling economic growth.'

'You're right,' Sarah conceded. 'We don't need more rules. You can have as many laws and regulations and punishments as you like, but that will never stop people from acting selfishly. People will always find ingenious ways to outwit regulations and find the loopholes. We need to rediscover integrity and build a society based on trust and honour instead of mindlessly accepting a market economy based on risk and self-interest.'

'You said it, sister!' Jimmy chipped in, always one to take the side of the underdog, perhaps forgetting he wasn't at a union meeting.

I reached into my pocket and took out the small white card. I handed it to Timothy. 'On second thoughts, I think you'd better take this back.'

He stood up stiffly. 'If that's what you want. I'd better go and see if Mum needs any help.' He walked away, tripping slightly as he passed Jimmy.

'Sorry, mate,' Jimmy smirked.

Sarah gave me a long look and smiled. 'I think you offended him.'

'Good!'

'You didn't pull your punches, either,' Dad said to Sarah.

'Always brutally honest,' I said proudly.

'How are the driving lessons going?' Jimmy asked awkwardly. 'Had any accidents yet?'

'I was bumped from behind... but Vincent sorted it out,' she replied.

'I bet he did –'

'Yes,' I interrupted quickly. 'A Vauxhall Astra drove into the back of us. It was nothing. A small dent in the bumper.' I glanced over at Simon, but he was talking to my parents and hadn't heard the exchange.

Catrina jabbed Jimmy in the ribs with her elbow. 'Behave, Jimmy, or I'll take you home.'

'Yes, please, pussycat.'

Sarah turned to speak to me, her voice raised against the background noise echoing around the village hall. 'Vincent.' There was a sudden lull in the conversations. 'You left your razor in my bathroom. I'll give it back to you at our next driving lesson.' Her voice travelled further than she intended.

Jimmy choked on his coffee, spraying hot liquid onto the table in front of him.

'Vincent!' Mum gasped.

Gavin started flapping. Catrina thumped Jimmy on the back, smiling at me as if we were sharing an enormous joke.

'Calm down, Gillian,' Dad muttered.

A surge of elation flooded my being. Sarah still wanted driving lessons!

'What did I say?' Sarah asked, taking in the reactions around the table. She patted Gavin on the knee.

'I don't know what all the fuss is about,' Nana declared, suddenly roused. 'They *are* married, after all!'

A bubble of joy inflated within me. 'Take no notice, Sarah,' I laughed. 'I'll pick the razor up later.'

Spasms of happiness welled up and overflowed, moistening my eyes and shaking my shoulders. Our relationship, if you could call it that, was out in the open. And I didn't care what anybody else thought about it. As I roared in amusement, I heard first Dad and then Catrina joining in. I'd turned down the possibility of working for one of the biggest banks in the world. But what did that matter? I wiped my eyes.

'That's the funniest thing,' Catrina gasped.

Then I noticed Simon staring gloomily at the floor, pretending he hadn't heard that I had taken a potential client away.

I rested my hot face in my hands, suddenly serious. I felt a soft touch on my arm. I opened my eyes. Sarah had taken the seat recently vacated by Timothy Hutchins. She took my hand in hers.

'That's my hand you're holding,' I said.

'I know it is.'

'Why are you holding it?'

'Because that's the hand I want to hold.'

'Good. Because I don't want to hold my own hand any longer.'

Chapter 31

Nearly a year has passed since I drove home that night with my few belongings and a despairing heart. It was a cold winter. Now it's almost Christmas again. I'm still in Elmsford, though no longer with my parents. I moved into Sarah's bungalow in October. Unfortunately for me she moved out at about the same time. She has gone to Cambridge to do a research Masters in modern and postmodern literature, in particular comparing structuralist theories (including the Paris School of Semiotics) with postmodern approaches to literary theory. It all goes over my head, of course, but we exchange emails and phone calls and I listen to enthusiastic accounts of her tutorials and her part-time job in the university library.

She passed her driving test on the second attempt. I introduced her to Simon after the fundraiser. He taught her about roundabouts, three-point turns and turning right. He has taught me how to make right turns too. Under Simon's tuition I'm learning to be a driving instructor. I sold my BMW and purchased a sensible hatchback with dual controls. I'll be taking my test in the New Year.

In the meantime I'm giving free lessons to a select few to increase my teaching experience. Despite his stance on the damaging environmental effect of private vehicles, Gavin is one of my pupils. Watching the DVD in Sarah's house ignited a dream that he could become a bus driver. Once he has gained his small vehicle licence, he intends to apply to a local bus company to become a trainee driver. He would be a knowledgeable employee, but he would need to limit his unending stream of information about the Suffolk public transport system if his bus were ever to leave the depot. I have learned, like Sarah, to tolerate his obsessive monologues. I think his chances of finding a job are small. But who am I to crush a man's dreams?

I have also been giving Janice lessons. Although she has used a mobility scooter since her riding accident, she has enough movement in her legs to drive. Simon is pleased I am developing a niche market of special needs clients: it's a unique selling point for Addington's Autos, of which I will become a junior partner when fully qualified.

We have overhauled the driving school's website together and I have looked through his accounts. By shopping around, I managed to identify savings on his car and household insurance policies and found a way to amalgamate his debts with 0 per cent interest for a year on the credit transfer. Liz applied for Sarah's old job at the local library, and much to her surprise was offered it. The money's not great but it helps to cover their mortgage repayments.

About a week after the fundraiser, I discovered Mum sitting at the kitchen table, looking distraught. Dad stood behind her with one hand on her shoulder. I guessed at once that Dad's hospital results had arrived and that the news was not good.

'Vincent,' Mum sobbed, 'your Father and I have something to tell you. He's been to the hospital and had some tests. Without telling us!' She blew her nose. 'He's just had the results – and it's bad news. How could you keep something like this a secret, Derek? I thought we told each other everything. You shouldn't have had to go through this alone.'

Dad shrugged helplessly behind Mum's back. He looked resigned, almost relieved that it was out in the open. 'I didn't want to worry you in case it was nothing.'

'But it's not nothing. It's serious! It's too much for me to take in.'

I mentally prepared myself for the worst, steeling my heart so I could be brave for my parents' sake.

'It's not so bad,' Dad interrupted. 'I'm going to be fine.'

'But it's incurable!'

'Yes, but not terminal.'

'Just tell me what it is!' I exclaimed.

'I've been diagnosed with coeliac disease. Basically I am allergic to wheat, barley and rye gluten. The food I've been eating has damaged the lining of my small intestine so that I can't digest my food properly. It will heal with time if I don't eat anything containing gluten.'

'But that's just about everything we eat!' Mum wailed. 'Bread, pasta, cakes, biscuits, pastries, gravy, sauces! What am I going to feed you? We won't be able to go out to restaurants any more. Our friends won't ask us round for dinner.'

'I've got a diet sheet. I can get special food on prescription. The supermarkets have their own ranges of gluten-free food. It will be a lifestyle change, but once we get the hang of it...'

'But you can never eat normal food again!'

'It could have been a lot worse,' Dad said, with a slightly stern tenor to his voice.

'I don't see how!'

Dad and I looked at each other. Neither of us would tell her of our earlier fears.

The following week I emptied all the cupboards in the kitchen and threw away everything containing gluten. I went to the big supermarket in Bury St Edmunds and read the ingredients on every jar and packet I put in the trolley. After I stocked up on gluten-free flours, bread, pasta, breakfast cereals, gravy mix, cakes and biscuits, I ordered several specialised cookery books online.

Slowly Mum adjusted to the new regime. As the weeks passed, Dad's body healed and he gained weight. We have taken up fishing again. Together we absorb the smell of the damp earth and the shimmer of wind and sunlight on the water. I feel my own spirit healing as if it too had been starved of nutrients.

Jimmy and Catrina are still together, though Catrina keeps him on a tight rein. He's drinking less and has lost some weight. He's travelling into work by train, having been banned from driving for two years. He keeps dropping hints to Catrina that she should let him move into her place in Bury St Edmunds, only a ten-minute commute on foot. But she's a clever girl and is keeping him waiting.

I am now an honorary member and treasurer of the Specials. We meet once a week at the village hall for socials and talks on the benefits system or access to services. Don't be fooled. Just because Micky tolerates me as treasurer doesn't mean he has dropped his suspicions. After all, I *have* moved myself into Sarah's bungalow. He likes to keep his enemy close, enjoying going through my accounts with a fine-tooth comb, searching for minor discrepancies or evidence of fraud. Simon and I also earn a little extra money as an informal taxi service for some of the members.

I have a growing sense of something missing in my life – not the money, or the rushing about, or the perfunctory night-time activities at Chloe's flat. I am missing the sense of being observed. I have been self-conscious all my life, so conscious of myself as far back as I can remember that I hadn't realised there were other people in the world who didn't operate in that way. I have watched myself living my life like an audience watching a play, or a reader reading a book. I have been split in two: both myself and the observer of myself. I used to glance at my reflection in shop windows, judge my actions after the event, and replay my words over again, wondering how they had been received.

I suppose I had got into the habit during adolescence, feeling the weight of my parents' expectations and wanting, then later resenting, their approval. I had tried to impress the teachers who hovered over my life, grading, evaluating, always expecting more. I had desperately sought the approval of my peers as they scrutinised my appearance and analysed every move and decision I made, looking for the slightest chink in my armour. And I had been putting on a performance for years with clothes, scenery, props and dialogue carefully prepared and adapted to suit my environment, never surrendering to instinct or impulse.

Being with Sarah has cured me of that pernicious habit. She doesn't want anything from me. She isn't waiting for me to slip up. She lives entirely in the present moment. To do otherwise would bring on an attack of crippling anxiety. I am taking a leaf out of her book. An enormous load has been lifted. For the first time in years I can feel the joyous freedom I experienced in childhood.

It's time for me to walk Bruce. I'm living practically rent-free at the bungalow, just picking up the bills and a percentage of the Council Tax on the understanding I'll look after the house and the dog while Sarah is away. She is returning soon for the Christmas holidays. We will have Christmas dinner with Mum and Dad and Nana. Lauren has offered to drive Nana home afterwards and put her to bed, as she does every night.

Sarah still sleeps in her single bed at the bungalow. I am hoping one night she might steal cross the corridor and visit me. In the meantime I have my own space and a little more dignity now that I'm no longer living with my parents. I don't know whether ours can ever be a complete love story. Looking back, I realise the journey I've been on has been one of self-discovery, of learning to accept myself with all my faults and limitations. I am grateful to Sarah for showing me a more authentic way of living. I am trying to put it into practice, with mixed success.

I have grown a beard to wean myself off personal grooming products. I am making an effort to engage my brain and my critical faculties so I can spot the lies that are constantly being peddled by the media, politicians and celebrities. I am thinking about starting an Open University degree sometime next year, if I can afford it on a driving instructor's salary, something in the area of economics or overseas development... and, of course, I have been writing this book.

I know it isn't possible to have it all, but it's possible to have some of it for some of the time. I'm also thinking more about those who have nothing and to whom my life, fractured and disappointing as it is, must seem like an impossible dream.

Sometimes I reflect on the irony that a predominant neurotype, as Sarah likes to call me, is learning how to be a better person by following the example of a minority neurotype, someone with autism. Perhaps the fact that I still find this surprising demonstrates how deep-seated my prejudices are, despite my desire to overcome them.

It's a bright December day, one of those glorious late autumn mornings when the sky vibrates with blue light, and the cool air is crisp and redolent with the smell of fallen leaves. I am going to walk through the fields where I first met Sarah and Bruce, fields which appeared flat and desolate at that time. Since then I have grown to appreciate the enormous emptiness of the landscape and am learning to see the subtleties and slight undulations that had been invisible to my inexperienced eye – fingerprints of God. I have seen the frost brush the fields with silver and the rain intensify the green of the undergrowth. I have observed the fields being ploughed and planted and watched the summer sun swell the corn and bleach the grasses until the landscape resembles the pelt of a vast tawny animal stretching beneath the hot sky.

And today, once again, the horizon stretches endlessly around me. A lone tractor drives across a distant field. The sky pulses with light. Clouds, luminously white, rush forwards – blown across the North Sea from Scandinavia. The light is so perfectly clear it is as though the landscape has been washed, or a grimy filter lifted, and my previously blurred vision restored. There is a big world, a big, big world stretching before me. And I am on the road.

K A Hitchins studied English, Religious Studies and Philosophy at Lancaster University, graduating with a BA (Hons) First Class in English, later obtaining a Masters in Postmodern Literatures in English from Birkbeck College, London. She is married with two children.

Stay in touch with the author via her website: www.kahitchins.co.uk

Follow her on Twitter @KathrynHitchins

or connect via her Facebook page: Kathryn Hitchins, author

If you would like any further information about some of the issues in this book, the following websites might be helpful:

National Autistic Society in the UK: http://www.autism.org.uk

Autism Society in the USA: www.autism-society.org

Mencap: www.mencap.org.uk

Mission Enfant pour Christ International: www.meciuk.org